*S*trathblair

Strathblair
THE NOVEL

Alanna Knight

BBC BOOKS

Alanna Knight has written thirty books and is well known as a Scottish historical novelist and author of the popular *Inspector Faro* crime series. She has written extensively on Robert Louis Stevenson and her work includes stage and radio plays.

This book is published to accompany the
television drama series entitled *Strathblair*
which was first broadcast in May 1992.
Published by BBC Books,
a division of BBC Enterprises Limited,
Woodlands, 80 Wood Lane,
London W12 0TT

First published 1993
© Alanna Knight 1993
ISBN 0 563 36778 4

Jacket illustration by Brian Smith
Set in Century Old Style by
Phoenix Photosetting, Chatham, Kent
Printed and bound in Great Britain by Clays Ltd, St Ives plc
Cover printed by Clays Ltd, St Ives plc

Credit List

Sir James Menzies	Ian Carmichael
Macrae of Balbuie	Andrew Keir
Andrew Menzies	David Robb
Alec Ritchie	Derek Riddell
Jenny Ritchie	Francesca Hunt
Flora McInnes	Kika Mirylees
Pheemie Robertson	Alison Peebles
Umberto Fabiani	Urbano Barberini
Robert Sinclair	Neil McKinven
Veronica Smythe	Ingrid Lacey
Marjorie Moresby	Angela Douglas
George Moresby	Ronnie Stevens
Great Aunt Ishbel	Julia McCarthy
Donald Telfer	Lou Hirsch
Lady Constance	Moira Redmond
Scriptwriters	Bill Craig
	Julia Jones
	Susan Boyd
	David Ashton
Script Editor	Margaret Graham
Producer	Aileen Forsyth
Directors	Ken Hannam
	David Blair

Acknowledgements

The author gratefully acknowledges the assistance of Aileen Forsyth, producer, in the production of this book. The series was created by Bill Craig who wrote Episodes 1, 2, 5 and 10. The author also wishes to acknowledge Julia Jones for Episodes 3, 4 and 9, Susan Boyd for Episodes 6 and 7 and David Ashton for Episode 8 of the BBC TV series.

To
Chloe Kathleen Knight
with love

April 1950

As Alec Ritchie parked the motorbike and sidecar that had carried them from Salisbury, Jenny leant on the fence, Thermos in hand. Far below the great range of the Cheviot Hills spread out like a faded quilt. So this was the no-man's land fought over by the Scots and the English for centuries. She wondered why, since there seemed to be nothing but mile upon mile of empty space as far as the eye could see.

Town-raised, with the comforting presence of houses and neat gardens, she had never imagined anything as desolate as this great empty land under brooding clouds. The wind, always from the east, blew in their faces and was far from welcoming.

April was a cruel month. There had been little sunshine or blue skies to cheer them, nothing but a scattering of wind-tossed wayside daffodils to nod them on their way.

Suddenly afraid without quite knowing why, she shivered. This bleak prospect stretching endlessly before them was like the beginning of creation. She sought comfort in remembering that the farm Alec had been promised – their farm – was waiting among the gentle fertile Perthshire hills. It would be different there – romantic and as lovely as its name: Corriebeg.

'We're making good time, Jenny.' Alec had spread out the travelling rug and was studying the route map. She watched him fondly. Her husband – of three days. When they first met, this twentieth-century soldier had reminded her of the eighteenth-century Highlander on a box of Scottish short-bread. All her girlfriends, movie-mad, had sighed: 'He's just like a film star, Jenny. You are lucky.'

Lucky – she felt proud and something else, too. She was just a little afraid of the steel beneath his gentle touch, of those dark eyes that could turn suddenly cold: a good friend and a fierce foe, one she wouldn't have liked to meet in battle. He didn't talk much about the war, eager to forget it. But the leather jacket, the Army raincoat, which he wore with such in-built style, hinted that the fighting man had not been completely shed. Such garments, innocuous in themselves, added to the exciting, but nevertheless dangerous, aura he carried with him, hints of a secret life she knew nothing about – and hoped she would never encounter.

She sat down beside him and opened the packed lunch, wishing that rationing would end. Grudgingly and frugally provided by the landlady at the last bed and breakfast, it contained the inevitable Spam sandwiches. Not that Alec would object. Constantly hungry, he took a sandwich and bit into it almost absent-mindedly. The Army trained its soldiers to eat for the purposes of survival only.

Jenny leant against his shoulder as he ate. 'You just can't wait to get there, can you?'

'The sooner the better.' Alec narrowed his eyes, staring north, always north, to Scotland and the new life waiting for him. Against all the odds, against the savagery of war and man's inhumanity to man, he had come home with his own particular dream unscathed.

Corriebeg symbolised the crowning ambition of the boy from the Dundee tenement who had never had a garden of his own in which to walk. Now he would have space beyond his front door, limitless green hills with birdsong by day and starlit skies by night.

Wrapped in the excitement of anticipation, he wished he was as certain that this was what Jenny, temporarily blinded by love, wanted as well. Sometimes on that long uncomfortable journey, he had looked at her, trying to read her thoughts and willing her to share his own feelings about the future, their future together.

They knew so little about each other really. Three months ago he was unaware of her existence, but now it seemed that life could never have existed without her. He looked at her with love and wonder, at the heavy honey-coloured hair, that English rose complexion; her eyes deep blue in gentleness and grey in anger. Such ire was concern for ill-treated animals, little lost dogs or neglected babies, never with him, of course.

She stood up, tall and slender. He didn't care much for women in trousers and jackets, but Jenny endowed them with her particular brand of feminine desirability. Now, raising her arms to tie on a headscarf, she smiled down at him, her lips, red even without the fashionably carmine lipstick, were inviting, just made for kisses.

Lost in the miracle that she belonged to him, bemused by his own cleverness at winning such a prize, he felt a sudden urgent desire to make love to her. Trying to sound casual, he said: 'Fancy stopping at a B & B somewhere or do you want to press on?'

Jenny laughed. 'Not after the last time. I'll never forget the indignity of that dreadful woman demanding to see our marriage certificate. What cheek!'

'And there was me, thinking that the last of the confetti had blown away on the Great North Road,' said Alec.

As they set off again, with Jenny on the pillion and their few necessities in the sidecar, Alec felt ashamed that he had not suggested stopping off at his home in Dundee.

Was he being too rough on this gently reared lass? The wedding and two nights of serious and prolonged lovemaking, in which it seemed they could never get enough of each other, had been followed by the long drive north. He had offered her the sidecar but she declined.

'Oh no. I want to keep my arms round you. See you don't escape. You're all mine now,' she laughed.

Every time they stopped to attend the needs of nature, what Jenny called politely 'comic relief', or to eat, they fell into each other's arms again, the temptation to make love in the hedgerows of that wild land, with the sky above them, almost irresistible.

It was marvellous, finding a lovely girl who fitted his body as if she had been specially made for it. He had never imagined as he'd listened to his mates in the Army with their dirty talk that sex could be like this. He thought back to his own early attempts with girls to prove his manhood. But this, this was love, this was what the poets wrote and the singers sang. And it was all his.

Last night, conscious of the thin walls that separated them from the suspicious landlady, as he held Jenny, his whole body radiant and fulfilled, he had whispered: 'How long do you think we'll feel like this?'

'For ever, silly.' Besotted, she couldn't imagine a time when they wouldn't want each other. And stroking his chest, she sighed contentedly. 'We can make it last. And we will.'

'And tonight we'll sleep in Corriebeg.'

But Corriebeg was still a long way off. Dundee was much, much nearer, he thought guiltily.

Jenny had accepted that his mother was a bit of an invalid and couldn't travel so far for their wedding and that his sister wouldn't come without her.

Jenny's mother, Mrs Moresby, had understood. Delicate since Jenny's birth, she did, however, secretly resent the fact that her only child had opted to marry this stranger within weeks of their first meeting and was going to live in Scotland. Looking at him sometimes, tactfully questioning him on his background, she decided Jenny was marrying beneath her. What did she find so special about him? Oh, he was handsome enough and that accent was quaint and attractive. And he did look smart in uniform, she had to admit, but what was wrong with an English boy, one of her own kind, for heaven's sake? There was always that nice, studious-looking Tim who worked in the bank and was crazy about her – and he'd be branch manager some day.

But Alec hadn't been absolutely truthful with Mrs Moresby. Neither his parents, nor his sister, had ever set foot in England, which they regarded suspiciously as a foreign country.

'It will be nice for your mother having you both living so close at hand,' she had said.

Alec smiled vaguely, for the situation she implied was far from the truth. Having seen the comfortable middle-class surburbia in which Jenny lived, the idea of taking her to stay in the Dundee tenement, with a shared staircase and toilet, was unthinkable. There was only one bedroom which his mother and older sister shared while Alec slept in the box bed in the kitchen. No, that wouldn't do for Jenny. She might react by being sorry for them. He couldn't bear that. He had his pride. Jenny's only flaw that he hadn't learnt to handle was her 'over-the-top' emotions.

As for Jenny she couldn't believe her good fortune that the darkly handsome, kilted soldier who had shyly asked her for the last dance at the Saturday night hop in the Memorial Hall had walked her home afterwards.

'My great-grandmother came from Aberdeen,' she had told him proudly.

'You'll be all right then, if you have a few drops of Scottish blood.' He had laughed, seemed pleased when she had said: 'I've always wanted to go to Edinburgh for a holiday.'

'Maybe you will some day.' He had tucked her arm under his as if this was the most remarkable ambition for any lass to confess.

For both of them that encounter had been love at first sight. A week later he had announced he was leaving for Scotland and had asked if she would like to go with him.

'That's a long way away,' she had gulped, fighting back the tears. She was going to lose him so soon. 'I don't understand.'

He had seized her hands. 'I mean – come with me – marry me, Jenny.'

She asked him to repeat it, not sure that she had heard properly. Then, before she knew it, she was in his arms, and he was holding her as if he would never let her go.

'Scotland?' said her friends making it sound like an alien land at the end of the world. They stared at her in horrified concern. 'But it's miles away – and so cold.' They wondered if she knew what she was taking on. She must be quite mad.

But Jenny smiled; love had made her poised and confident of the future and what it held – Alec Ritchie mostly.

Now, peering over his shoulder, hoping that the next rise would reveal Scotland and finding instead just one more road, one more steep hill, she had her first feelings of doubt. Maybe her friends had been right —

A signpost at last.

'Scotland!'

Breathless, they paused on the hill's summit to take in the scene of the great deep valley and undulating hills.

'Why isn't there any heather?' Jenny demanded.

'Idiot, it isn't the right time of year for heather. You'll see all you want in August.'

August. She sighed. By then they would be settled in. All their troubles would be over.

The motorbike's engine roared into life.

'Home, Alec. Home to Corriebeg!'

· · · · *Two* · · · ·

As Alec and Jenny continued their long journey north, four miles from Corriebeg a train puffed into Strathblair Station. From the clouds of steam an officer emerged sporting on his bonnet the red hackle of the Black Watch. With his wavy light hair, bright eyes and wide cheekbones, he bore the mark of race, the Viking inheritance of the Lowland Scot, undiminished through centuries of inbreeding.

At first glance, he was the typical fighting man strong, tough, who had helped to build the British Empire. The locals described Major Andrew Menzies as, 'A fine braw lad.' But today there were no flags waving, no cheering or bagpipes playing as might have happened in centuries past when the laird's son returned from battle – from many battles, as the scar from his left eyebrow to cheekbone testified.

As for Andrew, he had never expected to see Strathblair again or this station platform with its childhood memories of going off to boarding school and fighting back tears, trying to be brave. Memories sad and happy, but never had a homecoming seemed sweeter than today.

Walking towards the exit he watched passengers boarding the local bus which passed the lodge gates. He hung back. It was too soon, much too soon, to regather the threads of old acquaintance in hand-shaking, back-slapping, false jollity.

'Aye, the war's over,' they'd say consolingly.

But was it? For him would the war ever be over, forgotten? As the train slid out of the station he felt a moment's anger towards his absent parent. Typical of Father, of course —

A car pulled up. A fair-haired woman waved to him.

'Welcome home, Andrew. Sorry I'm late.'

'That's all right, Flora. I've just arrived.' They shook hands, smiling yet awkward. They were old friends in the Scots tradition where it was bad form to make public demonstrations of affection.

As they walked down the now-empty platform, she indicated the two pieces of luggage he carried. 'Shall I —'

'No. I can manage,' he replied stiffly. Did she think he had been mortally wounded, incapacitated? Flora McInnes might be his father's factor now, but he certainly didn't want her behaving like a servant.

At her side in the car, Andrew realised he had forgotten how pretty she was. The heavy blond hair, her deep blue eyes, but most of all that deceptively cool air of elegance and breeding. He often wondered since they were so alike in colouring and her family had served the laird for generations, if one of his ancestors had claimed the droit de seigneur.

Conscious that she was aware of his scrutiny, he asked hastily after the estate and was told it was breaking even.

'And you?' He had sent her a letter of condolence after her husband died at Anzio.

'Oh, I'm fine too.' She smiled, sad-eyed, then quickly looked away. 'John was a methodical man. He left the paperwork in apple-pie order. That helps a lot. Until I come across his signature on some document. Then it doesn't help at all.'

They were taking the short cut, the back road past the church. Andrew was disappointed. He wanted to absorb his surroundings, the upper reaches of the hills still ice-capped, awaiting something stronger than the fitful spring sunshine to transform frozen snow into a dozen thin waterfalls rushing down to meet the River Tilt.

He would have enjoyed lingering in Strathblair, driving slowly past grey stone houses and staring into the shop windows. Instead he wound down the car window and breathed in the peat-scented air. They never burnt coal in Strathblair and peat had not been rationed.

Smiling, he sat back in his seat, reassured that this was not another dream where he would awaken once again to the sickening reality of war.

'Old place doesn't change much, does it?' said Flora as they entered the drive of Strathblair House. Soon the rhododendrons which screened the house from the road would be in full bloom. Now the gardens were thick with daffodils as they had been every spring since Andrew could remember. One of his first recollections was toddling through them and gathering armsful for his mother.

His mother. She, too, belonged to a lost world.

Flora noticed his wistful expression.

'Pretty, aren't they?'

She was thankful they were still at their best, the only welcome for the returning son and heir. Where was Sir James? she wondered. Andrew, regarding the closed front door, was clearly thinking the same.

She realised, as he thanked her absently, that he had already forgotten her, looking up at the house as if he were seeing for the first time the handsome Georgian mansion which had replaced the sixteenth-century turreted house, whose narrow windows and arrow slits had been built for defence in a wild land. He regretted the passing of the original house where Sir John Menzies had entertained Bonnie Dundee; Sir John had died at his hero's side at the Battle of Killiecrankie.

As he opened the front door, he realised that even had he been blind he would have known he was home. The old familiar smells of dogs and polish mingled with good cigars and his father's favourite brand of snuff. That was Strathblair for him. But there was no sign of Sir James, or anyone else for that matter.

Glad of the respite, he wanted to shed this hated uniform, thrust it out of sight, with its memories of battle. It smelt less pleasant than the house, of sweat and fear.

He raced upstairs to his room. Mrs McKenzie and her minions had been busy. The room was so polished and sparkling that it seemed impersonal, all character sanitized out of existence.

Many of his old treasures had been removed discreetly to the attics. A rocking-horse and a fort with soldiers (had he really once loved pretending to be a soldier?); a moth-eaten teddy with only one eye. Presumably Father gave the order when questioned, that such possessions were too unmanly, too childish, for a returned soldier.

At least his wardrobe was undisturbed. It was good to be in civvies again. Thank heaven he'd not put on weight, he thought, buttoning the flannel trousers and tucking in the pristine white shirt. He hesitated for a moment over sweaters, decided on a Fair Isle pullover and his favourite Donegal tweed jacket, his worn but highly polished brogues felt hard inside, unfamiliar, like someone else's shoes.

'There now!' he smiled at his reflection as he folded a starched white handkerchief into his top pocket. 'Ready for anything.'

Preparing to face his father, man to man, he descended the oak staircase with its portraits, its Highland scenes darkened with age and the grandfather clock with its pastoral scene, which continued to tick away mortal lives, indestructible, relentlessly recording time.

Outside the front door, he hesitated, looking up at the windows. Should he go back to the sitting room, ring the bell for tea? Wait for Father?

No, not yet. He needed time to think, dreading the confrontation which would be worse than any school report. Somehow he had to bring up the topic of Alec Ritchie. He had already rehearsed what he would say so many times that he was dizzy. A debt of honour, Father. But how could he expect his father to understand anything which inconvenienced him in the slightest? Anything which presented a deviation from the normal running of Strathblair?

The peace of the daffodils was vastly preferable and he headed towards the little rose garden his mother had loved. There she had read him stories and although the roses would not bloom yet awhile, a stone seat held memories of the boy Major Andrew Menzies had been.

The sun was warm on his face. This was peace. No more wars, thank God, only a fractured future to piece together the untidy jigsaw of emotions his life had become. Seeing Flora again brought back painful memories of her elder sister, Janet, whom he'd once loved and lost.

Their father had been the local doctor, his two clever daughters had gone to the University in Edinburgh. When Flora came back and married the handsome young factor, some folk had whispered that it was a waste of all that education. Others, more sentimental, had sighed, delighting in the love match.

He looked up to see Mrs McKenzie waving to him indicating that his father had seen fit to summon him.

Almost expecting an irritable: 'Where the devil have you

been, Andrew?' there was no reprimand, no gladness nor indeed any expression of emotion in his father's hooded eyes.

Sir James was a master of the stiff upper lip. Grey-haired, his bearing military, Andrew had never seen him in shirt sleeves or less than immaculately attired. A velvet smoking jacket was his nearest concession to informality. But, worst of all, searching in the attics of memory, Andrew had never heard him laugh.

The war hadn't changed him apparently. He'd appeared unconcerned that, had his only son been killed, his line would have been rendered extinct.

They shook hands. 'Sorry I wasn't here to greet you.' And considering further explanation unnecessary, he continued: 'Good to have you home, Andrew.'

'Good to be home, Father.'

As Andrew followed him into the house, he was once again amazed that this austere man had ever had enough passion in him – lust was unthinkable – to beget a son. He searched in vain for any tender memories to console himself that he had been wanted by his father except as a necessary heir.

'When do you return to Germany?'

'With any luck, never. I've applied for a home posting.'

Most fathers would have been delighted, relieved, smiled even, but not his. As they walked through the hall and into the sitting room, Andrew noticed all the familiar objects that told his heart he had come home: the old and comfortable armchairs with their floppy shabby cushions, the ancestral portraits, the Landseer paintings.

His hand flew to the scar on his cheek. At one time, he thought he would be blinded and would never again set eyes on this house, nor this room of memories. Five years of war, another five in the Army of occupation. But here he was, the traveller returned, with everything as it had been when he went away. But he had changed.

'We'll be seeing much more of you then?' asked Sir James.

Andrew sighed. 'I hope so.'

'Do I detect a note of doubt?' Sir James said quickly.

'With the Russians and the Chinese cuddling up together, the international situation looks less than promising.'

'The domestic situation doesn't look much better,' was the gloomy response.

'Still, given the mood of the country, I suppose a Labour government was inevitable.'

'Like death and taxes.' Sir James headed towards the table with its array of decanters. 'Whisky?'

Andrew smiled. He could remember as a boy having been accused of some misdemeanour, quailing before his father's wrath, that he had watched his father pour himself a stiff whisky. He could hardly believe that here he was being given full honours as an adult and an equal as they raised glasses in the Gaelic toast: 'Slainte.'

Sir James drank thirstily and soon refilled his glass. 'I expect they'll tax places like this to the hilt if they don't decide to nationalise them first. Not that they'll get much for their trouble,' he added bitterly.

'Oh, I gathered from Flora that the estate was doing reasonably well.'

Sir James looked doubtful. 'It isn't losing money. It just isn't making any.'

'Are all the tenancies filled?'

'Except for Dalcardoch and Corriebeg. Dalcardoch hardly counts. The steading's almost beyond repair.'

'And Corriebeg?' said Andrew, aware that the dreaded topic could no longer be avoided.

'The house hasn't been lived in since old Robertson died. But the land's in fair condition. Alasdair Macrae took it over four years ago. I've been meaning to find a new tenant.'

Andrew took a deep breath. 'Well now, I think I may have done that for you. As a matter of fact, I have promised it to one of my jocks – Alec Ritchie, and his wife,' he added, his voice calm but defiant.

Sir James was momentarily speechless. Then he slammed down the glass on the table. The explosion Andrew had hoped to avoid was under way. 'Do I understand you correctly? You have promised the lease of Corriebeg to a complete stranger.'

'He isn't a stranger.'

'He is to me. Who is this man Ritchie anyway?'

'He was my platoon sergeant during the war – the Western Desert, Sicily, Salerno. He's a first-rate chap.' Suddenly, knowing that he hadn't a hope of getting through, Andrew desperately wanted his father to like Alec.

'I'm sure there were many first-rate chaps in your company,' said Sir James acidly. 'That doesn't oblige you to promise them tenancies on the estate! What on earth possessed you?'

'A place called Coriano Ridge,' said Andrew touching the scar on his cheek. 'Where I got this. Ritchie was wounded, too. A lot of men owe their lives to him.'

'But not you.'

I owe him more than that, thought Andrew, more than I can ever repay through Corriebeg. But Father would never understand.

'We ended up in the same hospital and we had time to talk about what we would do if we survived the war. His ambition was to run his own farm, be his own man. I promised to see what I could do. A rash promise, but a promise just the same.'

Sir James made a dismissive gesture. 'So why does he choose to remind you of it now?'

'He stayed in the army for another five years. Now he's out and newly married. I'm prepared to accept responsibility for Ritchie, Father. I've offered to guarantee his overdraft.'

Sir James eyed him coldly. 'What you do with your own money is your affair. What happens on the estate is mine. You've placed me in a damned awkward position, Andrew. If John McInnes had survived, he would never have countenanced an incomer taking over the tenancy. As it is, God knows how Flora will react. Not to mention old Alasdair Macrae.' When

Andrew didn't answer, he demanded, 'How much farming experience does he have?'

'None. But he has read books.' Andrew wanted to tell him that Ritchie was surprisingly knowledgeable about the Scottish Blackface sheep but Sir James snorted contemptuously. 'Books! And what exactly did he do before the war?'

'He worked in a Dundee jute mill.'

Sir James, struck dumb by the enormity of the situation, looked at Andrew as if he had taken leave of his senses. A moment later, his calm regained, he said, 'I'm sorry, Andrew, it won't do. You'd better get in touch with Ritchie and tell him so.'

Andrew took a deep breath. 'I'm afraid it's a bit too late for that.'

And before his father could interrupt again, he found himself stammering that the Ritchies were already on their way, reduced to the sweating schoolboy who had to explain the reason he'd failed his maths exam and probably wouldn't get into Oxford after all.

He was saved by the telephone ringing. As Sir James bellowed into the instrument, he seized the chance of escape. Daylight was fast fading as he walked swiftly down the gravelled drive. This was the gloaming: all nature stilled in the peace of approaching evening. The day's toil had been put aside, the trees motionless as if they, too, bowed their heads in sleep. Even in the battlezones of Italy, this hour, the time of Angelus, had filled him with longing for Strathblair.

Now, on his own land again, his heart soared. Andrew Menzies was home, home, against all the odds.

He thought of Flora's smiling face and made his way towards the factor's office in what had once been the old stable block of the estate. Perhaps she would understand his dilemma.

She had discarded the tweed swagger coat and was wearing a pretty cashmere jumper and neat tweed skirt which emphasised her slim figure. Andrew noticed with pleasure that Janet's rather plump younger sister had certainly fined down during those missing years – grief for the husband she had lost, no doubt.

The sympathetic response he had hoped for, however, was not forthcoming.

'You're a fool, Andrew,' she told him bluntly.

'Macrae'll get compensated for his ploughing. And he doesn't need the steading,' said Andrew reassuringly.

Flora shook her head, concealing her exasperation with difficulty. 'Why on earth did you do it?'

Andrew's face shadowed. 'My own reasons,' he said stiffly. 'Can we leave it at that?'

Rebuked, Flora was reminded once again of her place. She was merely a Strathblair servant, a fact Andrew reinforced as he continued: 'I won't be here when the Ritchies arrive. I have to report to Perth so if you could use your good offices with my father.' He added with a winning smile: 'Try to talk him round.'

'Since I happen to agree with him, that's asking rather a lot,' said Flora acidly.

But Andrew was not in the least contrite. He skipped out of the office leaving Flora feeling that she was gradually learning that factors were expected to do the dirty work, smooth the paths to the feudal mansion.

Imagining that Andrew would be different when he came back from the war, she was disappointed. He had never been able to face up to his father and that obviously hadn't changed.

'The Army will make a man of him,' she had once overheard Sir James telling the family lawyer. It had indeed. It had almost made a deceased man of him. Idly she wondered if Sir James would have cared if Andrew had not returned. Would he have shrugged it off as he did all emotions?

· · · · *Three* · · · ·

The Ritchies regarded the sun sinking below the hills with dismay. Jenny's spirits had risen as they reached Perthshire where the hills that had been shrouded in mist all day suddenly gave way to something like the Scotland of her imagination. Fickle sunshine had cleared the skies and grey misted land-scapes were once again in the hands of a celestial painter. Everywhere patches of barren earth bloomed in the purples and yellows of springtime flowers and the annual miracle of resurrection breathed new life upon skeletal shapes of winter trees.

Jenny had sighed with anticipation. If this was Strathblair country then she couldn't wait to get to Corriebeg. But now even closely following Alec's map, they were lost, well and truly lost.

Signposts had been few and far between. Presumably they had not all been restored since the war ended. They had passed one sign: 'Strathblair Estates Ltd' followed by a hopeful: 'Corriebeg 2½m' half an hour ago.

As Alec paused to look round, Jenny shivered. 'It'll be dark soon,' she said. She was cold and hungry, now regretting that she had so scornfully dismissed the B & Bs on the Pitlochry Road. The countryside, momentarily so welcoming, had long since petered out into twisting roads that had become mere cart tracks with no indication as to where any of them might lead.

'Listen,' said Alec.

Tramping hooves indicated cows approaching and with them the cheering sight of a human face, a farm hand in dungarees and boots. On closer scrutiny the herder was a woman, young-ish still, since her hair under the woollen beret was auburn.

'Corriebeg? You'll no' find anybody there.'

'You will tonight,' grinned Alec. 'I'm the new tenant.'

As she pointed the way, Jenny wondered if the woman was a neighbour. She must be quite old, past thirty, but had obviously been pretty once, before wind and weather roughened her complexion.

There wasn't much that missed Pheemie Robertson and as

the motorbike roared on its way, she was overcome by curiosity. Who could have put a tenant into Corriebeg without her or auld Macrae knowing? The lad looked tough enough but as for that young lassie, with that posh English accent, never a farmer's wife.

Pheemie laughed. They'd not last six months in Corriebeg. As for Macrae, she'd like fine to see his face when he heard. He'd have a fit.

'There it is. That must be it.'

Without Pheemie's directions the Ritchies would never have found Corriebeg. The motor cycle chugged up a rutted track and for a moment they both sat and stared, the engine still switched on.

The rain that had been threatening for the past hour had now resolved itself into a steady drizzle. In the fast-fading light veiled by mist on top of a sharp incline, a small steading stared down at them. Built of grey stone with a central door, a window on either side and a couple of dormer windows under a sloping roof, it was typical of the croft houses they had encountered since crossing the Border. Most were ruined and roofless, and this one, thought Jenny despairingly, seemed little better.

The farm gate hung by a broken hinge. Any garden that had ever existed had long since vanished under weeds. It was a sorry scene which told a story of long desolation and neglect and it added to Jenny's sense of foreboding.

'Well, what do you think?' asked Alec, trying to sound encouraging.

Words failed Jenny. All she could hope at that moment was that they'd made a dreadful mistake, taken the wrong turning. But she was so weary and tired that had she been alone she'd have sat down and had a jolly good cry. In a voice that was not quite steady she gulped: 'It looks nice.'

While Alec parked the motorbike and went in search of the key, she trudged round the outside of the house, staring into the windows, resolving to remain calm until they had set foot inside. It might not be as bad as she feared.

'Here's the key, where she told us,' Alec called and the door swung open onto a dark cavern smelling strongly of damp.

'After you,' said Alec and when she didn't move, added: 'Something wrong, Jenny?'

She forced a laugh. 'Our first home. Haven't you forgotten something?'

He stared at her and then, with a laugh, thrust his gloves into his pockets and picked her up, carrying her across the threshold, setting her down in the nearest room.

'I'm starving. Anything left to eat?'

'Ye-es. I'm sure there must be.'

'Good, I'll bring in the things. Don't go away,' he added archly. Jenny stared after him, amazed that he had neither remarked on nor apparently observed the horrors that surrounded him. She kept a steady rein on her nerves, determined not to give way to hysteria. Her eyes adjusted to the dim interior to reveal filthy bare boards on the floor, the sole furnishings an ugly solid wooden table and two kitchen chairs. The walls had been painted a ghastly shade of blue and some-one had made half-hearted attempts to scrape it off, but had given up or died in the attempt. Wallpaper had been con-sidered, but that, too, had fallen victim either to lethargy, damp or both. A particularly gruesome example, yellowed and faded, hung on one wall, curling at the edges.

Taking a deep breath, Jenny turned slowly round. What had once been a lace curtain was now a rotted string half-covering the window. The only shelf, hastily thrown up by the look of it and never painted, was occupied by a battalion of chipped mugs, faded cartons, old newspapers and empty beer bottles. And whatever surface she touched, her hand came away sticky with grease and damp. Spiders roamed in every corner and from a curtained recess which surprisingly held a mattress came a sickening stench of mice.

Dominating the scene was an antique range. Jenny lifted the hob cover gingerly and looked inside. She must be practical. They must eat and for that they must have fire.

Across the hall, a door hung off its hinges. Unfurnished but for one broken chair, with a few faded marks on the wallpaper once occupied by pictures, this had been the parlour, but was now put to more practical uses than entertaining the minister, or important guests. Its floor was covered in filthy straw and poultry droppings.

Next to the kitchen the door yawned on a lavatory containing a revolting toilet and a cracked wash-basin which made her decide a ditch outside would be infinitely preferable.

The stench of neglect was everywhere. Suddenly she felt sick, wishing she could run away and forget she had ever seen Corriebeg. Putting her hand to her mouth, she fought back the tears.

She had never set foot in such a hovel in her whole life. And this – this was to be her home. If only her mother could see her now, she thought. Her mother spent her life worrying about damp sheets, moths and spiders, not to mention the occasional mouse.

She heard Alec return, saw him looking up the stairs which led to the other rooms. Terrified at what they might find, keeping a tight hold on herself for fear she might howl with misery, she stood clutching her arms, gazing out of the window.

'Jenny.' Alec had his hands on her shoulders.

Biting back her tears, she stared ahead.

'Jenny, if you're having second thoughts, say so now.'

Oh, poor darling Alec. It was his home too. And he must be as shattered as she was, he was just better at concealing his feelings. After all, this was the dream he had set his heart on. Guiltily she realised at that moment how selfish she was being. Turning to him she went into his arms, hugged and kissed him reassuringly.

'Any progress on the food front?'

She nodded dismally, turned on the water tap but nothing happened. Alec tried the light switch. Nothing there either.

'There's a wee burn. That'll do for now,' he said seizing the kettle. 'I'll look for the header tank when it's light.'

There was just enough paraffin in the bottom of the stove to get it going and by the time Alex returned she had sausages and eggs frying in the pan, candles firmly fixed on the table.

'Electricity seems to have been cut off, too. Never mind,' Alec said, 'a candlelit supper's romantic.'

Jenny was glad he couldn't see her expression. Almost too tired to eat, her bones aching with weariness, she longed for oblivion. But worse was to come.

When Jenny asked: 'Where do we sleep?', Alec swept open the curtained recess with a dramatic gesture.

'The box bed. Where else?' he smiled triumphantly.

She was too tired to resist or protest as they settled down under their travelling rug. Alec's arms were warm and welcoming, they shut out the cold, the damp and the despair which were lying in wait for tomorrow. But neither had any heart or energy for lovemaking, and they both fell almost immediately into an exhausted sleep.

The country sounds of a cock crowing and the distant lament of sheep woke Jenny. A ray of sunshine flickered through the curtains of the box bed and she recoiled at what the light revealed. Evening's dark shadows had been kind. The reality was much worse than she remembered.

At her side Alec was still dead to the world. She crawled out and looking to neither left nor right threw open the kitchen door. For outside a miracle had happened.

It was as if the map Alec had consulted so frequently on the journey with its green, brown and yellow contours, and unpronounceable Gaelic names, had now come to life. Hills, wavy brown lines on paper, were huge towering snow-capped mountains, their lower reaches speckled with blue-white patches of hardened drifts that the sun never touched.

In a distant wood, birch trees were touched by a delicate nimbus, a shimmering green mist, ghosts of summer leaves to come. Somewhere close at hand a bird sang, unidentifiable, its echoing sound held the welcome note of springtime and the earth's re-emergence from winter's little death.

Jenny breathed in the air, so fresh that it made her dizzy for a moment. She threw her arms wide open as if to embrace the panorama of blue-misted hills and sky with its wisps of purple cloud that had replaced the dour greyness of their arrival.

Behind her the interior of Corriebeg had been despoiled by man's presence, by the detritus of civilisation he leaves in his wake. But out here, a careful nature husbanded waste, disposed of it neatly and discreetly. And those sheep moving on the hill were their very own sheep, she thought proudly. There were few trees to shelter and protect them, but somewhere near at hand, she heard the sweet music of a burn chattering its way to a distant river. Beyond it, she saw open pasture, coarse grazing, dotted with green broom and the rise of their own fields.

This was a world she wanted to belong to, to enfold in her arms like a lover. And this, she told herself, this was Corriebeg, where one day, this scene would be as familiar as the home she had left in Salisbury. She would have walked every part, touched every tree and stone. This would be the land of her memories, of youth and bridal days.

Rubbing her chilly arms she was overwhelmed by the prospect of a new day, a beginning filled with excitement and a sense of adventure, a determination to win against that dreadful scene she had left inside.

Going back, she surveyed the kitchen with hard eyes. It was indescribably dirty. The sooner she set to work and did some scrubbing, the better. Under the sink she found a brush and bucket, battered but nevertheless usable.

From the curtained recess came sounds of movement. Alec was awake. She looked at him with concern but his face registered no dismay as he took in their appalling surroundings. He kissed her and apart from yawning wearily was prepared to be extremely cheerful.

Breakfast didn't take long. Praying there was enough oil left in the stove, she cooked up the remains of the sausages, fried some stale bread. Alec finished his mug of tea eagerly. 'I'm away to explore the policies. Want to come?'

Jenny smiled. 'I rather think my kitchen needs me.'

She watched him go, walking jauntily, whistling hopefully. Picking up the scrubbing brush she set to work with great vigour, writing a letter in her mind to her mother, a somewhat expurgated description of Corriebeg and what they had found there.

As she filled the bucket from the water-barrel, she wondered rather proudly if they were the only people around at eight in the morning. Once she thought she heard a motor-car engine. Was someone coming? As it faded she remembered that sounds distorted by the hills can travel a great distance.

· · · · *Four* · · · ·

The distant traveller was Flora McInnes performing one of the less pleasing aspects of her factoring duties. She was heading towards Wester Balbuie where Alasdair Macrae would have been up and about since dawn. She wanted to get the bad news over with, tell him about the new tenant at Corriebeg before he disappeared into the hills for the day. She was just in time for he was already boarding his tractor.

At her greeting he walked towards her, a tall, upright old man who in his youth must have turned quite a number of girls' heads, she thought. Although he didn't appear to spend much on clothes or shaving soap these days, the vestiges of a once-handsome man with an impressive personality clung to him like beggar's rags. The battered hat he now raised politely, he'd worn for umpteen years.

His face showed no smile of welcome to her greeting. But then it rarely did. She mustn't expect miracles. Smiles and old Macrae didn't belong on the same planet.

Anxious to ingratiate herself before the blow fell, she said: 'I see your hoggs have wintered well.'

'And so they should at the price I paid.'

Flora laughed at his dour expression. 'I have never heard of you getting the worst of a bargain.'

'That's as may be. I see the major's back. Germany, wasn't it?'

Flora's eyes widened. 'You don't miss much.' She sighed. Here was the moment of truth. 'Alasdair, you'll be interested to hear you might be getting a new neighbour at Corriebeg. A man called Ritchie. He's arriving with his wife today.'

Macrae frowned, demanded sharply: 'Strangers?'

'Major Menzies knew him in the Army.'

Macrae's face expressed little, but Flora would have liked to know what he was thinking. He nodded curtly. 'You'll have some tea.'

Whatever disapproval he felt, Highland hospitality must be offered and the laird's factor must also be diplomatic.

As they walked up towards the house, Macrae, restraining his curiosity, politely said: 'I'm surprised that the laird's let it out to an incomer.'

'He hasn't. Not yet. Sir James wants to see what they're like first.' And Flora steered the conversation away from Corriebeg.

Later, watching her drive off, Macrae was inwardly seething. He should have been informed, consulted.

It was typical behaviour of these new lairds with their Sassenach ways. The Macraes had been on this land for more years than the history books could remember. They had worked and suffered and endured with the land. They had followed their laird to a thousand battles great and small, to wars not of their own making, whose reasons for conflict they only barely understood.

But they were lairds' men through and through. And how had this been repaid? He looked at his flock of sheep. Damned sheep; the lairds had sold out loyalty for a price, cleared the land of their clans and replaced man whose upkeep was too expensive with more productive sheep.

Sir James's grandfather had been just as guilty as the rest of them. As for young Andrew, each new generation was becoming more English. No Gaelic, no native language. To hear them speak no one would take them for Scots any more. And now Corriebeg had been given to foreigners.

Striding up the hill, with his dog, Fly, at his heels, he decided he might take a look, console himself with the certainty that they'd never last.

It was Fly's odd behaviour that alerted him that something was wrong. The bitch stopped, listened. Macrae couldn't hear anything, but she took to her heels and disappeared, leaping over the whins towards the burn which ran through Corriebeg where, a short while ago, Jenny had just finished scrubbing the kitchen floor.

Emptying the last bucket of filthy water, her back sore from such unusual exertion, Jenny had never felt dirtier or more dishevelled in her life. She looked longingly towards the small burn twisting away from the steading. Two days travelling without a proper wash was bad enough and then no running water in Corriebeg until Alec found the header tank. It was more than Jenny could bear.

But there, just a few yards away, was all the clean water anyone could wish for. She was tempted. There might be a sheltered spot where she could have a jolly good dip.

At the head of the burn, she found it: a tiny waterfall, screened by whins, perfect and so romantic. She'd managed to solve one more problem at Corriebeg – Alec would be delighted.

Stripping off, she stepped gingerly into the water. Then screamed! It was colder than anything she had ever imagined, so cold in fact that after she got her breath back, her whole body began to tingle. Rinsing off the last of the soap, her hair dripping wet, she stretched out her hand for the towel.

To her horror she discovered she was no longer alone. Standing over her clothes, snorting and pawing the ground was a great shaggy dangerous-looking beast with long sharp horns.

Jenny was transfixed with terror, aware for the first time how cold she was. She'd die if she had to stay in this burn for a moment longer.

'Help! Somebody! Anybody!' she yelled.

But who could hear her against the rush of the waterfall?

Praying for a miracle, she heard a dog barking. Then a black-and-white collie dog appeared. With almost human understanding it looked from girl to bull, took in the situation and rushed barking towards the bull which needed no second urging to a rapid departure.

'Oh, you lovely dog,' she gasped.

The dog looked round as if to make sure she was safe, wagging its tail.

'Fly! Here, lass.'

Alasdair Macrae, staring over the ridge, could hardly credit his eyes. There was a lassie, stark naked – well almost – a wee thing of a towel round her middle, standing in the burn. Embarrassed, Macrae didn't know where to look, but raising his hat politely as if this extraordinary scene was an everyday occurrence, said: 'Fine morning.' And calling his dog he continued on his way, leaving Jenny to stumble out of the water. Teeth chattering, she struggled, very damply, into her clothes.

Half a mile away Alec Ritchie was a happy man, exhilarated by all he surveyed on his first morning as a hill farmer. Thin sunshine revealed a fine land and a farmhouse that, while a wee touch neglected, would be a grand solid home once Jenny got to grips with it. But the land was his main concern. And it pleased him, for amid the red-brown of withered heather, there was a hint of the emerald-green of new shoots, of heather and rich grass protected by winter snow, greenness that meant food for winter-starved sheep.

He thought of Jenny's distress about the house. How could he convince her that it didn't matter a damn what kind of house you lived in? It was a transient thing, a shelter against the forces of nature, in a land that conquered and consumed man and beast, and the dwellings they made for their brief sojourn returning them to the dust from which they had sprung.

A car came up the hill. 'Mr Ritchie?'

As Alec nodded Flora's smile hid her exasperation. 'You weren't expected until today. I'm Mrs McInnes, the factor. I manage the estate for Sir James.'

Alec smiled. 'I know fine what a factor is, Mrs McInnes.'

'I've brought some things you might need. Groceries and paraffin for the lamps.' Opening the passenger door, she said: 'Jump in.'

As they drove into Corriebeg, Alec expected Jenny to appear, curious to see who the visitor might be.

'It's all in a bit of a state,' he said apologetically.

'It's been empty for years, Mr Ritchie.'

Opening the door, Alec called: 'Jenny.' And warning: 'Jenny, a visitor.' He ran quickly through the house from room to room, baffled by her absence.

'She must have gone out,' he said. Watching Flora putting the groceries away, he decided this was a very presentable woman. She caught his appraising glance and he said hastily: 'A bit unusual, isn't it, a female doing your job?'

'My husband was the factor. I took over when he went into the Army.'

'Didn't he want his job back?'

'He was killed at Anzio.'

'I remember Anzio.' Poor devil. As if mention of the war reminded her, Flora said: 'The major sends his apologies. He had to go to Perth. But it's Sir James not Major Menzies who handles estate matters. You'll be dealing with Sir James and you'll need a cash advance against your lamb sales in August. The usual procedure is for Sir James to make an arrangement with the auctioneer, Mr Wallace, to tide you over.'

'Sounds reasonable,' said Alec in tones of relief.

Flora realised a warning was needed. 'Mr Ritchie, I wouldn't take too much for granted at this moment —'

A disturbance outside interrupted them.

'Alec, you won't believe what I've been through.' Jenny burst into the room. Expecting him to be alone, she felt sick with embarrassment as he introduced Mrs McInnes.

'You've been running, Mrs Ritchie,' said Flora, tactfully concealing her curiosity for this bedraggled figure looked as if she'd been pulled backwards through a very wet hedge.

'I decided to take a dip in the stream and then this – this great hairy beast showed up and I'd still be there if a sheepdog hadn't showed up with an old tramp. He called her Fly.'

Flora suppressed a smile. 'That would be Mr Macrae of Balbuie – your nearest neighbour.'

'Sorry,' said Jenny. Now she had put her foot in it.

'Then we should be seeing quite a lot of him,' said Alec.

'He's seen quite a lot of me already,' said Jenny ruefully. She'd never be able to look him in the eye again. Wait until she told Alec —

Flora decided that her visit had lasted long enough. As she prepared to leave Alec indicated the groceries.

'Oh, how kind, Mrs McInnes,' said Jenny. 'What do we owe you?'

Flora smiled. 'Nothing. A gift from Strathblair Estate.'

Waving her goodbye, Jenny said, 'What a nice woman, so

pretty too. Can't imagine her doing a man's work. I thought you'd be dealing with Major Menzies. What did she want?'

When Alec explained and told her about the financial arrangement with the auctioneer, Jenny looked very enthusiastic.

'That's very kind of him.'

Alec looked at her and shook his head. 'Kindness doesn't come into it, Jenny.'

'I don't understand. He's lending us his money.'

'It's his business.' And Alec realised that he'd have to explain once more from the beginning the business of managing a sheep farm, how the laird owned all the land and the livestock on it, which he then rented out in lots to tenant farmers.

'Sir James has divided his estate into twelve farms and each farm is divided into two components, the fixtures, that's the steading and outbuildings, and the movables, the sheep and other livestock.'

'Why do you call them movables?'

'Because their value can and does change from year to year. We have five hundred breeding ewes and Mr Wallace might say they are worth two pounds per head and lend us a thousand pounds. With luck and no disasters like a late snowfall, if the majority of the ewes produce twin lambs and most survive, he might expect to sell, say two hundred and fifty lambs or more for us and that will repay our loan and hopefully give us money to keep us going for the rest of the year. Understand?'

Jenny smiled but Alec caught her look of uncertainty. He had expected that having worked in a bank she'd have a fairly acute grasp of financial dealings and hoped that would include house-keeping on a tight budget.

'I wish you could have seen me at the waterfall,' she said eager to change the subject. 'I was absolutely terrified —'

As she went over the disastrous episode, Alec remembered the broken fences and gates. 'That's how your hairy visitor got in. We'll need to see that doesn't happen again and that's where

Mr Wallace's advance will come in very handy.'

As Alec closed the door, Jenny set to work building a fire. She'd never been good at it, not even in her Girl Guide days. However, if they were to eat —

After several frustrated attempts she remembered that fanning the sluggish flame with a newspaper often helped. The next moment she was choking, blinded by the soot that shot down the chimney.

As she stumbled outside, scarcely able to see or breathe, Alec, alarmed, took hold of her and shouted: 'What's happened?'

'Everything. Everything,' she cried. 'Alec, I can't do this. It's not what I thought it would be! The house is damp. The place is falling apart. The chimney hasn't been swept for years. I can't work that range.' And turning from him she beat her hands against the door lintel and sobbed. 'This house hates me. Hates me!'

Gently Alec took her in his arms. 'Jenny. It will be alright once we've got things fixed up. Just give me time,' he pleaded.

But, as he feared, Jenny was beyond rational thought. She had had enough – more than enough for most girls. And he knew by the way she shook her head that she had made up her mind. Corriebeg was not for her and never would be.

As Alec got a fire going, tidied up the mess and boiled enough hot water to wash the soot out of her hair, Jenny could hardly see for tears. This hateful place. Tricked by a flicker of morning sunshine, why had she ever imagined it as lovely or romantic? How could it ever really be a home? She was sorry for Alec as she watched him repairing the gate as if glad of the opportunity to keep out of her way. It was just as well, for if he had been nice to her, she would have burst into tears again, angry tears directed against Major Menzies. She'd expected that he would be there to greet them. And if he'd really been the friend he pretended to be, he'd have made certain that Alec had a decent place to live. It was an insult to give this hovel to anyone.

She went to bed early but she couldn't sleep. She remembered how Scotland had been a dream place for her, based firmly on the film *I Know Where I'm Going*, with a castle and a loch and everyone dressed in tartan. A keen moviegoer from her earliest days, her knowledge of Scottish history was based on Katherine Hepburn, her favourite actress, playing the tragic Mary Queen of Scots.

Alec moved restlessly at her side.

'What are you thinking about?' she whispered.

'The best way to tell Sir James that we don't want Corriebeg.'

So that was that. Alec would never fail her. How could she have ever doubted him? With a sob she moved into his waiting arms and held him close, feeling safe and protected again, loved and cherished.

· · · · *Five* · · · ·

Flora gathered her papers together in the factor's office and prepared to join the Ritchies at a meeting she would have gladly avoided especially as she remembered her talk with Sir James.

She had found him in his greenhouse, brooding over his orchids with more anxious loving care than many men gave to household pets. To her assurance that the Ritchies seemed a decent enough couple, he replied: 'It takes more than just decency to run a hill farm.'

'Ritchie was in the Terriers when war broke out, so he was one of the first to go.' Flora looked out of the window, seeing far beyond the hills. 'He was also at Anzio.'

Sir James looked at her quickly. Pity John hadn't survived. He could have coped with this situation. 'I doubt if they fully appreciate what's involved. The best outcome would be if they changed their own minds about taking over the tenancy. Who better than you to tell them.'

Once again, elected to do the laird's dirty work, she walked towards the house.

The Ritchies had already arrived and Jenny was enjoying a glimpse into that romantic, affluent Scotland of her imagination. She was very glad to be wearing her pale blue serge 'going away' outfit, with navy hat and matching leather shoes and handbag. She felt smart, elegant and quietly confident in the sort of clothes she would have chosen to meet any of Daddy's influential friends or to go to a bank 'occasion'.

Alec, too, was looking very handsome in his Sunday suit. He was the sort of man who had in-built style and who looked good in anything, even his working dungarees, she thought proudly.

She was looking forward to seeing the inside of Strathblair House and wasn't disappointed. Impressed by the long winding drive and a glimpse of rolling lawns and well-kept gardens, the house came up to her expectations for it looked very old. She liked the sweep of the curved stair to the front door and the old stone was charming. Like many Scottish houses, Strathblair seemed to rise from the earth to be part of the land in a way that English red-brick houses never did.

The housekeeper opened the door and led them through the hall into the sitting room where, standing in front of a cheerful fire, Sir James was waiting to receive them.

As they shook hands, the laird's black labrador lumbered over to them and was restrained from a more voluble greeting.

Jenny considered the room was quite perfect. Glass cases of china and tiny tables held what were doubtless priceless ornaments. She noticed the huge glass-fronted bookcase with its old leather-bound volumes; the high ceiling and great windows with shutters that doubtless worked; silver candlesticks, tapestry firescreen and frayed brocade curtains, heavy with years, and although the chairs were shabby she felt that they managed to age with the dignity appropriate to a laird's house.

Everywhere showed the signs of wealth and tradition inherited from the oil paintings of bygone Menzies. She suspected that the faded but ornate wallpaper hadn't been changed since it was hung more than a hundred years ago; she suppressed a smile. Mummy would be impressed, and horrified, as she redecorated the whole house in Salisbury every five years.

Alec was telling Sir James about his early days on a Tayside farm and his ambition to be a farmer, so Jenny settled back into her chair happily. She felt quite at home in such surroundings and as the dog Prince came and laid his head on her knee, she decided that her ambition had always been to have a dog. Fondling Prince's ears, she abandoned her day-dream to hear Sir James saying to Alec: 'Staying on a farm isn't the same thing as being born to the land. You have no family background in agriculture?'

He was interrupted as Flora entered. Apologising for being late she took a seat and noticed that Sir James was looking more than a little ruffled.

He was, in fact, cursing his absent son for having landed him in this deuced awkward predicament, especially when he observed Flora's encouraging smile in the Ritchies' direction. All three heads now turned towards him expectantly.

'I cannot but feel embarrassed in having to say this, but my son had absolutely no right to offer you the tenancy of Corriebeg.' As Ritchie said slowly: 'I see,' Sir James continued hastily: 'I quite understand that in the atmosphere of wartime comradeship, certain rash commitments might be made. In the cold light of reality, it may be necessary to question the wisdom of making them —'

While Alec was thinking of a suitable reply, Jenny faced Sir James and said in icy tones: 'Is that a long way of saying that promises don't have to be kept?'

'Jenny —' Alec said warningly, but Sir James waved it aside.

'No, Mrs Ritchie. It's merely a way of saying that certain facts have to be faced. Corriebeg is a working farm. Your husband would be taking over a tenancy with about five hundred ewes on the hill. It has to pay its way in terms of the estate.'

'And that does mean a lot of hard work,' Flora put in quickly, rewarded by a nod of approval from Sir James.

'Quite so. Quite so. It can be a very harsh life.'

Looking at the Ritchies' downcast faces, Flora said, 'You will have help, of course. From your neighbours. And plenty of advice,' she added consolingly, ignoring Sir James's disapproving glare.

What the devil did Flora think she was doing, encouraging them? And, as all three faces again turned towards him, he added: 'In a community like this one always helps one's neighbours. Though, frankly, I don't know how they'll feel about newcomers taking over the tenancy.'

'At first.' Flora's smile completely ignored Sir James's furious look in her direction as he continued: 'And there are other considerations. From what you tell me, I have to say that I think you are somewhat under-financed. I understand that my son is prepared to guarantee you a small overdraft.'

'He kindly offered to do that.' And with a glance at Jenny's stony face: 'But if you think —'

'I did explain to Mr Ritchie that Mr Wallace would make him an advance against the lamb sales,' Flora interrupted, 'And the initial outlay on gear and equipment need not be too heavy. What he can't borrow, he could hire from the home farm.'

Sir James, his patience at an end, said: 'Yes, yes. But the fact remains you have no experience, no qualifications. Quite frankly – I don't think you could make a go of it.'

Alec rose to his feet slowly and said with great dignity: 'There isn't much more to be said, is there, sir? I'm sorry I've taken up your time.' And, turning towards the door, he murmured: 'Come, Jenny.'

Jenny, preparing to follow him, was close to tears. 'We seem to have come a long way for nothing.' And to Sir James, she said scornfully: 'Nobody asked what his qualifications were for fighting Rommel.'

Sir James looked helplessly across at Flora, taken aback by the boldness of the young woman who ought to have been sitting meekly and silently by her husband's side. 'It's hardly the same thing —'

Jenny faced him squarely. 'No. It isn't. The war's over and nothing that was done or said then matters now.' And ignoring his protest, she continued: 'It isn't fair, Sir James. If the major hadn't promised my husband this place he wouldn't have wasted his time coming here. And he wouldn't be leaving now feeling he'd failed —' She stopped, abashed at her outburst, not knowing where to look. She had never thought of herself as capable of such defiance, of standing up to authority before.

Sir James regarded her thoughtfully, then turned to Alec. 'What will you do now?'

'Oh, I'll try for some other place, sir.'

'You're a determined man, Mr Ritchie,' said Sir James.

Alec smiled. 'Yes. I am.'

Sir James sighed. 'Very well, I have done my best to dissuade you. But since you – and your wife –' he added glancing in Jenny's direction – 'obviously have your hearts set on the place, I don't seem to have much choice. Mrs Ritchie has stated the position most clearly. Indeed, forcefully,' he added with a wintry smile. 'My son made a promise. We shall keep that promise.'

Alec glanced at Jenny whose mouth had fallen open. What had she done?

'So I propose a seven-years' repairing lease, to be reviewed after three,' Sir James continued. 'If your husbandry isn't up to the mark, I will have a legal right to terminate it. But I want you to make me a promise in return. If, at the end of six months, you have not – in my sole opinion – run Corriebeg in a satisfactory manner, then I shall expect you to relinquish the lease.'

Alec looked desperately at Jenny. Was this what she really

wanted after all her protests and tears? But there she was, smiling wryly, nodding happily.

'Nothing in writing. Nothing legal,' Sir James went on. 'Just your word and your hand on it.'

Solemnly, the two men shook hands and a still-dazed Jenny followed Alec out to the motorbike. 'I must be mad.'

'You've only got yourself to blame from now on,' said Alec.

Watching them drive away Flora whispered: 'Well done.'

'You were not at all helpful,' said Sir James crossly. Matters had not gone the way he planned. As for Flora, she had betrayed him.

'John would never have approved of this,' he added reproachfully.

'John didn't come back,' she reminded him. 'Alec Ritchie did.' And she was pleased to see that his steps faltered momentarily before he walked swiftly away in the direction of his greenhouses.

There was a letter waiting from the major welcoming them to Corriebeg apologising that he had been called away to Perth before he could greet them in person.

The letter made Jenny feel much better towards him and in bed that night as they reviewed the extraordinary events of the day, she said: 'That was a lovely dog too. Did you see how he took to me? I'd love a puppy, Alec.'

'I can't guarantee a puppy, but a dog you shall have —'

'Oh Alec – a labrador, please?'

'No, a Border collie – a sheepdog. I'll need one to work the sheep. Not a pet lap-dog for you to spoil, but an intelligent, hard-working animal.'

But Jenny was beyond warning. All she could see was that she would have a dog of her own. She would have gladly accepted a mongrel. Then she remembered her rescue from the Highland beast at the waterfall.

'That dog I told you about. Called Fly. That would be a sheepdog, wouldn't it?'

Having been promised a dog that she was determined to make her own, for she'd soon overcome Alec's feelings about pets, Jenny was filled with new resolution in the days that followed. She'd turn Corriebeg into a proper home, whether it liked her or not. Still abashed when she remembered how she had spoken back to Sir James, she realised it was because she loved Alec so much and would never forgive herself if she had allowed the dream he had carried through those terrible war experiences to be shattered before it even had a chance to begin.

She would have made any sacrifice for his sake. At that moment she felt like her heroine, Mary Queen of Scots, who featured in the book she was reading, and was ready to follow her lover 'to the world's end in a torn petticoat'.

She put some Spam into a sandwich and carried it out to where Alec was repairing a fence. He regarded the steaming mug of tea gratefully.

'You never did say what was blocking the water tank.'

'You'd never drink from that tap again if I told you.' Alec grinned as he remembered the dead crow he'd fished out. He'd be wise to keep that information to himself.

Later that week they went to the factor's office where Flora had the tenancy agreement ready for Alec's signature.

'The official take over day is 28 May. Your first rent is due on 28 November, but you'll have the valuation before then.' And Flora explained that his tenancy was a commonty grazing – the Corriebeg sheep shared the hill with the other tenant's flocks. Once a year, they were all brought down and separated.

'That won't be easy,' Jenny commented. 'All sheep look the same to me.'

'Corriebeg has CB on the horn, Balbuie, WB.' Flora smiled at Alec's offer to help at the gathering. 'That would be neighbourly. How are you settling in?' she asked Jenny.

'All right. It'll feel more like home when our furniture gets here tomorrow.'

Flora stood up. 'Good luck, Mr Ritchie.'

Alec hesitated. Jenny suddenly remembered he'd said he'd only really feel accepted when he was called by the name of his farm.

He smiled at Flora. 'Corriebeg?'

Flora laughing, held out her hand. 'Good luck, Corriebeg.'

· · · · *Six* · · · ·

Over breakfast the next morning, Jenny tried to picture what the furniture, mostly discards from her parents' overcrowded home, would look like in Corriebeg. She sighed. It was a hopeless task, imagining a glass display cabinet and her grandmother's elegant Victorian tables in the dismal parlour.

As she got dressed, she watched the grey sky anxiously, willing it not to rain. What should she wear? Something smart but not too elegant, so she decided on a brown skirt and jacket, with a pretty home-knitted lacy cardigan. This had been her bank-clerk uniform, with a selection of tailored crêpe blouses. At least she looked neat and tidy and she intended to spin out the pairs of nylons hoarded for her trousseau by wearing ankle socks for all but formal occasions.

'Are you nearly ready, Jenny?' Alec called upstairs. 'Time we were going.'

As they drove down the hill she thought she felt spots of rain. Panic. What if the furniture wasn't on the train but was already standing at the platform? Her fears were groundless. All went smoothly and with some helping hands Alec soon had the furniture loaded on to the estate tractor and 'coup-cairt' Flora had lent them.

Jenny, having been told by Alec this was man's work and she was to go away and amuse herself, set off to explore Strathblair which until now she had seen only as a distant prospect of smoke-plumed grey stone houses nestling against the blue hills.

The original town had been set around a village green with an ancient Celtic cross. By English standards it was not much larger than a Wiltshire village but considerably busier.

The prosperous years for the Menzies Family who had built the new house had added the High Street, a main thoroughfare intersected by roads and terraces of handsome stone houses glimpsed behind high garden hedges.

In a kirkyard gnarled old trees and lichened, leaning gravestones with their skulls and crossbones told of a longer history than the church with its memorial hall, products of late-Victorian architecture and far from beautiful.

She returned to the main street. As well as food shops, there was a bank and post office, a haberdashery and a small and exclusive-looking dress and Scotch knitwear shop.

But what pleased her most was that the passers-by all gave her warm friendly greetings and smiles as if she knew them already. What a difference to the red-brick suburbia she had left where neighbours kept themselves very strictly to themselves and no one spoke to anyone else without an introduction.

'Jenny!' Alec came across the road. 'We're ready to leave. Did you get the groceries?'

She had forgotten the list which was still in her pocket.

Alec sighed. 'Well, I'll have a pint while I'm waiting.' Furniture loading was thirsty work. He made a face when Jenny said she wouldn't be *that* long.

Mr Forbes' shop was busy. As she waited to be served, Jenny looked round the shelves. There were plenty of tinned goods and brand names, far more than many small shops in her home town. It didn't look as if Mr Forbes had been hard hit by wartime shortages.

'And what can I do for you?' he smiled. Large, rosy and

jovial, the grocer's round cheery face suggested Father Christmas without the beard. He was a man who enjoyed his food and his drink, Jenny suspected, noticing the apron stretched around his ample waistline.

Mrs Forbes also served behind the counter. A small, neat woman, sharp-eyed and businesslike, who watched her husband as well as the customers. Jenny suspected that she kept a tight rein on his in-built affability, especially where young and pretty women were concerned.

Clipping the coupons from her ration book, Mr Forbes said: 'That'll be twelve and three pence ha'penny, Mrs Ritchie.'

Jenny looked at him in surprise. How did he know who she was? she wondered. She realised she had a lot to learn about communications in Strathblair where, rumour had it, word of mouth travelled faster than light!

Embarrassed, she discovered she didn't have enough to pay him.

Mr Forbes smiled, unperturbed. He delivered to the farms twice-weekly. He'd collect it then and take any eggs she had. At her look of astonishment, he said: 'You'll be keeping hens.'

Reporting the conversation to Alec as they walked back to the station yard, she asked: 'What did he mean about hens? Do we have to keep hens?' Secretly she hoped he would say no as she didn't much care for hens; they seemed noisy and messy.

'We'll need the eggs, Jenny, besides it's traditional that farmers' wives always keep hens. And the money from them will be yours to spend as you like. Think of that!'

Jenny mused. It was an attractive idea and would give her a small measure of independence and remembering the dress patterns and materials in the High Street, she'd be able to make clothes and things for the house.

As Alec drove the tractor up the hill to Corriebeg, Jenny leant happily against him. 'You'd better save your energies for unloading,' he said with an affectionate grin.

Moving was hard work. Jenny had never been good at lifting

heavy objects and had been warned sternly by her father that it caused 'woman's troubles'. She was struggling with a picture when a visitor arrived.

'Saw your furniture going by. My place is Carnban, two miles back.' Curiosity had overcome Pheemie Robertson and it was well rewarded by the sight of delicate wee tables and fine chairs with spindly legs and a glass-fronted cabinet. More suited to Strathblair House than Corriebeg, Pheemie sniffed. What on earth would the lass be doing with such clutter in a farm kitchen?

Recognition dawned on Jenny. 'Didn't we meet —?'

'Aye, that's right. You were lost,' said Pheemie, taking her hand in a wincingly iron grip. And without another word, she lifted a headboard as if it weighed no more than a bag of flour and disappeared into the house.

Half an hour later, the furniture more or less installed, Pheemie explained over a cup of tea that her cousin Archie had farmed Corriebeg. 'Well, he wasn't exactly a cousin but we were kin of some sort. There's a lot of Robertsons hereabouts.'

'Only one casualty,' said Alec coming to join them and holding up a now headless pottery dog. 'One of our wedding presents,' he said in mock sadness.

Pheemie looked contrite and embarrassed. 'Sorry, it just slipped through my fingers.' Jenny said hastily: 'He hated it.'

Greatly relieved Pheemie asked: 'Have you got any stock yet?' And having being informed they were getting a pony, a garron, on loan from the factor, she continued: 'Flora McInnes is a bit hoity-toity wi' being at the university. But nice enough.' She sighed. 'Sad about her man getting killed. Now, he was nice.'

By the time Pheemie took her leave, she had blackened Forbes, the grocer, as a wartime profiteer and promised to sell Jenny six hens for three shillings each.

'Five are good layers. You can wring the other one's neck

when you get fed up wi' it,' she added cheerfully and Jenny repressed a shudder. What a horrible idea!

In reply to Alec's question about getting a dog she said: 'Try Balbuie. You'll have met Alasdair Macrae?'

'Jenny met him, briefly,' said Alec with a sidelong glance which made her blush.

'He'll no' be pleased at you taking this place,' Pheemie grinned. 'Come to think of it as his own. Likes to act as if he's a wee bit saft in the heid. But he's all there when it comes to money.'

As Wester Balbuie, Macrae was apparently not displeased at the idea of selling one of his dogs and Alec was greatly impressed as the old man put a collie called Tam through its paces. 'Think he'll be my dog by the gathering on the 21st?' he asked.

'More likely the other way round. But he'll come to your whistles by then. A dog aye goes to the one that feeds him. So make sure that's you and not your wife.'

Alec looked round for Jenny. She was playing with Fly, her rescuer from the Highland bull.

'How much would you be asking for Tam?' said Alec.

'Oh, I'm thinking fifteen pounds at least.'

Alec and Jenny exchanged glances. Fifteen pounds was a bit steep, considerably more than they had expected to pay.

'And how much for Fly?' asked Jenny quickly.

'Fly? Och, you don't want Fly.'

Jenny came over. 'Is there something wrong with her?'

Macrae hesitated. 'No, no. Not a thing, Mrs Ritchie. But Tam's the best for you – well trained and obedient.'

'How much for Fly?' Jenny persisted.

'Seventeen.' Seeing the lass was keen Macrae went on hastily to sing Fly's praises. 'Aye, she's a gey intelligent dog, that one. And being a bitch, there's aye the breeding from her.'

Jenny bent down, fondled Fly's ears. 'She's lovely.'

'Aye, she's the one,' said Macrae aware of the bargain he was making. And as Alec hesitated, he added: 'It's up to yourself. I'd advise Tam. But Fly's trained to the hill, even if she is a wee thing less biddable. No offence, Mrs Ritchie. But she's a female and, like most women, she takes notions into her head at times.'

'Maybe Tam would be best,' said Alec. Jenny, still holding Fly, looked hard at him and he was aware that both dog and girl had very pleading eyes. 'As you say, Mr Macrae, they take notions.'

Jenny held on to Fly all the way back to Corriebeg. She couldn't believe her good fortune. After all these years she had a dog of her own. She'd wanted one since she could first remember, always pleading for a puppy. But her house-proud mother couldn't bear the thought of dog hairs on the sofa and muddy paws on her pristine kitchen floor. Her father, who would have given Jenny anything within reason, had a garden that was the joy of his heart and he couldn't bear the thought of messes to clean up or evening walks that were the alternative.

Fly, having been given a share of their evening meal, was temporarily housed in a cardboard box by the fire. Jenny, content at last, knelt on the rug stroking her while Alec practised blowing the bone whistle Macrae had given him.

As Fly pricked up her ears, Jenny said proudly: 'Fly must be a really good dog. That's why he tried to fob us off with the other one. I think we got a real bargain.'

'Seventeen quid?' Alec looked at the dog doubtfully. 'I can do without bargains like that.'

'Clever girl,' said Jenny and Alec, watching her nuzzle her face against Fly's soft fur, sounded a note of warning: 'Jenny, she's not a pet. And as soon as I get the outhouse fixed up, that's where she sleeps. And talking of that,' he added archly, 'if you're not too exhausted cuddling that dog —'

For Jenny, tired and happy, slipping between fine linen sheets and lace-trimmed pillowcases that had been her grandmother's was her idea of heaven. And it was wonderful to be making love in a proper nuptial bed at last. Tomorrow she'd finish the rest of the unpacking.

She hadn't realised how inappropriate those wedding presents would be. Granny's Persian carpet was far too big for any room except the kitchen where it would look ridiculous.

Alec was having similar thoughts as he eyed with dismay the bone-china dinner and tea set, fine table linen, crystal glasses and silver. Family heirlooms, he guessed, more in keeping with Strathblair House than a farmhouse kitchen; with its well-scrubbed wooden table.

And talking of misfits, Jenny realised Pheemie had been right about one of the hens.

Later that week, Jenny was in the yard with her henfood when Pheemie appeared on her bike. 'I was just passing. How are they doing?'

'They're all laying, except for that one over there.'

'That's the one for the pot, then,' said Pheemie cheerfully and pounced on the unfortunate creature. Jenny could hardly believe her eyes as with one twist of her wrist, she had wrung the bird's neck and was now handing it to her dead, but still twitching. How revolting.

Watching Alec whistle to Fly, Pheemie's eyes widened when she heard that Macrae had sold the dog to them.

'The auld devil.'

'Is there something wrong?'

'Aye, there is. He should have warned you that Fly's no good at the sheep dipping. Fair terrified, she is. One whiff of the dip and she's away like the clappers.'

Preparing the bird for the pot with a certain lack of enthusiasm and a great many flying feathers, Jenny decided that, given time, she might become as adept at plucking them as Pheemie was at killing them. Meanwhile, exhausted and frustrated, she went back to Fly who had graduated to a rug in front of the fire.

Hearing Alec's footsteps and concerned by Pheemie's remarks, she whispered: 'You won't let Alec down, will you?' And Fly wagged her tail as if she understood perfectly.

Looking at them, Alec said: 'You'll spoil every creature we get.'

Jenny stood up and retrieved the hen. 'I've got one less to spoil thanks to Pheemie Robertson,' she said wryly. 'I like Pheemie, but nothing seems to pass her by.'

'What was she saying?'

Jenny looked hard at Fly, and Fly wagged her tail somewhat apprehensively. 'Oh, nothing much.' Better to keep Pheemie's remarks to herself. There was no sense in worrying Alec unduly, sure that Fly would behave differently with him.

Alec picked up the bone whistle, weighed it in his hand. 'We've an early start and a long day.' Then added to Fly: 'My first gathering. You keep me straight, girl.'

But even Alec was unprepared for the morning's events, for the tide of sheep and the dogs that were their masters.

The dipping was a long ritual. Overseen by the local policeman, Sergeant Brodie, who had to be present to make sure that every sheep was dipped against infestation, it was an exhausting task, despite the ease with which skilled and trained hands carried it out.

The smell was awful and the noise of the sheep's terrified blaring not much better. But it gave Alec an enormous sense of pride to be part of this scene, the scene that would one day be a familiar part of his life. Someday he would remember that once, long ago, he had been afraid he'd make a fool of himself in front of these seasoned herdsmen.

Moving away from the sheep dip that was being prepared, he hurried towards the farmers driving their flocks downhill, among them Macrae and Pheemie with their crooks, whistling and calling.

In answer to his offer, Macrae shouted brusquely that help was needed over on the left flank.

'Fly. Here, lass.' Alec whistled. But Fly wasn't at his heels. Perhaps she had already moved to her place among the sheep – 'setting' they called it. But as the other farmers called their dogs, he realised that Fly had vanished.

He couldn't work the sheep without her and shame-faced, he hurried to Corriebeg, hoping that everyone was too busy to notice or to remark on his sudden departure.

Jenny came out while he was searching the outbuildings. 'Finished already?'

'Finished?' Alec shouted. 'I didn't even get started! Fly's disappeared. She didn't come back here, did she?'

'I don't think so. I've been working upstairs all morning.' And as Alec demanded: 'If she isn't here – where the hell is she?' Jenny wondered if she should tell him what Pheemie had said. But it was too late now. She would be betraying Fly. It would only increase his fury against the dog.

'She'll come back, Alec. She always does.'

'That's a big help.' Turning, he looked back at her and frowned. 'What do you mean – she always does?'

Jenny took a deep breath. Now he had to be told.

It was late when Alec returned to Corriebeg with Fly in the sidecar. He was in such a foul mood Jenny was glad his supper was on the table. Fly retreated to her cardboard box and eyed the scene with almost human anxiety.

'I've never felt such an idiot! In front of all of the others. They must have been laughing their heads off!'

Jenny looked across at Fly. 'Maybe she'll learn —'

'She'll learn?' Alec thumped the table angrily. 'She's supposed to know! I'm the one that's here to learn! If word gets back to Sir James about this —'

The tirade was interrupted by a knock at the door. Alec sprang to his feet. Macrae stood on the threshold.

'Would it be convenient to have a word?'

Pheemie Robertson had torn him off a strip about letting Ritchie have Fly. Pheemie was a gossip and in the interests of his pristine reputation and integrity, Macrae didn't want her spreading rumours around Strathblair, that he had more or less admitted it was an act of deliberate malice on his part, adding that if Corriebeg got too much for them, at least they'd have a house pet when they left.

'I'd like to have quite a few words with you, Mr Macrae.' Alec said grimly.

'I see you've got her back,' said Macrae motioning to Fly.

'She was at Dalscriadan.'

'Aye, she goes there sometimes.'

'Or any other farm within a five-mile radius,' said Alec furiously. 'I should know. I've been round them all. Mr Macrae, I think you should have warned me —'

'I did try to suggest that Tam might be better for you.' He glared at Jenny indicating that it was entirely her fault that Alec had taken Fly instead.

'Aye, you did,' said Alec ruefully and glared at the dog.

Macrae sighed. 'But fair's fair. I'll take her back and you can have one of the others.'

Mollified, Alec watched Macrae leading Fly away on a rope, while at his side Jenny stifled a sob as the dog turned once, tail down, and gazed back longingly in their direction, whimpering in protest as Macrae dragged her away.

Alec looked at Jenny. God, he hated making her unhappy. He watched her toying with the food on her plate, knowing that her eyes were full of tears and it made him feel wretched. Finally he suggested they might take a trip to Perth next week and go to the pictures.

'That would be nice. Something to look forward to,' Jenny said dismally trying not to look at the empty cardboard box.

Alec stretched out a hand, covered hers. 'Fly had to go.' And as she tearfully agreed, he added: 'I grant you she was a nice animal. I was getting quite fond of her. But she was unreliable.'

'If she scoots off every time there's real work to be done, I agree,' said Jenny, trying to be fair, conscious that this was, in fact, their very first quarrel. Over a dog. She wouldn't have believed it possible, she thought, as bravely they both picked up their forks and resumed eating. Tomorrow would be another long day for Alec.

The Corriebeg sheep were to be dipped, checked over and have new keel marks put on them.

As they watched the proceedings, Macrae agreed to let Alec have Tam as soon as the gathering was over.

'You were asking fifteen pounds for Tam,' Alec reminded him.

'Was I?' Macrae turned. 'I cannae just mind.'

'Fly cost seventeen,' said Alec firmly and returned his attention to the last of his sheep which were ready to be driven back to pasture. He was managing reasonably well until one broke away from the herd. Without a dog, there was nothing for it but to chase the beast himself. Louping after it, flapping his jacket, he caught his foot in a heather root and fell full length. Struggling upright, humiliated, he swore. 'There's an ill-natured heap of mutton if ever there was one.'

Macrae nodded dourly and Alec was suddenly aware of a dog on an outcrop of rock. Fly, 'setting', was awaiting his word of command.

'Get away out, Fly. Get away out.' As Fly raced ahead and cornered the ewe, sending her bleating back to the rest of the flock, Alec eyed Macrae triumphantly.

The last of the sheep gathered in, the farmers, weary but satisfied with the two days' work, prepared for home. While Alec was washing down with Fly beside him, Macrae brought over Tam.

'You did none so badly, Corriebeg. And here's the two pounds extra you paid for Fly.'

At Corriebeg, Jenny would be waiting, his supper on the table. Alec hoped it would be a better supper than last night for he had a surprise for her. Creeping past he knocked on the door and hid round the corner.

Jenny looked out. Who on earth could it be? There was no one there. A moment later a dog leapt over the gate and across the yard, jumping up at her in an ecstasy of tail-wagging.

'Oh Fly, what are you doing here? You'll get us both hung.'

Alec sauntered over. 'From now on she sleeps in the out-house, just as soon as I've got it fixed up.'

And Jenny, with a cry of delight, flew into his arms, hugging and kissing him, while Fly expressed her own delight singing like a kettle as she followed them into the house.

May 1950

Strathblair bloomed in the bridal greens of early summer. April's chill winds and sudden showers gave way to May mornings with the scent of yellow broom on the air and the pools among the moorland heather reflecting an azure sky with high sailing clouds.

Beneath Corriebeg's sheep-dappled hills, Alec and Jenny awoke to a full orchestra of larksong and cuckoo-call. Mild days had seen the lambing safely over. Another hurdle lay ahead: the valuation of their flock.

'Sir James owns all the sheep,' Alec explained to Jenny. 'You have to remember that we just rent our flock from him. So Mrs McInnes will appoint one of the Strathblair tenants, probably Mr Munro of Dalscriadan, to give a just price on Sir James's behalf. Mr Wallace, the auctioneer, will speak for us and hopefully between them they'll arrive at a figure which will satisfy Sir James and be fair to us. Naturally Mr Wallace will want as low a price as possible so that come the auction in August we'll make enough profit to pay back the loan he made us.'

'Sounds like a war in the making, another Munich. Do they ever come to blows?' said Jenny.

Alec smiled. 'They've thought of that. The referee, or oversman, is called in from neutral territory. Mrs McInnes says they've appointed a Mr Abercrombie from Braemar way to see justice done and to have the final say in any disagreement. There's no going back once we've agreed to accept their valuation.'

Jenny sighed. 'It all sounds very complicated.'

Alec kissed her. 'We just have to stand by and watch; we're not allowed to interfere. However, the farmer's wife has her part to play. She's expected to oil the valuers' geniality with whisky and provide plenty of food and drink for the neighbours.'

At her doleful expression, he laughed. 'Come on, Jenny. It's right up your street. You'll be great.'

In the past month Jenny had mastered the intricacies of the kitchen range, let it know who was boss. It responded with splendid cakes and roasts and the Corriebeg neighbouring would be her début. This was her chance to impress upon them all that a foreigner and an incomer she might be but where cooking was concerned she could equal and, she secretly hoped, excel any Strathblair wife.

A week ahead wasn't too soon to plan and she had already begun preparations with lists and menus when Pheemie arrived on her bike. Indicating the cockerel in the basket, she grinned: 'Just turn him loose among your hens with instructions to do his duty.'

Following Jenny into the house, she surveyed the scene of culinary activities with awe. 'My mother's recipe for fruit cake,' she was told, as Jenny abandoned the mixing bowl for a pot of tea. 'I've a list as long as your arm for Mr Forbes when he arrives.'

'You'll need a lot of whisky,' said Pheemie. 'It's gey thirsty business, a valuation. And I'll put in an appearance at the gathering beforehand just to annoy them. Och, it's one o' these daft things,' she explained at Jenny's questioning look. 'There's men's work and women's work and the men dinna like the womenfolk working the sheep. But I'll be there a'right. Me and my orraman.'

'Your orraman?' asked Jenny.

'Aye, a man that does odd jobs about the place. You know, bit planting, bit herding, this and that.'

Alec's motorbike arrived as Pheemie was releasing the cockerel. 'Something to keep your hens happy,' she grinned.

Jenny gratefully waved her goodbye and as the cockerel marched purposefully towards his new harem, she said to Alec anxiously: 'You don't think five shillings was too much for him?'

'Not for something that'll get you up in the morning. You always sleep through the alarm clock.'

'Cheek!' said Jenny knowing perfectly well what he meant. 'And whose fault is it that I'm so tired in the morning?'

Alec made a move towards her and, still holding the baking bowl, she flicked some of the mixture at his face. In mock anger he grabbed her, she twisted away and darted, laughing, into the outhouse, where Alec caught her and threw her on to the hay.

As they kissed and cuddled, Alec aroused, began to caress her with greater urgency. Suddenly Jenny remembered the precious ingredients in the baking bowl which she had abandoned. Pushing Alec away, she sat up in time to see Fly hungrily devouring the contents.

Well, that was that. And there were better things than making cakes – more rewarding hungers to satisfy. With a sigh, she returned to Alec's waiting arms. At last he sat up, smacked her playfully: 'There's planting to do. We can't all lie on our backs and think of England, like some I could name!'

'What a nerve! I'll remind you of that later.'

She watched him go and, as she prepared the henfeed, she heard the grocer's van coming up the brae. Once again, their transaction ended, she was in Mr Forbes' debt.

'Nae bother,' Forbes grinned. 'You can settle on Thursday.'

What a relief! She didn't want Alec to know. He hated them to owe money to anyone. As she handed Forbes the list for the valuation his eyebrows shot up. 'Four bottles of whisky. You're making a good start. And I hope you'll have enough coupons for this lot.'

As he drove off, two young lads carrying haversacks came into the yard wanting to buy eggs and milk. Glad of an unexpected sale, she poured some milk into a bottle while they told her the youth hostel was full.

'But we have a wee tent. Is there somewhere nice to camp?'

'Yes. Try up the hill just beyond the waterfall.'

Watching them go, she realised she should have reminded them about closing gates. But it would probably be all right. They seemed such a friendly pair and very polite. She imagined they were students.

As she went back into the house she heard a couple of shots on the hill and a cloud of crows rose filling the air with their raucous screeching.

Alec heard the shots, too, and found Macrae tying two dead hoodie crows to a fence. Greeting him he indicated the shotgun. 'I'll need one of those myself, Balbuie.'

'You'd better if you don't want to lose any more lambs.' And Macrae nodded towards the hill. 'It was one of yours newly dropped. The hoodies have taken its eyes.'

As they buried the pathetic wee creature, both men sickened and silent at the thought of the cruel birds who took such a toll of the newborn and helpless, Alec asked Macrae about Mr Abercrombie.

'Well, he's done it often enough and he's fair. Though maybe he talks too much. Great on addressing Burns' Suppers, I'm told. Wait till you hear him speechifying at a valuation.'

Alec laughed. He was a Burns' fan himself and he liked the sound of the man. 'I'll look forward to that.'

'If that's to your taste,' was the dour reply.

Half an hour later Alec was repairing the guttering when Macrae stormed into Corriebeg's front yard. Jenny was hanging out the washing. Ignoring her friendly greeting he turned to Alec.

'A word wi' you.' He looked grim, but then he always did. 'Two lads up by the waterfall with a tent. They've lit a fire and said your wife had given them permission to camp there.'

Jenny came over. 'They were just —'

As if she hadn't spoken, Macrae continued: 'There's a notice in the hostel that they're to keep off the hill during lambing.

There's two things we don't want – hoodie crows and hikers! It's a pity we're allowed to shoot the one and not the other.'

'I'm sorry, Balbuie,' said Alec with an uncomfortable glance in Jenny's direction. 'I'll tell them to clear off.'

'I've done that. Just you have a word with your wife.' And, turning on his heel, he marched through the gate.

Jenny looked after him furiously. 'Well, of all the – He doesn't own the hill!'

Trying to calm her down, Alec said: 'Jenny, he's right. It's a rule that the sheep shouldn't be disturbed during lambing.'

She hardly listened. 'He didn't have to be so rude, did he?'

In reply, Alec kissed her gently. Sentimental about animals, kind-hearted to Youth Hostellers. She'd learn – given time.

· · · · *Eight* · · · ·

The train that brought Andrew Menzies back home also carried a stranger to Strathblair.

His name was Robert Sinclair and his dark good looks suggested he might have tinker blood. At first glance he looked very young, his features still softly round and boyish. But a closer glance was oddly disturbing. It revealed something wolfish behind the ready smile; eyes never steady, always furtive, eternally watchful, as if those youthful years might already hold unpleasant secrets.

As he trudged up the road a car he'd seen parked outside the station came into sight. Its driver was the fair woman he'd seen meeting a Black Watch officer off the train. Robert signalled for a lift but she shook her head, indicating the back seat which contained large packages like pictures.

Too bad. A mile further on the grocer's van stopped for him. Forbes was intrigued: a smartly dressed laddie in a good suit and raincoat, with a suitcase, wanting Wester Balbuie.

'Travelled far?' he asked curiously. When told Edinburgh, he said: 'Ye'll be a friend of Mr Macrae.'

'It's hard to say,' was the enigmatic reply and his passenger continued to stare moodily out of the window. At last the van stopped at a farm road.

'Yon's Wester Balbuie,' said Forbes. 'I doubt if you'll find anybody there. He'll likely be up on the hill.'

'I can wait. Thanks for the lift.' And giving Forbes a wave he walked toward his destination. He stopped in the yard and took in the prospect before him. A steading built to the pattern he'd observed on the Strathblair estate so far, but one that looked prosperous and well-kept as if its owner took pride in possession. The green painted door with its horseshoe and polished brass also suggested that there might be money in the offing. There was no response to his knock, and walking round the outside of the house, lace-curtained windows defeated his curiosity.

There was nothing to do but wait, so he sat down on the doorstep, enjoying the afternoon sunshine. With the ability of the very young and the very old to sleep at any time, his comfortable doze was disturbed by a noisy animal near at hand. Annoyed, he saw a ram by the open gate, with its foreleg caught in the tines of a harrow.

With some difficulty he set it free. It looked like a nasty cut but no doubt sheep were hardy creatures. Watching it limp off up the hill he settled himself comfortably on the step again.

Heavy footsteps entering the yard aroused him from his reverie. At first glance it looked like an old vagrant seeking shelter. But he was mistaken; the air of authority, the sheepdog and crook denoted ownership.

'Hello, Grandfather,'

That halted Macrae in his tracks. He turned, stared unbelievingly at the boy for a moment. But there was no real doubt. One look at him and Macrae knew this was his daughter Mary's son. And the very last person in the world he wanted to see.

Without a word he walked past him and into the house.

If he had hoped that such a hostile reception would have sent the lad scurrying back down the hill, he was soon to learn that his grandson was made of sterner stuff. Robert Sinclair knew what he had come for and knew what was at stake.

In the kitchen he put down his suitcase and in the manner of an invited guest he looked round approvingly. The room was plainly but well furnished with good solid-oak furniture and leather armchairs. But this was obviously a man's house. Apart from a few plates, cups and saucers on the shelves of an old-fashioned kitchen dresser, there were no feminine fripperies, no pot plants, no ornaments or fussy cushions. The whole effect was monastic rather than domestic, suggesting a neatness which didn't extend to Macrae's ancient clothes and scruffy appearance.

Then Robert noticed the mantelpiece. Here then was the real heart of Wester Balbuie and Alasdair Macrae, sheep-farmer. The shelf was crowded with trophies for Blackface rams, best of breeds, and framed photographs of his grandfather with his prize animals. Otherwise there was only one that could be classed as personal: a faded sepia picture of a young woman whom Robert guessed was his grandmother.

'No photograph of my mother.'

'Why would there be?' asked Macrae harshly.

'I wrote to you about the funeral.'

'I got your letter.'

'But you never came.'

'Why are you here?' Macrae demanded impatiently.

'You're the only kin I have,' said Robert desperately.

'What's that to me?'

'And I'm the only kin you have,' Robert reminded him.

'That's no choice of mine,' was the grim response.

Unperturbed, Robert continued to look round the room. He smiled. 'I'd like to stay here. It's a fine big farm this.'

'Thinking it'll be yours some day?' Macrae said coldly.

Robert shrugged. 'You've got to leave it to somebody.'

This practical answer infuriated Macrae. Thumping his fist on the table, he said: 'By God, you're none so blate at speaking your mind. What makes you think you'll get it?'

'I'm my mother's son.'

'Aye, and your father's,' Macrae added viciously. 'And I've no wish to talk about either.'

Robert looked at him. He hadn't come all this way just to quarrel with his grandfather. He had urgent reasons of his own for seeking refuge at Balbuie. He hadn't expected it to be easy. His mother had told him her father was a cussed old devil. But, trying to humour him, he said: 'Look, I've learnt a lot at the Agricultural College. I could help you run this place until you retire.'

'Until I'm up in Strathblair kirkyard, you mean,' was the sharp response.

It was no use. 'Whichever,' said Robert wearily as he watched Macrae lay down on the table a frugal meal of bread and cheese. He was surprised to find two places set. Was this Highland hospitality being obeyed to the letter since all his attempts at conversation were met by stony silence?

After the meal, Macrae cleared away the dishes. 'You can't stay here.'

It was late. There was no bus. 'I've nowhere else to go.'

'You've been staying somewhere.'

'I had digs in Edinburgh. But I gave them up when I packed in college.'

Macrae stared at him. 'You've left?'

'Aye, I got fed up with it.'

'That's been a waste, hasn't it?' said Macrae angrily. 'Still it's no surprise. Feckless and footloose. You've got your father's nature as well as his face.' It wasn't true, he was Mary's image.

Robert looked at him and said with great restraint, 'Don't you say anything bad about my father.'

'I'll say what I like in my own house. She was carrying you when they left. Did you know that?'

'Aye, she told me.'

'If I'd known what was going on under this roof, I'd have libbed him.'

'They loved each other,' Robert said desperately.

'What's that to me?' Macrae demanded. 'He wanted to get his hands on Wester Balbuie. That's why he bairned her.'

'He was killed in the blitz.' Robert protested. 'Clydebank. Him and another three firemen. A tenement came down on them.'

Macrae hadn't known that. It didn't make any difference. He didn't want their bairn here to remind him of his daughter's betrayal, of the rancour that had eaten him for twenty years.

'I want you gone in the morning.'

Robert considered that remark for a moment and then took out a Savings Bank passbook and threw it onto the table. 'If that's how you feel, you can have this back.'

Macrae stared at the book. 'She wasn't to tell you. That was our arrangement.'

'She didn't. I found the savings book among her things.'

'The money was to see you through college. Keep it.'

'There's nearly thirty pounds left —'

Macrae pushed the book back at him. 'I said keep it.'

Robert regarded him slowly, shook his head. 'If you don't want me, I don't want your money.' Then, curiously, he added: 'If I'm not family, why did you send it?'

'She wrote asking for it.' He still had that letter, the first one she had ever written him, telling him that she was now a widow and that he had a grandson who was good with animals and wanted to go to agricultural college. She hoped one day his grandfather would be as proud of him as she was. Although she had never asked him for money, she had accepted the offer of fees gratefully. He never knew until too late that her reason for writing was that, knowing she was dying, she was making a last desperate bid to secure Robert's future.

Thrusting aside the memory, Macrae said viciously: 'Your

father was a wastrel and a liar. He betrayed my trust. So did she. So don't think you've come here to claim your inheritance.'

'Well, if that's how you feel, I'll be away in the morning.'

'You can sleep in the box bed down here, then.' And Macrae went upstairs without another word.

Robert slept fitfully and awoke several times during the night. Sounds outside? Could he have been followed? But these were animal noises not stealthy human footsteps.

He awoke to hear his grandfather in the kitchen. He wondered if the old man had decided he might be useful after all, when, handing him a crook, he said: 'Here, you can earn your porridge.'

Robert breathed again. He was safe. For a while, at least.

· · · · *Nine* · · · ·

Flora McInnes put on her grey crêpe-de-Chine jacket and dress with its pretty lace inset, and the pearls that had been John's wedding gift to her. No grand occasion, she was only going across the garden, but in Strathblair House one dressed for dinner. Even if Sir James dined alone with his son, he expected formal attire.

Traditions were not relinquished and codes of conduct were strictly adhered to whatever happened beyond its walls. Two world wars had threatened, scything servants and retainers. But the ancient feudal structure laid down by the first Menzies of Strathblair had survived, its values kept firm and inviolate. Even in Britain's darkest hour, food might have been scarce in the kitchen, scarcer, too, those who prepared and served it, but Sir James had refused to surrender candles on the table and guests hospitably received under the stern gaze of the Menzies' ancestral portraits.

Tonight the talking point was a new rare fruit, occupying the crystal bowl. Mrs Forbes had been collecting a crate of bananas from the station while Flora waited for Andrew, and had told her that some bairns had never tasted one.

'How are the Ritchies settling in?' Andrew asked Flora.

'Very well. Alec is coming tomorrow to sign the submission.'

'Have you met Jenny yet?'

'Oh yes. She's quite a determined young woman,' said Flora with a sidelong glance that made Sir James wriggle uncomfortably.

'Speaks her mind when she feels like it, I don't mind telling you,' he muttered, pausing to take a pinch of snuff. 'We have an understanding about the tenancy, but I did my best to discourage them.'

'I rather thought you would,' Andrew replied drily and, smiling at Flora, said: 'Thanks for looking after them.'

'Oh, I didn't do anything to help.'

'You did quite enough,' said Sir James acidly. However, as she prepared to leave, thanking him for an enjoyable evening with her most beguiling smile, he had quite forgiven her.

When Andrew returned his father held out a brandy. 'A nightcap?' And regarding his son thoughtfully murmured: 'An attractive woman.'

'Flora? Yes, very.'

Sir James nodded. 'Tell me, Andrew, have you formed any romantic attachments?'

'Not lately. No. Why do you ask?'

Sir James sat back in his armchair. 'I had two appointments in Edinburgh. Venables gave me a pretty thorough going over. Confirmed that I was as healthy as I could be for a man of my age.' Pausing, he added: 'I also saw my lawyer.' At Andrew's questioning glance, he continued heavily: 'Mathieson confirmed that even with the 45 per cent abatement on agricultural property, the estate could be pretty badly hit by death duties. So, without going into the legal technicalities, I propose to gift most of it to you. And then do my damndest to live for another five years.'

'I have no doubt that you will, Father.' Andrew smiled.

Sir James sighed. 'I want Strathblair to stay in the family, Andrew. Mathieson thinks there could be some means of setting up a trust to pass it on to you and your heirs.'

'If I had any,' said Andrew ruefully.

Sir James studied him for a moment. 'We've never been very close, Andrew.'

'Hardly surprising. Eton – Sandhurst – I was never here long enough to get close to.' Andrew tried to keep the edge of bitterness out of his voice.

Sir James nodded. 'The divorce didn't help.'

'I know.' Andrew looked at him quickly. This was the first time his father had ever referred to his mother running off with an American when he was ten years old. 'Since we've never talked like this before, I assume there must be some reason.' He paused. 'You're about to say it's time I got married.' When Sir James nodded, he asked: 'Anyone in mind?'

'If your affections were engaged elsewhere, I wouldn't dream of interfering. But you tell me they aren't. Flora would make an admirable wife for you. And since she's been widowed for six years it would be quite seemly.'

Andrew looked at him slowly. 'All a bit cold-blooded, isn't it?'

Sir James shrugged. 'Few of our line were the end product of grand passions.'

Andrew smiled sadly. 'I rather thought that I was.'

'We know what came of that,' was the icy reply.

Andrew thought for a moment. 'Aren't you overlooking something?'

'Flora's a sensible woman. I think she'd see the advantages of such a match.'

'Well, I'll have to think about it myself.'

'She's over thirty. Not much time left,' Sir James warned.

'Sons and heirs, you mean?'

'Just so.' And somewhat brusquely bidding him goodnight, in the manner of one who has said more than enough, Sir James left Andrew who, as it happened, was not at all displeased with his father's suggestion. In fact, he realised he had already been thinking along similiar lines ever since he came home.

Drinking the last of his brandy he thought about a new and novel campaign: a peaceful one this time, the wooing and winning of Flora McInnes, widow of this parish.

Next morning he began by telephoning Flora and suggesting that they might have a picnic lunch if she wasn't too busy.

She sounded delighted at the prospect, so, after giving instructions to Mrs McKenzie to make up a hamper, he turned his attention to the best way to go about his new project: establishing an art business. He had bought some excellent pictures at a Perth auction, at a good price. They would make a start. The more he thought about it the more enthusiastic he became. He would need a proper office or workroom, of course, but there was plenty of space in the attics, with good light.

The delivery van from the auctioneers didn't arrive until midday and after seeing the contents safely stored he realised he was going to be late for Flora.

He hurried across to her office full of apologies to find he had just missed Alec. He must try and see more of him. He had hoped that their wartime comradeship might continue in Civvy Street and that Alec would get out of the habit of saluting him each time they met.

He smiled at Flora.

'All ready for our picnic?'

Together they drove through the estate and settled for an idyllic spot by a rustic bridge with a flowing stream. While Andrew took out his sketchbook, Flora unpacked the picnic hamper: egg-and-tomato sandwiches, a fruit cake made by the housekeeper, and Andrew's contribution, a bottle of wine from Sir James's cellar.

Flora looked round. 'I used to come here with John.'

Observing her wistful expression, Andrew said gently: 'You still miss him terribly?'

She nodded. 'Oh yes. It doesn't seem fair. I married the factor and finished up with a soldier. We had such a short few months together.'

'You must feel very lonely at times.'

Flora shrugged. 'Sometimes. But I've made sure my life isn't empty. The estate keeps me busy.'

'Work's not much of a substitute for companionship.'

Flora sighed. 'It'll have to do, won't it, until something better comes along.'

Looking up from his almost completed sketch of her, so pretty, so soft and womanly, he said: 'I'm surprised it hasn't already.' The strange look she gave him made him fearful that he had offended her. 'Sorry. Didn't mean to be impertinent.'

Again she smiled. 'You weren't.' And, pausing, she added: 'Just after the war finished a friend of John's came to visit me. David Malcolm. He was stationed at Perth.'

'I know him,' said Andrew, 'Captain in the Second Battalion.'

Flora nodded. 'We saw quite a lot of each other. He would drive down almost every weekend.' She looked towards the flowing water.

'I was glad when he was posted elsewhere.' And when Andrew asked why, she answered: 'Because I could see what was going to happen.'

When Andrew queried whether that would have been so bad, she gave him an oddly penetrating look. 'Regular army, Andrew. I never want to go through that again.'

'The war's over now, Flora.'

She shook her head. 'Not for the professional soldier. There's always one more war to be fought somewhere.'

Andrew regarded her thoughtfully. He was going to need a very different tactical approach to this campaign.

'May I see?' And holding out her hand for the sketch, she remarked: 'That's very good, Andrew. Seriously, have you ever thought of doing it professionally?' Refusing a refill and watching him tip the last of the wine into his glass, she added: 'You never did tell me about your interest in those paintings you brought home.'

'Not in front of Father.' Andrew laughed. 'But seriously, I'm toying with an idea that I might be better at selling them than painting them myself.'

· · · · *Ten* · · · ·

Early on the morning of the valuation, Alec was preparing to bring down the Corriebeg flock.

'Five hundred sheep,' Jenny repeated, still in her dressing gown and stifling yawns. 'And how many people?'

'A dozen maybe. Mrs McInnes will bring over Mr Abercrombie, the oversman, and the two valuers. The idea is to put them in the parlour and leave a bottle of whisky handy. What about food? Have you got everything ready?' he asked anxiously.

'It will be by the time they get here.' And, giving him a little push in the direction of the door, she urged: 'You look after the sheep. I'll look after the neighbouring.'

As Alec departed whistling for Fly, Jenny saw the distant figures moving on the hill. Activity had already started. There were many willing hands for Alec among their neighbours.

Sighing, for she could have done with an extra pair or two, she covered the old table with a white damask cloth and napkins, set out her wedding silver, then the food.

She was proudly surveying the results of her labours when Pheemie arrived. 'I've just this minute finished.'

Pheemie's smile died as she looked at the table: plates with lace doilies heaped with tiny sandwiches, their crusts cut off, wafer-thin boiled ham, sliced eggs, jellies, chocolate eclairs and melting moments. It was the sort of spread Pheemie had only even seen in movies about the English upper classes, settling down for afternoon tea on the lawn.

But for a hill-farm neighbouring, it was totally inappropriate. 'In the name o' God,' was her awed whisper. Then, turning to Jenny, she said cheerfully: 'You've been working hard. I can see that.'

Jenny wasn't fooled. Regarding the feast in dismay she said: 'It's all wrong, isn't it?'

'Oh, they look fair nice. The wee tomato sandwiches. Fair tasty,' Pheemie smiled brightly.

'But it's all wrong,' Jenny repeated miserably.

'Oh, I wouldnae just say that,' said Pheemie carefully.

'Well, what would you say?' Jenny demanded.

'It's just that folk might be looking for something a wee bit more – well – substantial.' Seeing Jenny was almost in tears, she said: 'Like soup for a start.'

Jenny said, 'I've made soup,' and Pheemie looking in the pot could only say of the chicken broth, 'Fair nice, too. In its way.'

'I have spent all my coupons on those chocolate eclairs!' said Jenny tearfully. 'Pheemie, what am I going to do?'

'Maybe I've enough time to get round the other farming wifies, see what they've got. Mrs Forbes'll get us meat from the butcher. We need a nice stew going. And tatties. Lots o' tatties. Can ye make griddle scones?' And when Jenny shook her head, Pheemie smiled. 'You'll learn how this morning. First, some sheep's heid broth.'

'Where are we going to get a sheep's head?'

But Pheemie's knowing wink said it all. She would have no problems rallying round the neighbours.

An hour later the Corriebeg kitchen was once again the scene of anguished activity. Dicing vegetables Jenny was told firmly not to peel the potatoes, the goodness was in the skin.

By the time the broth was ready, Mrs Forbes had arrived breathless having nearly cleared out her husband's shop and triumphantly produced two pounds of stewing steak from the butcher.

When Jenny said she hadn't any coupons, Mrs Forbes was

reassuring. She would sort that out with her man later.

'It'll never be ready in time!' Jenny said looking at the clock as Pheemie inspected the soup and pronounced it was doing well.

'Umberto will fair enjoy that. He loves his sheep's heid.' And in answer to Jenny's 'Umberto?' she explained: 'My orraman. An Italian. Came over as a prisoner of war. He just stayed on.'

Alec was consumed by an anxiety equal to Jenny's. According to neighbouring farmers, the Corriebeg sheep were in good condition but he was worried that the valuers would not reach agreement on a price that, when they were auctioned, would leave him enough profit to pay off some of the overdraft that Andrew had guaranteed him, buy animal feed for the lean winter days, as well as keeping Jenny and himself existing above the starvation margin.

'*Buongiorno*. Mr Ritchie of Corriebeg?'

Alec was surprised to hear Italian being spoken in Strathblair by a tall fair-haired young man who smilingly introduced himself. 'Umberto Fabiani, I'm Pheemie Robertson's orraman. She has gone to Corriebeg to help Signora Ritchie.'

Despite encounters with light-complexioned, blue-eyed Italians during the Anzio campaign, Alec still expected the men to be a race of tenors, short, dark and olive-skinned. As for this one, there was an undeniably distinguished quality about his good looks, tempered with an air of self-confidence.

'Aye, it's not a bad wee place you have over there. I give you a hand when I have time. I'm good with machinery, though I say it masel'.' His English was good but accented with the local idiom.

Thanking him, Alec turned his attention again to the three men. There seemed to be a certain amount of dissension, with agreement reached on the beasts being well-fleeced, but their real value lay in their meat. With half the world starving, it was the meat that mattered. From this vantage point he could only see much shaking of heads and waving of arms, with a smooth-looking gent, who had to be Abercrombie, in a dazzling waistcoat and elegant suit, occasionally intervening.

Alec watched the scene helplessly. He could do nothing to influence them, but knew that Flora was on his side and that she would have already oiled the wheels of diplomacy and the valuers' throats with plenty of drams before they left the factor's office.

'How do you think it's going?' he asked Umberto.

'*Buona, buona*. Not sae bad,' was the enigmatic reply.

The three men, deep in earnest discussion, were now walking towards the farmhouse where they would finalise their deliberations. If only he could be a fly on that parlour wall.

An anxious half-hour passed before they emerged. Abercrombie held up his hand for silence. 'Ladies and gentlemen, if I could have your attention, please. Loons and quinies, just a wee bit o' hush. Mr Munro of Dalscriadan, whom you all know, and Mr Wallace, whom you know just as well, and myself, whom you have seen afore now, have reached agreement on the valuation of the Corriebeg flock. The beasts are in fine condition, as you might well expect, seeing as they were looked after by Mr Macrae of Balbuie this while back.'

Alec couldn't see Macrae, but he spotted Jenny and Pheemie and, near the back of the crowd, Flora and Andrew. He must have a word with Andrew later, thank him for Corriebeg.

'But before I come to the bit,' Abercrombie continued, 'since this is Mr and Mistress Ritchie's first neighbouring, I know you would wish me to welcome them to Strathblair with a few words. And what better words than those penned by the Immortal Bard when he wrote: "The cottage leaves the palace far behind, What is a Lordlings' pomp? A cumbrous load. Disguising oft the wretch of human kind Studied in arts of Hell in wickedness refin'd . . ."'

Alec groaned silently. He had been warned that the man had

verbal diarrhoea. Did he think he was addressing a Burns' Supper? 'For heaven's sake, get on with it, man,' he muttered.

But Abercrombie was enjoying himself. '"O Scotia my dear, my native soil, From whom my warmest wish . . ."'

Other people were impatient, Alec realised, aware of good-humoured stirrings in the crowd.

'". . . Long may thy hardy sons of rustic toil Be blest with health and peace and sweet content."'

Jenny came over. He could feel her shiver of apprehension as he put an arm round her and they joined in the polite applause – not too much in case Abercrombie felt obliged to give an encore. Bowing, smiling, thoroughly pleased with himself, the oversman held up his hand: 'It is our unanimous finding that the Corriebeg valuation is one thousand and sixty one pounds ten shillings.'

Alec hugged Jenny in delighted relief, making a quick evaluation of his own he joined the thirsty neighbours drifting towards Corriebeg. Five hundred sheep, that worked out at just over two pounds ten shillings each.

In the already crowded kitchen, Pheemie ladled out soup while Jenny dispensed stew and tatties.

Wallace came over. 'You did none too bad, Corribeg. We'll come to the usual arrangement and I'll sell your beasts at the mart. Aye, and I'll get you a cow. No bother.'

As the food vanished, the simple meal declared a great success, Alec and Jenny exchanged happy proud glances. This was their début. Corriebeg had arrived!

'Where's Balbuie?' Wallace asked. 'It's not like him to miss a free feed and a few drams.'

'He found one of his champion tups with an injured foot when we were on the hill this morning. He was getting the vet to take a look at it —'

'How about a song from our host?' shouted Abercrombie. Having completed his Burns recital he had been threatening the company in the kitchen with 'Ye Banks and Braes'. Sundry groans and cat-calls suggested he give up good-humouredly.

Alec, reluctantly but with surprising good voice, launched into 'The Bonnie Lass of Fyvie' while in a quiet corner Mrs Forbes and Pheemie were indulging themselves with fruit cake, a well-earned rest, and entertaining Jenny to some local gossip.

She was surprised to hear that the absent Macrae whom she had thought of as a crusty old bachelor had once been married.

'Eighteen she was and him old enough to be her father,' said Mrs Forbes. 'The daughter, Mary was born within the year. But it was a bad birth. Jeannie was never the same. She died not long after. He got some wifie in to look after the bairn and keep house for him.'

'He fair doted on Mary,' said Pheemie. 'We were at the school together.'

'The only chance she ever got to play wi' other bairns. When she was in her teens, and should have been daffin' wi' the lads, he kept her at home up in Balbuie. So I suppose it had to happen.' Mrs Forbes looked at Pheemie and the story of Mary and Macrae's orraman, Gavin Sinclair, was interrupted by loud applause for Alec's final chorus.

Joining in, Jenny noticed Flora bending over the major who was slumped at the table and rather drunk. She was obviously urging him to leave as he looked up dazedly at her.

Fine head he'll have tomorrow, she thought, and Alec, too. Oh well, a house-warming, as they'd call it in Salisbury, didn't happen every day. It had been great, but none of it could have happened if it hadn't been for Pheemie whom she'd seen casting wistful glances in Umberto's direction. There were hints that the handsome young Italian performed other duties than those required of an orraman.

Having got to know Pheemie, Jenny realised she had a fine bone structure, the kind that would wear well, and a good figure. All she needed was a stylish haircut, some feminine clothes and a dash of make-up. Even Alec agreed that she could be a real smasher if she put mind to it. Perhaps Umberto had recognised that too, she thought.

Jenny didn't see Macrae pushing his way through the crowd.

He was a very unhappy man. The vet had come quickly enough, but there was nothing he could do to save the beast. It was too late, the whole leg was poisoned. If only Macrae had spotted it sooner.

The short cut to Corriebeg, and what was left of the neighbouring, led down past the waterfall where something glinting on the ground caught Macrae's eye. He hurried towards the house, heard the singing. He'd soon change their tune and, by God, someone would pay dearly for this day's work.

Jenny came to greet him. All the bottles had been empty for a long time, but her smile was welcoming. 'Mr Macrae, you were able to come.'

'You've missed a fine neighbouring, Balbuie,' said Pheemie proudly. 'She's done well wi' her first.'

'Ay, her first and maybe her last,' shouted Macrae.

Flora stepped forward. 'What are you talking about?'

'A dead tup. That's what I'm talking about. And this.' And into the remnants of the feast on the table he hurled the shard of broken glass which he had picked up.

Alec looked at it. 'What's that to do with my wife?'

'I found it up by the waterfall. The place where she told those lads to camp.' And turning to Jenny in an accusatory tone, he added: 'You'll not deny that.'

Jenny, horrified by the implications, shook her head miserably. 'No. I'm very sorry —'

'They'd no business being there. And you two have no business being here. Go back to where ye belong!'

Andrew, sobered by the scene before him, staggered to his feet and said, in tones of authority: 'Steady on, Balbuie.'

Flora touched his arm. As factor she once more took

command of the situation. 'Mr Macrae, if you have anything to say, it should be said in private.'

'No,' shouted Macrae. 'Let it be said where folk can hear it. The Ritchies are only in Corriebeg because he was friendly with the major here.'

'You're forgetting yourself, Balbuie,' said Andrew coldly.

'There's no other reason and it's a gey bad reason.'

Trying to save a worsening situation, Alec interrupted: 'I can understand you being upset, Mr Macrae, but there's no reason to be offensive —'

'Man, Balbuie,' said Wallace entering the fray, 'you've got to keep a sense of proportion. You lose beasts every year —'

'I don't lose a champion tup because of a daft woman's damned stupidity,' was the furious reply.

That was too much for Alec. 'Macrae, I am not having my wife spoken to like that. Get out.'

'Oh, I will that. And maybe you'll not be long behind me.'

'I'm sure Mr Ritchie will compensate you for your loss,' said Wallace, ever the voice of reason.

'Will he now? There's no a tup in the Corriebeg hirsel comes anywhere near to the one I lost.'

'You've no proof that your tup was injured on a broken bottle,' said Alec angrily.

'Have I not? That glass is from one of Forbes' bottles. Where would they get it if not from there?' There was nothing Jenny could say as Macrae went on: 'That's proof enough for me!'

'Look,' Flora intervened, 'I think you and Mr Ritchie should come around to my office tomorrow and we'll see what can be sorted out.'

'Oh, I'll be there, all right. And if I don't get satisfaction, it's the laird I'll be wanting to see. Not his factor.' And, turning to Wallace, he said shortly: 'I suppose you'll have had some thoughts on handling Ritchie's business.'

'And if I had?'

'That's up to you. You've been handling mine for long

enough. But you're not the only auctioneer in the district.'

'I'll not be threatened by anyone, Balbuie,' said Wallace.

'You choose. Him or me. Come away, Robert, out o' this.'

Outside, Robert could hardly keep up with him. At last he reached his side. 'I've got something to tell you. Your tup,' he panted. 'I found it wandering about the close. The day I arrived. Someone had left a gate open.'

'Did it have a bell-mark on the brow?'

'Aye. Got itself caught in the tines of an old harrow.'

Macrae halted in his tracks. 'Why didn't you say so then?'

Robert shrugged. 'I forgot all about it —'

'You forgot!' Macrae roared.

'Aye. That welcome you gave me put everything else clean out of my mind,' said Robert bitterly. 'It's your own fault. If you hadn't raged at me, I might have remembered and you wouldn't have lost your damned sheep.'

And turning on his heel, Robert strode angrily ahead of him in the direction of Wester Balbuie.

· · · · *Eleven* · · · ·

The neighbouring which had begun for Jenny in disaster had ended the same way. She could have wept. Alec had been so proud of her. Now all she could moan was: 'Oh Alec, I'm sorry.'

But all Alec wanted at that precise moment was to lie down and sleep. When he was sober he would realise this was just one more result of her misplaced kindness. Dear God, would she ever learn there was no room for sentimentality in a farmer's wife?

Jenny slept little that night and felt dreadful as she watched Alec leaving in his Sunday best again for the meeting in Flora's office. 'What will you do if he insists on seeing Sir James?' she asked.

Alec looked at her. 'I can't lie to him, Jenny.'

'I'm sorry,' she whispered again as he kissed her goodbye.

And as he drove off she realised they both knew how inadequate those words were. Guiltily she was aware that she had failed him once again.

At Balbuie Robert also watched his grandfather grim-faced preparing to leave for the Strathblair estate office, an occasion which warranted his best suit, despite the fact that it smelt abominably of mothballs so infrequently was it aired at weddings and funerals.

Macrae hadn't spoken to Robert since his revelations on the road home. Perhaps he would never speak to him again for he realised this was the worst thing that could have happened. If Grandfather had to apologise, then he would lose face and the words would choke him.

While Macrae made his way to the factor's office brooding darkly that none of this would have happened if Major Menzies hadn't been such a fool as to give Corriebeg to strangers, the cause of his anger was blissfully engaged on a painting of Strathblair House.

Andrew was hoping that fresh air and an escape from his father's disapproving presence might rid him of the crippling hangover that was his legacy from the Corriebeg neighbouring. He could not pretend that was the sole reason for his depression.

It was much more than that. When Alec had started singing 'The Bonnie Lass of Fyvie' he had been transported back to the storming of Coriano Ridge and to the gates of death which had almost engulfed him.

Prime Minister Winston Churchill had dismissed the invasion of Italy as attacking the 'soft underbelly of the Axis'. For Andrew, Salerno to Monte Cassino through Anzio to Coriano Ridge felt like climbing Italy's hard backbone. And, even in 1944, he had been sick of war. Would he ever cease to taste the sweating fear of horror as he relived his own lack of courage, or cease to feel his guilt for the unnecessary blood shed by the men who died, but might have lived, had he given the command to retreat?

Engrossed in his dismal thoughts, he was surprised to hear his father's voice. 'I didn't see you at breakfast, Andrew.' And when he replied that he hadn't felt like any, Sir James, looking over his shoulder, said rather awkwardly: 'It'll be nice when it's finished.'

Andrew sighed. He'd better get it over with. 'I've been thinking, Father, about resigning my commission.'

There was no explosion this time, but Sir James had the look of a cautious man with a lot of questions who didn't know quite where to begin. 'What future do you see for yourself?'

Andrew flourished a brush towards the painting. 'This.'

'I agree you do have a certain talent,' Sir James admitted with considerable restraint, since this was not what he had in mind for the heir to Strathblair.

Andrew smiled at his father's doubtful expression. 'It's a very modest talent, I'm afraid, a competent amateur rather than a professional artist. However, I have a fair idea how the business side of the art world works, enough to make a successful dealer or curator. I've thought about it and that's what I'd like to do.'

Sir James's reaction was surprisingly mild. There were no reproaches, no recriminations. 'I see.' He nodded slowly and turned to face the painting. 'You've caught the colours very well.'

Watching him walk away Andrew saw his father for the first time with a touch of pity. A rather lost, unhappy old man whose only son, a soldier bred of generations of soldiers, had let the family down. Andrew sighed. They all thought he was so brave and valiant. Yet sometimes he fancied that Flora was regarding him quizzically, when he quickly changed the subject to safer ground. He wondered if she knew, guessed intuitively. If he intended to marry her, then some day she would have to know the truth about the gallant Major Menzies.

Flora, too, was less than happy. She had slept badly, puzzled and worried about Andrew's behaviour. He was drinking too much and he had behaved like a man with a lot on his mind during the Corriebeg neighbouring. She could have done without the interview between Ritchie and Macrae which promised to be both difficult and unpleasant; it was another disagreeable aspect of factorship.

'Now, gentlemen, since you've slept on it, let's hear your own sides of the story and see if we can resolve this matter amicably.'

Calling upon Macrae to reiterate his accusation, she said: 'You have no real evidence that your tup received its injury on Corriebeg land, Mr Macrae, or that the campers left the broken glass there,' she added thoughtfully. 'After all, to get to Corriebeg from the hostel, they wouldn't go through Strathblair. So where did they get the milk?'

'Jenny gave them some in an empty bottle.' Macrae was surprised to hear that, as he expected Ritchie to defend his wife's negligence. 'This isn't about campers, injured tups or anything else,' Alec went on accusingly. 'You've resented us from the minute we set foot in Corriebeg. And you've shown it.'

'I've given you all the help you asked for —'

'Helping a neighbour, as you well know, has to do with survival, not goodwill. Your real feelings came out last night —'

'I have something to say about that,' Macrae interrupted. 'I shouldn't have spoken to Mrs Ritchie the way I did. Or the major. I'm sorry. I was upset about losing my prize beast.'

'Which brings us back to the subject of compensation,' Flora sighed.

'Aye well, it was gey valuable, a Champion Blackface and border bred. I paid thirty pounds for it, but I've been offered fifty.'

'Fifty pounds!' said Alec angrily. 'That settles it. I don't have fifty pounds to spare.'

'So we're back where we started,' said Flora wearily. 'Do you still want to see Sir James, Balbuie?'

Macrae shook his head. 'No.' And, as the other two exchanged looks of astonishment, he added: 'There's been enough ill will I'm thinking. I'll accept one of the Corriebeg lambs and leave it at that.'

'One with a bell on the brow,' Alec told Jenny later. 'Like that wee fellow I showed you.' Having spent the morning anxiously awaiting his return, she was surprised and relieved at Macrae's decision.

The following day Flora arrived with Macrae to see the matter settled. Robert came too for his own private reasons. As Macrae inspected the newly born lamb Jenny cradled in her arms, he said: 'It'll do. A fine beast right enough.'

Robert rubbed the lamb's bell mark and grinned. 'You might have another champ here if it was sired by your one.'

'At least it's all in the family,' said Jenny delighted with this peaceful settlement.

'Aye. Best to keep things in the family,' Robert grinned, giving his grandfather a significant look, well aware of the old man's discomfort and his relief that Robert had kept the truth about the injured tup to himself.

Carrying the lamb, they returned home silently where Robert's first action was to put his mother's photograph on the mantelpiece. Macrae made no comment and the two sat down to supper, each wrapped in his own thoughts.

Robert sighed. He had found a safe refuge. No one would think of looking for him at Wester Balbuie.

June 1950

· · · · *Twelve* · · · ·

June brought clover-scented fields and bees booming among the first blossoms as flowering heather created faint shadows of smoky amethyst in sheltered slopes. Rosy bird-haunted dawns with hills shimmering under cloudless skies meant one anxiety less for the annual sheep-shearing at Corriebeg.

The days had been hot, and matronly ewes, despite some argument and noisy blaring, celebrated the loss of heavy winter fleeces by scurrying up the hill with a return to skittish lambhood.

Two experts who toured the farms made shearing look deceptively easy, and Jenny was determined to 'give a hand'. Although she was skilled with shears when it came to cutting out frocks and skirts, managing a heavy recalcitrant ewe required dexterity as well as brute strength.

'You have to let it know who's boss,' said Pheemie and Jenny gave up, terrified lest she injured the struggling animal. Under Macrae's critical gaze she resorted to folding the fleeces where she could do less damage. After all, she decided, wrinkling her nose, it wasn't so different from folding blankets only a lot smellier.

Summer weather agreed with her and she had been feeling pleased with life. Corriebeg was responding to her loving care by slowly emerging as a comfortable home, with flowers, books, ornaments and pictures, and the odd pretty cushion. But Alec seemed not to notice her additions, only her omissions, such as her inability to keep within their strict budget. He was annoyed to find her owing money to both the grocer and to Collins the butcher.

These minor domestic issues weren't serious and any daily differences were soon settled in bed. In fact, their lovemaking had improved greatly in comfort and expertise since their honeymoon days though neither would have believed that possible.

But the main problem was Fly. Try as she may, Jenny couldn't help treating her like a pet. Fly was devoted to her and, when they were alone in the house, liked nothing better than to sleep with her chin resting on Jenny's ankles. Conscious of the master's disapproval the two sprang apart almost guiltily when his footsteps approached.

At the gathering that morning, Jenny was hurt and angry when Alec reprimanded her in front of everyone for 'fussing Fly' who had cleverly rounded up a very truculent ewe.

'She's only doing her job,' he told her irritably.

Sighing she returned to the kitchen to do what she did best. No one complained about her mugs of tea and carrying out a tray she overheard Pheemie saying to Alec: 'You look as if you've lost sixpence and found a penny.'

'I seem to be two ewes short. And I'm sure I counted right.'

Pheemie's shrug indicated that people often count wrong.

'Sheep can't just disappear, Alec,' said Jenny.

'Oh Jenny, for heaven's sake,' he said shortly.

This second reprimand was too much for Jenny. Still feeling sore about Fly, she turned sharply away as Macrae came over and flounced back to the house.

'You're not the only one,' Macrae told Alec. 'I've lost a couple, and Dalscriadan's lost three. What about you?' he asked Pheemie.

'I'm alright – so far.'

Macrae pursed his lips. 'Somebody's been busy. We'd better have another look.' Alec followed him up the hill where they were alerted to the fact that something was wrong by Fly's behaviour. They found her standing over a dead ewe.

Macrae straightened up after inspecting the animal. 'Pheemie's. Must have exhausted itself, most likely running away from the thieves. I'll speak to Sergeant Brodie.'

Meanwhile Pheemie had followed Jenny into the kitchen. As

she washed the mugs, anxious to justify herself, Jenny said: 'I don't know why Alec has to be so bad tempered with me. It's not my fault the sheep are gone.'

'That's men for you.' Pheemie was sorry for Jenny. Men were difficult creatures at the best of times, she thought cycling back to Carnban, and Jenny would have to learn to put up with things and be less sensitive if she were to survive.

An army lorry emerged from the farm road watched by Umberto.

'Who was that?' Pheemie demanded, drawing up next to him. Umberto told her it was some man who had come selling gates. 'Pity you missed him.'

The same lorry's next point of call was Corriebeg. 'Quality gates, sir. Metal. They'll last a lifetime.'

Alec stared at the man. There was something familiar about him. The limp and that dark auburn hair worn longer than the last time they'd met triggered off his memory. Then he remembered: the wide boy with the innocent expression who got into all kinds of scrapes.

'Corporal Speirs, isn't it?'

'Oh – Sergeant Major Ritchie!' The man saluted, grinning.

'How's the leg?' He'd been wounded at Coriano Ridge.

'Took a while to heal, but I get around.' And, taking the cigarette Alec offered, he sighed: 'Could be worse.' The look the two exchanged said they'd been the lucky ones. They'd lived on.

'This your farm, then?'

'Aye, all mine.'

Speirs nodded. 'Nice place. Tell you what, sergeant-major, I'll sell you a gate at half price – for old times' sake.' And, before Alec could protest, he called: 'Open up the back, Rory.'

Alec was surprised to see a smart young woman in a khaki uniform and army boots.

'My partner,' but Speirs's look indicated there might be more than business to this relationship.

Observing the girl's army cap, Alec said: 'Ex-ATS?'

'Aye, sergeant driver.' Alec had met her type before: pretty once, but now tough as old boots, aggressive as hell, with all the femininity knocked out of her. She represented a new breed of woman the Army had created, equipped to live and survive in a man's world.

As he looked into the lorry at the gates, she said: 'They come in two sizes. You'll need the big one – thirty bob.'

At that moment, Alec wasn't sure whether he wanted to do business with this pair, despite memories of the brief comradeship which brings together ill-assorted men under fire. 'I'll have to think about it. Meet you at the pub later, eh.'

Alec took Fly out again after supper. He loved the evening stillness, the fine, clear light on the cloud-feathered hills. It was a time for a man to feel at peace with himself and the world. But Alec couldn't get those damned missing sheep out of his mind.

He wasn't alone either tonight. There were two men on the road below him, scanning the hill with binoculars, with a green van parked near by. It was obvious they were strangers acting too furtively to be up to any good. He'd better find out if Macrae knew anything about them.

He watched them until they drove off. There was no nightfall in midsummer and the sky was like green crystal with a faint echo of light left over from the sunset that would linger to join hands with the sunrise.

In the hope of stumbling on some clues to those missing sheep, or the thieves, he stayed on the hill, watchful and wary. When at last he returned home, he was exhausted. He must have walked miles.

As he prepared for bed, Jenny, eager to make amends, sat up and told him proudly Macrae said she was 'doing not bad' at the fleece-folding. 'Praise indeed from him, wasn't it?'

But instead of laughing and cuddling her, Alec merely nodded absently. 'I never reckoned to have to cope with sheep thieves.' With his back towards her, he turned onto his side and minutes later, she knew by his even breathing, he was fast asleep.

Miserable she lay awake, longing to touch him, but for the first time she was afraid. What is happening to us? she thought. What could be more important than making love to her?

The next day as they cleared up after the shearing, Macrae made a point of telling Pheemie that Brodie was on the look-out for the sheep thieves.

'Someone who knows the area, he reckons. The comings and goings of the folk.' And, giving her a hard look, he said: 'Not seen much of your Eyetie lately. What's he up to?'

At this none-too-subtle implication she said angrily: 'An errand for me, Macrae.'

As she stormed off she remembered uneasily that she had seen Umberto in Strathblair – talking to Collins the butcher outside the slaughter house in the lane behind his shop. This was not one of her errands. As she watched the two men light up their cigarettes, there was something in their expressions that suggested that a satisfactory deal had been struck.

Eternally curious, irritated as always by Umberto's secretiveness, Pheemie moved closer, hidden by a parked van.

Umberto had a resonant voice that carried. 'Is it the same as before?' When Collins murmured in assent, he said: 'Then I can do. But the money. Perhaps it will need to be more.'

That scene returned constantly to haunt her. If Umberto had a hand in this sheep stealing, she'd kill him. And then, with a sinking heart, she realised he would be sent to jail, or deported to Italy. She'd never see him again. Damn all missing sheep. She didn't care if the whole herd went missing, if only she could keep Umberto.

· · · · *Thirteen* · · · ·

Morning found Alec in an ill humour, feeling guilty about Jenny, knowing he had no right to take his worries over the missing sheep out on her. Storming into the house after dropping a bag of nails, he knocked over a saucer of milk which was standing on the doorstep.

Hearing the noise, Jenny sprang to the door. 'Alec, didn't you see the cat?' She had almost succeeded in taming a wild cat. Now terrified, it would never come back.

Alec shouted: 'I don't want to hear about any bloody cat!'

That was too much. 'Stop swearing!' she shouted back.

'I've been awake half the night with blasted sheep on my mind —'

'You're not in the Army now!' she interrupted coldly.

'I wish I was!'

Following him into the kitchen, her heart thumping she whispered: 'What do you mean?'

'You know what I mean. You cannae hold a sheep for shearing. You ruin my dog —'

That hurt but Jenny ignored it. 'What did you mean – wishing you were back in the Army?' It couldn't be that bad, living with her, not worse than the desert war or Italy where men died.

She stared at him in horror as he shook his head miserably. 'God knows.' Then looking straight across at her, his eyes full of that cold steel light she had hoped never to see, he said: 'I'll tell you something I do know though. You cannae be sentimental on a farm.'

She was rather tired of being reminded of that and turning on her heel with great dignity she swept out of the kitchen. Carefully refilling the saucer of milk, she fed the hens and in defiance of Alec's ruling, she brought Fly into the kitchen and cuddled her for comfort, crying into her soft fur. Fly whimpered in return and put a paw on her knee, as if she, too, understood the fickle moods of men.

News of the sheep thieves had reached Strathblair House. The Menzies of the eighteenth century who glared down from the walls would have had a swift cure, thought Flora. They would have hung them from the Gallows Tree in the garden: it would have been a public event to which all the tenantry would be invited as entertainment – and warning.

But at that moment Flora, meeting Andrew on her way to the factor's office, was rather more interested to hear that he had told Sir James he was thinking of resigning his commission.

'That's a big step, Andrew.'

Andrew shrugged. 'Father's getting on. I should be thinking of settling down here,' he added with a sidelong glance in her direction.

'He seemed concerned your interests might lie elsewhere.'

Wondering what the devil his father was up to, Andrew said cautiously: 'Would you be happy working for me? You wouldn't suddenly take off to fresh fields?' he added quickly.

'Why should I? I like it here.' Flora stared at him astonished by the question.

'I've got a lot to learn and I'll need your help – to show me the ropes.' He took a deep breath. 'And also – I'd like to —'

Flora got into her car. Smiling, she looked out at him. 'I know – get on with your art dealing. I'll help all I can but I imagine your father will be around for a while yet.'

Andrew watched her drive away; she'd left him feeling that his wooing campaign still had a long way to go. He returned to the attic where he was clearing away some of the debris to create a workable space for his art business, when he made a surprising discovery. An hour later he was delighted to see Flora's car had returned.

In her office she was busy with ledgers, frowning over the accounts. He couldn't honestly pretend that she welcomed this intrusion although she politely offered him some tea.

'I've just found some of Mother's paintings,' he said, taking a seat at her desk. 'They're rather good. And there's a splendid self-portrait. I'd like to show you if —'

Flora looked over her shoulder. He was holding a photograph she had received that morning of her sister Janet whom he had once loved.

In answer to his question she told him Janet was still unmarried and lecturing at Edinburgh University.

'Two clever sisters,' he smiled. And, remembering how he had lost one sister and didn't want to lose the other, he said anxiously: 'Will you have dinner with us tonight?'

But Flora turned down his invitation without explanation. Was he still interested in Janet? Was that why he seemed so thrown by the photograph?

Jenny had a visitor. Umberto was out shooting rabbits. Hanging out the washing on the line, she had shouted a cheery greeting and Umberto, who had an eye for a pretty woman, didn't need a second invitation. He made polite and flattering remarks about all the improvements as they walked round the outbuildings.

In the barn, she pointed to an old wreck of a bicycle. Alec had promised to do it up for her so that she could use it to go into Strathblair. Bearing in mind Alec's preoccupation with lost sheep and the uneasy climate of life within Corriebeg at present, she said: 'I need transport. I can't always be waiting for Alec to be free to take me into the village or into town.'

Umberto smiled, looking down at her. He was very tall. 'You could ask Umberto.'

'To transport me?'

'To fix the bike.'

'Really?' And watching him examine the machine, she remembered that Pheemie had told her he was 'awfu' guid wi' his hands'.

He nodded. 'It wouldn't be any trouble. I have a saddle and other things. Yes. Seven shillings?'

Jenny frowned. Alec might be offended. 'Well —'

Misunderstanding her hesitation he dropped the price: 'Six shillings then?' He smiled. 'A bargain. I am a good worker.'

'Alright. Thank you,' she said smiling gratefully as he pushed the bike across the yard. She accompanied him to the gate. She liked Umberto. He made her feel like a pretty, desirable woman again and she knew from the man-woman expression in his eyes that he found her attractive. He was very good looking, she thought, and being foreign set him apart, made him that bit different, sexy and mysterious. He had a nice deep voice and that accent – she wondered how her girlfriends in Salisbury who were man-mad would react to Pheemie Robertson's orraman. And thinking of Pheemie, if rumours were true, then she was a very lucky woman.

Waving him goodbye, laughing and suddenly pleased with life again, she was suddenly aware of another presence. Looking up, she saw Alec watching them from the hill. He was very still. Discomforted at being spied on, she went into the kitchen and was busily setting supper when Alec came in.

'What was he doing with that bike?'

'He's going to mend it for me.'

'I said I'd fix it,' was the furious reply.

'You said you'd fix it days ago. I need it now.'

Alec paused. 'And what does he expect in return?'

That was too much. Jenny raised her hand in blazing anger but it was seized before it reached Alec's face.

'Eat your supper and I hope it chokes you.' Then, rushing upstairs, she banged the door furiously behind her, returning ten minutes later to clear the table noisily.

Alec stood up and seized his jacket. 'I'm going for a drink.'

Jenny's answer was to turn her back coldly on him as she prepared to wash the dishes. Hearing the motorbike leave, she stared miserably at her hands clutching the sink. A month ago she could never have believed such a scene would ever take place between them.

She went to the door, gazed across the hills, so tranquil and benign in the heavy-scented gloaming, the sky still flying the gold-and-saffron banners of a stormy sunset. But such beauty no longer deceived Jenny. It wasn't Alec, or the sheep thieves. It was this land, Corriebeg itself, that was their enemy, the destroyer of their love. And if she hoped to survive, she must never forget it.

· · · · *Fourteen* · · · ·

In the Atholl Arms, Alec found consolation in men's company and the familiar faces of neighbouring farmers.

The strangers he had seen surveying the hills with their binoculars now occupied their own corner of the bar-room. They were ugly-looking customers on closer scrutiny, tough and watchful, here for the sole purpose of making a deal.

Alec was ordering a drink when Speirs came in with the woman, Rory. She went straight over to the bar. 'Two halfs and two pints.'

The other customers were shocked into silence. Such a thing had never been heard of in their pub before. As far as decent, respectable folk were concerned, there was only one kind of woman who ever entered bars. And they didn't have *that* kind in Strathblair – or if they did, then no one was letting on about it.

Alec smiled at her. 'Brave lady.'

Rory shrugged. 'I've drunk in pubs all over Britain. What was good enough in the war is good enough now.'

Their route across to Speirs took them past Umberto, conspicuously the only man drinking alone. He leant forward and said to Rory: 'What we were talking about, I fix for you.'

She looked evasive. 'See me later.'

I'd like fine to know what that was about, thought Alec, as he said to Speirs: 'Busy day? I saw your lorry out there.'

'It's no' his lorry,' Rory corrected him sharply. 'It's mine. I bought it wi' my gratuity. It was pretty clapped out and I patched it up myself.'

'Clever girl.'

Such flattery was wasted on Rory. 'I'm a good mechanic, but who wants a good female mechanic in peace time?' Downing her whisky like a man, she continued: 'So I started my own haulage business. This is my first vehicle.'

'I've hired her,' Speirs put in quickly.

'Thought you were partners?'

'Aye, we are. In a way.' Again Alec noticed the swift intimate glance. 'Seen anything of the major at all?' Speirs added casually.

But Alec's attention had wandered. Collins had just come in and was chatting to the two strangers.

'Funny, isn't it, you ending up in the major's part of the world?' Speirs's quizzical look invited more information on this coincidence.

'We met – when he came out of hospital.'

'Good for you.' Tom's expression clearly indicated that he was delighted that at least one jock had played his cards very successfully, getting on chummy terms with his superior officer.

'Another drink?' asked Alec shortly.

Macrae, who preferred to drink at home, was collecting his usual half-bottle wrapped in brown paper. He was also watching Collins who was now deep in conversation with Umberto.

Suddenly Alec felt angry, frustrated and reckless. Damn the lot of them. 'Make it doubles,' he said. He'd not go home sober this night.

He was good to his promise.

At Corriebeg, Jenny was in bed when he arrived home, sobered somewhat by the ride through the cool of evening, but not quite steady. Glancing scornfully at the bread and cheese she had left out for him he clattered his way upstairs hoping to waken her.

But from her gentle breathing he realised she was fast asleep. The peaceful scene accentuated his feelings of rage.

He seized the bedclothes, wanting to tear them off her, to hurt her, take her body whether she wanted him or not. But he couldn't do it – not to his gentle, loving Jenny. And sobered again, he went quietly downstairs.

As the door closed behind him, Jenny's eyes shot open. She hadn't been asleep. Hearing his menacing breath over her, feeling his hand on the bedclothes, she had been terrified. She realised she had narrowly missed an encounter with that other Alec whom she always suspected lurked behind the gentle exterior of the man she had married in Salisbury. It would have been a brutal encounter which would have destroyed her love and the now-delicate fabric of their marriage.

With a shiver, she realised she was safe again. Tired, wretched, she pulled the covers over her head. Tomorrow morning he'd say he was sorry, she'd forget her wounded pride and try to sort things out with him, before their life became any worse. For it certainly didn't show any signs of getting better of its own accord.

The following morning, seeing him sitting at the kitchen table, his head resting on his arms and realising he had slept there all night, Jenny wanted to rush to him and hold him like a little hurt child. However, afraid of her reception she went to the fire and began to rake the ashes.

Alec gazed at her sleepily and came over, desperate to stretch out his hand and touch her, to ask her forgiveness. But instead he opened the door, called Fly and she watched him disappear across the field.

Macrae was waiting for him. 'I'm missing another ewe,' he said grimly, nodding in the direction of Carnban. 'I checked with Pheemie. She's only lost the dead one we found.'

'Lucky Pheemie,' said Alec heavily.

'Aye.' They exchanged glances which indicated they were of one mind. 'What do you think of the Eyetie?'

'Oh, him.' And remembering the incident with Jenny's bike, their laughter that had excluded him and his jealousy, Alec said acidly, 'Smooth type. Wouldn't trust him much.'

'No,' said Macrae and closed his mouth firmly. No more words were needed. They had marked down their chief suspect. All that remained was to tell Sergeant Brodie. The Eyetie had never been a favourite of his either.

Unconscious of the danger looming over him, Umberto whistled as he worked on Jenny's bicycle. As Pheemie approached, he looked up and smiled: *'Buongiorno, signorina.* This is for Signora Ritchie. I have mended it.'

Now it was Pheemie's turn for jealousy. 'Maybe you should do something for my old rattle trap.'

Umberto beamed. 'It would be my pleasure.'

Pheemie glanced round the neat garden by the side of the steps which led to Umberto's bothy. Under his care that barren earth had yielded flowers and vegetables. 'It's looking good here.'

He smiled. 'I make it like in Italy.'

Pheemie remembered the faded photographs in the bothy – some older folks, three children. 'My family,' he had told her proudly. To her more urgent question, he had answered: 'They are my children. No, I have no wife.' But he had refused to respond to any deeper probings, merely staring at her bewildered, almost as if quite suddenly he no longer understood English. Being Pheemie, she had persevered, hoping to get under that reserve. 'Why do you never go back, Umberto?'

'There is nothing for me there. And I like the people here.'

'Well, lucky me.'

Pheemie was drawn back to the present as he looked up at her tenderly and then started to pick some flowers. 'I pick for you.'

'It's a long time since someone gave me flowers,' she said wistfully. But ten minutes later, watching him stride off down the road, she wondered where he was going now. Sometimes they were so close and she thought that he loved her a wee bit and wasn't just taking what she gladly offered. If only he wasn't so secretive. There were so many other questions she was afraid to ask – like why was he so flush with money lately?

She might have been less than pleased to discover that he was heading towards Corriebeg. When he arrived he slapped a rabbit down on the table and said with a bow: 'For you, Signora.'

'How very kind,' muttered Jenny regarding this offering with dismay. 'I'm fond of rabbit. It'll need skinning, of course,' she hinted hopefully.

'It'll no' bite,' said Umberto. 'Ah yes, the fleas perhaps.' When Jenny dropped it hastily he laughed. 'You are so English.'

'Why? Because I don't like fleas.'

'Your eyes, your face, your voice.'

Jenny smiled, basking in the admiration that told her she was still attractive to men. And to provoke him further she said in her most English voice: 'Please do sit down.'

Returning her smile, Umberto chose Alec's chair. As he settled down his eyes never left her face. 'You see, so English,' he said softly.

Jenny turned away wondering what she had started. It was all very gratifying but even she could sense danger everywhere.

Danger of quite a different nature was threatening Robert Sinclair. Two days earlier he had received a letter from his friend Mackintosh in Edinburgh. It contained only one line.

'They're on to you. For God's sake, watch out.'

Now every footfall in the byre startled him and although it was only his grandfather spying on him, it gave him a nasty turn.

This time Macrae wanted to know why he hadn't finished flooring the byre. When Robert told him that he had run out of nails, Macrae's patience, never his strong point, snapped: 'Then go into town and buy some.'

Worse was to come. That morning Robert had seen his pursuers. Hidden in the barn, he'd watched them look around. With a sinking heart he knew they had tracked him down and next time he might not be so lucky. But where else could he run to? Where else could he hide?

· · · · *Fifteen* · · · ·

In Corriebeg a cold wall had sprung up between Alec and Jenny. They went about their daily routine, coming together for meals in silence, each hurt and unforgiving, deeply pained by the other's lack of understanding.

Matters weren't helped when Alec returned from Strathblair on his motorbike in time to see Jenny riding round on her mended bicycle, watched by Umberto. They both looked very pleased with themselves.

'Wonderful,' laughed Jenny. 'It's like new. I must pay you.' As she disappeared into the house Alec eyed him coldly.

'Lost any more ewes at Carnban?'

'No. We are lucky.'

'You certainly are,' said Alec heavily as Jenny appeared and handed some coins to Umberto and treated him to her most winning smile.

Umberto bowed. 'My pleasure, *Signora*.'

As he departed the couple's eyes met. At that moment it would have been so easy to have said: 'I'm sorry. I do love you,' but neither of them could make that first move.

Instead Jenny declined Alec's lift into Strathblair, saying: 'I want to try out my bicycle.' It wasn't the right thing to say. As she rode off Alec was still staring after her resentfully when Rory's lorry appeared.

'We brought your gate,' said Speirs.

'I didn't know I ordered one, Corporal.'

'Half price, five bob down and the rest when you can manage.'

Alec looked at the gate. 'Seems OK. All right then. I'll square up with you by the end of the week.'

Returning to Carnban Umberto found Pheemie in conversation with Sergeant Brodie.

'He's not here,' he heard her say. Turning she saw him dodge out of sight and had to call him twice before he approached them. 'Sergeant Brodie would like a word with you.'

'Just a general check. This sheep thieving —' said Brodie.

'Ah – this is very bad thing —'

Brodie took out his notebook. 'Mr – er – Fabiani.' He looked cross as Umberto corrected his pronunciation. 'Well now, on the night of the sixteenth of this month —'

'What about it?' demanded Pheemie sharply.

'I'd like Mr – Fabiani,' he enunciated carefully, 'to give me an account of his movements on that night.'

'Movements?' Umberto frowned.

'Two hoggs went missing at Balbuie, Mr Fabiani.'

'I am sure I was not at Balbuie, sir.'

'No, he wasn't,' Pheemie interrupted coldly.

'Can you be certain of that?'

Pheemie nodded looking at him defiantly. 'Fairly certain.'

Brodie pocketed his notebook, a disappointed man. 'I shall be looking further into the matter – Miss – Robertson.' His emphasis on 'Miss' and his mocking glance told her that he'd heard the gossip about them and had not misinterpreted her meaning.

There were lots of questions Pheemie would have liked to ask Umberto, but he seemed to have forgotten Brodie's visit as they lifted Speirs's new gate into place.

'You are strong – like a man,' said Umberto admiringly.

'I've had to be,' was Pheemie's somewhat withering response. Watching him test the gate, she nodded approvingly. 'Well worth the price. I got a bargain.'

Umberto shrugged. 'Perhaps. But I could have mended the old one.' As they walked back to the house, he put an arm around her shoulders. And that was nice, she thought, making her feel like a woman, for a change.

'Communist North Korea invaded the independent southern half of the nation at dawn today. The invasion came without warning and within a few hours troops and tanks of the Northern army had stormed across the 38th parallel, the agreed border between the two states, and had occupied all the territory of the Imjin River. The shock of this attack is ringing round the world. It seems certain to bring the Western Allies and the Communist bloc into conflict . . .'

The situation Andrew had most dreaded had come to pass. He switched off the wireless. Later on, as Sir James's car dropped him off in Strathblair High Street, he noticed Alec.

Hailing him across the road, Alec responded by saluting smartly: 'Sir!'

'Has Brodie made any progress on the sheep thieves?'

'Early days, sir. I just hope Balbuie doesn't catch them first. He'd like to settle matters with a shotgun.'

Andrew laughed. 'He's too canny for that.' Then he lowered his voice. 'What about this Korean business?' When Alec looked puzzled, he gestured with his newspaper. 'The invasion.'

'Oh, aye,' said Alec. 'I'm not up to date. Don't get to read the papers much these days.'

'Latest is that Truman's sent in air and naval forces to support the south. Endorsed by Atlee, I might add —'

But Alec's attention was elsewhere. The two strangers had dashed out of the newsagents and jumping into their green van, set off in hot pursuit of the bus Robert Sinclair had just boarded.

On the other side of the road Umberto had emerged from the butcher's shop with Collins and was counting some notes. A successful deal concluded by the look of it, he thought grimly.

'I tell you, Alec,' Andrew was saying, 'they'll have us back at war before they're finished.' Conscious that Alec was no longer listening, he said: 'We should have a dram sometime.' And he drifted off, wishing his ex-sergeant-major would show a little more interest in the grave situation confronting the nation. But Alec couldn't think past the mystery of his stolen sheep.

On his way home he passed the green van leaving Wester Balbuie. What were they up to? If it was sheep stealing then Macrae couldn't be involved, he had lost sheep himself. But what about young Robert? Macrae would never recover from the shame of that. It would be a worse blow even than his daughter Mary's betrayal.

At that moment Robert was emerging from the duck pond, extremely shaken and extremely thankful to be in one piece. He had been surprised in the barn, seized in a powerful grip.

'Mackintosh tip you off?' When Robert denied it, his attacker said: 'We'll sort him out when we get back. You owe us, remember.'

Robert kicked him viciously on the shin, slid down the ladder and ran across the yard. Hotly pursued by his tormentors he splashed through the duck pond which happened to be in his direct line of flight. It was his undoing, slowing him down. They caught him and, forcing his head under water, held him down repeatedly as he fought for breath, certain he was going to drown.

'If ye cannae pay, don't play,' said one.

'Twenty-five quid's a lot of dough,' said the other.

'I'll get it for you!' Robert screamed. 'First thing tomorrow, I'll go to the bank. I have money. I'll get it!'

They looked at each other, nodded and let him go. With a

final warning: 'You'd better,' they thrust him back into the water. Robert, spluttering, half-crying, knew he was in deep trouble. If Grandfather ever found out about his gambling debts, it would be the end of his high hopes of a future at Wester Balbuie.

Pheemie met Jenny wheeling her bike back up the hill to Corriebeg, her baskets loaded with groceries. Pheemie, a good strong cyclist, asked: 'Want a push?'

'Don't show off,' laughed Jenny breathlessly as Pheemie dismounted and walked with her.

'Saw Alec in town. Thought you usually went with him.'

'Well, thanks to Umberto, I now have a measure of independence. Which I like.'

Pheemie looked at her. 'You don't look yourself.'

'No,' said Jenny bleakly, fighting back the tears. The cold war with Alec was getting her down. She felt poorly these days, so tired all the time, weary and dispirited.

Back at Corriebeg, as Jenny made the tea, Pheemie regarded her new friend anxiously, aware that all was far from well between Jenny and her man. Glancing at the unpacked groceries spread on the table, Jenny smiled wryly.

'Mummy would die seeing me offering you a biscuit from the packet. She likes everything to be perfect – afternoon tea on the little table with the little silver cake forks and embroidered napkins.'

'Do you miss it?'

Jenny sighed, staring out of the window. 'Yes, I miss my friends. It was great at first. There was so much to do, everything new and exciting. And it was so lovely just being with Alec.' Turning to face Pheemie, she said desperately: 'He doesn't understand the way I feel. He says I'm not a farmer's wife. I'm not. He says I'm very silly with animals – though why one can't like animals and be a farmer's wife I don't know. It's ridiculous.'

Pheemie nodded. 'He's taken on a lot. So have you.'

'It's just not what I thought it was going to be. Not at all. Farms where I come from are – well – lush.' Wearily she sat down. 'Here it's like a fight from start to finish.'

So she'd just discovered what I've known all my life, thought Pheemie. 'You ought to get out more,' she said.

'Out?' Jenny laughed. 'I spend my whole time out. I dread to think what I'll be like in the winter.'

'No. I mean – we should go out. To the pictures. There's a travelling show in the village hall. And you could join the Rural Institute.'

'Is that like the WI?' Jenny remembered all her mother's stuffy middle-aged friends who belonged to worthy causes. She didn't want to become one of them or join them. Not yet. How awful.

Seeing her expression Pheemie said: 'It's saved a lot of lonely women going mad. Is that the time? I must go.'

Outside, the great bowl of hills was filled with shadows, the rim of the sun, held in a ragged blaze of clouds that had gathered out of a clear sky, rested on the shoulder of Schiehallion. All the mountains westward bloomed with the slow dark of evening while the last light burned on the hillside.

Such unearthly beauty bred a new intimacy, invited confidences. Pheemie felt it, too. 'Sergeant Brodie's been questioning Umberto again. About the sheep thieving.'

'Surely he can't suspect Umberto,' said Jenny.

'Just because he's a foreigner, everyone's suspicious. Look, Jenny,' she added desperately, 'I can vouch for Umberto's whereabouts most nights.'

At that moment, Alec's motorbike came into the yard. There was no time to say more, not that any explanation was necessary. Waving goodbye, Jenny thought how lucky Pheemie was with her Latin lover, and turning her back on the sunset she went to prepare supper for her own man. At one time I wouldn't have envied any woman. I loved Alec so much –

correction, I still do – but where has he gone? Will he ever come back? Will things ever be the way they were before? Perhaps in bed tonight —

But Alec disappeared after supper and she was asleep by the time he crept in beside her. He looked down at her and the old tenderness came back into his face. She was so young really, young, stubborn and vulnerable. He was sure he loved her, but the words he yearned to say still stuck in his throat.

· · · · *Sixteen* · · · ·

Next morning Alec went down to Strathblair to pay Speirs for the gate. He spotted the green van parked by the bank and Robert coming out counting some notes which he handed to the driver.

What the devil was young Robert up to? Puzzled and deeply suspicious, Alec went in search of Rory's lorry. He found it empty in a side lane near the pub. Prepared to wait, he lit a cigarette. Suddenly he noticed some wool – sheep's wool – attached to the back board.

He climbed up. There was more inside and fresh droppings on the floor. He jumped down as Speirs and Rory approached.

'Saw the lorry. Thought I'd hang on and pay you,' he said handing over the notes. 'Where do you get the gates from?'

'Friend of Rory's,' Speirs exchanged a quick glance with her. 'What else do you deal in?'

'Oh, this and that,' said Rory, jumping into the driver's seat. Speirs leant out. 'Be seeing you, Sergeant-Major.'

The meeting was to be sooner than he expected. That evening Alec was in the yard when he noticed the lorry driving along the road below Corriebeg on its way to Strathblair. He came to a rapid decision and, to Jenny's consternation, he leapt on to the motorbike and set off in pursuit, following it to the lane behind the butcher's shop. Keeping close watch, he saw Speirs emerge and say to Collins: 'I think this should be the last.'

'Why?' Rory complained. 'We're just getting into the swing of it. Come on.'

Alec watched the money changing hands. 'Delivering a gate, Corporal?' They both stopped, open mouthed as Alec stepped forward. Speirs was momentarily speechless, but Rory said boldly: 'No. Mr Collins here was just settling his account with us.'

'Seems like I saw a lot of money for a gate.'

'Well, he bought more than one,' was the defiant reply.

Alec turned to Collins. 'Do you mind if I look in your shed?'

Collins hesitated then laughed. 'Have you a search warrant?'

'I could fetch Brodie,' said Alec quietly.

'Look if you want to,' said Collins uneasily.

Alec stepped inside the slaughter house. There was no sheep's carcass as evidence, but the place had been recently cleaned.

'You've been slaughtering in here.' When Collins shrugged Alec said furiously: 'My lambs. And Balbuie's and Dalscriadan's —'

'Aye, if you bring them here,' was the calm reply.

'Or if someone else were to steal them.'

'You should be careful what you say, Sergeant-Major,' piped up Rory. 'You're no' in the Army now. There's a law of libel.'

'You're too clever by half,' said Alec contemptuously.

'I know.' She smiled. 'I'm wasted selling gates.'

Alec looked at them. He had no proof of their illegal activities. 'Right. You've made your packet. Now get out of this area —'

'Oh, we were leaving for Glasgow tonight anyway,' said Rory smoothly.

'Good. Stay there and don't show your faces round here again. Or I might just take the law into my own hands.' Alec turned on his heel. 'And, Corporal, find yourself another partner!'

Macrae narrowly escaped being run down by the lorry as it departed at high speed. He followed Alec into the pub. Andrew was there reading a newspaper and Umberto, alone as usual.

Alec ordered two whiskies and Andrew smiled. 'Thought you were a beer man.'

'I need something a wee bit stronger right now.' And to Macrae, he added: 'A slight altercation – over gates.'

'You've not been had by the two crooks?' said Macrae.

Alec downed his whisky and saying: 'We've all been,' he took the second glass and handed it to Umberto. His gesture of reconciliation was not lost on Macrae.

'We made a mistake, Balbuie. They are our sheep thieves, but unfortunately as they've pointed out to me, we've no real evidence.'

Macrae nodded. 'Collins is in it too then. We'll talk to Brodie in the morning.'

Alec went over to join Andrew who had ordered him a drink. Picking up the newspaper he read the headline: 'ROYAL NAVY TO AID AMERICANS. ONCE AGAIN, AMERICA AND BRITAIN FIND THEM-SELVES ASSOCIATED IN A NOBLE CAUSE . . .'

'If there's real trouble, you could be affected. You're a reservist,' said Andrew.

Alec smiled. 'Aye, but the thing is, would I go?'

Next day, Collins closed his shop for the last time under the eagle eye of Sergeant Brodie while on the hill above Corriebeg, his sudden departure was eagerly discussed.

'I knew his father for the best part of forty years,' said Macrae and when Pheemie agreed that Collins senior was a fine man, he added, disgustedly: 'To think his memory's tarnished by that wastrel of a son.'

'Aye, well, maybe we're all a bit the wiser,' said Alec.

All three looked at Umberto, who agreed with them, quite unaware until he learnt from Pheemie later, much to his indignation, that he had been under suspicion.

When Macrae returned home, Robert was reading a book instead of playing his eternal games of Patience. He had been busy, there was a fine smell of cooking.

'Your dinner's ready, Grandfather.'

Macrae went over to the peat fire that was never allowed to die. Although it was summer outside, he felt the cold in his bones these days. He was getting old. As he poked the fire into a good blaze Robert held out a dog-eared pack of cards.

'Here ye are, Grandfather.'

'What am I meant to do with them?' said Macrae, eyeing them with distaste. 'Tell your fortune?'

Robert smiled. 'I know my past and my present. That's enough for me. They've got me into enough trouble for one lifetime. I never want to see another card game as long as I live. Go on, —' and thrusting them at him, he said, 'Now, burn them.'

Watching the cards burn, Robert told him about the gambling debt that was now settled. Macrae just listened. For once there was no reprimand.

'Aye, an expensive experience, right enough,' was his only comment.

Alec walked back down to where the little world of Corriebeg was still at peace. Before any political storm could destroy them, he too resolved to be wiser, count his blessings.

Jenny was at the door, the wild cat drinking from a saucer. She straightened up as Alec appeared, saw a new gentleness in his face. 'I think she's got kittens somewhere. If I could find them – I'd like to keep one,' she said wistfully.

'Take a look in the old shepherd's bothy above the burn.'

'You've seen them?'

Alec grinned. 'Aye, but they're too wee to leave their mother just yet.' He followed her into the kitchen, where the table was spread for dinner. There were flowers in a vase and Alec smelt the rich aroma of roast meat as he washed his hands.

When Jenny set the platter before him to carve, he asked: 'Where did you get this lamb from?'

'There's only one butcher.'

'*Was* only one butcher,' he corrected.

They both looked at each other and back to the meat as realisation dawned.

'He sold us our own lamb!' Jenny laughed.

'Well, at least we know the meat's good.'

Alec's laughter had been lost for many days. Jenny was smiling back at him, her heart in her eyes. And suddenly it was all over.

He held her close murmuring the words she had longed to hear, words so simple really. 'I'm sorry, Jenny. It's been awful. I do love you.'

'And I love you.'

'I'll try to be more understanding. About Fly, I mean. And all the other —'

She put a hand over his lips. 'I know, I know.'

As they kissed again, with growing urgency, both of them realised the lamb would be eaten cold that day. Hand in hand they went up to their bedroom and closed the door. All the bad things that had divided them were already past and gone, just as if they had never been.

The lost lovers had found each other again.

July 1950

· · · · *Seventeen* · · · ·

Long hot days alternated with chill mists on the hill as if in the hands of a celestial weatherman with an unreliable calendar. In Strathblair roses bloomed radiantly against grey stone walls, nodding dazed heads battered by sudden torrential rain, and in every hedge harassed birds tended noisy nestlings. Keen gardeners found plenty to keep them busy and on drowsy afternoons an army of unseen humming insects vied with the constant whirring of lawnmowers.

Up the hill in Corriebeg where fragile harebells and wild pansies grew by the roadside, the plaintive lament of sheep, added to the call of peewit and oyster catcher, was the only music.

The midgies attacked silently, murderous and inescapable as in the turnip field Alec worked long, gruelling hours. He was kept company by a hungry hawk who hovered in an all-day vigil for young grouse with not enough sense to keep under cover.

As for Jenny, she had never before faced the prospect of back-breaking labour in a temperature soaring into the eighties, while constantly fighting off clouds of flies and more predatory insects. She almost welcomed rain and the sudden drop to a shiversome 50°.

A year ago she wouldn't have believed any of this was possible. Last summer she didn't even know of Alec Ritchie's existence and still believed that sunshine was for deckchairs and tea on a neatly manicured lawn. She thought wistfully of the garden in Salisbury, where Daddy's roses would be at their best.

The day that was to change it all began like any other. As she was preparing to take Alec his mid-morning break, Mr Todd the postie brought the mail, eager to tell her all it contained. Business letters (that meant bills) for Alec and a letter from her parents (who would be missing her! Todd said).

In the field Alec was anxiously awaiting her arrival, ruefully flexing a blistered hand.

'Oh, you poor thing,' said Jenny, all concern.

'It's OK. Just give me the tea. My throat's like sandpaper.' Watching Jenny read her letter, he slipped a crust to Fly.

'Oh dear. It's from Daddy. Mother's ill in bed and the doctor says she's to stay there. Tired heart they think.' She looked up at Alec. 'He'd like me to go home.'

'Well, if she's ill,' he said grudgingly. 'Does he say how long you'll be needed?'

'Oh, just till she's on her feet again,' said Jenny cheerfully.

'That could be weeks,' Alec said dolefully.

'He doesn't seem to think so,' Jenny replied brightly, seeing the welcome prospect of a break slipping away from her again. 'I couldn't stay too long.' And, ignoring his stricken expression, she asked: 'Could you manage?'

'I'll have to, won't I?'

'I could always ask Pheemie —'

That was too much. 'I'll ask Pheemie if I need her,' said Alec shortly.

Jenny decided to leave the following day. She packed feeling guilty that she was really looking forward to seeing her parents and her friends again, as well as getting away from singling neeps. She had hoped that things would ease up in the summer, but no such luck. Each season brought a new kind of drudgery.

As for Alec and herself, it seemed that for two blissful weeks the honeymoon had magically returned. But the land was against them. Sometimes it seemed as though it had never heard of summer and Corriebeg itself appeared to hate them, no longer home but a grim steading in a dark land of bleak hills.

Relations between them, like the weather, blew hot, then cold as Alec once more began to show his impatience when Jenny overspent the housekeeping allowance or couldn't keep up with the relentless daily chores. Sometimes she felt as if she were walking a tightrope, her emotions as carefully controlled as an acrobat without the safety net.

Jenny was so flustered the next morning – there was so

much to do, so many last-minute things to pack, with Alec shouting upstairs: 'Hurry, woman,' that she almost missed the train.

The guard had blown his whistle as they raced across the bridge to the platform. Alec pushed her and her suitcase into the compartment. There was no time for anything but a brief kiss, not even a proper goodbye hug. Her last sight was his sad face disappearing into the steam clouds from the train. As Strathblair folded back into the Perthshire hills, the first heavy drops of rain splattered on the window. Like tears she thought, hoping poor Alec got home dry.

A storm of a different kind threatened Strathblair where Flora and Andrew were listening to the wireless in her office.

'Losses have been heavy and among the ranks there is resentment at the lack of allied support. In the House of Commons today, Mr Churchill's warning of a Third World War serves only to increase pressure on the Government to despatch British troops to Korea.'

'Why can't we leave Russia and America to fight it out?' said Flora. 'I mean standing shoulder to shoulder's one thing, but the entire issue –' she shrugged – 'it's so obscure.'

'Whatever the rights or wrongs, I can't resign my commission. Not until it's over.'

'But you've done your bit,' Flora protested.

'I know. I know. Oh, I wish I'd been born ordinary. I mean without responsibilities.' One war had cost him Janet, he didn't want another to lose him Flora.

'And all my plans for the art business. I've found several of my mother's paintings. It's strange she never mentioned leaving them behind.'

'You've kept in touch with her?'

'Yes. Father has no idea.' Flora was surprised and gratified that Andrew had been defying Sir James all these years.

'Just as we're beginning to see some kind of a future,'

Andrew went on. 'I feel as if I'm on a treadmill, continuously turning a wheel I hate!'

Flora looked at him. 'Andrew, if you felt it to be the wrong sort of war, if you weren't sure you were on the right side, would you still go?'

Andrew straightened his shoulders. 'I'm a soldier. We're not permitted to ask questions. Just fight, that's all.' Turning, he glimpsed an expression deeper than polite concern on her face as she came over to him.

'I shouldn't try to stop you, I know, but —'

'Would you want to?' he asked softly.

'I don't want you to go. Of course I don't want you to go.'

'Well, that's good to know.'

'Is it?' she asked looking up at him sadly.

And suddenly the whole atmosphere between them became electrified, charged with longing. In that moment, he was sure she loved him. He yearned to take her in his arms, ask her to marry him. It was all going to be so easy, after all.

He took a step towards her, and she closed her eyes, ready for his kiss. And then it happened. The violent blast of a motor horn and the screech of car tyres braking shattered a moment as fragile as gossamer.

Andrew pulled away from her. 'Oh hell, that'll be my cousin Veronica.'

They looked at each other, the air still charged with emotion. To kiss or not to kiss. Better not. It wouldn't be the same now. Perhaps the moment would come again. Perhaps not, thought Andrew bitterly, cursing Veronica for her ill-timed arrival.

Sir James had told Flora they were expecting a guest, but she wasn't quite prepared for the young woman who stepped out of the little red sports car. Tall and slim, her blonde elegance was emphasised by a pale yellow suit and matching headscarf which had obviously been bought in Paris.

'It is Andrew, isn't it? It's been a long time – school hols – before the war.'

'Correct,' Andrew smiled.

'Golly. You have grown military.'

They both laughed and Andrew gestured towards Flora, introducing her, adding: 'Our factor.'

Hanging back Flora said coldly: 'You'll need to drive to the front of the house —'

'Oh, have I come to the servants' entrance?'

Flora's face darkened slightly. 'Not quite.'

'I'll come with you,' said Andrew.

Flora watched them go, Veronica driving faster than was necessary, showing off. She decided in that moment that she didn't like Andrew's cousin, not only because her entrance had ruined a precious moment, but because she resented the memories of those distant childhood days the cousins had shared which excluded her.

Going back into the office she realised the reason for these new emotions was rather obvious. After all these years, she was falling in love with Andrew.

Veronica stood by the drawing-room window. As Andrew poured drinks, he studied this new stranger cousin. She was certainly eye-catching, extremely smart. As a man he appreciated style, remembering the rather plain little girl who had such an embarrassing crush on him. He hadn't liked her much then. He wasn't sure whether he would like her now either. All that elegance was a brave try, but somehow it didn't succeed in making her particularly warm or feminine. In fact she exuded a sense of deep still waters in which he would on no account want to make any waves.

'You haven't been well?' he said for something to say.

She turned very sharply to him. 'Really?' she demanded.

'Your mother wrote that you needed a rest – you were recuperating.'

Veronica's lip curled as she took the glass from him. 'Good old Mummy. So, what's been happening to you now? Will you be off to Korea?' she added lightly.

'God knows.'

'Heard you did very well in the last lot.' When Andrew merely shrugged, she continued: 'Don't be coy. I got all your gen from Mummy.'

'I heard you did very well. Special Ops, wasn't it?' And when she, in turn, shrugged, he asked: 'Where were you stationed?'

'Oh, here and there.'

Her tone was dismissive. Aunt Amelie had told him that she had been dropped in France, a very rough mission. There was also a broken romance. Aunt Amelie had added a warning note: 'She never talks about her wartime experiences. Even to us.'

Looking up, Andrew saw her admiring an Italian watercolour. He told her it had cost him fifty cigarettes and the few lira he had on him at the time. 'We were on the move – I couldn't do more.'

'You've got a bargain. He'll be tops one day.'

'If he's survived.' Reference to the war provoked for them both a flood of scenes best forgotten, of horrors best unnamed.

Veronica lit a cigarette, drew on it as if it were life blood. Sir James was in Perth and Andrew was relieved when she retired early. This was not going to be an easy visit, he decided, his cousin's devils were manifold and very tricky.

Next morning he suggested that Flora would be delighted to take her on her rounds, show her something of the estate. However, Flora, not having been consulted, was less than pleased.

As they drove up the track to Corriebeg, Pheemie came out of the byre where she had been milking Jenny's cow. Introduced to Veronica, she murmured a greeting and they followed her into the kitchen. 'Alec's just finishing off the neep thinning. Jenny's not here. She's gone home. Her mother's poorly.'

Bored, Veronica went outside. The two men coming across

the yard were both young, handsome and well set up. What luck.

She awaited their arrival smiling. 'Veronica Smythe.' And, looking from one to the other, continued: 'Alec Ritchie?'

The younger of the two smiled, held out a bandaged hand.

'A casualty?' she said.

'Put it down to inexperience.' He grinned, eyeing her with approval. She was a good-looking, classy woman. You could tell the real breeding a mile off. She had the voice of authority, too, the officer breed. A glance at Umberto told him the Italian was thinking much the same thing.

Flora appeared at the door. 'Can you let me see the valuation papers, Mr Ritchie? It's for insurance purposes.'

As Alec went inside Veronica drifted over to where Umberto was lounging against a wall. Noticing his uniform jacket, she said: 'Washed up by the war, eh?'

Umberto frowned. 'No. I am not a sailor.'

'I was speaking figuratively.'

'*Si?*' Umberto shook his head. She returned his smile and he responded to its warmth, to eyes that invited. A very nice lady, this one. *Si!*

'What keeps you here?'

A shadow loomed between them. 'Umberto works for me,' Pheemie said sharply. Ignoring her, the smile that Veronica turned on Umberto spelt nothing but trouble. 'I thought I'd walk back.'

'It's a long trek to Strathblair,' said Pheemie shortly.

'I'm a good walker,' And to Umberto: 'Is there a way over the hill?'

Pheemie answered for him. 'Yes. But if you don't know the way, you could get into difficulties.'

'Perhaps Umberto can set me on the right track.' Veronica's eyes had never left him. Her smile held an unmistakable challenge.

'It will be my pleasure, *Signora*.' Umberto bowed, grinning delightedly.

'Umberto, you've got work to do,' said Pheemie crossly.

'But I'll no' be long!' Umberto replied sweetly.

Pheemie watched them go helplessly. Of all the nerve! A brazen hussy, that, if ever she saw one.

In the kitchen, Flora was preparing to leave. 'How are you getting on with the garron?' she asked Alec.

'Fine. Jenny's in her element. Shades of the Pony Club and all that.'

Flora smiled. 'Don't let her spoil him, will you? Monty's a working beast.'

As she was leaving, Alec said: 'That lady you brought with you – who is she?'

When Flora explained, Alec nodded. 'I thought she might have been in the services.'

'She was,' said Flora, 'but it's all very hush hush.'

Waving to Flora as she drove off, Alec went back to the neep field where Pheemie was working on her own. 'Where's Umberto?'

'Showing Miss Smythe the road to Strathblair.'

As Alec picked up his hoe, the two exchanged looks that spoke volumes about the absent Miss Smythe.

'How long is she staying?' asked Pheemie.

'Don't know. Seems she's recuperating.'

'Oh aye?' said Pheemie doubtfully. 'From what?'

Alec shrugged. Pheemie had stopped hoeing. 'It's just I don't want Umberto upset.'

And that, thought Alec, considering Miss Smythe's impact on every man in sight, was putting it mildly. He didn't want Pheemie upset either. She had been good to him since Jenny left.

Having supper at Carnban that evening there was no mention of Umberto's afternoon expedition. He had prepared his specialty: Spaghetti Carbonara. Having refused a second helping, Alec sighed.

'Jenny would love this. I want to take her to Italy.'

'I keep asking him to take me,' said Pheemie. 'Sun. Flowers, I'd love it,' she added with a wistful look in Umberto's direction.

'The people were so generous,' said Alec. 'They took us into their homes, fed us. Even though they'd little for themselves.'

'With the Germans gone, they would be glad to see you,' said Umberto.

'And their own lot. *Fascisti. Appendile per le palle.*' Alec's laugh wasn't echoed by Umberto who left the table abruptly and, picking up a newspaper, said solemnly: 'Times were not easy.'

Alec and Pheemie exchanged puzzled glances. Alec knew Pheemie was crazy about the Italian, guessed she would have married him like a shot if he'd cared to make an honest woman of her. For her sake, he hoped it would work out in the end.

And a *femme fatale* like Veronica Smythe was the last thing she needed. Or himself, for that matter.

Going home to his empty bed, he wondered what it would be like with another woman.

God, how he missed Jenny.

· · · · *Eighteen* · · · ·

In Salisbury, Jenny wasn't missing Alec at all. Had anyone asked her, she would have denied it, of course. She wrote him long loving letters; his replies on one sheet of lined paper consisted of two stilted paragraphs about what was happening at Corriebeg and were signed 'Your loving Alec'. She looked in vain for some passionate response, some reassurance that he was lost without her.

She sighed, feeling vaguely let down. But at least there was no shortage of love here at home. Smothered by her mother, she danced with her father. Once a superb performer on the ballroom floor, he had some super Ivor Novello records. Bliss! She had only danced with Alec once, at their wedding reception, but alas, he was so stiff and unyielding she felt as if he still had his army boots on.

Besides it was such joy to be back in the cosy sitting room with its pretty chintz covers, with all the pictures and ornaments she remembered. And, best of all, her very own bedroom, with her doll's house and her favourite toys and teddies looking down at her.

In the spartan surroundings of Corriebeg she'd forgotten just what comfort was: hot water, lots of baths, elegant china. Everyone was so civilised. Mummy, of course, was a bit of a trial, never forgetting to remind her of all she had given up. Jenny had to forgive her; she wasn't well and that's why she was a bit petulant and sorry for herself. But never sorry for her appearance.

At fifty Marjorie Moresby looked like a faded Dresden shepherdess, with worn vestiges of the doll-like features, the delicate small bones that had captivated suitors in her youth. Alarmed, she had discovered early that Jenny had inherited her father's bone-structure and she could never quite forgive Providence for the gift of a daughter with none of her own delicate beauty. Even as an invalid, she insisted on her prettiest négligé, slept in pin curls and made up her face conscientiously each morning.

'How do I look?' Jenny smiled. She was as vain as ever.

'Very pretty.' Oh, she did like that.

And, eyeing the lunch tray, she said in a voice of doom, 'Oh Jenny, not Spam again. I don't know how I ever got through the war, Spam and chips for ever.'

But she ate it just the same. There was nothing invalidish about her appetite, thought Jenny, offering her an oatcake which she declined, adding rather nervously: 'Did you make them?'

Rather proudly Jenny said: 'Yes,' and this made her mother more apprehensive than ever. 'I'm awfully sorry, darling. I don't fancy one just now. I feel a bit queasy.'

'Mm. You don't know what you're missing.'

'Oh, all right,' and taking a bite Mrs Moresby's eyes widened appreciatively. 'These are good. You've actually learnt to cook while you've been up there.' She sighed. 'I can't think why Alec had to take up farming. And in Scotland of all places.'

'Well, he is a Scotsman, Mummy.'

'That's no reason why he couldn't have found a nice little place down here. I mean, darling, we quite like the Scots, you know,' in a tone that implied some doubt whether or not this was advisable.

And as Jenny removed the tray she commented: 'Oh my darling, your poor hands. They used to be so pretty.'

Jenny hastily put her hands out of sight and said defensively: 'Well, I work hard.'

Mrs Moresby sighed. 'Daddy says he's never seen you look so –' she paused searching for the right word – 'so worn. And your hair, darling,' she continued reproachfully. 'I know you're a long way from a hairdresser. And of course, it can be so difficult finding a girl who understands one's hair.'

With a feeling that this wasn't getting through to Jenny, she said encouragingly: 'Don't you get to Edinburgh at all? It's a really big town and I bet there's a decent hairdresser there. You're having tea with Pam and Joan tomorrow,' she sighed. 'Perhaps you'll listen to them.' Her tone carried a simple message: you never listen to me.

The girls met at Tiffany's, a very smart teashop frequented by elegant customers. Jenny had been looking forward to seeing her old school friends. Joan, the youngest, blonde and slight, was Mrs Moresby's idea of the perfect daughter, the prettiest girl in the class with an enviable number of boyfriends. Pam, dark-haired and brown-eyed, was the most vivacious of the trio and the first to marry. Jenny's hopes that this would create a closer bond between them were soon blighted. Dismayed, she discovered that, as with her mother, she had outgrown her friends whose conversations seemed dominated by the latest in hand-creams.

Noticing Jenny's expression, Pam interrupted hastily: 'I

know you're on the land now, Jen. But you can't let yourself go!'

'Do you actually enjoy it?' Joan sounded surprised.

Jenny brightened at that. 'It's simply super, so beautiful, first thing in the morning – opening the kitchen door and it's there.'

'What is?' Joan looked puzzled.

'Why, the hills and the sky.'

'We've got sky here,' Joan reminded her sternly.

'Yes, but there it goes on for ever. And we've got hens. I sell the eggs and we've a garron. A pony,' she explained. 'He's lovely.'

When Pam asked if she could come and stay with her husband Freddie, Jenny agreed weakly and, with a sudden vision of Alec's reaction to these visitors, added a warning that she didn't have much spare time.

'We'll amuse ourselves, darling. Help out and all that. Collect eggs. Another cake?'

Suddenly the sight of all that sticky icing made Jenny shudder. 'No, thanks, I won't. I feel a bit sick.'

'All that plain fare up North,' said Joan soothingly. 'Spoiled your appetite.'

The two friends exchanged glances, aware that Jenny's mind was elsewhere. She was studying their reflections in the mirror. It had never struck her before that apart from their colouring, Joan and Pam could have been poured out of the same mould. What a contrast, her own straight hair and weather-beaten face made to their immaculate make-up, varnished nails and pretty dresses.

'You do like it up there, don't you?' Pam was regarding her anxiously.

Jenny laughed. 'Yes, of course.' Kissing them goodbye outside the teashop, she made a sudden decision.

Returning home later from her two last-minute appointments, both of which filled her with apprehension for very different reasons, she went straight upstairs and found her mother dozing. She opened her eyes and said: 'Jenny. So pretty. You look just like my little girl again.'

Jenny looked in the mirror. She was still apprehensive about having had her hair trimmed and waved and she wasn't at all sure she wanted, or could ever be, her mother's little girl again.

'The doctor says you can get up tomorrow.' Mrs Moresby didn't greet this news with any great enthusiasm, knowing full well that the longer she could stay in bed, the longer she'd have Jenny here at home where she belonged.

Her father watched her reading Alec's once-weekly letter. 'Alec's missing me,' she said. 'I must be thinking of getting home. Mummy's so much better.'

'Are you sure you're up to it?' her father asked anxiously. She'd seen him studying her and sometimes she wondered if he suspected the truth.

Discussing plans for her departure as she and her mother wound wool together, her father sat in his special armchair. In the background the gramophone was playing his favourite dance medleys and Jenny wondered when – if ever – she would be this comfortable in Corriebeg.

'Surely, darling, if Alec really cared for you, he'd find a more congenial job down here, where you can be near friends? And near me.' When Jenny protested that she was making new friends, her mother said sharply: 'But are they quite suitable, dear?'

Ignoring George Moresby's warning: 'Marjorie!' she continued: 'I have to say what I feel. She's my daughter and I am concerned about her!'

'She has her own life to lead now,' he grumbled.

'It seems to me it's Alec's life she's leading, George. As for friends, she only seems to know an Italian ex-prisoner of war and a beefy woman farmer.'

He watched Jenny, wearied by the argument, go over to the gramophone. 'Do you miss us at all, darling?' When she said she did, he suggested they might come for a holiday.

'That would be lovely, Daddy. It's a bit rough, of course,' she added glancing nervously at her mother who asked: 'Well, is there an hotel?'

'Yes. A nice one. Victorian affair.' As she looked through the records, seeing her wistful expression, her father said: 'Jenny, how would you like to have the gramophone up there? We can get a new one.'

She threw herself into his arms. 'Oh, I'd love it.'

When Jenny went to say goodnight, her mother sat up in bed looking forlorn. 'I didn't mean to upset you —'

'I would have gone anyway, Mummy. Moved out, I mean —'

'Yes, but darling, to have gone so far —'

'Don't you understand, it could have been a lot further, if I hadn't married Alec.'

'To get away from Daddy and me?' was the reproachful reply.

'Not really. To find myself.'

'Oh, Jenny, you sound so hard.'

'I'm trying to be hard. I think I married Alec because he was ready to take chances. To move on,' she added desperately. 'I couldn't have married a nice, cosy little bank manager who left home at the same time each morning and came back at the same time every night and worried if he were five minutes late, like you do with Daddy.'

'How cruel!' Mrs Moresby whispered and she began to cry.

'It's all very difficult, Mummy,' said Jenny, hating to see her tears. And suddenly they were in each other's arms and Jenny, crying, was her little girl again, which was just the way her mother wanted it. Consoling her, she realised she hadn't the least idea what Jenny had been trying to say.

That night Jenny wrote a letter to Alec:

'Mummy is out of bed and doing well. But I feel I'm about ready for bed now. Yet I've not worked like I work at home. It must be the emotional tension. Mother treats me like a child. I seem to be in a sort of limbo – a sort of nothing. I met my friends Pam and Joan. They are so carefree and pretty and I feel very old. I seem to have outgrown them. And do I care? I seem to. Perhaps you were right. Perhaps I'm not meant to be a farmer's wife . . .'

· · · · *Nineteen* · · · ·

'. . . Perhaps you were right. Perhaps I'm not meant to be a farmer's wife . . .'

Jenny's words added to Alec's alarm. He had already had a letter from her father saying she wasn't well and they had persuaded her to stay on for a few extra days.

Alec threw down Jenny's letter with an exclamation of disgust. What was going on? Were her parents trying to break up their marriage? He felt desolate and alone in his despair. Looking round the kitchen, he had to get escape from his gloomy thoughts.

He could go to the pub and get drunk, but he was learning fast that it wasn't worth a hangover when you had a hard day's work ahead singling neeps. A better idea would be to go to the pictures. *The Third Man* was on at the village hall.

It was a good exciting thriller, well acted with a haunting theme tune. So he was feeling quite cheerful until he watched the newsreel which was devoted entirely to the Korean war. The Americans had been badly mauled in their first major engagement and, beleaguered, they were wondering where the Allies were.

'According to a military spokesman there was no Dunkirk in sight. There is no doubt we are going to come out on top of the heap. We have got the means to handle the situation. Give us time and we will take the ball away and start going up the field . . .'

Alec decided he had had enough. As he went out he noticed

Robert Sinclair, his eyes rivetted to the screen. Lads who had never fought didn't find war as repellent as he did. He was surprised when Veronica Smythe followed him out.

'Seen one war, seen them all,' he said, offering her a cigarette. And, as they lit up, he grumbled: 'Don't know why I went in there.'

'Nostalgia?'

'Come off it,' he said scornfully.

'One is always drawn back to the highpoints in one's life.'

Alec regarded her steadily. 'No newsreels of the sort of thing you did.'

'No. Mostly it was boring.' She looked at him, sizing him up. 'Do you want a lift home?'

For a moment he thought he was going to take up her offer – and whatever that might lead to. 'Got the bike,' he said instead and turned his back on her. When he looked round, she had driven off and feeling suddenly alone and empty, he wandered into the Atholl Arms.

Andrew Menzies listened gloomily to his account of the newsreel. He very clearly didn't want to go to Korea and Alec said: 'You fought in the last war with credit. Why should you worry about what people think?'

'That's not the point, Alec, and well you know it.'

'Well, if I decide not to go then I won't. But I reckon I'll be exempt, being a farmer now. You could say the same.' And downing his beer he said: 'I often wondered why you became a soldier.'

'I never felt I had much choice in the matter. My father thought that Sandhurst would be good for me. It worked up to a point. I acquired a veneer,' he added ironically. 'Another beer?'

'Thanks. Your cousin, Miss Smythe. She seems a bright girl.'

'Yes, she's all right I think . . . reasonable veneer.'

Alec thought about Miss Smythe quite a lot on his return to Corriebeg. He reckoned he had probably seen the last of her.

Just as well, really. She was what the Americans call 'a ball of fire'.

Sitting at the kitchen table, he viewed the squalor surrounding him, the piles of dirty dishes in the sink, the general air of neglect. He'd have to set to work and tidy the place up a bit for Jenny's homecoming – if she decided to come back.

His thoughts were interrupted by the sound of a gunshot in the distance, closely followed by another. He went to the door. Who could be shooting over the hill at this hour?

Balbuie had been similarly alerted and for a very different reason. He came home to find his gun cupboard open, shotgun and cartridges missing, as well as his grandson. What the devil was the young fool up to now? Intending to wait up to give him a piece of his mind, he fell asleep.

The next morning, Robert's bed hadn't been slept in. Trying to be unemotional about the fact that he had stayed out all night with a gun, Macrae made porridge as usual but had little heart to eat it. He was a very worried man.

Outside Strathblair House the next morning, Andrew watched some pictures being loaded into a van as Flora approached.

'More rich pickings?' she asked.

'The last perhaps. You've heard the news. They're sending in our chaps. Shinwell's just announced it in the Commons.'

'Well, look on the bright side,' said Flora. 'It can't mean everyone. There's a good chance the Black Watch won't go.'

'My CO's been in touch. They want me back at Regimental Headquarters.' They regarded each other helplessly and, with a despairing gesture, Andrew turned and headed towards the gardens.

In the office, Alec was waiting with the valuation papers but, still disturbed by Andrew's news, Flora found it hard to concentrate. Only when he was leaving did she remember to tell him: 'Someone's been disturbing the grouse, the keeper found a few dead birds with gunshot in them.'

Alec said he'd heard shots last night and promised to keep a look out. As he went to his parked motorbike, Veronica sauntered over wearing riding breeches and a jacket. He greeted her cordially enough, but he hoped he'd indicated that he didn't particularly want her company.

'Heading home?' When he said yes, rather brusquely, she smiled. 'Room for a reasonably small one?'

'Meaning you?'

'Who else? I need to stretch my legs.'

'You won't do that in a sidecar.'

'No, but it'll get me out to the hills.' Her sidelong glance suggested this request wasn't as innocent as it sounded.

Hoping to put her off, he said: 'The sidecar's not too clean.'

'Then I'll sit with you,' she replied cheerfully, with her most brilliant smile.

Alec hesitated, wanting to refuse. Then, with a shrug, he got on the bike. Behind him Veronica clasped her arms very firmly around his waist. This close contact with her body made him uneasy. He could feel the soft roundness of her breasts against his spine, the pressure of long, slender thighs. He was aware of the quickness of his own heartbeat. He hadn't been this close to any woman since Jenny. Such intimacy awoke desires, images that should remain dormant during her prolonged absence.

At Corriebeg, she thanked him. 'Finished the neeps?'

'Almost. We've started grubbing – clearing weeds.'

'Want a hand?'

He smiled. 'I thought you were going to walk?'

'Oh, any sort of exercise will do. And company would be nice.'

'Company.' Alec's glance slid towards the silent house. He nodded. 'I know what you mean.'

'Your wife's still away?'

'Aye.' He walked towards the field where Macrae and Pheemie were working the grubbing machine. Veronica went straight to the garron and began to guide it between the rows of neeps.

'Mrs McInnes thinks there's a poacher about,' Alec told Macrae. 'And I heard shots last night.'

'Seen anyone?' asked Macrae, scarcely able to conceal his relief when Alec said, 'No.' Robert still hadn't returned home and the postie had brought a letter clearly marked with: ON HIS MAJESTY'S SERVICE. Was the lad being called up to fight in Korea? Was that what was troubling him? If only they could talk to each other. But stubborn silence was the one thing Robert Sinclair had inherited from his grandfather.

They had reached the end of the line and Veronica was turning the garron's head. She was very competent and looked just like a land-girl in that outfit, Alec thought, as she smiled across at him. No fuss, no dithering, she just got on with the job.

'Brings back happy memories,' she explained. 'I lived near a farm as a child. We used to help out – my brothers and I.' Unaware of Macrae's cynical look, she went on: 'Lots of horses, for work and play. We used to hunt and all that —'

'Rich farmer,' Alec commented.

She shrugged. 'Oh, Daddy owned the farm.'

'Sheltered childhood,' said Alec.

'Oh, I wouldn't say that. A lot was expected of us.'

It was time to break for lunch and she followed Alec into the kitchen, where he noticed gratefully that Pheemie had been busy. There was a clean tablecloth and she set before them a plate of cheese-and-tomato sandwiches.

'Where were you stationed?' Alec asked.

'London mostly.'

'You moved about?'

'A bit.' But Veronica refused to be drawn. No, not the Middle East, or India. And when Alec persisted, she said reluctantly, France, and looked away as if she wasn't going to discuss it any further.

To Alec's question: 'After D-Day? Before?' Veronica's smile didn't reach her eyes. 'My lips are sealed.'

'I see,' said Alec slowly.

'Do you?' she said earnestly.

Alec knew all too well the appalling dangers that those who were dropped in France faced every day to help the partisans blow up bridges, maintain radio contact and distribute arms. All that was required of them was superb French and for the women, superhuman courage. He looked at her with new respect.

'You saw a lot of action,' she said. 'Does one ever forget?'

'In time – perhaps,' said Alec consolingly, knowing how hard it was to talk about experiences still too close for comfort and too vivid ever to be forgotten.

The silence between them was broken by Pheemie impatiently tapping the table with a matchbox. They had been oblivious to her presence, but were now aware of her watching them, tense and resentful.

Veronica glanced across the table and suddenly strode out of the kitchen. Alec followed her, with an apologetic smile at Pheemie. It was not well received.

Veronica was leaning against the wall. 'Sorry to rush out like that. Sometimes I just have to get into the air.'

Alec looked towards the hills. 'Right through North Africa and Italy, I dreamt of this – a farm of my own.'

Veronica smiled wryly. 'And I dreamt of beauty parlours and hairdressers. Now, I don't give a damn about them. But I suppose it kept one sane.'

A sharp voice broke the quiet between them as Pheemie demanded: 'How are you getting home, Miss Smythe?'

'The same way she came. On the back of my bike.'

Pheemie watched them drive off together, dismayed by what she felt was in the air, the attraction of like to like. Anyone could see that a mile off. Oh, poor Jenny.

Robert Sinclair made his way wearily home to Wester Balbuie. The blood lust aroused by the Korean newsreel was now assuaged. He'd never handled a gun, but he'd seen himself out there in the thick of battle, mowing down the enemy.

Why not practise on a few birds and rabbits with Grandfather's gun? Get the feel of it. Up on the hill, taking pot shots at everything that moved, he lost all track of time. Man, it was great. He saw himself as a great hero, until he came across the mangled body of a rabbit he had shot. Bloody and terrible, he suddenly realised that not only animals but the broken bodies of men, terribly wounded but alive, could look like that.

Turning away, he vomited and sweating with exhaustion, he knew he didn't really want to fight. In fact, he was bloody scared. He'd always been a bit of a coward where physical violence was involved and still smarting over his beating by the two thugs over his gambling debts, he'd been trying to prove something to himself.

Well, he had proved it. He was no fighter, the birds and rabbits were safe from him. He was going home.

Luckily his grandfather was asleep by the fire when he opened the door cautiously, carrying the gun towards the cupboard. He almost jumped out of his skin when the old man spoke up angrily: 'I'm awake. Look at you. A gun is not a toy.'

'I never said it was.'

'If I catch you touching my gun again —'

'Aye?' he said defiantly.

'I'll personally thrash you.'

Suddenly the humiliation of that other thrashing resurfaced. He couldn't manage two strong young bullies, but he could cope with one old man. As his grandfather rose slowly out of his chair and came towards him, he levelled the gun.

'Watch it, Grandfather, I'm a big boy now. Don't push me too far.'

Macrae stared at him unbelievingly. Surely it couldn't come to this between them. He shook his head. 'There's a letter for you. It'll be a request from the Army to attend your medical.'

Certain now that he was safe, Macrae took advantage of the

uncertainty on Robert's face as he stared at the letter on the table. 'You'll be pleased to go, no doubt. They'll give you a gun and no questions asked. Then you can go round blasting men's heads off to your heart's content. Better than birds and rabbits, eh?'·

That touched a sore point, a sickening memory and Robert screamed at him: 'Shut up. Shut up!' He felt the tears pricking his eyes and shouted at Macrae: 'You just don't understand, do you? You don't understand.'

Macrae didn't. He had failed to respond to that cry for help which could have brought them close, ending the acrimony for ever. He watched the lad fall sobbing to his knees, then he gently took the gun from his grasp. Returning it to the cupboard, he saw that the barrel was empty. He had never been in any real danger. Only in Robert's mind.

Macrae went silently up to bed while Robert took his letter and climbed the hill outside. Reading the call-up papers, he tore them into small pieces, and threw them into the face of the setting sun, in a kind of frenzied exorcism. And then as if pursued by devils, scattering the sheep before him, he raced back down to Wester Balbuie.

· · · · *Twenty* · · · ·

Alec was milking the cow, at peace with the world. Jenny was coming home. Tomorrow he'd meet her off the afternoon train. He was smiling to himself thinking of that homecoming when a shadow in the doorway cut across the evening sunlight.

'Pheemie?'

'No.' It was Veronica. What did she want? As if he didn't know. It had been obvious from their very first meeting. Ignoring her, he went on with the milking.

'Interesting life, farming. So fundamental,' she commented.

Alec looked up at her angrily. 'It's damned hard work and you're disturbing my cow.'

'Sorry,' she said and left. When Alec came out with his pail there was no sign of Veronica but he caught sight of Pheemie in the upper field. He waved to her, hoping she hadn't seen Veronica arrive and come to the wrong conclusions, that there was something going on between them. Pheemie was no fool, that was for sure.

But when he opened the kitchen door, Veronica was sitting at the table waiting for him.

'You've been busy,' he said. The dishes had all been washed and put away.

'I'm a tidy person,' she said.

Taking the whisky bottle and two glasses from the shelf he sat down. 'In other people's homes?'

'It depends.' And, to his questioning glance, she clarified her meaning. 'On the mood I'm in.' She took a cigarette, then offered the case to him.

'You smoke too much,' he said shortly.

Ignoring that, she said: 'I hid in a cow shed once. Under a cow. It shat in my face.' When Alec laughed, she went on: 'I couldn't move.' He asked why and she shrugged. 'Someone was looking for me.'

'I'd have moved.'

'No, you wouldn't.' Her face expressionless, she added: 'There are worse things than cow shit in your face. Civilians have no idea.' When he agreed she leant across the table, looked deeply into his eyes and said softly: 'We are able to say things to each other and not explain.'

Alec nodded. That was one answer to their mutual attraction, the other was pure honest lust.

'Do you talk about the war to your wife?'

Alec wriggled uncomfortably. 'Never.' He didn't want Jenny's name dragged into this, making him guiltily aware of his feelings for Veronica.

'You're not married?' he asked. When she shook her head: 'Boyfriend?'

'I'm here to escape one.' She paused. 'I don't fancy men who didn't go through it all. And I can't get close to those who did.'

'So you mean you just settle for —' His shrug was significant enough for her smile to confirm the same thought in both their minds.

'It's getting dark,' he said abruptly. 'You may have difficulty finding your way home.'

She smiled. 'Oh, I'm used to finding my way in the dark.'

Alec left her and went to the window. The invitation was there. It had been fairly shouted at him. How easy it would be with this experienced woman – no questions asked, no tears and recriminations afterwards. And Jenny need never know.

'Trouble is,' she said, 'there are no wild places any more. No new places to explore. One feels the need to be on the move after – you know. I suppose I should have been an intrepid Victorian lady traveller crossing deserts on camels and all that sort of thing.'

'I got to know the desert a bit too well,' said Alec grimly.

He heard the scrape of her chair as she got up and came over to face him. She stood very close and took his hands, palms upwards. 'All healed?' Her grasp was surprisingly warm.

'Now I make the callouses Umberto says.'

'Interesting man, Umberto,' she said idly.

'You should know.'

'*Peut-être*.' Her shrug gave nothing away.

'I suppose you speak French like a native.'

'My mother's French.'

'That accounts for it. Your *savoir-faire* in certain things.'

The look she gave him said it all. And as Alec thought what the hell, now is now, to hell with tomorrow, he let burning desire for this woman thrust conscience aside. He stretched out for her but before their mouths could touch, the moment was interrupted by a plaintive miaowing.

Ironically, as Veronica's arrival destroyed a poignant moment for Andrew and Flora, so was hers with Alec lost for ever. Jenny's wild cat, neglected and hungry was demanding its supper.

As the train approached the platform at Strathblair, Jenny looking round for Alec, saw Flora and Andrew waiting for the Perth train. Totally absorbed in one another, they didn't see her. Andrew was in uniform. Had he been recalled for Korea?

Where was Alec? She waited outside the station but when he failed to appear, she decided to jump on the local bus where she sat, staring out of the window, consumed with anxiety at his failure to meet her.

What had happened while she was away? She thought of those brief letters, without warmth or loving words.

At the main road, she struggled off with her suitcase and the gramophone. They were heavy so she put them on the ground and watched the bus move off.

Then, turning, there he was. All she could feel at that moment was relief at seeing him again. 'I thought you'd be at the station.'

'Trouble with the bike. Couldn't get it started. Sorry.' As she walked towards him, he said anxiously: 'You look pale.'

'Lack of fresh air.' She smiled sadly, with the odd feeling that this man to whom she had given her life and her love was suddenly a stranger. 'I was afraid to come back.'

'I was afraid, too.' His face was expressionless.

'You were? Why?'

'That you might not come home.' The intensity of his words surprised her, hinted at shared anxieties of pain and fear. Relieved, but awkward still, Jenny smiled. 'Well, here I am.'

'And you're glad to be back?' he said anxiously.

'Yes.' She looked around. It wasn't, as she had feared, a lie. She had known from the moment she stepped off the train that this was her home as no other place could ever be. The world she had left in Salisbury was the empty chrysalis of youth. She could no more return to it than a butterfly to its cocoon. She had stretched her wings and Corriebeg had drawn her into itself. Taking in the surroundings that had now grown so endearingly familiar, she said softly: 'This is where I want our child to be born.' She looked at Alec as she said the words. But his face was stony. Panic seized her. What if he didn't want a baby?

'What did you say?' he demanded.

'Our child,' she said proudly. Then she realised as his eyes filled with tears that he was in a state of shock, that he couldn't believe it either.

'Jenny,' he whispered and, with a whoop of delight, he gathered her into his arms. As they kissed long and deep, Jenny knew how much she loved and wanted this man. How could she ever have doubted him? As for Alec, lost in the wonder of reunion, smelling Jenny's hair, her soft body scent and feeling again the urgency of their love, how could he have ever thought of another woman?

And releasing her at last, they walked hand in hand together, sharing their dreams, up the road that led to home.

August 1950

· · · · *Twenty-One* · · · ·

As Strathblair fields, heavy with the fruits of the earth, turned to gold, the once-bleak hills above Corriebeg cloaked in purple heather were transformed into the romantic Highlands of Jenny's imagination. To her parents and her friend Pam, she wrote: 'I wish you could see the scene from my kitchen door. The colours are unbelievable. It's every painting you've ever seen come to life.'

She still found it difficult to believe that a new life grew inside her. There was no outward evidence and apart from the tendency to feel rather queasy in the mornings, she had never felt better, or looked more radiant, in her whole life. If this was all there was to having a baby, then it was a walk-over. She smiled to herself as she saw a future with Corriebeg echoing to the laughter of a growing family.

When her parents' doctor in Salisbury had confirmed her suspicions she had initially been scared, even a little resentful. Alec and she had been married only four months and the possibility of a baby had never been discussed between them.

How would Alec take the news that in addition to his trials at becoming a farmer he was now about to become a father?

She need not have worried. The forthcoming baby appealed to everything that was gentle and kind in Alec.

He watched over her anxiously. She was not to get over-tired, he told her sternly. She was to leave all the heavy work to him. One day he came in with a box of pills from the chemist.

'You've been looking pale. I thought you might need an iron tonic.'

The other bedroom would make a fine nursery. 'I'll get some paint. Might as well make a start. And we'd better set aside a few shillings a week towards a layette for the wee one.'

Jenny smiled. She found herself cherished as never before. This was a new Alec, worried and even a bit over-protective, she thought fondly when she wheeled out her bicycle.

'No more cycling for you,' he said, firmly removing it. 'From now on you go down with me or you take the bus. Understand?'

And waiting to get on the motorbike behind him, she saw that the sidecar had been cleaned, empty but for a neatly folded rug.

'No more pillion riding either. From now on you travel in comfort and safety.'

When she bought her first ounce of baby wool and a knitting pattern, word spread around Strathblair with the speed of light that Corriebeg's wife was expecting.

Jenny didn't resent the shopkeepers' questions about her health and their smiling, meaningful glances. Would her man be called up for Korea? they asked apprehensively. Jenny was confident that he would not, her euphoric state excluding all but the coming baby.

The fruit crop had been good this summer and under Phee-mie's expert guidance, Jenny wanted to try her hand at making raspberry jam. Buying sugar from Mr Forbes, she heard bagpipes in the street for the very first time.

'That'll be the McPhees. Tinkers,' Mr Forbes added dourly.

'Gypsies?' asked Jenny.

'No. Tinkers. You'd best keep an eye on your chickens,' warned his wife as Jenny went over to the window.

The piper in shabby but tidy clothes and an ancient hat was accompanied by a brown-skinned woman who looked tough and strong. She was soliciting contributions from the citizens of Strathblair while a pretty young girl with butter-coloured hair led the pony pulling their living quarters, a hooped, tarpaulin-covered cart.

The woman wasn't having much success, but Jenny noticed that Robert Sinclair was also fascinated by the tinkers. At least, he was obviously taken by the young girl and she watched him shyly thrust some coins into her hand.

Jenny didn't see what happened next as Sergeant Brodie's large frame blocked her view temporarily. 'Come on, Donald,' she heard him say sternly, and the pipes thereupon ceased.

What a pity, thought Jenny as the door opened to admit the tinker woman whose presence clearly wasn't welcome. Jenny could feel the Forbes' hostility. They kept their eyes glued to her as she wandered round the shop, asking her sharply what she wanted.

'Salt, just salt, mister,' she replied with quiet dignity.

Jenny, embarrassed by the Forbes' behaviour, gave her a friendly smile as Alec came in.

'What did the doctor say?' he said anxiously.

'Said I was doing fine.' As she paid Mr Forbes, Alec picked up the box of groceries. And when she protested, he said sternly: 'I don't want you carrying anything like that.'

As she sat in the sidecar with their purchases, Alec stopped to give Robert Sinclair a lift. He had missed the local bus and said vaguely that he had been to Perth. Setting him down at Wester Balbuie road end, they continued to Carnban where Alec happily handed over five shilings to Umberto for the pump he had repaired.

'Do you think you might be called up again?' Umberto asked.

'I'm on the reserve, and as an ex-NCO I'm bound to get my papers,' said Alec. He hadn't told Jenny that.

'But what about your farm?'

'Might keep me out. The word is that farmers will be exempt. Great, isn't it? Four months out of the Army and they start another bloody war,' he added bitterly going over to a dismantled grasscutter.

'Got it cheap,' said Umberto. 'I buy up bits of gear that are broken, repair them and sell for profit.'

Following him into his crowded workshop, impressed by its neat shelves of tools and pieces of machinery and somewhat envious of Umberto's apparent wealth, Alec said: 'Nice little business, eh?'

Inside the house, Jenny was unpacking the sugar.

'I hope you watched Forbes weighing it,' said Pheemie.

'I never took my eyes off him,' laughed Jenny. 'It'll be nice when it comes off the ration.'

'Not for Forbes, it won't. Oh, he was a power in the district that one, during the war when everything was rationed. Mind you, some that were prepared to do a favour never went short of the scarcities.'

'What sort of favours?' asked Jenny innocently.

'Favours of a personal nature. In his back shop. When his wife wasna' there,' was Pheemie's straight-faced reply.

Jenny's eyes widened. 'I don't believe you.'

'No?' said Pheemie casually. 'Been there a couple of times myself,' she added idly enjoying Jenny's shocked expression. But it was too much for her. She began to laugh and Jenny realised she was being teased.

Preparing the fruit, she sighed. 'I think you'll have to teach me quite a lot, Pheemie. I'm going to have to start economising. In a few months' time, we'll have another mouth to feed.' And Pheemie, who knew already, pretended to be taken by surprise and hugged her delightedly.

Jenny hadn't seen Umberto since her return. When he came in, she greeted him warmly. 'Alec was telling me what a wonderful help you were to him while I was away.'

'It was no trouble. No trouble at all. The Miss Veronica did as much as I did.'

Jenny looked faintly puzzled and Pheemie shot him an angry look. 'Umberto, just pour the tea and leave us to get on with the jam, will you?'

Home again, Jenny proudly placed her jars of neatly labelled raspberry jam in the cupboard. They looked so good and smelt of summer that she'd have preferred to display them where they could be admired. But there was no sign of the shelf Alec had promised to hang while she was away. He just hadn't had time, he said.

After supper, she took out her knitting and Alec grinned. 'How many wee jackets is that?'

'Still the same one. I've unpicked it a few times. I'm afraid I never was much good at knitting.'

'I'm sure your mother will come to the rescue.'

'Yes, but baby clothes are so expensive. It'll save a bit of money if I have a few made.'

Alec sighed. Always money. He returned to his newspaper. 'Says here there's a farm sale next week at Aultbreac. Might be able to pick up some bits and pieces quite cheaply.'

'You can't run a farm without tools,' Jenny agreed. 'Or help.' She paused. 'What was she like?'

'Who?' asked Alec, trying to sound innocent. When Jenny said 'Veronica,' he shrugged. 'Oh, you know . . .'

'No, I don't. Tell me.'

Alec thought for a moment as if he was having difficulty in describing her. 'County set. Huntin', shootin' and fishin'. Big woman.' He made a vague gesture. 'You know.' And putting aside the paper, yawned: 'Think I'll turn in. Got a long day tomorrow.'

He stopped to kiss Jenny and seeing her worried expression, he grinned. 'Hey, she's the type that wears Harris Tweed knickers.' They both laughed and Jenny, reassured, relaxed with her knitting. She knew the type well. Her mother's circle was full of them.

Tidying the garden the following morning Jenny became aware that she was being watched. Looking up, she recognised the pretty young tinker girl. Prepared to be friendly, Jenny greeted her, but she backed away nervously.

'I was just going to get a drink. Would you like something? A glass of milk.' The girl didn't reply and Jenny, smiling, asked: 'What's your name?' There was still no response. 'Not very talkative, are you?'

A shadow appeared around the side of the house. It was the tinker woman she had met in Forbes' shop. 'Her name's Bel. She was born that way.' And, looking at Jenny, she remarked:

'Ye're carrying yersel', aren't you?'

When Jenny looked surprised, the woman smiled. 'Not second sight, missus. I seen you at the grocer's. You'd been to the doctor's and your man was gey attentive. Mind you, I do ken things right enough, I kenned we'd find folk living at Corriebeg and I told my man,' she explained. And, regarding Jenny thoughtfully, she continued: 'If you need anything fixing, your pots and pans or knives sharpened, McPhee'll dae it. You'll find us up there on the Corriebeg burn.'

Jenny couldn't think of anything and she felt menaced by the woman's presence, by these strangers prowling uninvited about her yard. The anxious look she darted towards her hens wasn't lost on the McPhee woman, who gave her a mocking glance.

'Himself mends horses' harness and if ye need tatties lifting or hay coling, we're good workers.'

Suddenly Jenny wanted to be rid of them. 'I'd have to ask my husband,' she murmured.

The woman came close to her. 'Aye, you ask him, missus. Folk about here are aye glad to see us. We bring good luck.'

Jenny watched until they were out of sight. The girl was all right but her mother – she didn't know what to make of her. Alec would be furious with her for encouraging tinkers. If anything went missing she'd be blamed.

The presence of the McPhees had also affected Robert Sinclair. He had told the Ritchies the same story as his grandfather, that he had been to Perth for his medical and that he had passed fine, no bother. When Macrae asked when would he be called up, Robert turn on him irritably: 'Just can't wait to get rid of me, can you?'

'If you hadn't left college, you'd have had deferment. Though what the army wants wi' the likes of you, I don't know.'

'A tinker's get?' said Robert bitterly.

'You're the one that said it.'

'And you're the one that thought it.'

But Grandfather was right. That's what he was and what's more he was proud of it. The McPhees fascinated him. They gave him a sense of identification, for the same blood ran in their veins as his. Bad blood, Grandfather would call it. Besides they might have known his father, Gavin Sinclair, since they'd been coming to Strathblair for years. And then there was the lass Bel.

He got a shock when he realised she couldn't speak, imagining that she was just shy. Strangely enough, it didn't matter. In a curious way, beauty marred by affliction made her even more appealing. Such vulnerability roused all that was strong and manly in him. Unsuccessful with girls, now he couldn't think of anything else but what it would be like to hold Bel in his arms and to make love to her. She seemed to have taken possession of his mind in an extraordinary way and he was discovering in common with lovers all round the world, that attraction doesn't have a time clock. A minute or less is all that it takes to fill the empty space in one's destiny by a heart overflowing with love.

Desperate to see her again, he was considering devious methods of getting closer acquainted. Then by chance an opportunity arose. He found McPhee at one of his snares and greeted him politely.

'Fine morning.'

'Fine enough,' was the cautious reply. 'Your snare?'

When Robert nodded, McPhee said: 'Good eating on this one. I'll give you sixpence for it.'

'Keep your sixpence.'

'And the rabbit?' said McPhee eagerly.

'Keep it. They don't belong to anybody.'

In return McPhee took Robert back to the camp where Jess McPhee was weaving a basket while two blackened tins with wire handles which served as cooking pots were simmering above a fire. Looking at the cart and their meagre possessions,

Robert was wondering how they managed to make a living when they told him that there was no shortage of work. They'd picked up a few shillings at the neep thinning and soon there'd be help needed with the hay.

'Then it's off to Blairgowrie,' said Robert. The two looked surprised as he grinned. 'Aye, the berry picking. My father used to talk about it. Where do you winter?'

'South.' Robert was looking round for Bel, who suddenly appeared with a mug of tea for him. Although she had no words, she let their hands linger, their fingers entwine in a manner that set Robert's blood pounding, as her shy smile told him she was delighted by this unexpected visit.

There was a shrill whistle and a dog appeared. It was Fly, followed by Alec who, with a curt nod, walked on.

Feeling suddenly awkward, Robert turned back to McPhee who was asking: 'And who would your father be?'

But they seemed to know nothing about Gavin Sinclair or if they did, were wary about discussing him. Robert was disappointed, as he had hoped to establish this as a further bond between them. Instead he got the impression that his father, only part-tinker, a social outcast, had succumbed to that despicable way of life of sleeping under a roof at night and being another man's slave. Like Robert himself, he had been a misfit in both respectable Strathblair and the tinker clan.

Still inhabiting a fantasy world with Bel McPhee, Robert was totally unprepared for the violent reception on his return to Wester Balbuie. His grandfather was lying in wait. He pounced upon him and hit him hard across the mouth shouting: 'Liar. A liar and a fool. You never went for any medical.'

Robert wiped the blood from his lip and as Macrae lunged again he put the table between them. 'So what if I didn't?'

'You made me a liar as well. Sergeant Brodie was here.'

'What did you say to him?' Robert couldn't keep the anxiety out of his voice.

'Just what the hell do you think you're playing at?'

'What did you tell him?' Robert persisted.

'That you'd gone to Glasgow and were staying with friends. Why did you say you'd been to your medical?'

'I meant to go. I went to Perth on the bus. I even got as far as the front door.' Robert shook his head, remembering that awful moment of indecision. 'Well, I changed my mind about going in. I went to the pictures instead.'

As his grandfather erupted with rage, Robert shrugged, confident again. 'As far as Brodie's concerned, it's like you've told him. I'm in Glasgow. You don't know where, or when I'll be back. They'll forget about me in time.'

'Like hell they will!' said Macrae furiously. 'You'll go down to the police station tomorrow with your papers and tell them you got the date wrong!'

'I can't. I can't. I tore them up,' he added desperately.

'You stupid, feckless – What the hell are you going to do?'

'That depends on you, doesn't it? Somebody was saying that people who run farms don't need to do National Service.'

'But you're not running a farm,' Macrae reminded him.

Robert smiled. 'No, but I would be if you retired and handed this place over to me.'

Macrae stared at him, speechless at such effrontery. When he spoke again it was in a quiet, but deadly, voice. 'You can think again, my mannie. And I'm sheltering no fugitives under this roof! First thing in the morning, I'm telling Brodie you're back. After that, it's up to you!'

· · · · *Twenty-two* · · · ·

'Nothing's ever straightforward in the British army,' Andrew told Flora on his return from Regimental Headquarters. 'And I've been given a home posting.'

Suprised and delighted to see him again so soon, Andrew's short absence had given Flora time to examine her new feelings for him, feelings she suspected were mutual. The prospect of becoming Lady Menzies when Andrew inherited was rather pleasing. She loved Strathblair House and the thought of sharing it with Andrew was very agreeable. True, theirs would not have the rapture of first love, but it would be something stronger and more mature, based on common interests and her intimate knowledge of factoring a Highland estate.

There was, as far as she could see, only one fly in this particularly delectable ointment – the threat posed by Andrew's army career. She knew she couldn't go through all that again and risk losing a second husband to yet another war.

All Andrew had wanted when he arrived home was to get out into the hills. The Strathblair horses were seriously under-exercised while he was away. And Flora had never enjoyed riding alone.

She kept pace with Andrew who rode superbly and they climbed high into the purple-clad hills above the estate. The violent thunderstorm, which had reverberated back and forth hours before and killed off armies of midges, had left no trace upon the greedy earth. The sky above them looked as if it had never heard of rain, it was so serenely blue. The heather drying in warm sunlight steamed gentle clouds filling the air with its fragrance. Tiny brown pools glittered like secret mirrors as their horses' hooves kicked up the warm, sweet smell of damp earth.

By a high-standing rickle of stones they dismounted, the remains of ruined crofts that remembered the Clearances of a century ago. That desolate chapter of Scotland's history had been repeated in every Highland glen, every hillside dotted with these sad monuments of man's inhumanity to man. Now the only sound was the eternal sighing of the wind like the ghosts of forgotten sorrows breathing through a vanished door and window.

In the shelter of the wall, Andrew lit a cigarette. 'What's the latest on Korea?' Flora asked. She had promised herself she would forget everything but the magic of this day with Andrew, but so much hinged on the battles raging in that far-away land. There one general's wrong decision or miscalculation could destroy for ever any hope of a future for Andrew and herself in Strathblair.

'It's getting damn serious, that's for sure,' said Andrew. 'They're sending in masses of armour and artillery and infantry, of course. My old battalion's still in Germany.'

Flora was relieved to hear that but Andrew smiled wryly. 'It's not as simple as that. The Argylls are in Hong Kong. It doesn't take a genius to work out where they'll be posted soon enough. They're under-strength apparently and may have to second officers from other regiments. I'm afraid by applying for this home posting I've made myself rather available. Hoist with my own petard, as the saying goes.'

Flora shook her head sadly. 'When will you go?' she asked seeing all her rosy dreams fading.

'I don't know, but I think it'll be sooner rather than later,' was the gloomy reply.

Would wars never cease? Andrew thought desperately. All of this land had been blood-soaked in battle. Far below them stood a bright jewel in an emerald landscape, Blair Castle. Nearly two hundred and fifty years ago, Bonnie Dundee 'Iain Dhub Nan Cath' fighting in a lost Jacobite cause was slain by a musketball at Killiecrankie. His body was carried back to the castle by his loyal Highlanders with a piper playing 'Lochaber No More'. When he was young Andrew sometimes fancied he could still hear that sad lament echoing through the mists of time.

At his side Flora sighed. 'I suppose we should be thankful for these few days.'

She looked so sad, Andrew said helplessly: 'Flora, if all this had only happened six months later.'

Flora looked at him. 'I know, but life's just not like that, is it?'

Andrew was forced to remember that, but for Veronica's ill-timed arrival, he might have proposed. Flora, he suspected, had never liked his cousin and had not been sorry when later that week she announced that she was returning to the fleshpots of London, as she called them.

'No experience should last for ever,' she added, inviting them all to a farewell dinner.

Veronica's visit was almost over, the damage almost, but not quite, done.

Alec enjoyed his evenings out at the local with the other farmers, although he felt a bit guilty about leaving Jenny on her own. It would be different of course when she had a bairn to occupy her time. True, she never made any fuss about him going, always comforted him with a mention of vague 'things to do' or a programme on the wireless she wanted to listen to. But sometimes he caught her looking wistful as he got ready.

'I'd be happy to take you along,' he said apologetically. 'But it's not the thing in these parts for women to be seen in pubs. Not respectable women.'

'Do you meet the other kind?' asked Jenny curiously.

'In Strathblair? You must be joking. It's all male talk, farming and so forth. Business really.' When she sighed, he said: 'Look, Jenny, I wish you'd say what you mean.'

'All I meant was – can we afford it?'

Alec laughed. 'Is that all? Don't worry, I can make a pint last the whole night.'

'That's all right, then.' Money was so tight these days, as she had discovered when she took over the accounts. She was good with figures, a relic of her bank-clerking days.

Putting on his jacket, Alec said: 'I meant to tell you, we've got tinkers camping up by the waterfall.'

'I know. I had a visit from a woman and a young girl this afternoon, wanting to know if we had anything needed mending.'

'More like wanting to see if there was anything worth lifting.'

'I don't think so. They've been coming here for years. They

couldn't do that if they were thieves.'

Promising not to be late, Alec found his cronies already gathered at the bar. The older men who had missed the war were keen on his reminiscences. He told a good story, avoiding the unpleasant aspects and concentrating on the lighter side of a soldier's life, particularly exploits with the Italian girls.

He realised this was gaining him quite a reputation as a ladies' man when Wallace said: 'With all the high jinks you got up to, I'm surprised you had time to win the war.'

'Oh, he'll have had some friends helping him,' put in Todd the postman.

And Alec saw vividly the faces of those whom he had called comrades, smiling faces he would see no more. He raised his glass in solemn toast: 'To absent friends.'

Bailley polished more glasses. 'You'll be on the reserve then?' Alec preferred not to brood on that either. 'What about big Umberto?' the barman added.

'They canna conscript him,' said Todd. 'He's too auld and he's an Eyetie.'

'Maybe he's in the Italian reserve.'

This raised a laugh and Forbes said: 'They should send Pheemie Robertson out there. Let her slander the Koreans to death.'

Wallace, who had done well out of his auctioneering, lived in a big house a mile down the road from Strathblair. Drinking with 'the lads' was a shrewd matter of business for, in other company, he was apt to give himself gentlemanly airs. A bit shocked by Forbes' ungallant remarks, he changed the subject abruptly: 'You'll be going to the roup at Aultbreac, Alec?'

'Aye, if there's anything interesting for sale.'

'There's a Fergie tractor, in poor working condition, so it's likely to go for scrap.'

'Drink up, gentlemen,' said Bailley as, on the stroke of nine, Sergeant Brodie put in an appearance. When he drifted over

Alec thought he'd better mention that the McPhees were at Corriebeg burn.

'It's as well to know. Though they don't cause any trouble.' said Brodie, but Alec wasn't convinced. 'Last time I had folk camping up there, it cost me a lamb.'

'I heard about that.'

'Well, Balbuie can hardly blame me if anything happens this time. Not with his grandson encouraging them.'

This was all the information Sergeant Brodie needed. He was in his element, he'd found crime at last. Even if it was only a lad evading his call-up it was better than tracking down poachers and rescuing old wives' cats from trees. Next morning he presented himself at Wester Balbuie and demanded: 'Do you still deny that boy's here?'

'I've said everything I've got to say, Sergeant,' was the evasive reply.

'He has until the end of the week to turn himself in. If he doesn't he's in trouble. And so are you.'

A noise above their heads alerted Brodie who rushed past Macrae into the house. He was too late to see Robert disappear around the corner of the byre.

To everyone's relief, the day of the Aultbreac roup dawned fair. A roup was regarded as a great occasion for socialising as well as for getting bargains, although neighbours felt compassion for old Mrs Fraser who was leaving Strathblair and the home she had come to as a bride forty-two years ago. Since Charlie Fraser took sick and died, the farm had proved too much for her.

Flora, as factor, had already settled the business side and was leaving for the auction when Veronica arrived at her office.

'My, what a busy social life you lead.'

'It's my job to keep an eye on what's going on. Why don't you come along? You might find it interesting.'

'It's not really my sort of thing.' Veronica suppressed a slight shudder. 'Besides, since I'm off tomorrow, I thought I'd like to make some farewells.'

Watching Flora depart and declining a lift, Veronica set off to her own destination. Corriebeg.

Alec, counting his notes with that tractor in mind, found Jenny somewhat preoccupied.

'Are you sure you don't want to come with me?'

Jenny walked away without replying and Alec, who was feeling guilty about having been late home from the pub last night and somewhat merry, said: 'Oh, for God's sake, how can you stay in a huff so long?'

'I'm not in a huff. I've got things on my mind. One of the hens is missing.'

Her search was interrupted by the arrival of a red sports car. A very elegant young woman emerged wearing an expensive-looking cashmere cardigan and tailored slacks which empha-sised her long legs and a film star's figure. Her hair was long and blonde, her face immaculately made up.

Conscious of her own shabby working attire, Jenny won-dered who on earth this visitor could be.

She wasn't kept in the dark for long. The newcomer approached smiling. 'Hello there. You must be Jenny.' At her questioning look, she smiled again. 'I'm Veronica.'

Jenny's mouth dropped open. So this was Alec's big beefy woman, the huntin', shootin' county type of the Harris Tweed knickers. She stared at him as he came out of the house, dismay written all over his face as Veronica drawled: 'Hello, stranger.' Her voice became soft and sexy.

'Hello there.' Alec gulped, looking as if he'd like to have been anywhere but standing in his own yard with his wife never taking her eyes off him.

'It's hello and goodbye, I'm afraid.' Veronica pouted. 'I'm leaving tomorrow.'

Alec breathed again. That was one piece of good news. 'I see you've —' He nodded towards Jenny whose tight-lipped expression boded him no good as she said, 'We've met'.

'Well, then, safe journey,' Alec offered with awkward cheerfulness. 'And thanks for your help.'

Veronica came close to him, her smile brilliant. 'I enjoyed it. All of it,' she added significantly, without bothering to lower her voice. 'Good luck, Alec. Nice to have met you, Jenny.'

They watched her drive off, then Jenny turned to Alec. 'Not quite what I expected,' she said coldly.

Alec smiled vaguely. 'Well, I'd best be on my way,' he said, and jumping on to the motorbike he drove off with considerable alacrity.

The roup was already under way, the accumulated possessions of Mrs Fraser's lifetime spread rather pathetically over the yard, with her household goods on tables. She sat apart, looking tearful as each lot was knocked down to the highest bidder.

'Aren't you taking anything from the house at all?' Pheemie asked gently.

Mrs Fraser dabbed at her eyes. 'Nothing big, lass. My daughter's house is gey well furnished seeing as her man's got a good job wi' the Glasgow Corporation.'

And so Pheemie found herself the possessor of a rather dreadful Victorian vase, much to Flora's amusement.

'I don't know what came over me, I just got carried away,' she said looking round for Umberto whose main interest was the Fergie tractor. When Macrae assured him disgustedly that it was only fit for scrap, Umberto flew to the late Mr Fraser's defence.

'The man was sick, Balbuie.' And as they walked towards the house he said: 'Your grandson, Robert.'

'What about him?' Macrae demanded.

'The policeman was up at Carnban asking if we'd seen him.'

Damn Brodie, thought Macrae, and seeing the postman talking to Mrs Fraser, decided to ask him a few vital questions.

They were interrupted by Alec's arrival, wanting to know when the farming implements were being auctioned.

'The auctioneer's still working his way through the rubbish,' said Macrae. 'I'm only interested in the beasts myself.'

After a moment's hesitation, Alec said: 'Balbuie. I think I might have put my foot in it the other night with Sergeant Brodie.' And Macrae's face revealed nothing of his anger as Alec related the incident. He had many faults, but he was proud of his integrity. Known as a man of his word, he resented the fact that now the lad was turning him into a liar, ruining the reputation he had treasured all his life.

Wallace was about to auction the Ferguson tractor. This was the moment Alec had been waiting for.

'I won't pretend that it's in tip-top condition, but who'll start me off at thirty pounds,' shouted Wallace. 'Twenty-five then? Twenty?'

'Twenty,' said Alec confidently. He seemed to have the field to himself. This was going to be easy.

'Twenty-two.' He turned and found Umberto bidding.

'And ten shillings,' said Alec.

Wallace laughed. 'Come on Corriebeg, no ten shilling bids.'

'Twenty-five,' said Umberto.

Alec quickly counted his money. 'Twenty-six.'

'Twenty-eight,' said Umberto.

'Twenty-nine.'

'Thirty.'

But Alec couldn't match that, not even with the loose change in his pocket. Angrily he saw what he had already regarded as his tractor knocked down to Umberto for scrap. It was too humiliating and he waited no longer, hurrying away with the auction still in full swing.

His road home took him past the McPhee's camp where he thought he glimpsed Robert chatting to the girl Bel. But at

Alec's approach he darted out of sight.

Jess was stirring soup in a can over the fire and McPhee was repairing a harness.

'I'm missing a hen,' said Alec.

McPhee looked up. 'I never took your hen, mister.'

'Somebody did.'

'There's foxes hereabouts.'

'Aye,' said Alec and going over to the soup pan, he tipped it with his foot. As its contents hissed into the fire he saw the chicken bones. 'And they're dab hands at making chicken soup.'

Jess rose to her feet and said coldly with great dignity: 'There was no call for that, mister. That bird was bought and paid for.'

Alec gave her a disbelieving look. 'Next time I come up here, I want you elsewhere,' he said to McPhee and walked quickly away.

In Corriebeg he found Jenny peeling potatoes at the sink. She kept her head averted not wanting him to know she'd spent most of the afternoon lying on her bed crying. He'd lied to her about that woman and that could mean only one thing. He had something to hide. And Jenny knew exactly what had been happening. While she'd been in Salisbury, he'd been carrying on with – with that Veronica.

But Alec had other more important things on his mind than noticing Jenny's distress. 'Beaten by a pound,' he said. 'A lousy pound. And you should have seen the look on Umberto's face. Smug. That's the only word for it. All that and a bunch of thieving tinks in one day.'

When she asked how he knew the tinkers had been stealing, he replied: 'I saw the bones and giblets in their soup, when I —' He paused.

'When you what?'

'When I kicked it over.'

'Alec!' Jenny was horrified by such behaviour.

'Then she came out with this load of rubbish about having

bought the hen!' And turning on her furiously, he shouted: 'When will you learn to stop encouraging people like that?'

'Encouraging them? They've been coming here a lot longer than we have!'

'You know what your trouble is, Jenny. You get taken in too easily. Just because some tinker woman shoots you a sob story —'

Jenny threw down the potato knife. 'Stop talking to me like that! It's been going on too much lately. I'm your wife, remember? I'm carrying your child!'

'What's that got to do with it?' Alec demanded irritably.

Jenny stared at him for a moment. 'Wasn't she your type?'

'What are you talking about?'

'Your type. That's what I'm talking about. No wonder you didn't have time to put up the shelf for me. You were too busy with her, Veronica whatever-her-name-is.'

'Where does she come into all this?' Alec asked wearily.

'You tell me, Alec Ritchie, you tell me. I'm glad you had company while I was away. I'm glad you both enjoyed yourselves.'

'For God's sake, woman —'

'Don't woman me. She's not exactly the way you described her, is she?'

Alec sighed. 'Jenny, I don't know what you're thinking.'

'I know what I'm thinking. I'm not a fool. Why did you lie to me?'

Again Alec sighed. 'I didn't want you to get the wrong idea.'

Jenny thumped her fists on the table. 'Don't patronise me!'

'We only talked,' said Alec desperately.

'Oh, I bet you did. What did you talk about?'

'The war. Death. Danger. She'd been through it too —'

'She said you had a lot in common,' Jenny interrupted him furiously. 'You're talking like a married man who's been caught out!'

Alec stared at her and then shouted: 'I've had enough of this!'

She ran out into the yard and as he drove away, she yelled after the accelerating motorbike: 'Harris Tweed knickers! What were they really like?'

· · · · *Twenty-three* · · · ·

In the Atholl Arms that night the talk focused on the Aultbreac roup. Great bargains, a grand day out and everyone right glad Jeannie Fraser had done well from the proceeds, especially getting thirty pounds for the old tractor they'd expected to go for scrap.

'Umberto knows a bargain when he sees one,' said Forbes.

The barman nodded. 'Aye, he's quite smart when it comes to business. Maybe a wee thing too smart at times.'

'Macrae got the beasts. Any word about that grandson of his?' said Forbes.

'Why should there be?' asked Wallace curiously. He'd been too busy with the auction to pick up the latest gossip.

'Seems the boy's missing. Sergeant Brodie's gey anxious to get hold of him.'

'He's been up to something serious, I'll be bound,' said Forbes. 'Bad blood will out.' And they shook their heads, remembering the scandal of Macrae's tinker orraman, Gavin Sinclair, who had eloped with his only bairn Mary, having got her pregnant first.

'I think I could maybe hazard a guess, though I don't know that I should say anything seeing I'm what you might call a Government employee,' Todd put in.

'Would another pint maybe help you forget the glamour of the postie's uniform?' said Wallace.

'A half-pint?' suggested barman Bailley.

'Since you're offering and since I'm only guessing. Old Balbuie had a word wi' me at the roup. Wanted to know if the letter I'd delivered was the boy's call-up papers.'

'So that's it,' Forbes whistled. 'The boy's a deserter.'

'Hardly a deserter if he's not in the Army,' Wallace reminded him. 'What did you say?'

'I told him I thought I minded seeing them.'

'You only thought.'

'Well, I cannae remember every letter I deliver. I do hundreds every week' – the others exchanged glances at this slight exaggeration – 'and that'd be a while ago.'

'Supposing it got lost in the sorting office or something. Half of these damned Department of Agriculture forms do. At least so the farmers say,' said Bailley, as this was the constant excuse for lack of funds.

'That's what Balbuie was hinting at but I told him straight. If I've got a letter to deliver, delivered it is —'

He was interrupted by Alec's arrival.

'Just in time,' said Wallace. 'It's Mr Forbes' round,' he added with a sly look at the grocer, well-known to be 'grippy' with money.

But Alec nodded briefly and went to the far end of the bar. The three men exchanged puzzled looks as they heard him ask for a large whisky, instead of his usual pint.

Umberto came in and stood alongside him. Producing his large roll of notes, he looked towards the three men and said: 'Four large whiskies, please. What's yours, Alec?'

'Nothing, thank you,' was the cold reply.

'Manage to get the Fergie back to Carnban without the wheels falling off?' Wallace asked Umberto.

'Don't worry. I get it fixed.'

Forbes laughed. 'Aye, you're a great fixer, Umberto. I hear you're entering for the hill race again? Man, you're an optimist. You finished sixth last year.'

'Aye, but no' this year, I'll win. I've been in training.' Umberto continued confidently: 'This year I'll be first.'

Alec looked up. 'Aye, he'll win.'

'See, Alec agrees.' In response to Umberto's smile Alec murmured contemptuously in Italian.

Umberto stared at him, speechless for a moment. Then he hit him hard across the face. Alec stumbled and fell. He got up, wiping blood from his lips, and lunged at Umberto.

'Enough. Enough,' shouted Bailley. 'I'm not having that in here. Outside the pair of you!'

The two went out without a word, eagerly followed by the customers. Most of them could hardly remember the last time they'd seen a fist fight in Strathblair's High Street.

They were well rewarded, it was a fight they talked about long afterwards, a fight men might have paid good money to see. The two were fairly evenly matched for although Umberto was taller and heavier, he was also older than Alec. They lunged, punched, thumped, grappled and flailed at each other. No holds barred, finally they both went down rolling in the road, more through exhaustion than defeat.

As they lay there panting, wiping the blood from their noses, a shadow fell across Alec. He looked up to find Sir James staring down at him with a face like thunder.

Sir James said nothing. He took in the scene and without a word went back to the car that was taking him, with Andrew and Flora, to Veronica's farewell dinner.

As they drove off Sergeant Brodie arrived on his bicycle demanding to know what the fight was all about, at which the two protagonists decided they'd had enough and, stumbling to their feet, staggered off on their separate ways.

Jenny woke at dawn to find Alec's side of the bed had not been slept in. Alarmed she went downstairs and found him slumped over the kitchen table snoring. She had had plenty of time to get over her rage and putting a gentle hand on his shoulder, she said: 'What's this then? I missed you last night. Oh Alec, what have you been doing now?' she cried as his battered face gazed up at her. Rushing away she returned with a bowl of warm water.

'Umberto hit me,' he murmured as she dabbed at his swollen bloodied lips.

Jenny was astonished. The two seemed to be the best of friends.

'It was something I said.' When she wanted to know more, he said wearily: 'Oh, I can't remember.'

Alec Ritchie's behaviour was the main topic in Strathblair House as Sir James and Andrew breakfasted the following morning.

'You'll help him out, won't you, Father?'

'Certainly not. I have no authority. And I don't feel inclined to use my influence.'

'Ritchie's a good sort,' said Andrew defensively.

'Good sorts don't brawl in public —'

'I wouldn't call it a public brawl.'

'What would you call it?'

'A heated discussion,' said Veronica who had just dumped her cases in the hall. They both looked at her. 'All packed and ready to go. I take it you're talking about last night. Oh come on, Uncle James. Most men have squared off like that.'

'Not outside the Atholl Arms in Strathblair.'

'Outside the Oxford Union then,' said Veronica sweetly.

'What did you say?' Sir James demanded.

'Daddy told me. You took on three fellow undergrads, didn't you?'

'I've never heard about this,' grinned Andrew delightedly.

'He was almost sent down,' said Veronica sternly.

'I was not. Your father had a legendary capacity for exaggeration —'

'You would have been sent down,' Veronica insisted, 'if certain strings hadn't been pulled. Was it a fight over some girl?'

'It was over a matter of high principle. After a civilised debate,' Sir James added primly.

'Followed by a public brawl,' Andrew put in.

Sir James's face flushed scarlet. 'It was not the same thing at all.'

'Oh, I see, gentleman and players,' said Andrew mockingly.

'I decline to continue with this conversation,' said his father coldly and picking up his newspaper he departed in high dudgeon leaving Andrew and Veronica exchanging gleeful looks.

Pretty certain they had Sir James over a barrel and that Alec Ritchie was safe, they were not surprised when no further mention of the incident was made as Veronica took an affectionate farewell of her uncle, with Andrew promising to call her if he came through London.

Flora hadn't come to see her off. The omission was noted and she said pointedly, 'Say goodbye to Flora for me.'

As the car drove off taking her to the station Sergeant Brodie cycled up the drive.

'Sir James, I wonder if I might have a word with you about the business outside the hotel last night.'

Andrew watched his father carefully as he replied: 'Boisterous bit of horseplay, wasn't it?'

'Horseplay, sir?'

'Of course. You're surely not thinking of bringing charges?'

'I certainly am. We don't need riff-raff like that in Strathblair,' said Brodie stiffly.

'Oh, come now, Ritchie might be something of a rough diamond, but I'd hardly call him riff-raff.'

Brodie smiled. 'Not Ritchie, sir. The Italian. Fabiani. To the extent that the witnesses will say anything at all, they do say that Fabiani threw the first punch. Don't know why they don't send the likes of him back to Italy.'

Sir James ignored that comment. 'Still, it's difficult to see how you can charge one without charging the other.'

'That's for the sheriff to decide.'

'Of course. I quite agree. Sound man, know him quite well. I'm sure he'll be as even-handed as he can be. In the absence of witnesses,' he added walking towards the front door.

'Now, sir, that's where you can help me —'

Sir James halted in his tracks. 'I doubt it, Sergeant. I doubt it.

All we saw were two men rolling on the ground.' He paused. 'They appeared to be laughing.'

'Laughing?' said Sergeant Brodie. Thwarted once again, he could have wept as yet another miscreant was allowed to slip through his fingers.

In Carnban, Pheemie was dealing with her wounded warrior. Going out to tell him breakfast was ready, she found him working on the tractor. He didn't want any breakfast, he told her. He wasn't hungry.

'Don't be daft. You're aye hungry. And look at me when I'm talking to you.' Slowly he looked round and Pheemie's mouth fell open when she saw his bruised face. 'In the name o' God!'

'It was an accident.'

'Accident. You look as if you've stuck your head in a thresher. Come on.' And taking him into the house where she administered first aid she managed to winkle the story of the fight out of him.

Ten minutes later she was cycling to Corriebeg where Jenny was blacking the range. One look at her face told Pheemie she'd heard.

'Men are such weans,' said Pheemie. 'I've told Umberto he's to come and apologise.'

'Will he?'

'No. Will Alec make up?'

Jenny shook her head. 'No. What was this fight about?'

'Aye well, they were talking about the hill race. Alec said he thought Umberto would win it —'

'So?'

'Because the Italian army was so good at running.'

Jenny was first appalled and then suddenly both of them began to laugh. It was too absurd. As they went out to the hen house to collect the eggs, Jenny said somewhat shamefacedly: 'It was partly my fault, I suppose. We had a fight – and then he lost the tractor to Umberto. And then there was trouble with the tinkers.'

'Och, you poor lass. What were you and Alec fighting about?' she asked curiously.

'Well,' Jenny hesitated. 'That Veronica woman came here to say goodbye. Pheemie —'

'I'll get the ones in here.' Pheemie had her own ideas as to what had been going on between Alec and Veronica and she wasn't prepared to be questioned by Jenny. Fortunately the discovery of a folded note in the henhouse provided a timely change of subject. Opening it, Pheemie handed Jenny half a crown.

'They did pay for the chicken,' Jenny said but Pheemie, reading the scribbled note, shook her head. 'Oh, it was paid for all right. But not by the tinkers.'

'Then who?'

'Young Robert.'

Jenny had forgiven Alec, blaming her silly jealousy on her condition. Relieved, he said he was sorry too.

They had kissed and made up.

But Alec still felt he owed others an apology, too, and went in search of the tinkers. They had taken him at his word and moved camp. He caught up with them on the old drovers' road that joined the Pitlochry Road.

'A word with you, Mr McPhee.' The tiny cavalcade kept moving. 'I was wrong,' he called. 'Come back to Corriebeg. You're welcome.'

'Aye well, you're ower late, mister,' said Jess. 'You've seen the last of us. Aye, and the last o' any luck we brought with us.'

'Look, I know you didn't take the hen. I know it was paid for.' Seizing the pony's head Alec brought the cart to a halt. 'Are you in there, Robert? What the hell do you think you're playing at?'

Bel stood defensively by the tarpaulin flap.

'Look, I'm not going into the Army and I'm sure as hell not

going to jail,' came Robert's muffled voice.

'And you won't hide for long the way you're going. It was obvious where you'd be once the money was found.'

Robert looked out. 'I didn't think your wife would say anything,' he said reproachfully.

'She didn't. And neither will I.'

'My grandfather, he would turn me in.'

Alec shook his head. 'That's not the way I hear it.'

'What do you hear?' Robert asked anxiously.

'I'll tell you when we get back to Balbuie.'

Robert hesitated, looking at Bel and at her parents.

'Away back there, son,' said Jess. 'You've no place wi' us.'

'Then I've no place anywhere,' said Robert bitterly.

'You too, McPhee. Come back to Corriebeg,' said Alec.

'Aye, we'll be back, mister.'

'Good. So we're friends.'

'We'll be back to lift your tatties and help wi' the hay. We'll be back because you need us and we need you. But we're no' friends.' With that McPhee urged on the pony.

Robert took Bel in his arms. They kissed and then, with a longing backward look, Bel followed her parents.

A week later, Alec met Robert getting on the local bus in Strathblair. Wearing his best suit, he had been for his medical. When he asked how it had gone, Robert grinned and said: 'Fine.'

'Och, you'll find the Army's no' so bad after all,' said Alec consolingly.

'I'll not find it at all. They don't want me. I had 'flu a few years ago.

'Come off it! You don't get rejected because you've had flu!'

'You do if it leaves you with a burst ear drum!'

Alec watched him go. Robert had been forgiven. Relieved at not being called up he would settle down at Wester Balbuie again and get over Bel McPhee. As for himself, he had nothing to get over. If he and Veronica had met in some other time and place . . . But he recognised she'd never be the faithful, domesticated type. He was far better off with his Jenny and soon he'd have a son to take care of. Jenny was certain sure the baby would be a boy.

Forgiveness was in the air. All except Umberto. There was still unfinished business to settle when they next met.

· · · · *Twenty-four* · · · ·

Jenny's rapturous letters to Pam Clayton-Hill brought an unexpected result. Pam had to see these glorious Highlands Jenny was going on about and had persuaded Freddie that he must take her to Corriebeg – immediately!

When Freddie murmured that it might not be convenient to descend on the Ritchies at such short notice, Pam impressed upon him once again that Jenny's very last words on her Salisbury visit were: 'Come and see us any time. You and Freddie'll always be welcome.'

'In fact, between you and me, darling, she sounded a bit desperate for civilised society. And now with a baby on the way, this will be a lovely surprise.'

'I suppose you're right.' Pam thereupon took all arrangements into her own hands. She knew that letters to Corriebeg in the back of beyond would take for ever, so opted to send a telegram instead.

Thus it was late one Tuesday afternoon, when Mr Todd puffed up the way to Corriebeg on his bicycle. Jenny's heart almost stopped at the sight of the yellow envelope, traditionally the harbinger of bad tidings. Thrusting it into her hand, he grinned: 'Aye, lass, ye'll be having visitors.'

For once, Jenny blessed the postman for his nosiness. In that short interval she'd decided Mummy must be seriously ill – or worse. But her relief at Pam's message, 'Expect us Friday', was short-lived. It quickly turned to dismay as she thought about breaking the news to Alec. How would he react to this unexpected visit from her friends?

As she suspected, Alec was not pleased. The grim silence with which he greeted her announcement was far more voluble than angry words, and much more difficult to deal with. Valiantly pretending that all was still sweetness and light between them and that he wasn't sulking, she watched him put on his jacket. Once again he was making plain his displeasure by going down to the pub, which had become his place of refuge in times of domestic strife.

She could bear it no longer. 'For heaven's sake, Alec. Say what you're thinking.'

He shrugged. 'I'm thinking, can we afford to have visitors?' They both knew this wasn't the real reason, but it was kinder than the truth.

'These visitors are my very best friends.'

'So? They still have to be fed. We have to make a bit of a spread. And where does the money come from?'

Jenny was in bed asleep when he came back earlier than usual, guiltily aware that once again he had been selfish and unfair. She did need congenial company, especially at this time with a baby on the way. Full of remorse and anxious to be loving and reassuring, he climbed in beside her. But his gentle touch failed to stir her. Groaning sleepily, she turned away from him.

The next morning, he awoke to find Jenny's side of the bed was empty. She was already in the byre milking Buttercup. Leaning her head against the cow's warm flank she felt thrilled and excited at the prospect of seeing Pam and Freddie, despite Alec's reaction. She planned to spend the rest of the day baking and thanks to Pheemie she was now a dab hand at stews, broths and Scotch trifle, none of which would seriously tax the housekeeping budget.

Suddenly above her head, she heard a strange sound like distant weeping. How odd. She looked up, but saw only crossbeams and the roof. Yet she was sure that was where the sound came from.

Pigeons cooing, no doubt – they made weird courtship noises. But she felt chilled as she returned to the milking. The temperature in the byre had dropped alarmingly, as if someone had opened the door to admit an icy blast. She was aware of something else. The weeping sound had been followed by a curious stillness. A silence as heavy as the silence of death was the thought that occurred to her. It was as if for a moment, all time had ceased.

Buttercup felt it, too, for she moved restlessly and as a shadow filled the doorway, Jenny jumped up almost upsetting the pail.

'Alec. Oh, it's you.'

He smiled. 'Who else were you expecting? Any chance of some breakfast this morning?' Taking the pail from her as they went towards the door, Jenny looked back. 'I thought I heard something just now. I thought there – there was somebody else here.'

'I hope you're not going to go all fey on me when I'm dying of hunger,' said Alec, but his tone was gentle. She did look scared, and Jenny was the practical sort, not the kind who imagined things. Och well, just her condition, no doubt. Better than wanting to eat coal! He'd better be nice to her, humour her a bit after last night.

When he didn't immediately tackle the porridge she set before him, she asked: 'Something wrong with your breakfast?'

'No, no. It looks very good.' And picking up his spoon, he said sheepishly: 'I'm assuming there's no ground glass in it.'

'Not this time,' was her acid reply.

Alec stretched out his hand. 'Come on, Jenny. Talk to me.'

Throwing down her spoon, she said: 'All right, I will. Bidding at the roup for a tractor with money we don't have.'

'We discussed that —'

'Fighting with Umberto outside that wretched pub –' She

stopped suddenly, a hand to her mouth and rushed out to the lavatory where he heard her throwing up. He sighed, knowing the real reason for her anger wasn't money or Umberto but his failure to enthuse over Pam's and Freddie's visit.

He finished his breakfast and went out to gather his tools. When he came back she was washing up. 'I'm off now. Are you feeling better?' And, turning her around to face him, he kissed her.

'You mean you're not even going to be here when they arrive?'

'I can't. Those fences up on the hill won't mend themselves. And anyway, they're your friends. It's you they want to see. Especially Freddie, eh?' he added with a teasing smile.

Jenny froze. 'What do you mean?'

'You know —'

'We went about when we were children. That's all,' she said coldly. 'And we were in the Pony Club together.'

Alec looked at her. There was nothing more he could say. He'd tried to make amends by making a joke about Freddie and that had gone down like a lead balloon. He shrugged. 'Well, I'd better be off.'

He looked back and smiled but there was no softening to her look of indignation.

Pheemie would have sympathised with Alec. She, too, was having a visit she could have done without, a yearly visit calculated to try the patience of a saint.

Her Great Aunt Ishbel. A seemingly frail old lady who played heavily upon being Pheemie's oldest relative, she had an indomitable will for making others do what she wanted, reinforced by a tongue dipped in vitriol.

But it was her extraordinary effect on Umberto that both amused and irritated Pheemie. A great big man, terrified of Aunt Ishbel, living in almost superstitious dread of her visits, he was sure she was a witch. Every year they had a fight when

Pheemie made him take the tractor-trailer to meet her train and every year he pleaded: 'Can you not go?'

'No, I've got far too much to do here. What's wrong? You're surely no' scared of a wee old woman in her eighties, are you?'

But he was.

The same train brought Pam and Freddie to Strathblair. Umberto noticed them vainly searching for a taxi – a taxi in Strathblair! That would be the day!

Freddie came over looking desperate. 'I say, would you happen to know how we get to – Corriebeg?'

'I can take you.' To Pamela's horror, Umberto indicated the trailer where a gimlet-eyed Aunt Ishbel, already settled, was taking careful and disapproving stock of their appearance, including their most unsuitable city clothes which she wanted to describe to Pheemie in minute detail. She observed their dismay and evident misery expressed in those posh English accents with silent amusement. Especially when they were deposited at the short cut to Corriebeg – across the fields.

Her last sight of them was one of Pam staggering along on those high heels, crying indignantly: 'This is so typical of Jenny.'

At the sound of the tractor outside, Pheemie quickly stubbed out her cigarette, emptied the ashtray and hid it under a cushion, trying to eliminate the smell of stale smoke by fanning the air with a newspaper.

'And here she is at last!' She greeted her aunt.

'I've never missed a Show yet and I'm not starting now.' Pheemie suppressed a smile. Aunt Ishbel always made it plain that this event was the only reason for visiting her niece.

'How was your journey?'

But instead of answering, her aunt turned to Umberto who stood framed in the doorway. 'What are you hanging about for? Away and put my case up in my room,' she said sharply.

'Please, Umberto' said Pheemie sweetening the reprimand.

He was hardly out of hearing when Aunt Ishbel grumbled, as she did every year, 'Why didn't he go back to Italy when the others did?'

'Because he works for me, that's why.'

'Because someone somewhere has forgotten his existence, you mean.' And releasing the pins anchoring her hat, she grumbled: 'Your cousin Jamie would give his eye teeth for a job like that one's got. Instead he has to go labouring in the town. Jamie would be glad to work here, you know,' she added.

'Aye, maybe he would, Aunt Ishbel, maybe he would.'

Pheemie's tone was non-committal and her aunt sniffed, knowing full well the scandalous reason for the Eyetie's continued presence. She'd get in a dig about that later.

'And don't think I haven't noticed that you're still smoking.'

Ignoring that remark, Pheemie said: 'The tea's ready. You'll be needing a cup, I dare say.' She had done some special baking but the old woman ate in silence, sighing occasionally and pausing to examine the insides of the scones and the egg sandwiches as if they were a penance rather than a treat. Pheemie didn't worry, she had long since given up expecting praise, aware that her aunt's sharp tongue wouldn't spare her if the food set before her was less than excellent.

Tea over, Aunt Ishbel seized Pheemie's empty cup and after upending it consulted the tea leaves. 'There's a woman. See, aye and she's a strong woman. But she's carrying a burden that's too heavy for her.'

'That must be me all right,' Pheemie admitted wryly.

'It is you. But my, oh my, who have we here?' she asked holding the cup beneath Pheemie's nose.

'What am I supposed to be looking at? That blob?'

'That blob is the man in your life.'

'God forbid!'

'Oh, there's no two ways about it. There's a man on the horizon.'

'And that's where they always stay too,' was the bitter

response. 'So, tell me, who is this tall, dark stranger?' Pheemie added idly, seeing Umberto out of the window.

'He could even be a foreigner,' said her aunt reluctantly.

'Oh goodie. I'm going to marry a pygmy from darkest Africa!' And much to her aunt's resentment, Pheemie roared with mirth.

'When you are quite finished, Euphemia.' And as her niece subsided she continued: 'The other person who fits that description is, of course, that useless orraman of yours.'

'Oh aye, now you mention it, so he does,' said Pheemie with elaborate casualness.

Laying aside the cup, Aunt Ishbel studied her intently. 'Then tell me, is what the gossips and fishwives say about you and him the truth?'

Pheemie rose from the table. 'You tell me, Aunt Ishbel. You're the one with the second sight,' she said. Smiling at her aunt's frustrated expression she cleared the teacups and taking out a baking bowl and some flour, she set about preparing supper, confident that, for once, she had had the last word.

But Aunt Ishbel was not to be defeated. As Pheemie slapped down a dollop of pastry on the board and pummelled it flat, she remarked: 'You'll ruin that pastry. You'll kill it stone dead. Bad feelings when you're cooking go into the food and spoil the taste.'

'Then how come your cakes win all the prizes?' Pheemie demanded sweetly.

'And what's put you in such a mood, may I ask?'

'Nothing, Aunt Ishbel, absolutely nothing.'

'Was it me mentioning the gossip about you and the orraman?' Aunt Ishbel asked slyly. 'If so, I'm sorry, but all I told you was the truth. They say he's your fancy man,' she added heavily.

'Let them say whatever they like. I'm not bothered.'

'No? Then why are you in such a temper?'

Pheemie raised the rolled pastry in one hand, all her instincts demanding that she hurl it across the room, as the old woman added: 'Och well, I suppose it's just your age.'

No, not an old witch. An old bitch was nearer the mark.

In Corriebeg, Alec heard their laughter long before he entered his kitchen. Soothed with cups of tea, their shoes with the worst of the mud removed had been set to dry. Pam, regarding her high heels ruefully, decided they would never be the same again. They'd cost the earth and were probably ruined for ever.

Freddie jumped up to greet Alec. 'How are you?'

'Busy,' said Alec shaking hands, and kissing Pamela, he said: 'Hello.'

He had only met the couple once when Pam was their matron of honour. She was pretty in an upper-class way. Her voice tended to be too shrill and she giggled a lot. She would never have attracted him and he felt slightly awed by a latent snobbery she carried with her, a tendency to look down on what she considered 'vulgar' as appertaining to 'the poorer classes', the class to which Alec undoubtedly belonged by birth.

It was difficult to imagine why Jenny with her passion for the underdog, canine and human, had chosen Pamela as her best friend. He was baffled by what two girls so completely dissimilar could have in common.

As for Pamela's husband, he had heard more than enough about Freddie Clayton-Hill from Jenny's mother. Mrs Moresby never tired of telling him how well Jenny's friend had married.

'Freddie's father was our local MP and the Clayton-Hills are very well connected. Freddie's about your age but he's very high up in the civil service. So handsome too.'

Alec was surprised by this last remark, considering that Freddie's dapper looks, his plastered hair and thin moustache, only narrowly missed qualifying for the 'chinless wonder' of the English aristocracy. All that he lacked was the monocle.

'He and Jenny were childhood sweethearts,' Mrs Moresby

had added with a wistful smile that spoke volumes about her own feelings on the matter. That and the hyphen did little to endear Freddie to Alec Ritchie.

Jenny offered him some tea. Eyeing the delicate china teacups which were making their début, Alec said: 'I'll take a mug out with me. I'm short of just one fence post.'

'Well, Alec,' said Freddie heartily, 'you certainly won't be troubled by neighbours here, will you?'

'Oh, don't be too sure,' smiled Jenny.

Pam rested her chin upon her hand and regarded Jenny intently. 'I'll bet a place like this is an absolute hotbed of old family feuds.'

'Blood vendettas,' added Freddie dramatically. As all three dissolved into helpless giggles. Alec couldn't see the joke.

'There's this old boy up the hill, Macrae,' said Jenny. 'His grandson moved in with him recently and they can't stand the sight of one another. If you mention young Robert to Macrae, he positively growls.'

'Isn't that just the accent around these parts?' Freddie's remark sent the two girls into shrieks of mirth.

Suddenly conscious of his own Scots accent, which could be broad at times, Alec said: 'I'll just go and get on with the fences.'

'What was that, old chap?' asked Freddie.

'I think he was just growling, Freddie.' Jenny looked up and seeing Alec's expression instantly regretted having cracked such a joke. 'Excuse me,' she said and dashed out after him. 'Please, don't be touchy.' And encouraged by Alec's smile, she comforted him. 'They are my oldest friends. And they won't be here for ever. I'm sorry.' She put a hand on his arm.

'I know.' Alec put down the fence post and took her into his arms. 'And I'm sorry too.'

As they kissed, Freddie and Pamela emerged from the door.

'Ooops, bad timing,' said Freddie, dragging Pam back inside.

Without another word, Alec picked up the fence post and went back to his repairs. Jenny watched him go, sensing his exasperation. This visit wasn't going to be easy, and this was just the first hour, she thought anxiously as Pam and Freddie appeared with exaggerated caution.

'Coast clear?' whispered Freddie. 'Are we safe to come out?'

They all laughed and suddenly Pam whistled. 'Rather a good-looking chap.'

'Nice of you to say so, darling.'

'Not you, idiot. Him!' And she pointed to the garron who had trotted over to the fence.

'That's Monty.' Pam stroked his nose. 'I've entered him for the Highland Pony Section at the show. It's for the working ponies, really. I think he has a good chance.'

'Depends on the others,' said Pam surveying him critically. 'There might not be too much competition in a small place like this.'

'Ah well, a chap knows when he's not wanted,' said Freddie. 'Too much competition for this one. I'm off to explore the policies,' he added with a cheery grin, heading in the direction of the top field where Alec, repairing the fence, had found support from the most unlikely quarter.

Struggling to put in posts and taking ten times as long as it should have done with a helper, he found the stake being steadied by strong hands.

'It needs two people,' said Umberto simply.

He was right. 'Thanks, Umberto.'

As the post was firmly fixed Umberto said: 'No problem. No hard feelings?'

Alec grinned. 'No hard feelings. But my jaw ached for a week.' Gladly the two shook hands.

'Still friends?' said Umberto.

'Still friends. What brings you up here?'

'I'm having a run, training for the hill race. Plus I am keeping out of the way of Pheemie's auntie. She's visiting. And she's an old witch.'

'Hallo there!' Freddie was coming up the hill. He stumbled and fell a couple of times before he reached them. Then looking round, he whistled appreciatively. 'Spectacular views you have here. Mind you, it must get terribly lonely for poor old Jenny.'

At Alec's sharp response that he didn't think so, Freddie said: 'I should think it does. Jenny's very gregarious. Always has been since I've known her and I met her when she was ten or so.'

It was hardly a remark calculated to please her new husband, but Freddie, blissfully unaware, rubbed his hands together and said: 'Looks as if you two chaps could use an extra body on this job. Shall we get cracking?' His self-confidence was boundless, but in more practical matters he proved utterly incompetent. 'Handless' was the only word either man could have used to describe him. At last he was prevailed upon to continue his afternoon stroll, where he could do less damage.

Watching him go, Alec sighed deeply. He didn't know how long his patience would last. To Umberto's sympathetic grin, he said: 'You're not the only one with visitors they could do without.'

· · · · *Twenty-five* · · · ·

Now that she had Jenny alone, there was a question Pam had been dying to ask. 'Promise you won't be offended.'

Jenny smiled. 'You're not going to insult my beautiful pony, I hope.' And to Monty she whispered: 'Don't you listen.'

Pam leant on the fence beside her. 'How long do you think you'll be able to stand it here? I'm sorry, but it's just not quite the glorious Highlands you wrote about or the way you described it. I got the impression farms here would be like ours at home. You know, lush countryside, lots of dairy cattle and horses, the Young Farmers Club, lots of dances and socialising with wealthy young men.'

As she spoke, Jenny gazed across the misted hills, the only

sound the forlorn bleating of distant sheep. She could apologise for over-exaggeration, but she couldn't work miracles for visitors where the weather was concerned.

At her side, Pam shivered. 'Somehow I never imagined anyone could live in such a bleak and isolated place. Especially you, Jenny. Don't you ever feel just a little cut off from the good things in life you used to enjoy so much? Theatres, dances – things like that?'

Jenny shrugged. 'On days when the weather's awful, like this, and there isn't another soul to be seen for miles, then I wonder what possessed me.'

Pam smiled. She loved Jenny and wanted her to be happy. 'Give it time. It'll work out, I'm sure it will.' When Jenny agreed, Pam added: 'Change isn't easy. Look at me and Freddie. I literally keep forgetting I'm married to him.'

'How's that working out?' asked Jenny eager to remove the focus of attention from herself.

Pam smiled. 'Freddie's a sweetheart. But sometimes he's such a twit. It's infuriating. But then you know.'

The two exchanged glances. Freddie was a good sort, but Jenny could never have contemplated marrying him. She knew him too well to have ever fallen in love with him.

'I must groom Monty,' she said. 'Want to lend a hand?'

'Delighted. It'll be just like being back in the Pony Club. Have you got a hoofpick?'

Jenny frowned. 'Somewhere. In the byre, I think.'

Leaving Pam with the dandy brush, she went into the byre where she had thrust her riding tackle when it had arrived from Salisbury with the furniture. She noticed there was something underneath it.

She unearthed an ancient yoke, the kind worn by milkmaids in Victorian paintings of pastoral scenes. What a fascinating find! Examining it more closely, she decided to try it on. That would surprise Pam! And then she heard it again – the sound of weeping.

Throwing down the yoke, she called: 'Who's there?' A beam creaked and that was all. 'Is anybody there?'

'Who are you talking to?'

Jenny almost jumped out of her skin. It was Pam. 'Can't you hear it?'

'Hear what, Jenny?'

'A sound. Like someone crying. A woman.'

Pam listened. 'I can't hear anything.'

'Every time I come in here, I hear it. And I feel cold – and terribly sad.'

Pam looked round. She could sympathise with both feelings in this dreary place.

'Listen, Pam, you must have heard that. A woman crying – again – listen.'

But even as she said the words, the sound faded.

'I didn't hear a thing, Jenny. Now, where's that hoofpick?' And picking it up, Pam said firmly: 'I'll attend to that later. Let's have another cup of tea, shall we?'

Following Jenny into the kitchen, she watched her thoughtfully. She didn't like this business of hearing things, obviously brought about by spending too much time on her own. What a good job she'd persuaded Freddie to bring her to Corriebeg. It seemed their visit was opportune; she could put up with a few days' discomfort if it would help Jenny.

'Now what about that baking you were doing for the show?'

Jenny sighed. 'Yes. I suppose I'd better make a start.'

'Good. I'll read your famous recipe.'

To her relief, Jenny seemed to have forgotten her voices or whatever they were as she took out the mixing bowl and heaped the ingredients on the table. 'How many eggs?'

'Take three eggs – good Lord, haven't they heard of rationing?'

Remembering her very productive hens, Jenny said: 'Only three. Let's not be stingy.'

'Well, you may die of boredom here, but at least you'll be a well-fed corpse.' But Jenny was regarding the result of her generosity in dismay. 'Oh dear, perhaps five'll have made it too gooey.'

Pam sighed. 'Not to worry. Personally I've always felt I wasn't put on this earth to make cakes.' And, as Jenny smiled wanly, she added: 'But it's all part of the job-description, is it? Farmer's wife bakes cakes, enters them in contests at the local show?'

Jenny shrugged. 'Yes, well, it's sort of the done thing. The WRI like women who join in.'

And Pam remembering how they had giggled about the WRI as the absolute end, said reproachfully: 'Jenny, how can you?'

'It's not that bad.' She smiled. 'Grown-up version of the Pony Club, really.'

'Rubbish. The Pony Club was about having fun, not comparing wretched sponge cakes.'

'Well, they do lots of other things. They're all right.'

And Pam, noticing her defensive tone, realised this indeed was a new Jenny. Going to the window she watched curiously as two women, one youngish and one old, came across the yard.

'Hello, are these two members of the grown-up pony club or the local coven?'

They were Pheemie and her aunt, the latter driven by curiosity to inspect the newcomers at Corriebeg. As Pheemie introduced her, Jenny was thankful that the house was presentable, all spruced up for Pam's and Freddie's visit.

After a cup of tea laced by a chronicle of Pheemie's shortcomings much to her annoyance, Aunt Ishbel indicated the main purpose of her visit. She wanted a tour of the house.

That didn't take long and Pheemie, glad of a respite, said: 'You've made it really lovely in there. Hasn't she?'

Her aunt had said nothing, but touched a few of Jenny's antique pieces which she had inherited from her grandmother with a gleam of approval. As they were leaving, she said: 'Not to my taste, but anything had to be an improvement. This place was no better than a sheep fank a year ago.'

'Well, it's a right cosy wee place now,' said Pheemie.

'Apart from the spooky noises in the cowshed, that is,' said Pamela.

Aunt Ishbel and Pheemie halted in their tracks. They looked at each other and then at Jenny. It was too late to warn her friend so she could only say: 'Pam, don't be silly.'

'Jenny thinks she can hear someone crying when she goes into that barn.' Pam's remark obviously disconcerted the two women and Jenny said quickly: 'I'm sure it's just my imagination.'

But Aunt Ishbel who seemed to know her way around pretty well had marched to the byre. She stood silently looking up at the beams for a moment. 'This where you've been hearing things.'

'Yes. Silly, I suppose.'

The old woman didn't seem to hear; her attention was rivetted on the milkmaid's yoke. 'Nice, isn't it?' said Jenny. 'An antique. I was thinking of cleaning it up and hanging it somewhere.'

But Aunt Ishbel just looked at her like someone searching for the right words and as Pheemie and Pam approached, she said briskly, 'Well, we'd better be off. Come along, Euphemia.'

As they walked down the road, she remarked: 'Maybe we should have told her.'

'No, not right now, Auntie. Not when she's expecting.' That was the end of the subject as far as Pheemie was concerned.

Back in Carnban, Aunt Ishbel sewed a delicate piece of lace as Pheemie set the table for supper. 'A bride's garter. What's this for?'

'I'm putting it into the show. I only wish I was making it for one of my own. You, for example. And why not? Or are you going to continue living in sin with that Eyetie?' And at the sound of his footsteps outside, she added: 'Well, talk of the devil and he'll appear.'

Umberto had little to say and joined them at the table in gloomy silence. Preparing to help himself, as he always did, he was halted by Pheemie's aunt piously folding her hands together.

'Dear Lord, for what we are about to receive, make us truly thankful.' And opening her eyes she squinted at Umberto and added for his special benefit: 'Miserable sinners though we may be.'

'Amen.' And catching her eye, he crossed himself elaborately before taking a generous helping of stew.

'My God, what a hypocrite,' remarked Aunt Ishbel.

'You talking to me?'

'All that palaver of making the sign of the cross, and there's your plate heaped with meat.'

Umberto regarded his plate: 'So, what am I supposed to eat, grass?'

'Correct me if I'm wrong but I'd aye heard that those of Catholic persuasion never eat meat on a Friday.'

'Oh, is it Friday today?' Umberto asked innocently.

'Aye, it is,' was the grim response.

'He's got special dispensation. Haven't you?' asked Pheemie hastening to the rescue.

'Er – oh – aye, I have special dispensation.'

'From whom. The Pope?' demanded Aunt Ishbel.

'No. Father McConnell,' said Pheemie.

'Very nice man,' added Umberto approvingly.

'And for what reason has he given you this – this special dispensation?'

'For the hill race – tomorrow,' Pheemie and Umberto responded in unison. Rather pleased with themselves getting the better of the old witch, Pheemie smiled. 'Come on, Umberto, eat up. Your food's getting cold.'

Umberto threw down his fork. 'I'm not hungry any more.'

'Come on. You need to keep your strength up,' Pheemie urged.

'For his fornication tonight, no doubt,' was Aunt Ishbel's dry comment.

Umberto frowned. Fornication? What was that? 'What'd she say?' he asked Pheemie.

'Never you mind. She was just making a wee joke.' And with a dagger-like glance in her aunt's direction she countered: 'Though not a very funny one, I have to say.'

Supper at Corriebeg was hardly a spectacular success either, although it had started well enough, with Freddie agreeing that the air around there certainly gave a chap an appetite.

And Jenny, watching Alec down his glass of wine in one gulp – wine which the Clayton-Hills had provided for the meal – said pointedly: 'Wasn't that lovely of them?'

Alec had the grace to mumble thanks as Freddie asked: 'What happens at this show?'

'Oh, all kinds of things. Highland dancing, games, judging of farm produce as well as classes for cattle and sheep.'

'Wouldn't have thought they had a lot to learn. "How not to get fleeced" perhaps?' Freddie's witticism threw them into gales of mirth.

'You've forgotten the baking,' said Pam. And to Freddie, she explained: 'She's been baking all afternoon. Would you believe it?'

'Heaven forbid,' Freddie shuddered. 'I remember some appalling things you baked once years ago.'

'Rock cakes,' laughed Jenny.

'Aptly named. You could have killed a man with one of those things.' Freddie's remark reinforced the merriment. They all laughed except Alec who, excluded from their shared past, sought solace by applying himself vigorously to the wine.

'What on earth is "Best Polished Shoe competition"?' asked Pam, reading the programme.

'Oh, that's for me,' said Freddie cheerily. 'Not many people can polish a shoe the way I can. Boarding school and the Army and all that.'

'Why don't you go in for the hill race?' Alec's question was challenging as well as slurred and Jenny gave him a sharp look and said warningly: 'Alec!'

'The hill race?' Freddie beamed. 'What would I have to do?'

'Oh, just run up a hill and down the other side.' Draining his wine, Alec added: 'Easy.'

'What's the catch?'

'There isn't one,' was the innocent reply.

'Do you think I should?' Freddie turned to Pamela.

'Up to you, my sweet.'

'You don't have to, Freddie,' said Jenny putting in the voice of reason. 'It's quite some hill we're talking about.' And with a hard look at Alec, she warned: 'More like a mountain.'

'Well, I'm pretty fit, I think. Yes, I'm game, why not?'

It was Alec's turn to smile, certain that Freddie had fallen into the trap. He wouldn't dare go back now. Old school tie and all that sort of thing. Serve him right too. Let Jenny see what he's really made of, he thought, seizing the opportunity to finish the last of the wine.

· · · · *Twenty-six* · · · ·

Alec wasn't quite so jubilant when Jenny relentlessly awoke him the next morning with a cup of tea. 'I feel like I've died and woken up in hell,' he groaned.

'I hope you're not asking for sympathy. You behaved appallingly last night, drinking twice as much wine as anyone else and then goading Freddie into entering the hill race.'

'I'm sorry. Do you still love me?'

'You're not getting off that easily, Mr Ritchie,' said Jenny but her glance was tender as she climbed into her riding clothes and boots before going in search of her two friends.

Pam greeted her smart appearance with: 'You look lovely, doesn't she, Freddie?'

Freddie agreed but seemed fairly subdued. He was having second thoughts. Although a good sprinter at college, the euphoria of last night had worn off, and he realised a hill race was quite different.

'You don't have to do it, if you don't want to,' Pam had said reassuringly.

'I know. But I'd feel such an awful fool saying I'd changed my mind.'

Pam sighed. She appreciated that he was worried about loss of face and all that sort of thing, but it was hard for a girl to understand when it was just a silly local race that no one would ever remember. 'Well, it's up to you, Freddie my sweet.' And going over to Jenny who was harnessing Monty, she said: 'Pretty as a picture.'

'He is looking so smart,' Jenny agreed. 'He's just going to walk off with first prize, you know.'

'Stranger things have happened,' was Pam's doubtful reply.

Alec emerged from the house also looking very smart in his best suit and the four made a handsome quartet as they set off. The sound of pipes was audible as it echoed across the hills.

'Oh, listen, how romantic,' said Pam. 'We are being spoiled. I hope you remembered the camera, Freddie.'

Jenny and Alec leading a very well-groomed Monty smiled proudly at each other. Sunshine and bagpipes all in one day. The Clayton-Hills would remember this when they had forgotten all Corriebeg's other shortcomings.

As they drew nearer the distant mingling of voices, in various tones, varieties and ages, told them that the show was well under way. Excitement and enjoyment was the order of the day as all of Strathblair gathered in the field, intent on having a jolly good time.

There was a medley of entertainment: irresistible side-shows, fortune tellers, tannoys bawling out popular songs, coconut shies, guess-your-weight machines, roll-a-penny stalls offering tempting 'fabulous prizes': huge pandas and teddy bears in revolting colours and cheap glass ornaments. All melded together by the sound of dogs barking, babies crying, children yelling and the hurdy-gurdy music of merry-go-rounds.

This was humanity in holiday mood, laughing, pushing, eating, shouting. The air was filled with the smoke from steam-traction engines working the roundabouts, the smell of bruised grass, of boiled sweets and hot cooking fat. And for everyone, rich and poor, the irresistible nostalgia of remembered childhood days.

The sheep judging had just finished and they were in time to see Macrae leading off a champion Blackface with a first prize rosette.

'He's done it again,' said Alec and to Pam's question whether he always won, he answered: 'There's no one knows more about sheep than he does.' Watching Robert walk up to his grandfather obviously congratulating him, he even thought he saw the vestige of a smile on Macrae's face. Good for Robert. The lad was going to be a humanising influence after all.

As the cattle judging was announced, Pam and Jenny drifted towards the Highland dancers, four very serious-looking little girls. 'How sweet. If you have a little girl, Jenny, maybe she'll do that one day.'

Jenny smiled. And I'll be as proud and as anxious as any mum waiting to see her own precious darling win and being furious with that prejudiced judge for not seeing that she was not only the best dancer but by far the prettiest competitor.

'I say, who's that?' Pam interrupted her day-dream.

Alec and Freddie had drifted away from the ring and were talking to Andrew. 'He's the laird's son.'

'Mm,' said Pam approvingly, eyeing the good-looking Highlander in bonnet and kilt. 'Is he spoken for?'

'No, but you are,' Jenny reminded her.

Pam laughed. 'I told you, I keep forgetting,' she said as she tripped rather eagerly towards the trio who were heading for the refreshment tent.

'Not before you run the race, Freddie,' Pam whispered.

'Just a quickie, darling. Want to chat to Major Menzies here.'

Pam gave Andrew her most fetching smile as they were introduced. 'Seems the major and I have something in common. Did the same course during the war,' said Freddie. 'Intelligence.'

Alec was impressed. Intelligence work was about the last thing he would have associated with Freddie Clayton-Hill.

'Didn't have the brains for anything else,' Freddie smiled at Andrew who laughed. 'My story exactly. Come on, a quick drink. I'm stewarding in the working pony class.'

Jenny looked at her programme. 'Pam! The cake judging!'

In the tent, the line-up of home-baking was impeccable – all beautifully risen, all magnificently iced. And sticking out like a sore thumb, the one less than perfect, Jenny's plain sponge cake. 'It didn't look quite that bad this morning,' she groaned.

'I expect it's been deliberately sabotaged.' Pam nudged Jenny in Aunt Ishbel's direction. 'I bet she's put a hex on your cake.'

Mrs McKenzie, the housekeeper at Strathblair House, was tasting a tiny sample from each cake, accompanied by Flora McInnes. As they moved on hurriedly from her contribution, Jenny whispered: 'I think I'll die of embarrassment.'

'. . . And as so often in previous years,' Flora was saying, 'I'm pleased to announce that first prize has been taken by that well-known character, Miss Ishbel Robertson . . .'

The old woman looked proud and delighted.

'Black magic, I'd say,' said Pam as everyone applauded. Then observing Jenny's expression, she asked: 'What's wrong? You're not upset at not winning, are you? You surely knew you didn't stand a chance.'

'I know,' said Jenny miserably. 'But I just feel I'm not very good at anything,' she added unaware that Aunt Ishbel was standing right behind her until she heard her say: 'You put in ower many eggs.'

When Jenny shrugged sadly and said she'd got carried away, Aunt Ishbel smiled: 'Young lasses like you shouldn't be too bothered about baking or winning prizes. Leave that to the old ones like me, for we've precious little else to live for.'

And Jenny at that moment quite forgave her for going off with first prize. It was true. She was young and she had Alec and a baby on the way and her best friends on a visit. Life couldn't be better.

'Now for the hill race. But where is Freddie?' said Pamela.

Freddie had found a soul-mate in Andrew Menzies. They had the same public-school backgrounds and Alec found himself a polite listener to the reminiscences of the officer-class.

'Remember all that code-breaking stuff,' said Freddie. 'I still can't look at *The Times* crossword without trying to decipher it as enemy information!'

Andrew laughed and asked why he didn't stay in the Army after the war. Freddie said he had considered it. 'I prefer a duller life. Don't want to pack up and go overseas at the drop of a hat. Especially not now.'

'Korea, you mean?'

'No, the lovely wife. It wouldn't be fair to her.'

Andrew smiled at Alec, in an effort to draw him into the conversation: 'She's Mrs Ritchie's oldest friend, I hear.' And indicating his empty glass: 'Another Alec? And what about you, Freddie.'

'I'd better save myself. For the hill race.'

'Oh, go on. One for the bend,' said Andrew.

Freddie weakly allowed himself to be persuaded. He had taken only a few sips when he heard the announcement: 'Gentlemen taking part in the hill race please make yourselves known to the stewards.'

'Good Lord, that's me.'

After putting the final flourishes on Monty with the hoof-oil Pamela abandoned a downcast Jenny who was viewing Monty's rivals and rushed off to the starting-line.

Freddie greeted her arrival with tones of relief. 'Oh, there you are, I thought you'd forgotten about me.'

'As if I would,' said Pam hugging him. 'Silly billy.'

She saw the runners off and found herself standing next to Pheemie whose face was flushed with excitement. Then Pam realised why. The handsome Italian was in the race. Jenny had given her the low-down on their relationship and Pam, who never failed to appreciate an attractive man, or an illicit romance, was intrigued.

A man handed Pheemie a pair of binoculars. 'Oh, Umberto's going great guns. If he keeps that up, he'll win the race for sure,' she added with a gleeful look at her aunt's disapproving face. Umberto had already fallen foul of the old woman that morning. Innocently admiring the spread Aunt Ishbel was entering for the show, he was told in no uncertain manner to keep his dirty mitts off them.

Seeing Umberto's outraged expression as he pushed past her, Pheemie had asked Aunt Ishbel what was wrong.

'I said nothing. Foreigners are like that. Temperamental.'

Now as she announced huffily that she wasn't going to waste her time missing all the shows, Pheemie realised with delight that one person was going to be very upset if Umberto came in first.

As Pheemie was handing back the binoculars, Pam said, 'May I?'

She groaned. Poor Freddie was well to the rear of the runners and she hurried back to the pony judging where Monty wasn't doing too well either.

'The suspense is killing me,' Alec told her as they watched the judge make his decision. Monty was nowhere —

And then Andrew announced: 'Special prize.' And smiling at Jenny said: 'This is the first time Mrs Ritchie has competed.'

Seeing Jenny's sad expression the judge said kindly: 'He's just a wee thing common. He'll make a grand horse in the croft, but he's hardly a show beast – and just watch that bit, it might be all right for the pony club but it's no use in working harness.'

'Well, she won fourth prize,' said Pam consolingly to Alec and dashed off again to watch Freddie as the runners came in sight of the winning-post.

She found Andrew at her side. To his question she said: 'I don't know who's winning, but it certainly isn't Freddie. In fact I can't even see him.' And pleased to change the depressing subject. 'So? No more stewarding for you?'

'All finished. Done my duty. I hope Mrs Ritchie wasn't too disappointed.'

'If I'd been judging, I'd have placed them in exactly the same order.'

'You know about these things, do you?'

'I know a bit about horses, yes.' And shading her eyes, she added: 'Not so sure when it comes to men, though. I think Freddie would be a bit of a long shot for Cheltenham.'

Andrew laughed as he gave Pam an admiring glance. He liked her husband, too. They had a lot in common. Freddie was his class and he would have enjoyed having the two of them to dinner to meet his father, if they'd been staying longer.

The winners were approaching the tape. Umberto was first, followed closely by Robert Sinclair much to everyone's surprise and delight.

Pheemie rushed to hug Umberto. 'I wish I'd had a bet on you.'

'You mean you hadn't?'

They were interrupted as the ice-cream man thrust a cone into Umberto's hand. The two obviously knew each other and apart from gathering that his name was Tonio, Pheemie's curiosity went unappeased. She wished she knew what they were jabbering about in Italian.

But at that moment she saw Robert Sinclair who had spotted

his grandfather in the crowd watching the winners come in, looking almost as proud of his grandson as he did when his champion tup won first prize. Wonders would never cease, thought Pheemie. Balbuie was learning how to smile.

Surprises weren't over for the day for Robert either as Pheemie came up to him and said: 'Here, you're a good runner.'

'Not good enough,' was the rueful reply.

'Now don't do yourself down, lad. Do you know who you put me in mind of? Your mother. We were at school together.' Pheemie smiled remembering. 'Run! She was like a hare. No one could catch her, not even the boys.'

'You knew my mother?'

'Aye, we were best friends.'

Robert would have liked to ask her a lot more, but Pheemie's attention was diverted to Umberto and his Eyetie chum. There was something conspiratorial about the way they were whispering, and Pheemie would have been gratified indeed if she'd understood this particular conversation.

Tonio, who was now living in Perth, was urging Umberto to get wise and settle down, marry a local girl like he had done. In fact, she had a sister Sheena, beautiful too, if Umberto was interested. But Umberto had something other than marriage on his mind at that moment. He had a favour to ask.

'Remember it's our secret,' Umberto warned him as Alec came up to add his contragulations.

'So all that haring about in the hills paid off.'

'Aye, one thing to thank the old witch for.'

'You didn't happen to see my husband in your travels?' asked Pam. As Umberto shook his head, she recognised in the distance a tiny figure stumbling down the hill. It was Freddie and he was undoubtedly last by a long chalk.

The show was almost over and a very foot-sore Freddie gratefully accepted Pheemie's offer of a lift home in the trailer.

Cheering them off, the Ritchies, leading Monty, headed

homewards and Alec agreed with Jenny that it wasn't so bad after all, having visitors.

'But it'll be just as nice when it's just the three of us.'

Alec smiled at her tenderly. He sometimes forgot about the baby for a whole day. Perhaps it would never be real for him until he held his son in his arms.

· · · · *Twenty-seven* · · · ·

On the day Pam and Freddie left, Jenny was sweeping the yard when she looked up and saw Aunt Ishbel watching her. She hadn't heard her arrive and with a shiver wondered if she had been transported on a broomstick.

Perhaps Umberto was right and she was a witch. Aunt Ishbel said nothing, simply marched purposefully towards the byre where Jenny found her staring up at the overhead beams. 'Aye, it's as I thought. Rona.' And, turning to Jenny, she explained: 'The spirit that's haunting you. Her name was Rona Hepburn. Remember me, Rona. Ishbel Robertson. Aye, you mind me all right.'

She really is crazy, thought Jenny, talking to a ghost – or whatever – as if she exists. Wait until I tell Alec.

Aunt Ishbel turned and smiled thinly, as if aware of her thoughts. 'Don't worry. Spirits mean no harm. They're just a pest when they can't find their way through to the other side.'

Better humour her, thought Jenny: 'Who was she?'

'A poor soul who worked here sixty years ago. She used to milk the cows for the tenant, a man called Ferguson. Poor, poor Rona,' she said shaking her head sadly.

'Why do you keep saying that?'

Aunt Ishbel considered that for a moment before replying: 'Some of us never find a resting place in this life. We aye want to be elsewhere. Rona was like that. It wasnae exciting enough for her here, so one day she just upped and went to Edinburgh. Not a word of warning, left the beasts standing in the field lowing to be milked, for Ferguson to find when he came off the hill that evening.' And, nodding towards the beam, she continued: 'Aye, you were a bad girl, Rona. Three years later she was back, just as suddenly. And whatever happened to her when she was away, she wasnae right in the head when she came back.'

The beam overhead creaked and the old woman smiled. 'Aye, she hears us.'

'You mean, she went mad,' said Jenny, thinking that there were two of them now, one alive and one long dead.

'Mad but harmless. She went about saying she was secretly married to an earl, that he'd be sending for her soon and then she'd live in a palace. But she had to wait because his family were plotting against her. Now, nobody's sure of the truth, but it seems when she was in Edinburgh, she was in service to a rich family. The son got her pregnant and the family put her out on the streets.'

'How awful.'

'It was common practice then. Some call them the good old days, but I don't, and I bet you don't either, eh, Rona? Then the bairn was born dead. So she didn't even have that. She had nothing. But Ferguson took pity on her and gave her back her old job.'

'Thank heavens somebody was good to her.'

'There were one or two of us. But not enough, eh, Rona? Not enough to heal the hurt in you?'

Jenny was certain she heard a faint answering cry as the old woman continued: 'Five years passed and Rona's earl never sent for her, of course. So she tended the beasts by day and cried herself to sleep at night. Till one day Ferguson came down off the hill, and what did he find? The cattle lowing in the field, unmilked and unattended, just as it had been the day Rona ran away to Edinburgh.'

'And had she – run away?'

'Aye, for good. She hanged herself. From one of those beams up yonder.'

There was no mistaking it this time. Jenny definitely heard a woman sobbing.

'Wheest, Rona. I've come to help you. Trust me now. There's nothing for you here. Take the strength you need from me and depart in peace. I'm old now, too, so it won't be long before I'm joining you. Go now —'

Jenny felt hardly able to breathe as she watched Aunt Ishbel's face change as she concentrated all her powers on exorcising the milkmaid's sad ghost. Then, quite suddenly, she knew it was over, the atmosphere which had been so cold and sad was now restored to that of an empty byre.

Aunt Ishbel's eyes opened. 'That's it. What were you saying?'

Jenny hadn't been saying anything, but she had been thinking plenty. 'I can't stay here. This house hates me. It'll drive me mad as it did her,' she said desperately.

'The house did nothing. It was people that drove Rona to kill herself. The house is only trying to tell you its secrets. And you don't tell your secrets to somebody you hate, do you?' She paused and smiled at Jenny. 'You tell them to someone you've begun to trust. So don't betray that trust by running away. Because you've felt like it sometimes, haven't you?'

Jenny hesitated and then whispered: 'Sometimes.'

'Don't. There's great things in store for you here, you'll see.'

Suddenly Jenny wished, with all her heart, that she could get a glimpse of the prophetic vision that was passing before the old woman's eyes. It was obviously an attractive sight, for she smiled and said: 'Now, are you going to give me a cup of tea or not?'

'Yes, of course.'

With no more than a backward glance from Aunt Ishbel to make sure that all was in order, they walked towards the house as if the extraordinary incident in the byre had never happened.

'I'll see if I can find you a biscuit or something. Pamela and Freddie have eaten us out of house and home. It was like the descent of the locusts.'

'Well, you can aye offer me a piece of your cake.'

'I gave it to Monty. He quite enjoyed it.'

'There's no accounting for taste,' said Aunt Ishbel drily.

Over supper, Jenny told Alec all that had happened, wondering how he would react to the ghost in his byre. He listened in silence and at the end she expected him to laugh and say, 'There's no accounting for imaginations, either.'

Instead, he just nodded. 'You'll get used to it, Jenny. There's more things in heaven and the Highlands than are dreamed of in man's philosophy. You have to remember that people here live closer to the forces of nature than folk in towns. They are more in tune with senses we had before what we call civilisation destroyed them.'

'But I heard the crying and I'm not psychic, Alec. I've never had any ghostly experiences, in fact until now, I'd have said quite firmly there weren't any ghosts.'

Alec put his hand on hers. 'Until now, Jenny. That's the secret.'

'What do you mean?'

'It's probably because you're pregnant that you have this extra sensitivity. Don't worry, it may never happen again.'

In bed that night, before they turned out the light, Jenny said: 'Alec, have you ever seen – well – anything.'

'No, but my grandmother was Highland and we all took it for granted that when she told us something was going to happen it did. The nearest I've ever had was during the war, acting on instinct, that something was right or wrong. Perhaps that was more self-preservation than second sight.'

Jenny snuggled closer to him. 'It worked, or we might never have met. So whatever it was I'm glad.'

'I'm glad too,' he whispered and took her in his arms.

September 1950

· · · · *Twenty-eight* · · · ·

In every field golden stooks stood high like the discarded wigs of a race of forgotten giants. The McPhees, true to their promise, had returned to Corriebeg for the haymaking.

Cool, crisp mornings with the merest hint of autumn gave way to warm, mellow afternoons and cloudless nights, bright with the light of a million stars. As shadows lengthened and days shortened, Jenny drew the curtains on longer evenings. The wireless was company and she enjoyed listening except to the news bulletins. United Nations' troops were pouring into the Port of Inchon in Korea and, according to the broadcaster, the brilliant operation had been carried out with General McArthur's old flair. That distant war, unreal and unimaginable in Corriebeg, remained a source of anxiety despite Alec's reassurance that he wouldn't have to go. Apart from this one nagging uncertainty, she was happy and contented.

The summer had been kind and no longer feeling sick in the mornings, Jenny was blissfully fit and energetic. She loved haymaking with its nostalgic memories of holidays on a schoolfriend's Wiltshire farm. Glad to be out of doors, she was only too eager to lend the McPhees a hand.

'You make it look so easy,' she said to Jess.

'We've been bringing in hay and howking tatties since we could stand up straight.' She smiled. 'How's that bairn of yours? Can you feel it moving yet?'

Jenny touched her stomach. 'Not yet. But it's early days. Is it showing?'

'Only if you're looking for it. And that's a wee lassie you're carrying,' she added with a tender glance.

'Well, well,' said Jenny. She didn't want to offend the tinker woman by contradicting her second sight, but she was quite certain and always had been that it was a boy.

'Well, if it isn't my ain wee soldier laddie?' said McPhee as Robert Sinclair hurried towards them. 'So you're not away to foreign parts after all. Faraway places with strange sounding names?'

Robert grinned. 'Like Korea? 'Fraid not.'

'You must be broken hearted.' They all laughed as Jess asked: 'Are you here to give us a hand?'

'Aye,' said Robert. He had had a blazing row before he left Balbuie which had ended with Macrae shouting at him: 'Go then. Away down to Corriebeg with the tinkers. Join your own tribe. Water aye finds its own level.'

But Robert had a sweeter reason for seeing the McPhees. Looking round eagerly, he asked: 'Where's Bel?'

'She's away down Argyll,' said her mother.

'What's she doing there?'

'She met this young laddie and now she's upped and married him, and they're away off thegither.'

Robert couldn't believe it and McPhee, seeing his stricken expression, said gently: 'Did you no'ken?'

Robert shook his head miserably. He had been so certain that Bel felt the same way as he did and that she would be waiting for him when the McPhees returned. And now it seemed it was all over. Another chapter in his life closed almost before it began.

As they worked Robert told the McPhees about the row with his grandfather.

'He can be a thrawn old devil,' grinned McPhee. 'Mind you he can be decent enough, too.' Robert found that hard to believe. 'But never underestimate him. He's clever.'

'D'you not mean "crafty"?'

'And that, too. He's treating you the way he does because he wants to test you out.'

'Just like God does in the Bible,' Jess put in.

'He's not God. He just thinks he is.'

'Ach,' smiled Jess. 'He wants to see if you measure up.'

'Maybe I don't need my own kin making me jump through hoops.'

McPhee stared at him. 'Look, son. Have you never thought of moving on?'

'Where to?' asked Robert bitterly.

'Anywhere. A moving target is aye harder to hit.'

When Jenny noticed Robert she was surprised to see him hard at work. 'I thought you'd be up at the sheep fank with your grandfather.'

'He doesna' want me around.'

Jenny gave him a sympathetic look. 'Well, his loss is our gain. I'm glad you're here.'

Robert smiled at her gratefully. At least three people seemed to welcome his presence.

But Bel, oh Bel, why weren't you here too?

Inside Corriebeg, Jenny had worked wonders. When winter came and there was less work to be done outside, they would concentrate on the decorating. Meanwhile the house was warm, comfortable and weatherproof. That is, all except the roof. A heavy thunderstorm revealed ominous damp patches on the bedroom ceilings and Alec's inspection uncovered loose slates. The factor was responsible for repairs and Flora told him these might take about six to eight weeks.

'If you give me the materials I could do it myself. I'd rather not leave it; if we get an early winter we could have whole ceilings down. It would be even costlier then.'

'Well, if you're sure that's what you want.' When he asked about the major's whereabouts she said he had looked in briefly, but he had gone to play golf.

As Alec was leaving he saw Sir James welcoming Mr Laidlaw from the Forestry Commission.

'Sir James is considering selling off some land.' Seeing his expression, Flora added hastily: 'Nothing to worry about, Mr Ritchie, early days yet.'

Alec saw Laidlaw occasionally in the hotel chatting to Wallace, his next-door neighbour. But whereas the auctioneer was prepared to associate with humbler mortals, Laidlaw kept his distance. In his mid-fifties, smoothly groomed with an impeccable accent, and the aura of a senior civil servant with a keen sense of his own importance, Laidlaw tended to be contemptuous of farmers as uneducated peasants, who knew nothing about trees. They, in their turn, dismissed him as 'een o' those celluloid collared craters' who knew nothing about farming.

Flora, watching Alec ride away, realised that her consoling words might carry very little sway. Earlier that day she had to remind Sir James that the estate was costing increasingly more to run than it could possibly bring in. Since the war, the cost of labour and materials had shot up and the foreign investments that the estate had once relied on were yielding less and less.

Now she watched Laidlaw spread out some maps on her office table with a sense of foreboding. 'The days of small mixed-economy farming are over. They've gone the way of the run-rig system, I'm afraid. We are on the eve of the second agrarian revolution,' he added dramatically. 'Sad as it may be, estates such as this are faced with a choice: meet the future in future terms, or go to the wall.'

'You don't think that's too bleak a view?'

'I'm afraid not, sir. But the overall picture is far from bleak. A great deal of the land that the forestry has planted in recent years has been of little real value to its owners. Hopeless for cash crops or even beef, ground only fit for sheep, but ideal for tree-planting. I would hazard a guess that Scotland's future lies in timber.'

'Do I detect a note of bias?' asked Sir James.

Laidlaw smiled. 'Well, take Scandinavia. Small countries, small populations, but healthy economies based on afforestation and the timber industry.'

Sir James looked thoughtful. 'Are you suggesting an outright sale or some form of leasehold?'

'Both are options.'

'What about the tenants?' Flora demanded sharply as she examined the map more closely. 'This area includes a tenanted holding. Corriebeg,' she pointed out to Sir James.

'Their home would be unaffected,' said Laidlaw smoothly.

'But you would have the use of all this land around the steading?' said Flora. And when Laidlaw agreed, she explained: 'I'm sure you realise that without it their livelihood would be seriously affected.'

'Don't let's jump to conclusions, Flora,' Sir James put in. 'There are some vacant properties – Mrs Fraser's for instance at Aultbreac, or Dalcardoch.'

'But the Ritchies have been at Corriebeg for such a short time,' Flora protested.

'They are a young couple. Incomers,' Sir James explained.

'Ideal,' said Laidlaw. 'It would be easier for them to move elsewhere than for someone whose ties with the property run more deeply.'

'And of course their tenancy is only temporary at present.'

'Sir James!' Flora was shocked that he could be so heartless, so indifferent to the Ritchies who had tried hard and were making an excellent job of running Corriebeg.

He turned to her irritably. 'Just let me think about this, Flora.'

Alec approached the golf course where Andrew and his fellow members, correctly attired in the fashion of plus fours and Fair Isle sweaters, were finishing a round.

'Hello, Alec. What brings you down from the hills?'

Alec explained about the roofing problem and that he'd persuaded Mrs McInnes to let him do it himself.

As they walked off the fairway, he said: 'Any word when you're off to Korea?'

'No news is good news, I'd say.' From the end of August four thousand British troops had been put ashore with instructions from their Commander-in-Chief, Sir John Harding, to: 'Shoot quickly, shoot straight and shoot to kill.'

Andrew looked at Alec curiously. Surely he hadn't re-routed his return to Corriebeg via the golf course to talk about Korea? He was right. Alec wasn't convinced by Flora's attempt to cover up what might be a real threat to Corriebeg. 'What about this business of your father's?' he demanded.

Andrew was as shocked as Flora had been. He hurried home to find his father was contemplating the maps and plans Laidlaw had left.

'So, it is true, Father. You really are thinking of making a forest out of Strathblair.'

'A small part perhaps. Just liquidating some assets.'

'I see. Don't you think I might have been consulted?' Andrew added heavily.

'You?' said Sir James.

The surprise in his voice angered Andrew still further. 'After all, you did say you proposed to gift the estate to me.'

Sir James made a dismissive gesture. 'A fat lot of interest you've ever taken in Strathblair.'

'It's not that I've been uninterested. It's rather that you have refused to allow me any involvement.'

'You're never here for long enough to involve yourself in anything! First the Army, now this art business.'

'And you behave as if running the estate is some kind of arcane secret! It's the same old story, Father, you only ever see anything from your point of view.'

Sir James sighed. 'I've told you countless times. I am more than willing to hand this place over to you, lock, stock and barrel. Just settle down. Produce some heirs. What could be simpler than that? And don't for God's sake bring up Korea again. You've used that as an excuse for long enough to dodge any real commitment.'

'Yes? And what about you?'

'What about me?' Sir James demanded heatedly.

'You may be laird here, but you couldn't be more removed

from the earth of Strathblair. And now you're prepared to change this place for ever, simply to preserve a comfortable existence. It's sickening.'

Without waiting for a reply Andrew stamped out and went in search of Flora who confirmed that the estate had been doing quite badly recently. Andrew pointed out that did not justify shoving the Ritchies round like serfs and Flora tried in vain to reason with him, saying that he wasn't helping matters by arguing with his father who seemed determined to make major decisions without consulting him.

'Don't you see that this is symptomatic of our whole relationship? As far as he's concerned, I simply don't exist,' he added and scowling, he left her, the bitter, hurt, small boy he had never quite outgrown.

· · · · *Twenty-nine* · · · ·

Returning happily from the hayfields, Jenny found Alec waiting for her. One look at his face told her that something was wrong.

Alec was reluctant to tell her at first. He should keep the bad news to himself and spare her worries at such a time, but he was a poor actor and his denials were in vain. Putting her arms around him she said: 'Hey, it's me. Your wife, remember?'

He sighed. 'Sir James is thinking of giving over some of his land to the Forestry Commission.'

Jenny looked at him blankly for a moment, then the awful significance dawned. 'You mean – this land? Our land?' And as Alec protested that he didn't know exactly and wasn't sure if Corriebeg would be included, she cried: 'He can't do that! Just move us around like pawns.'

Alec looked at her. 'Oh yes, he can, if he really wants to, Jenny.'

'But Andrew wouldn't let him, surely?'

'I don't know how much say the major actually has.' Their talk had left the distinct impression that Andrew might not have much control over estate matters. Jenny's mind raced ahead, painting a series of dismal pictures.

'We could end up like the McPhees,' she whispered. 'Wandering around from place to place with babies strapped to our backs.'

'It won't come to that.'

'How can you be so sure?'

'Oh, Jenny, this is ridiculous. Never ask me to tell you what I'm thinking ever again. Right?' Then, with a sigh, he continued: 'Anyway, they'd have to offer us somewhere else.'

'I don't want anywhere else,' said Jenny looking around the kitchen tearfully. 'I want to stay here. This is my home.'

Alec regarded her helplessly. 'I'm away to the sheep fank. Try not to worry.' There was nothing else he could say.

Worry? Jenny could have sat down and wept. This just couldn't happen. Life – or Sir James – couldn't be so cruel. They had overcome so many trials since they had arrived in Corriebeg and were just beginning to make a success of it. Surely he knew that. Andrew must have told him. And Flora. She was sure they were both on her side.

Driven by curiosity about Andrew's workroom, Sir James had found his way to the attics where Andrew was studying the auction sheets from the picture sales at Perth and calculating an encouraging profit. He wasn't pleased by this interruption. 'Do you want me for someting?' he asked coldly.

Sir James ignored the question and moved over to the window. 'A good north light. I know nothing about art, but I do know that is essential. May I sit down?' As Andrew indicated a chair he continued: 'I know you won't want to hear this —'

'Then why say it, Father?'

'Because some things have to be said. You missed your chance with Flora's sister – through no fault of your own,' he added quickly as he noticed Andrew's angry expression. 'But you're in great danger of losing Flora, too, if you don't get a move on.'

Andrew considered his father for a moment. 'You are extra-ordinary. I know what war means, Father. And so does Flora.' But he had lost his father's attention.

Sir James was staring at the portrait of his ex-wife. 'Where on earth did that thing come from?'

'I'm going to clean it up.'

'To sell to some rich American? You ought to burn it.'

'It's a portrait of my mother,' Andrew reminded him. 'After all these years, can't you stop being so bitter about her?'

'I'm not bitter, I just despise the woman, that's all.'

'And how do you think that makes me feel? Has that thought ever crossed your mind? Well, I'm tired of you taking out the past on me, Father, and your snide remarks about my interest in art.' He grasped the papers on his desk. 'This isn't just a hobby. I know what I'm doing. I have Americans interested and I can turn buying and selling pictures – and antiques – into a lucrative business. A business that might allow Strathblair to make changes gradually and with a little bit of dignity —'

That was too much for Sir James who made his disapproval clear by leaving abruptly in a similar manner to his son's earlier exit from the sitting room.

As Jenny rejoined the haymakers once more, the sun still shone radiantly in a cloudless sky. Nothing had changed and she bit back her tears. This perfect summer's day seemed all wrong for Alec's bombshell, a disaster which belonged to sad rainy days when all the world weeps.

The McPhees were taking a well-earned rest from their labours and Jenny sat down beside Robert who was still brooding about his grandfather's treatment. He had told him that if he didn't work for his keep – for Wester Balbuie – then he'd better move on.

'Just because my dad, who ran off with his daughter, was a tinker like the McPhees. He can neither forgive nor forget that.'

'That's not your fault.'

'Try telling him that.'

'He must have loved your mother very much to take it so badly.'

Robert found it difficult to imagine that thrawn old devil loving anyone. 'Who knows? Maybe he just liked being in control and didn't like her having a mind of her own.'

Jenny regarded him thoughtfully. 'Well, whatever the reason, he should have got over it by now. Why did you come back, Robert? Was it because he's the only family you have?'

Robert nodded vaguely. The other less creditable reasons for his flight from college he preferred not to discuss.

'Do you think you'll stay then?' Jenny asked.

'I certainly won't let him drive me out. Any advice to offer?'

'Just keep trying.'

As Jenny gathered up the mugs and picnic boxes Jess McPhee who was lying against one of the stacks smiled up at her. 'What were you two looking so serious about?'

'Just wondering what the future will bring.'

'Now that's what I'd call a waste of time.'

'Don't you ever think about the future?' asked Jenny. 'Life can be so uncertain.'

Jess shook her head. 'Not my life, lassie. If it's spring you'll find me down by Kintyre. Summer and I'm here or hereabouts. And when the berry picking's finished and the tatties are out of the ground, me and McPhee'll be headed south towards Galloway where it's a wee bit warmer. So, what's there to worry about?'

'The unexpected,' said Jenny, trying not to think about what losing Corriebeg would mean to Alec. And to herself.

'You cannae worry about that, lassie. You just have to allow for it. Count your blessings instead. You've got a good man and a grand wee place here.' Jenny's smile was understandably bitter when she added: 'A secure tenancy and all.'

Robert took the basket from her. 'Aye, and the lamb sales

are coming up. You should do well there.'

Jenny was silent as together they walked back down the field. In the byre Buttercup was waiting to be milked. Watching her Robert said: 'You're a wee bit afraid of hurting her, aren't you? You won't, you know. Haven't you watched calves nursing? They're not exactly gentle.'

Jenny nodded and tried again, harder this time.

'Aha. I think I begin to get the idea,' she said as the milk flowed more quickly. 'Thanks!'

Robert grinned. 'Hope you didn't mind me speaking to you back there – about my problems.'

She looked up at him. 'Why on earth should I? You mustn't let your grandfather destroy your confidence, Robert. He's only one person in a world full of people.'

Robert nodded. 'I just wish he'd accept me, that's all.'

'And what if he never does?'

Robert looked as if that thought had never occurred to him. He stood silent for a moment and then announced that he'd get back to work.

'You don't have to. We can manage.'

Robert shook his head. 'No. I came to help and I'll stay till the hay's in. And if ever there's anything else you'd like me to do, just say.'

Jenny had just put the kettle on when Flora's car drew up in the yard. Andrew emerged alone, so Jenny offered him some tea. He followed her inside and stood looking round the kitchen.

'I know it doesn't look much,' she said watching his expression, 'but Alec and I have put a lot of work into this place: we've scrubbed, put right and planted. I suppose you're here to warn me we may not see them grow up?'

Andrew looked uncomfortable. 'The Forestry Commission is particularly keen on this area because of the easy access. But they could just as easily make use of some of the commonty grazing land. I came to put your mind at rest, so look on the bright side.'

As far as Jenny could see, the only light on the horizon was the forthcoming lamb sales. But at that moment they, too, were under dire threat.

Macrae with Munro who farmed Dalscriadan were making their way up to the sheep fank. Armed with brooms and a scythe they aimed to give it a clean before the lambs were collected into it for the sale.

Macrae was out of breath and begged Munro to slow down.

'Ach, you're getting soft, Balbuie, that's what it is.'

Macrae turned and saw Alec striding quickly towards them, apologising as he caught them up for being late.

Munro grinned. 'You're lucky Alasdair here's so slow. Me, I'd have been away up at the top of the ben by now,' he added proudly.

'Aye, you're fit, I'll give you that,' said Macrae grudgingly.

Sixty-two years old, strong and wiry, Munro had never had a day's illness in his life. When Alec asked his secret, he said: 'Drink your whisky neat. And smoke a good strong tobacco. Between them they'll account for every germ in your system.'

'Dalscriadan never made the mistake of saddling himself with a wife and bairns. That's how he'll live to see us all buried,' Macrae contributed gloomily.

'Oh, you don't expect me to go along with that?' said Alec.

'You'll find out,' was the grim response. Watching Macrae stride off ahead Munro grinned: 'A cheery thought for every occasion, that's our Alasdair.'

Work was progressing well on the fank when Macrae's dog Tam began barking at a ewe. Macrae went over to see what it was about and called to Munro. Alec followed and found them examining the animal's fleece.

'Dear God,' said Macrae in a voice of doom.

'What is it?' asked Alec.

'There's this one over here too, Balbuie,' called Munro.

'What is going on?' Alec demanded.

Macrae released the sheep and said angrily: 'If you hadn't been city born you'd know what was going on!'

'Now then, Balbuie, it's not the young lad's fault. These things can happen when the sheep are away off up the hill for a while.'

'Will someone tell me what has happened?' said Alec desperately. 'Is it something I've done?'

'Use your eyes, man!' yelled Macrae and as Alec went closer he saw that the ewe's fleece appeared to be moving. 'Maggots,' shouted Macrae. 'Maggots! And they could all be riddled with the damn things!'

Alec was stunned as he helped the two men inspect the neighbouring ewes, dipping them in the burn. 'Will this do the trick?'

'It should get rid of the worst, but they'll all need to be looked at,' said Munro.

'Will we have time before the lamb sales?'

Munro sighed. 'That's the big question, isn't it?'

An hour later, a careful inspection revealed that the lambs had escaped – so far.

'I've got an idea,' said Alec, straightening his shoulders.

'Oh, have you now? Let's hope it's a good one. Maybe there's some bit of animal husbandry that us old country folks haven't heard yet', Macrae added sarcastically.

'Well, there's nothing more we can do today. It's getting late,' said Alec and when the two agreed that there was no point starting again till morning, he suggested they adjourn to the pub. 'It'll take our minds off it and I'll stand the first drink.'

Munro grinned. 'Well now, that seems like a very sensible idea, wouldn't you say, Alasdair?'

Macrae nodded curtly and headed down the hill while Munro whispered to Alec, 'He's pleased you suggested that, but he'll never show it.'

As they walked towards Strathblair, the sun was setting, the hills were darkened majestically and the first evening star appeared. Despite his outward cheerfulness, Alec wondered how he was going to break the news of this second disaster to Jenny.

At Corriebeg, Jenny was taking Jess's advice to heart and being thankful for small mercies. At least the weather had been kind and they had got the hay in dry.

As McPhee put Monty back in his field and they prepared to move on, she paid Jess and gave her a brown-paper bag. 'I've put in some eggs and a bottle of milk.'

Jess smiled at her. 'God bless you, lass. They'll aye come in handy. So, we'll likely see you again the same time next year. God willing.'

If we're still here, if we still have Corriebeg, thought Jenny as she repeated: 'God willing.'

'God keep you, lass,' Jess whispered and taking her hand pressed a good-luck charm into it.

As she went to lock up the hens at the end of the day, the dew had already fallen and the barn smelt dark and earthy; she looked up and saw a young moon hanging over Schiehallion ghostly in the still azure sky. Clutching the charm she held it up and whispered: 'Please, please make it work.'

In the kitchen the clock ticked loudly. When you're afraid it's such an ominous sound, she thought, wishing Alec would come home. He couldn't be at the sheep fank in the dark. The house felt so empty, desolate and anxious, as if it knew that it was under threat.

Alone and scared, she needed him close in her arms, to reassure and comfort her with his love.

· · · · *Thirty* · · · ·

It was quiet in the Atholl Arms that night, the reason being, according to Munro, that a cowboy film was being shown on the local hall.

'Your very good health,' Munro said as Alec fetched over the drinks. 'And may all your children be twins.'

Alec shuddered. 'Forget it. I wouldn't know what to feed them on.'

'You could aye do what they do in the Australian outback,' said Macrae. 'Feed them on maggots. If we'd thought, we could have collected them, sold them to Sir James's upper-crust friends that come for the fishing.'

'He thinks he's funny,' said Munro with a sigh. 'Didn't we agree we weren't going to mention those damned things again tonight? So, how about a song to cheer us up.' And off he went, glass in hand, to join a group of hikers. Although Alec didn't understand the words, the song sounded anything but jolly. Suitably impressed he said: 'Gaelic's a terrific language.'

'If you ask me, folk talk too much, whatever the language,' said Macrae drily.

'I'll shut up then, will I? Oh, here's young Balbuie.'

Macrae's glance in his grandson's direction was less than welcoming.

'I thought I might find you here, Grandfather,' Robert grinned. 'Having a bit of celebration?'

'Don't judge others by the standards of your tinker cronies,' Macrae scowled and Alec intervened hastily: 'We're not so much celebrating as drowning our sorrows. The sheep are riddled with maggots. And earlier on I heard —' He stopped and shook his head. No point in adding to the gloom and despondency. They'd all hear soon enough. He looked at his watch. 'I'd better be off.'

Macrae declined his offer of a lift up the road, which was taken up eagerly by Robert. They left Munro enthusiastically beginning another song warning his small, but captive, audience that, 'It was a wee touch sad. About the clearances and this poor widow and her six bairns being driven off the land when it was wanted for sheep. And how they all died of starvation, one by one.'

Jenny was waiting up for Alec. Her face troubled, she turned to greet him as he walked in. Expecting wrath, he held up his hand: 'Don't say a word. Yes, I've been down the pub again, but I've a good excuse. Oh God, she's really angry this time.'

'I'm not angry. Oh, if it was only that.' So she told him about Andrew's visit. 'Seems the Forestry people are particularly interested in our inby land.'

'That's all the land that lies next to the hill. I just can't believe Sir James would do a thing like this.'

'The major was very apologetic. He's against the idea, so we'll just have to hope he stands up to his father.'

Jenny could think of nothing else but the threat hanging over Corriebeg, and Alec decided it would be cruel and unnecessary to add to her depression by telling her about the maggots. After all, the lambs didn't seem to be infested. He'd have to cling to that hope. In bed he picked up the book on animal husbandry he only had time to read before he fell asleep.

'How can you read that as if you didn't have a care in the world?' Jenny asked reproachfully.

Alec put the book aside and kissed her gently. 'Would you rather I was worrying myself sick the way you are?' When she said yes, he cuddled her to him and sighed. 'I'm glad you're here.'

Stroking his chest, Jenny said: 'Mrs McPhee advised counting my blessings.'

'Why not? It's a good idea.'

'Well, we've got the hay in and paid off the McPhees,' she said, counting them off on her fingers.

'Aye, and gave them half the food in the house,' said Alec.

'Well, I wouldn't fancy their life.'

'Maybe they wouldn't fancy yours.'

'That's true.' And, seeing her despondent expression, Alec said: 'Keep counting.'

'We've got the lamb sales coming up. I'm looking forward to that. And – oh, I can't think of anything else.'

'You can't? Well, I can.' And Alec kissed her again, more

passionately and demanding this time. Love was good, it didn't give all the answers, but it did help along the way. In each other's arms, they became one body, their souls united. In that moment of ecstasy it seemed impossible that anything so trivial as the world could come between them. A couple of months ago he had come very near to losing Jenny and that, for him, would have been the ultimate disaster. He felt certain he could survive anything but that.

As long as they had each other . . .

If only we had each other, everything would be different, thought Andrew, as he went across to Flora's office that evening.

'Still busy?' he said.

She smiled. 'I'm never too busy for mysterious parcels,' she answered eagerly unwrapping the package he handed to her. It was the portrait Andrew had been sketching on the day they had picnicked by the river.

'I thought you might like to have it,' he added awkwardly, hoping he hadn't made another mistake.

She turned to him, momentarily speechless. 'Oh, it's lovely. And very flattering.' Setting it on her desk, she said softly, 'Thanks, Andrew.'

And what began as an affectionate kiss of gratitude turned into a lover's embrace. He had to be content with kisses that grew deeper in intensity while his body, aroused, longed for her. Caressing her slender waist he wanted to crush her against his body, allow his hands to stray. But he was afraid that such behaviour might shock and scare her off. That would be too embarrassing for both of them.

He felt it would be better to draw back now and, as he did so, he saw a flicker of disappointment in her eyes. Could it be that she wanted him, too? After all, it was a long time since John died.

He kissed her again, gently this time, and slowly released her, confident that he could face anything the future chose to throw at him with Flora McInnes at his side.

As long as they had each other . . .

A far-from-confident Pheemie was celebrating her birthday – except that celebrate was the wrong word to describe another dreary milestone nearer forty. That was all that birthdays meant to her these days – a solitary card, ornate and flowery, from Aunt Ishbel.

Reading the gushing sentimental verse, Pheemie shuddered. 'Trust her to remember I'm one year nearer the grave.'

Umberto stared at her over his shoulder. 'Oh, is it your birthday today?' he asked innocently.

'You ken very well it is. But don't worry, I'm in no mind to celebrate,' she said bitterly, intensely hurt that Umberto had forgotten.

He had been very forgetful all day, come to think of it. He had returned from Strathblair without the paraffin which was the main reason for his trip, but with a large square box instead which he said contained spare parts for a bike.

A letter had arrived for him, addressed in an unknown hand, post-marked Perth. Pheemie wondered who was writing to Umberto, since he never got letters from one year's end to another, but he thrust it into his pocket without a word of explanation.

Her curiosity was aroused, so when the envelope dropped out of his pocket unnoticed as he carried some logs out of the barn, she had no compunction about looking inside.

It contained the photograph of a pretty young woman, and the back was inscribed with a message, written in Italian. All she could recognise was 'Umberto', a heart, and a row of kisses. Her own heart was thumping now, torn between a desire to inflict physical violence upon him and burst into tears. Oh dear God, don't tell me that he's got a secret love tucked away in Perth.

She had barely time to thrust it into her pocket and contain her fury when he looked in and said: 'I'll away down and get that paraffin. Is there anything else you need?'

'Aye, some arsenic.'

'Who for? Me or you?' He was laughing at her.

She scowled. 'What do you think?'

Now solemn, mistaking the reason for her anger, he said: 'Pheemie, I'm really sorry I forgot the paraffin.'

'I'm sure you are,' she replied sarcastically.

'It's not the end of the world, is it? Just paraffin, not medicine for a heart attack.' And when she didn't respond he continued: 'Pheemie, we all make mistakes.'

That was too much. She turned on him angrily. 'You don't have to tell me about making mistakes.'

Clearly baffled, Umberto discreetly withdrew. She watched him go, seething as she re-examined the photograph with a sinking heart. Young and pretty. What chance would she have against such a rival? Wisely Umberto made himself scarce all day, but that didn't improve her mood.

When she needed help, she had to go in search of him, yelling that he was a lazy devil. Hammering on his workroom door and finding it locked, she looked through a crack and saw what looked like a red carnation. Bewildered, she wondered what the devil Umberto was up to. Did he have a date with the girl in the photo? Was that it?

Feeling betrayed and helpless, and in a furious mood, she went back inside and poured herself a very large whisky.

When he came in she refused even to look round. How dare he treat her like this? It was no consolation to know Aunt Ishbel would readily provide the answer. She had made herself cheap, so what could she expect. And from an Eyetie. Foreigners were after all they could get from women. Maybe she should have listened.

'Pheemie. Happy birthday, Pheemie,' he said softly.

Reluctantly she turned round and beheld an almost unrecognisable Umberto resplendent in his very best and only suit, with a red carnation in the buttonhole and an immaculate white shirt. He was carrying the box he'd brought back from Strathblair that morning.

'This is for you.' Opening it, Pheemie discovered a beautifully iced birthday cake decorated with a sugar heart and roses. She was speechless; she blinked back tears.

'Remember Tonio I met at the show?' said Umberto. 'He made it specially. I had to collect it off the Perth train. That is how I forgot the paraffin – and this is to go with it.'

He put down a bottle of wine. Pheemie still hadn't got her voice back. 'The cake. Do you like it?' he asked anxiously.

'It's the best cake I've seen in my life.' She almost added, 'The only birthday cake I've ever had.' As they drank the wine and consumed large slices, they declared it the best cake either of them had ever tasted.

'You happy now, Pheemie?' Umberto smiled tenderly.

Should she risk spoiling it all by asking about the photograph? She knew she must, even if her curiosity ruined the whole moment between them, perhaps for ever, if what she suspected turned out to be true. Then he would go, leave her for this woman in Perth. What she had always feared most would come to pass. She'd never see him again.

And before she could change her mind, she took out the photo, demanded: 'Who is this?'

Umberto stared at it and then shouted angrily: 'It's – where did you get this? Have you been going through my things?' When she told him she'd picked it up in the yard, Umberto, mollified, said sulkily: 'It's nobody – nobody at all.'

'It looks very like somebody to me,' Pheemie said grimly.

'It's – only –' Umberto thought rapidly – 'Tonio's wife. That's who it is. Yes, Tonio's wife.'

'He sent you a picture of his wife?'

'Aye. He's awfully proud of her.'

'He certainly must be.' It sounded weird to her, but maybe

Italians were like that – impulsive, sentimental. And taking a gulp of wine, she said with studied indifference: 'And here was me thinking you'd got yourself a girlfriend.'

'Now, would I do a thing like that?' Umberto's reproachful tone sounded sincere, caring. And when he went back to his bothy later, Pheemie climbed the stairs after him.

What a lovely way to end a birthday, she thought, lying in his arms. As an orraman he might have his faults but as a lover he was perfect. He knew all the secret ways to bring a woman's body to dazzling fulfilment, and to keep her there. Sighing, she kissed his bare shoulder, entwining herself around him again.

As he responded, murmuring to her in his own language, she thought blissfully, we have each other, now at this moment, so what is there to fret about?

There was no love waiting for Robert Sinclair that night in Wester Balbuie. He had lost Bel McPhee and had only his thrawn old grandfather to wait for. He mentioned the sheep maggots and asked: 'Will you be able to clear them up in time for the sales?'

'I've aye been a dab hand at getting rid of parasites,' said Macrae.

The cruel remark stung Robert for there was no mistaking the malevolence in his grandfather's face.

When he went upstairs Macrae was already asleep. A pillow had fallen on the floor beside the bed. Robert picked it up and stood looking down at his grandfather's face. Sleep did nothing to soften the harsh expression bitter to the very bone.

If only Wester Balbuie was mine. If only he would die. It would be so easy. Just one movement, that's all. If only I could summon up the courage.

He was holding the pillow tightly when the old man's eyes suddenly opened. Staring up at Robert, he smiled, his face transformed: 'Mary. Mary lass, I thought you were dead.'

As Robert, hoping to escape unnoticed, gently replaced the

pillow on the bed, Macrae now fully awake, demanded harshly: 'What are you doing in here?'

'You'd fallen asleep. With the light on. Shall I turn it off?'

'Aye, do that.'

But for a long time Macrae lay awake. Was it only because Robert was so like her that the vision of Mary had been so real? Had she been sent to warn him? Was he in some kind of danger?

Sighing, he felt like a very old done man. He wouldn't mind dying either if he could see his Mary again.

· · · · *Thirty-one* · · · ·

If Sir James needed further convincing that Andrew was serious about this art business, it was the announcement that two of his business associates were to dine at Strathblair House. Using the excuse of a meeting in Perth that evening he left Andrew and Flora to entertain these unwelcome guests.

Theirs was a simple evening meal most often served at Sir James's table: home-made soup, followed by meat – venison in season, salmon or whatever fish was being caught in the river running through the estate – and some excellent vegetables grown in the kitchen garden. Dessert was also simple: Scotch trifle, fresh fruit and cream in summer, or in winter, apple tart or 'clootie' dumpling, to keep out the cold.

It was the venison that won Donald Telfer's heart. With an ecstatic expression, he munched happily and declared it was 'A Royal beast!' And waving a fork, he added: 'I want a twelve pointer tomorrow. Nothing else will do, Andrew.'

'We'll have to see what we can do for you,' Andrew smiled.

Despite his name, Telfer was from Brooklyn. A shrewd and able businessman, he was unimpressed by wealth. He had plenty of money and had sat at many millionaires' tables. His one weakness was tradition: a Scottish castle backed up by a title, however impoverished, was calculated to hit the spot and go straight for his pocket. Since meeting Andrew, Telfer's ambition was to take back a stag's head for his Fifth Avenue home. He longed to be able to proudly announce to visitors: 'That's one I shot myself, folks.'

Looking around at the ancestral portraits, Telfer smiled at his partner. 'What do you say, Charles, is this gracious living, or what?'

'Most gracious and much appreciated.' No two men could have been more dissimilar. Charles Somerville was a sedate and anaemic-looking, upper-class Englishman with his roots – or so he said – in Eton and Oxford. A bond between two such men seemed unlikely, except that Somerville's background gave them access to families with high-sounding names whose stately portals would have remained stoutly closed against his partner. But where money talked, Telfer's spoke very loudly indeed.

Somerville raised his glass. 'If I may propose a little toast to our host and hostess —'

'Oh, not hostess,' interrupted Flora hastily, 'I'm only an employee.'

'Hardly,' said Andrew with an affectionate glance. 'You're a friend first and foremost.'

Telfer giggled. 'Hey, Flora, if I thought I could get a pretty lady factor like you, I'd buy myself a piece of the Highlands.'

'Here's to the two of you —' said Somerville.

'Whatever you are,' chortled Telfer, giving Flora a wicked look. And, turning to Andrew, he said eagerly: 'About our little proposition. I can sell your stuff in New York, that's easy, but Charles here has connections all the way down the East Coast.'

As Somerville protested mildly at this exaggeration, Flora asked if he lived in America.

'On and off. My father was on the staff of the British Ambassador to the States during the war. I pop back and forth, you know.'

'Pop!' exclaimed Telfer. 'What connections he don't have,

aren't worth having.' And turning to Andrew, he remarked:
'It's a big market, think you can handle it?'

'Possibly.'

Telfer grinned. 'There speaks the canny Scot.'

'My clients would be interested in anything of tradition and
value,' Somerville put in.

Telfer regarded a cabinet of Sèvres china directly in his line
of vision. 'And that's what they've got to sell in this country.
Tradition. All these big houses with estates, stuffed full of
family heirlooms – antiques. No money after the war, so how
do they pay the bills? They sell. Bit by bit. Then lock, stock and
barrel. Now if we've got somebody here with a good eye for
antiquity, somebody who knows the value of things – someone
they trust, speaks the local lingo, we could clean up. Think of it
as helping to fill the dollar gap.'

Andrew, aware of a figure in the open doorway, saw that his
father had returned. His disgusted expression indicated that he
had overheard Telfer's eulogy.

'Hello, Father. How was your Chamber of Commerce
evening?'

'Dull,' was the laconic reply.

Telfer bounded to his feet. 'Sir James – we've spoken on the
phone. I am immensely pleased to greet you at last, sir.' As
Andrew introduced them, Telfer continued: 'And this is a
colleague of mine, Charles Somerville.'

'So pleased to meet you, Sir James. And thank you for this
wonderful hospitality.'

'Yes. So sorry you couldn't dine with us, Sir James,' said
Telfer.

'Well, business matters, you know.'

'Don't I just!' Telfer's loud laugh was countered by a frosty
smile from Sir James who turned to Flora.

'Good evening, my dear. You look very nice.'

As she graciously acknowledged his compliment, Andrew
said cheerfully: 'Can I get you a drink, Father?'

Sir James eyed the table. 'Is that by any chance my fifteen-year-old brandy?' he said acidly.

Well-mellowed by wine, Andrew was unrepentant. He smiled. "Fraid so, Father.'

'In that case I will have one, thank you.'

'I hope to make a killing on your land tomorrow,' Telfer piped up.

'I beg your pardon?'

'Andrew's going to take me on a shoot. Get myself a stag.' And as if aiming an imaginary gun, he joked: 'That's if the old Army training holds true.'

'Oh, we have quite a few stags,' said Sir James casually. 'If you miss one you'll probably hit another.' And with a wintry smile he turned to the other guest. 'Somerville? Any relation to Alistair Somerville, the whisky exporter?'

'No, unfortunately. Diplomacy runs in the family, not whisky.'

'Well, they both oil the wheels of the state, do they not? So here's to diplomacy,' he added lifting his glass and giving his son a withering look.

At breakfast the next morning, before Sir James could pronounce judgement on his new business associates, Andrew said: 'I don't want to get us into yet another conflict, Father, but I promised Mrs Ritchie —'

'I haven't yet decided one way or the other —'

'They're both worried sick.' When Sir James shrugged, Andrew said desperately: 'I'm sorry, but giving good grazing land over to planting trees just seems to me such an exploitation.'

This was the opening Sir James had been waiting for. '*He that is without sin* – Your friend Telfer was telling me about his plans to pillage our ancestral homes and ship the spoils overseas to our rapacious American cousins, using you, I believe as some sort of pointer to sniff out where the biggest profits are. Now that is what I would call exploitation.'

And for once there was nothing Andrew could say in his own defence.

Pheemie had been up early that morning helping Alec and Jenny load the lambs into the lorry. Alec should get a good price for them. They were in excellent condition. To everyone's relief, the threatened maggot infestation had been confined to a few ewes.

Returning to Carnban, she decided to smarten herself up for the sheep sales as she was being accompanied by Umberto, who was taking his time getting 'spivved up' as she called it. When he at last appeared, he looked the picture of elegance, sporting his best suit, white shirt and the tie she'd bought him last Christmas. At closer quarters she noticed his immaculately groomed hair was heavy with the smell of Brylcreem applied with a liberal hand.

'Well, well, you don't look as ugly as usual. Almost present-able in fact,' she said thinking: just too damned attractive. Suddenly she was jealous again. Surely this couldn't be all for her benefit? Other women had eyes, too, and they might fancy him. Younger, prettier women. She hated them all as she looked at him, weakly aware that he only belonged to her in bed and she couldn't keep him there for ever.

Mistaking her expression, Umberto, who so rarely saw her in anything but dungarees and a man's shirt, searched for some flattering words for Pheemie dressed in her Sunday best: a tailored jacket, smart jumper and land girl's hat. He'd have preferred a more feminine vision in a pretty frock for once, but didn't want to hurt her feelings. 'You look – very nice.'

She seemed pleased with his verdict and they set off for Strathblair and the bus for Perth. In festive mood, they shared a bag of liquorice allsorts while Umberto surreptitiously eyed a pretty girl sitting opposite them, an occupation shared by Robert, who was accompanying his grandfather to the sales.

Not far behind the bus were Alec and Jenny on the motorbike. As they turned a corner they paused to let Andrew's hunting party pass. Armed with guns and leading a pony, they were heading across to the hills.

As Alec greeted him, Andrew said: 'My American friend here wants a stag's head for his wall.'

'Seems such a waste,' said Jenny with a reproachful look in Telfer's direction. For once Telfer was subdued, having failed to make any headway in the gun room. Willie, the head stalker, with thirty years' experience behind him, knew and loved his deer herd and had his own private opinion about American so-called sportsmen with too much money and too little ability.

He made it a rule never to hand over the rifle until the shot was about to be made. This didn't suit Telfer who wanted to carry his gun, even when Willie insisted that this was a well-established safety precaution on the estate. Neither did Telfer relish being told by a mere lackey that deer had acute hearing and didn't like conversation. In other words: Keep your mouth shut.

Aware of Jenny's distress, Andrew said gently: 'Deer have to be culled.'

'And have you seen the damage they do to the trees?' Alec put in quickly. He didn't like her implied criticism of the major's guests.

'I should have thought the less trees around here, the better,' she said sharply.

Andrew looked embarrassed. 'Well, I'd best be on my way. Good luck at the market, Alec.'

'Good luck with the shoot, sir.' And he started up the engine, furious with Jenny. What did she think she was about, putting down the major in front of all those other men?

When they reached Perth and left the motorbike in the market car park, Jenny was still taking it out on him because Andrew hadn't told them then and there what Sir James had decided about the Forestry Commission.

'The major has a duty to his father, Jenny, as well as trying to help me.'

'Duty?' she said contemptuously. How like a man! 'Now we're back to being soldiers again.'

'There's nothing wrong with being a soldier,' Alec said huffily.

Jenny took his arm. 'Oh, I'm sorry. Look, let's just try to enjoy the day out.' They joined the throng of people heading for the ring – buyers, sellers, farmers and their families – all auction addicts.

Robert was there, smiling hopefully at a couple of likely lasses, who were not much older than himself.

Even to Alec's undiscerning eye, they were in army parlance 'a couple of fresh tarts', two lasses on the make, wearing frocks they'd been poured into, with short skirts stretched tightly over their bottoms, which they hoped waggled provocatively as they tottered along the uneven ground in their high heels, hardly able to see through mascaraed eyelashes, the paint and powder an inch thick.

Alec, reeling against a cloud of cheap perfume as they sailed past, grinned at Robert's hopeful expression. Good for you, lad. He didn't care much for his taste in females, but that's how he should be behaving at his age, testing the local talent instead of moping about Wester Balbuie, becoming warped by an old man's bitterness.

Suddenly Macrae hailed him from a group of farmers. 'I was just talking about you, Ritchie. Just saying to the lads here, if they need any advice on how to get a good price for their sheep, you're the man to contact.'

Alec smiled – spite and sarcasm, that's what old men were made of.

Pheemie struggled through the crowd towards them. As she approached, Jenny suddenly clutched her stomach. 'Ouch, I just realised, I didn't have time for any breakfast and the bump is starving.'

Umberto overheard her and much to Pheemie's astonishment offered to buy her a sandwich. 'Every time he takes a coin out of his pocket, Britannia blinks at the light.'

If Umberto understood, then he took this in good part. 'So what will I get you?'

Jenny asked for a cheese-and-tomato sandwich, and Pheemie for a gammon roll. 'And you can slam on the mustard!'

As he hurried away, Jenny smiled. 'He's looking very handsome today, our Mr Umberto.'

Robert had trailed the two girls with little success. Their haughty expressions made it quite clear that it was men they were after, definitely not boys. In the café he saw them again, sitting at a table with Umberto who was lighting a cigarette for one while her companion ogled him across the table. Pheemie had better not see that, thought Robert, or the balloon would go up with a vengeance. Taking his coffee to the next booth, he listened hopefully wondering what he could learn from the Italian's technique.

The older, bolder of the two girls was called Anne-Marie. Purring at Umberto, she repeated his name. 'That's a nice name. It's like a film's star's.' And when Umberto wished that he was, she said encouragingly: 'Oh, I think you look like one, doesn't he, Mae?'

'Aye, Lassie,' replied her companion, upset that she wasn't doing as well at claiming Umberto's attention.

'No,' drawled Anne-Marie. 'More like Cary Grant or Bing Crosby.'

'Crosby?' Although Robert couldn't see it, Umberto's demonstration as he said, 'What about the – ears?', raised a laugh.

'I like foreign men,' Anne-Marie continued relentlessly. 'They're very – attractive.'

'Who was that woman we saw you with earlier?' asked Mae. 'Was that your mother?'

Robert heard Umberto choke on his cigarette. 'No. She's a neighbour.'

Did they really believe that? Or that he had a farm? There followed a lot of suggestive innuendo between the two girls about how big and how broad it was. This threw them into shrieks of mirth, but Umberto who was slow on British humour and dirty jokes just looked bewildered, and Robert watched him slope off with a promise to see Anne-Marie later. Ho hum, thought Robert, I don't fancy your chances, chum, of evading Pheemie's eagle eye.

Umberto didn't fancy his chances much either, when he finally tracked down a scowling Pheemie at the ring to be greeted by: 'What took you so long?' Jenny was grateful for her sandwich but, of course, in the excitement generated by Anne-Marie, Umberto had forgotten the mustard for Pheemie's gammon roll.

'Ye daft Italian gowk!' she yelled at him furiously.

Fortunately for Umberto, the auction, the event of the day, was about to begin.

· · · · *Thirty-two* · · · ·

'Right, ladies and gentlemen, if you'll give me your attention, we'll begin today's sale,' said Wallace. 'I have seventy-five wether lambs being sold by a weel-kent local sheepman, Macrae of Balbuie. We all know his reputation for sound, healthy stock —'

Macrae could not resist a dig at Robert who had just joined him. 'Aye, I have mair luck wi' sheep than family.' Then he devoted his whole attention to the bidding, listening intently as it went from forty to fifty-six shillings per lamb.

'Come on – fifty-six for God's sake,' he whispered. The bidding went on, once again: 'Fifty eight – sixty?' There were no more bids and Wallace banged down his hammer. 'All done at sixty shillings '

'That's pretty good, isn't it?' said Robert, only to receive in return a grim look from his grandfather who had been hoping for more.

Corriebeg's lambs were led into the ring. 'Now our next lot is fifty wether lambs from Alec Ritchie, a newcomer to the area. What am I bid?'

The bidding went swiftly to fifty and Alec turned to Jenny. 'Well, at least we're off and running.'

Among the bidders, Umberto fell foul of Pheemie by putting up his hand, a pre-arranged signal to Anne-Marie. Intercepted by Wallace, it was taken as a bid.

'What do you think you're doing, you daft gowk?' Pheemie hissed.

'I was just – bumping it up.'

'I'll give you bumps. You keep your hands in your pockets from now on.'

Umberto looked around nervously. What had he done? But he was saved by a larger bid.

'Sixty-four shillings. All finished now at sixty-four shillings.' Down went Wallace's hammer. 'The best price of the day.'

Alec and Jenny hugged each other, knowing this meant they could safely face the future, if they had a future at Corriebeg.

One person didn't share delight in their good fortune and Alec caught sight of Macrae's angry expression as he stamped out. But Robert's cheery grin and thumbs up in their direction made it clear that he wasn't disappointed to see the old man bested. Robert tried to console Macrae. 'Never mind, Grandfather, we'll do better next year.'

'You won't be here, next year,' he was told.

As they were leaving the ring, Macrae was greeted by an old acquaintance, Geordie Gibson, a hill farmer now retired, as good-natured and placid as Macrae was grim and dour. 'Aye, aye, I suppose you've made your usual mint at the sales, Balbuie.'

'No bad, Gibby, no bad. Fair to middling,' was the cautious reply.

But Gibby was staring at Robert. 'Is this Mary's boy?'

When Robert nodded proudly, Gibby said: 'I might have

known. You look just like her across the eyes. Aye, you're yer mother's son all right.'

Clearly embarrassed by this remark, Macrae made an excuse to collar Wallace about his conduct of the sale. Gibby watched this exchange with some amusement. 'There's Alasdair laying down the law as usual.'

'It's his speciality.'

Gibby laughed, then looking up at Robert, he sighed. 'He and I were rivals in love, you know. For your Grannie's hand. Jeannie. But he was aye a better dancer than me, so that swayed her somewhat.'

'My grandfather . . . dancing?' Robert could hardly believe it.

'Aye, at the ceilidhs. Once he'd had a few. He danced her right off her feet.' He sighed. 'A lovely woman. She died early, not long after Mary was born. So your mother was all he had. The apple of his eye. When she left, it must have broken his heart.'

As Macrae stared suspiciously in their direction, adopting the manner of one who knows he is being talked about, Robert grinned. What a surprise, discovering that his grandfather, the old devil, had been a great dancer.

Further afield, Pheemie was in danger of a less pleasant surprise. As she searched for Umberto, Mae, who also fancied him and whose friend Anne-Marie had deserted her, was furious. In a spiteful mood, she recognised the woman they had thought was Umberto's mother.

'Are ye looking for him?' When Pheemie stared at her, she said: 'The Eyetie?'

Scenting trouble, Pheemie demanded: 'What business is it of yours?'

'Ye'll find him back over there.' The girl pointed towards the stables. 'And he's got company.'

Still not realising what was going on, Pheemie opened the door. She was about to call his name, when she heard sounds issuing from one of the stalls – heavy breathing, a few moans and cries. Unmistakable sounds to any woman who has made love.

And then she saw Umberto, her Umberto, in a decidedly sexy clinch with a heavily painted female, his hands groping her thighs. Like a fury, Pheemie descended upon them. Seizing the girl by the hair, she screamed: 'Get away from him, you dirty wee Jezebel.'

'Ow – leave me alone.' Wriggling out of Pheemie's grasp, Anne-Marie shouted: 'Who do you think you are? You stupid – old – bitch.' As Pheemie made another grab at her, she ran towards the door, wailing in a terrified voice. 'I'm going to tell my Daddy on you.'

Now it was Umberto's turn and Pheemie attacked him with her fists. 'Ye dirty, smelly, lecherous thing! The first wee bitch on heat you come across, you cannae wait tae glue yourself on.'

'*Per favore,*' said Umberto with a desperate attempt at dignity. 'I have a right to look at a pretty girl.'

'You have no rights,' said Pheemie through gritted teeth. 'You're here on borrowed time, Mr Spaghetti. One word from me and you'll be shipped back to Italy where you belong, hanging upside down from a lamppost like your pal Mussolini.'

White-faced and scared, Umberto stared down at her. 'You're my orraman. That's all you are. And if I catch you wi' another wee whore, you can kiss goodbye to Bonnie Scotland. *Arrivederci.*' Seizing his coat lapels she put her face close to his. 'Have you got that?' she hissed and stalked out of the stable.

Badly frightened, Umberto followed her to the bus which was waiting to take them back to Strathblair. There was no joking this time, no bag of sweeties to be shared. They sat as far away from each other as was humanly possible on one seat in a crowded bus.

Across the aisle, Macrae looked to have even fewer laughs in him as he stared grimly out of the window, while Robert dozed at his side.

A gloomy ending to a day that had begun so well, but there was worse waiting when they got home: Major Menzies was missing.

· · · · *Thirty-three* · · · ·

Andrew had no heart to go with the hunting party in the first place. Telfer, whom he was beginning to like less and less, was as excited as a schoolboy, especially when the whisky flask was solemnly passed around.

'Good old Scottish custom, huh?' As Andrew swallowed a dram, Telfer asked: 'Well, have you thought about it?' And, pointing his thumb and forefinger, he continued: 'Got you in my sights, Andrew.'

Knowing perfectly well that Telfer was anxious for a decision about their business deal that he wasn't quite ready to make, Andrew excused himself and walked over to a small belt of trees where he took a large swig of whisky from his own hip-flask. God, I shouldn't do that on an empty stomach, he grimaced. But Telfer was just about the end. He didn't know whether he could stand a whole day of him, since he was proving even more obnoxious than he had been last night.

Willie, meanwhile, had returned with his telescope and rifles. 'I've spotted a wee herd and there's a stag or two. We'll leave the ponyman here and from now on, you'd better keep the noise down.'

Andrew drifted back to them and they set off up the hill where Willie handed the telescope to Telfer who exclaimed: 'That's what I'd call a Royal.'

'All right,' said Willie, 'see that wee bank up there? That's a perfect place for the shot and that is where we'll go.' As Willie loaded the rifle, Andrew knocked back some more whisky. Guns being loaded triggered off too many memories, stirred murky depths he'd rather not explore.

Seeing Somerville at his side, he offered his flask which

Somerville declined, giving him a curious look that suggested it was bad form for the laird's son to be drinking so much.

Lying on a hillock overlooking the herd, Telfer took careful aim and fired. Andrew winced as the shot echoed across the hill. Guns, dear God, how he hated them.

'You missed it by miles, sir,' said Willie.

'It moved. Just when I fired,' Telfer protested.

'Sir, you couldnae hit a barn door if you were standing on the padlock.'

The candid reply did not suit Telfer. 'I'm not used to this gun,' he said sulkily. And as Andrew began to laugh, he spun round. 'What the hell's so funny?'

'Sorry. I was just trying to imagine you – standing on a padlock.' Conscious that he was more than a little drunk, Andrew said: 'Don't worry yourself, partner. Plenty more stags. And we've got the whole day.'

Somerville and Willie exchanged glances. Somerville was no sportsman and a cold Scottish moor was his idea of hell. He hadn't wanted to come on the shoot. As for Willie, he went off stalking another herd, thinking mutinously that if there was one thing he hated, it was working with amateurs who fancied themselves as lords of the isles once they got a rifle in their hands.

As the little group awaited Willie's return, Andrew seized the opportunity to apply himself to his flask again. Telfer watched him, frowning. 'Don't you think you ought to go easy on that stuff, Andrew?'

'Drunk or sober, I'm still a better shot than you,' Andrew bragged recklessly, turning away with a contemptuous laugh.

Scenting trouble brewing Somerville said smoothly: 'I'm sure Donald was just unlucky —'

But Telfer was watching Andrew through narrowed eyes. 'No, he's right, Charles. After all, I was at the back during the war – supplies. Andrew, here, was at the sharp end, weren't you, Andrew?'

'Sharp enough.'

'Coriano Ridge and all that stuff,' Telfer nodded genially. 'OK, I'll tell you what. When and if Willie finds the next stag, you make the shot. Show me how to do it. For the honour of the British Army.'

Suddenly sobered, Andrew realised he had fallen into the trap, hoist, once again, with his own petard. His prayer that the deer had taken cover for the day wasn't to be answered either. At Willie's signal they followed. There, in the gully, stood a solitary stag.

Andrew stretched out his hand for the rifle. He knew even as he lay down and looked along its sights that he was no longer in any condition to shoot straight. But there was no way out. It was a magnificent stag, a 12-pointer, exactly what Telfer had ordered.

He squeezed the trigger and as the rifle kicked back against his shoulder, Willie laid down the binoculars and called: 'You've downed him, all right. Well done, sir.' And Willie raced down the gully followed closely by Somerville and Telfer, who turned and shouted: 'One up for the Black Watch, Andrew.'

Andrew scrambled after them. He was the last to arrive, but he heard what he dreaded most, the grunts of agony of a mortally wounded stag.

'No' such a good shot after all, sir,' said Willie. 'You hit him along the back.' Taking the rifle from Andrew he loaded it and stepped out. 'Now stand back please, gentlemen, if you will.'

Willie aimed carefully, fired. Then it was all over. But for Andrew the sound of the beast's agony remained still in his ears. He was surprised to realise that there was so little difference between dying creatures and dying men. Then he remembered his own mortally wounded men, screaming to be put out of their agonies. And as he watched Willie gralloch the stag, he saw, too, that there was little difference between the blood and guts spilling out of a dying stag, or out of a dying man. They smelt the same as they soaked the earth.

Willie looked up. 'I'll give the ponyman the nod, sir.'

'I'll do it,' said Andrew, relieved by an excuse to quit the gory scene. 'I'll catch up with you later.'

Watching him go unsteadily, Somerville said disdainfully: 'I thought the Scots could hold their drink.'

Telfer smirked. 'Oh, he's all right. We need him, Charles.' He nodded vigorously. 'And I think we've got him.'

Having alerted the ponyman, Andrew continued to stagger along, putting as much distance as he could between himself and the hunters. He felt sick, terrible. Suddenly he was very sick indeed. It failed to clear his head, the trees around him continued to move in a menacing way, threatening to fall on him. As for the ground beneath his feet, that wouldn't stay still either. It heaved up and down like the floor in a fun-fair house.

His unsteady progress gathered momentum, but was finally halted when his foot caught in a tree root. The motion of being flung violently forward stunned him and he lay still.

Once the stag's carcass was loaded on to the pony's back, Willie looked around for Andrew before they began the descent.

'He'll catch up with us,' said Telfer reassuringly.

Willie looked doubtful. 'Aye well. Most likely he's away home to put his feet up,' he said, not wanting his master to lose face in front of these foreigners.

Telfer stood squarely in front of him. 'Now I want another shot. So, how about it?' he demanded.

Willie wanted to refuse the man. He had no right, not without the major's say-so. 'Aye. We'll try and find you a big herd.'

'You mean if I miss one, I might hit another, right?'

'That's the idea.'

Andrew opened his eyes, his face pressed into the damp earth. Bewildered, he looked round. Where the hell was he? As it all came back, the unholy mess he had made of the damned shoot, he struggled to get to his feet and was halted as pain screamed through his leg.

He'd done something stupid to his knee. Dammit. Reaching for the whisky flask in an effort to dull the pain, he raised it to his lips. Incredibly, it was empty.

'Now isn't that just like the bloody thing?' And angrily hurling it away, he stood up and dragging his injured leg he began to weave his way slowly and painfully through the forest. The sky had darkened, the trees were very black and still. He was lost, with no clue as to which direction to take. He listened intently. For a moment the heavy silence was broken by a dog-fox barking, followed by the distant sound of a rifle shot. Then another.

The nightmare had begun. He was on familiar ground. He had been in a forest like this once before in his life. He knew it well. Now as the gun shots echoed around him, they became the mortar fire at the battle for Coriano Ridge. The next moment he was back with the dead of his battalion, the dead and the dying. He could smell the stink of blood, hear the screams of those afraid to die and of those afraid to live hideously maimed, pleading for death to end their agonies.

He staggered on from one corpse to the next.

'Private Chalmers – dead; Private Findlay – dead; Private Chisholm – dead; Private Macintosh – dead. CSM Slattery – dead.'

Now there came another voice. Sergeant Ritchie, shouting above it all. 'We have to pull back, sir. We haven't a hope in hell. They've cut us to pieces. We must pull back, sir. For God's sake, sir, do something. Give the order . . .'

And then he was hit. He was blind. Blind. He screamed against this monstrous obscenity of never seeing the sunlight again. Then the entire world went black, was lost as the forest rolled upon him and with it he fell into the peace of infinite space.

· · · · *Thirty-four* · · · ·

Flora's first intimation of disaster was when Sir James appeared at her office. 'Ah Flora, I wondered if Andrew might be with you.' He managed to sound both worried and irritated at the same time. 'Obviously not. You haven't seen him, have you?'

Mystified, Flora said: 'No.' Sir James nodded. 'Well, they're back from the stalk.' And trying to sound casual and failing miserably he added: 'Seemingly Andrew left them some time ago. And there's no sign of him in the house.'

'That's strange.' It didn't sound at all like Andrew.

'Also it appears he has been drinking,' said Sir James disapprovingly. 'Probably wandering about lost somewhere.'

With that he left her, returning to the house where Telfer and Somerville were anxiously awaiting him.

'Is there anything we can do, sir?' asked Telfer.

'You have done quite enough already,' was the acid reply as Sir James went into his study and shut the door.

'Don't worry, Charles,' said Telfer. 'They'll find him.'

'I hope so, Donald. For all our sakes.'

Flora, staring out of her window, frowned at the darkening sky. The sun had set an hour ago. The hills looked black and menacing. For the first time, she felt both afraid and helpless.

Sergeant Brodie took the matter of the major's disappearance very seriously. Taking his bike and alerting the farms along the way, he ended up at Corriebeg.

He found Alec and Jenny happily doing their sums, allocating money from the sheep sales among housekeeping, animal feed and farm maintenance.

'Sorry to disturb you. I don't suppose you've seen Major Menzies at all?' And when Alec said not since morning, Brodie continued: 'Seems he might have gone missing, somewhere out on the moors. Sir James has just telephoned. I'm organising a search-party, I wondered if you —'

'Sure. How long has he been missing?' asked Alec seizing his jacket and crook.

'I don't know. Could be four or five hours.'

Alec swore. Why hadn't the alarm been raised earlier? Four or five hours was enough time for an injured man to die out there, especially as the temperature dropped dramatically after dark. 'Will you be all right on your own?' he asked Jenny.

'Of course. On you go. Good luck.'

Brodie eyed the piles of bank notes sternly. 'I'd put that money out of sight if I were you, Mrs Ritchie,' he said importantly. A town-bred policeman, he believed Strathblair, where no one ever locked their doors, was thick with thieves.

He had arranged that the search-party should assemble at the hill path which led to the deer forest. Macrae was already there with Robert and Pheemie. Pheemie hadn't bothered to tell Umberto. She was still furious with him and when they arrived back at Carnban, he had gone straight to his bothy and wisely stayed there.

In the flickering light from their flashlamps, Alec recognised his cronies who had been rounded up from the pub where they'd been enjoying a post-auction pint: Wallace, Munro, Todd and Forbes.

'Everyone here?' said Brodie importantly. 'Right. We'll split up into groups. One last thing, if any of you come on any sign of Major Menzies, a member of your party should raise the alarm. Now, if my group's ready —'

Pheemie stepped forward. 'If you're going up the slopes, then I'll take the lead. I ken that land better than anybody.'

'She's right, Brodie,' said Macrae.

The sergeant obviously didn't want a woman taking over. 'Well,' he said doubtfully, 'if you think you know.'

'I know,' said Pheemie firmly. She'd been walking these hills all her life and knew them far better than any policeman whose beat was mostly confined to local farms and the village street.

'Well, after you then.' Brodie stepped aside and there was a flutter of amusement in the group as Pheemie marched ahead.

Robert, secretly enjoying the drama of the search and still glowing with his success in the hill race, was confident that there wasn't a hill in Strathblair that could beat him. Enthusiastically, he joined in the calls of the searchers as they kept in touch with each other in the darkness: 'Major Menzies? Major Menzies?'

The flash of a torch piercing the dark was soon the only link between the parties as they separated to cover a wider area. It was a pitch-black night without a moon. Macrae and the more experienced searchers soon realised that if the major had wandered into the forest, and was badly injured and unconscious, they'd have the devil of a job tracking him down.

Robert, plunging forward over-confidently, missed his footing and slipped down the bank. His cry for help had Macrae rushing to his assistance, peering into the darkness. 'Robert? Are you all right, son?'

'Down here. My backside's all wet.'

Macrae went forward and giving him a helping hand heaved him back. 'And you're a pain in mine, right enough. From now on watch where you're going.'

'Sorry.' But Robert had been surprised to hear the note of concern in his grandfather's voice when he thought he might be hurt – as if he really cared.

From Strathblair House, Flora had followed the distant pinpricks of light thrusting into the darkness like demented glowworms. She looked at her watch. They had been gone nearly an hour.

Suddenly the lights disappeared. What had happened? She felt panic rising. Had they found him – dead? Was Andrew lying somewhere with a broken neck? Then she realised that the lights no longer visible meant they had penetrated deep into the deer forest.

There was no point standing out here, shivering. She

thought of Sir James. Presumably he shared her anxiety, although his stiff upper lip might never quiver; feeling sorry for him she made a pot of tea in the kitchen and carried it through into his study.

Finding it empty she went in search of him. He was in Andrew's workroom, staring balefully at the portrait of his ex-wife, as if he'd like to blame her for their son's disappearance. He jumped as Flora knocked on the door.

'Come in.' Seeing the tea tray, he said gratefully, 'Thank you so much. No news, I suppose?'

'Not yet.'

'What an absurd fuss to be making. What an idiot that boy is!' he said angrily, glad to have someone with whom to share his feelings.

'We don't know it's his fault,' said Flora defensively.

'He should not have been drinking.'

'He's had a lot on his mind lately, Sir James.'

'So he keeps telling me! Going on and on about the Forestry business and Ritchie. Well, frankly, this sort of behaviour just makes me think I should ignore him and go ahead with the whole project.'

Flora looked at his flushed countenance. Realising he was taking refuge in this furious tirade to hide his anxiety, she said quietly, 'I think the most important thing is to get Andrew back safely. After that – well, it's your decision.' And having said her bit, she returned to her lonely vigil.

In the forest the searchers had reached an area that required great caution, even in daylight. A high crag fell steeply down to the burn. It was hard going and extremely dangerous. One false step and they would be in trouble.

They inched their way along, calling, 'Major Menzies!', but now with little hope of getting any answer. It had turned very cold and they were all feeling the effects despite their exertions.

Pheemie stood on the top of the crag. Far below, a tiny glimmer and the sound of fast-rushing water marked the burn.

'Well, wherever he is, it's no' up here,' she said to Brodie who struggled to her side.

Out of breath, he shivered. 'No, that's for sure. It's getting colder, too.'

'If he's in this neck o' the woods, I hope he's wearing his long underwear,' said Pheemie grimly.

The Corriebeg party led by Willie and Alec were a short distance away from them on the steep forest path.

'All right,' called Willie. 'We'll move round to the head of the crag.'

Alec shone his torch toward the sheer drop. 'What about down there?'

'Ach, you'd have to be daft to launch yourself over that. Right lads, round we go.'

Aye, daft or drunk, thought Alec. As they trailed away, he remained, still shining his torch in some fleeting hope of finding any evidence to indicate that the major had come this way.

Suddenly, far below him, the tiny beam touched something glinting among the fallen leaves. Glass perhaps? For a moment he hesitated, then he clambered down.

It was a silver hip-flask, engraved with initials: 'AM'.

Heartened by the find, Alec inched his way down, yard by tortuous yard, calling: 'Major Menzies! Major Menzies!'

There was no reply and he had almost given up hope when the torch's beam touched a white face, a body sprawled at the base of a tree.

It was the major. Alec blew his whistle, alerting the others. Then he bent over Andrew's still figure, praying that he was still alive.

'Major Menzies. Are you all right, Major?'

Andrew stirred. His eyes flickered open. 'Sergeant Ritchie?' he whispered. 'The men —'

'They're coming. They're coming, sir,' Alec replied, indicating Willie and the search-party stumbling down the slope.

Andrew struggled to sit up and groaned. At least he could still see. He touched his eyebrow. There was no blood. So he wasn't blind, after all. Thank God for that.

'Where am I?'

'At the bottom of the crag, sir.'

Andrew blinked, looked around in the faint torch light. The bodies of his dead company, sprawled like broken dolls had all disappeared. 'Not the Ridge?'

'No, sir. Not the Ridge.' Andrew was obviously badly concussed, imagining he was back in the war again. 'Come on, sir, let's get you home.'

Alec hoisted him to his feet, half-carrying him towards Willie and the others who were waiting with hands outstretched to heave him to safety.

'You've saved my bacon once again, eh, Sergeant?' Andrew gasped. 'It's getting to be a habit.'

And Alec knew exactly what he meant.

Half an hour later Alec strode wearily into Corriebeg. Jenny had probably gone to sleep hours ago. She had left him a note:

'Hope you found the major. Have gone to spend all your money on baby clothes and tree-felling equipment. Your loving woolly wife Jenny. PS. Come to bed, quick.'

Alec grinned. Pregnancy did strange things to many women, he'd heard, but he hadn't bargained that it would turn Jenny into a very sexy lady. Going upstairs, he remembered she had read to him from one of her books: 'In the third month of pregnancy, it is advisable now and again to take a little exercise.'

Seeing him working on his accounts, she had put an arm around him and had said: 'I don't suppose you've time to – to help me with a little bit of exercise.'

There was no mistaking the glint in her eye, and when he had answered: 'What a cheeky wee baggage you're becoming,' she'd grinned.

'It's being so close to nature, I suppose.'

Alec had followed her upstairs thinking they'd better make the most of this time together. Once the baby came, with broken nights and crying evenings, they might never again have it so good.

Robert looked with compassion on his grandfather's face, grey and weary, as he slumped into a chair. He was an old man to have spent all these hours trailing about in the hills. They'd had no time for any tea either and saying: 'I'm starving,' Robert took over the cooking.

Macrae was feeling his age, and more exhausted than he would ever admit, he was glad to let Robert get on with it. He sat at the table and counted the money he'd got from the sheep sales, still smarting that he'd been beaten by Corriebeg.

At last a cooking pot was banged down in front of him. 'What's this?' he demanded suspiciously.

'Elephant stew,' was the laconic reply.

Macrae gave Robert a hard look and tasted it gingerly. 'Too salty,' he said. But it wasn't half-bad. In fact, it was perfect. However, he had no intention of letting praise go to Robert's head, so he grumbled in his usual irritable fashion. 'Still I suppose it's better than nothing.' And, looking across the table, he added: 'Like many other things.'

Robert smiled, refusing to rise to the bait. 'Is there a ceilidh about here soon?' When Macrae puzzled, asked why, Robert shrugged. 'Oh, nothing. I just fancied a wee bit of a dance, that's all.'

And he had the satisfaction of seeing his grandfather wriggle uncomfortably, wondering what the devil that old fool Gibby had been telling the lad.

In Strathblair House, Flora opened the door to Sergeant Brodie. One look at his smiling face told her all was well.

'They've found him,' she said to Sir James who had followed her into the hall.

'They're bringing him back on the pony now, sir.' And to Sir James's anxious question, Brodie said: 'Could be worse. He's got a gey bad knee, suffering a bit from exposure. Got him just in time, sir. It's turned a damned cold night out there.'

'Where was he?' Sir James asked.

'In that wee forest at the bottom of the crag, sir. God knows how the major found himself down there. It's a place I'd never have thought of looking. Nor anybody else for that matter.'

'Who found him then?'

Brodie smiled. 'Alec Ritchie. You have him to thank, sir.'

Flora gave him a look of triumph. She suspected that he was going to find it very difficult to dispossess Alec Ritchie now that he owed him his son's life.

She waited to see Andrew carried up to his bedroom, too exhausted for more than a wan smile when she took his hand. She stayed until the doctor arrived, and assured that there was no real damage, made for home. When she returned early the next morning she was surprised to find Andrew awake and remarkably perky after his ordeal.

'One good thing,' he said after greeting her, 'my father has just been in. Told me he wasn't going ahead with the Forestry Project. Not this year, anyway.'

'Alec Ritchie will be pleased,' Flora said, sitting on the bedside.

Andrew smiled. 'I owe Alec some good news, wouldn't you say?'

'Well, he was the hero of the night.'

'Not for the first time.' He looked beyond her. 'You knew Alec and I fought together at Coriano Ridge?'

'Yes, but you've never really talked about it.'

Andrew leant back against his pillows. This wasn't going to be easy. He dreaded telling Flora. But now it must be said. This was the moment.

'It was what they like to call "a subaltern's battle", in other words an appalling bloody mess. We were supposed to secure the ridge, my company spearheading the attack. We came under heavy enemy fire almost immediately we advanced and lost radio contact.'

He paused and looked at her. 'That's like fighting blind. Anyway, we pressed on and were hit by intense mortar fire on our right flank, which shouldn't have been happening according to the recce chaps. It was a slaughterhouse really: what a bloody business.'

Again he paused, remembering. And when he spoke it was slow, painful, the words pulled out of him. 'That's when Alec Ritchie appeared by my side. He was extraordinary – and do you know, he was my youngest sergeant, just twenty-four years old. He told me that the Signals Officer and the CSM were both dead and that we should retreat. I said we had to stick where we were. He said the right-flank platoon had been pretty badly cut up, over 50 per cent casualties, and that we really should pull back.'

He stopped, shook his head. 'And what did you do?' asked Flora.

'Nothing,' said Andrew bitterly. 'It was probably only a minute or two, but it seemed like an eternity. I just couldn't decide. Then I was hit. It turned out to be a chunk of shrapnel but at the time I thought I'd been blinded. A lot of blood, couldn't see a thing.'

Pausing again, he closed his eyes. 'I thought I was dying. Then above the din, the last voice I heard before I passed out was Ritchie's. He took command, in effect, supervised the withdrawal. He was, by all accounts, remarkably brave. Altogether my company suffered about 70 per cent casualties.'

His voice trembled. 'God knows how many died while I was still making up my mind.'

Flora looked at him. 'I lost my husband at Anzio remember.'

'I know that. I know the kind of man you had, Flora.' He

looked into her eyes and said bleakly: 'I just wanted you to know the kind you might be getting.'

Flora took his hand, held it tightly, as she wondered if Andrew was actually asking her to marry him. At last – and in such strange circumstances.

October 1950

Summer days had given way to warm insect-free afternoons on the hill, where pine woods remained a dark and sombre ribbon in a rich spectrum of yellow, orange and crimson.

Beneath an outsize autumn moon the land echoed to the eerie primeval sounds of stags bellowing, the thud of antlers as young bucks challenged old warriors for supremacy over the herd. Prehistoric tribesmen had listened and moved uneasily closer to their fires, for in that forgotten past, before annual culls or guns had been invented for the convenience of the deer's new predator, Man, the rutting season was Nature's own way to ensure that only the fittest survived.

In Strathblair this was also the time of the harvest festival. Gardens lay stripped of their fruits, the first red berries appeared on holly bushes, and the air throbbed with the robin's sweet melancholy song, not for the entertainment of humans, but as a dire warning as he staked claim to his territorial rights.

Meanwhile, up at Corriebeg, the potato crop was being lifted by many willing hands, Umberto driving the spinner-digger which helped to take some of the back-breaking out of the job, Alec, Pheemie and Robert gathering, examining and Macrae on the sidelines dourly pronouncing judgement.

Pheemie straightened up. 'The makings of a fine crop, eh, Balbuie?'

'Aye, plenty to the shaw and free of scab. Or so it appears,' he added, unable to resist a warning to the over-optimistic.

'We should be done by nightfall,' said Pheemie.

'As long as the rain keeps off,' Macrae told her, casting a doubtful eye on a sky innocent of clouds, as they paused to watch the grocer's van heading for the house where Jenny was gardening.

'Keeping well are you?' Forbes asked her as he counted out the eggs.

'I've never felt better in my life.' And, taking the money he handed to her, she enthused: 'Wonderful! More nappies for the son and heir,' she returned to her planting.

Her work done in the fields, Pheemie looked in with a rabbit for the pot. 'What have you got there?'

'Daffodils, crocuses and the odd tulip,' said Jenny proudly.

'Aye. It'll be the Strathblair Flower Show next.' And when Jenny said she just hoped they'd be in bloom to welcome Master Ritchie in the spring, Pheemie grinned. 'Don't be disappointed if it's a girl.'

Jenny smiled. 'Oh, I won't be. It just feels like a boy, that's all.' She'd never even considered girl's names and up to now favoured Christopher or Geoffrey, although she couldn't get Alec to share her enthusiasm. He understood and sympathised that the coming baby absorbed all her emotions and had awakened an intensity of maternal feelings. After the first flush of excitement at the baby's conception, he was happy to play a minor role until he held his new-born son or daughter in his arms.

As Pheemie followed her into the house Jenny said: 'Funny, isn't it? How you change.' At Pheemie's questioning look, she smiled. 'I never cared for babies. I wasn't interested, just wanted to get out in the world and do things.'

'And then Alec came along, eh?'

Jenny nodded. 'And now his baby's coming along.' She looked up and saw once again that strange, sad expression she'd observed on Pheemie's face as her pregnancy progressed. Poor Pheemie, all this talk about babies must be making her broody, aware that time was no longer on her side either. Especially as Jenny suspected she was desperate to marry Umberto.

'How will you manage, Jenny? Will your mother come?'

'I'm not sure how kindly Alec would take to having my mother here for that length of time.'

'What's a couple of weeks?' Pheemie demanded. 'Breathing

space till you got back on your feet, that's all.'

'You don't know my mother, she'd probably be more of a hindrance than a help.' And when Pheemie suggested Alec's mother: 'She's an invalid, poor thing. I haven't managed to get to Dundee although Alec's been to see her. She's hoping to come with his sister when the baby arrives. You lost your mother early, didn't you?'

'A long time ago. I grew up in a man's world,' she added bitterly. 'Just my father – and a brother.'

'A brother?' Jenny looked at her in surprise. Pheemie had always given the impression that she, too, was an only child and Jenny asked curiously: 'What happened to him?'

'Ended up in Australia.'

Jenny wanted to ask more, but something reluctant in Pheemie's voice and her withdrawn expression warned that this was a sensitive area. It hinted at deep waters not to be stirred, even a bitter family quarrel, especially as Pheemie closed the subject very firmly by talking about a film with Stewart Granger she wanted to see in Perth next week – if she could get Umberto to take her.

Jenny would have been even more mystified by Pheemie's behaviour if she had seen her return to Carnban and walk up into the field overlooking her house. Lately she had come more often to sit by two flat stones the wall sheltered, staring across the field as she smoked a cigarette, as if keeping vigil.

And Umberto, who imagined he knew her every thought and action, was a great deal more sensitive to atmosphere than Pheemie gave him credit for, watched from the doorway of his bothy. He found himself oddly troubled these past few weeks by her attitude to Jenny's baby. Somehow it was quite out of character, something for which he, a mere man, could find no name.

Often as if she craved his company she'd come to sit silently with him these evenings, her gaze lingering on the few faded family photographs, particularly his three small children.

'You must miss them.'

'Yes, I miss them very much,' he said without looking round.

'You could always go back, I suppose.'

'I told you many times —' he said wearily for he had assured her constantly that he didn't want to go back. He was happy here in Scotland. This was his life now. Would she never understand and accept that the way they lived here in Carnban was best for both of them?

As for Pheemie, she was a little confused by Umberto's ambiguous statements and hoped that it was really because of her that he stayed, because they had each other.

'I mean, go back for a visit. Just to see them.'

'It is not possible.'

Just that. No explanation. Tonight it wasn't enough. Ignoring the irritation in his voice, she said hastily: 'Umberto, I need to know.'

Turning he faced her. 'You always need to know,' he said coldly. 'I've told you everything I know.' And jumping up from his chair he grabbed her roughly by the front of her cardigan as if he'd like to shake her, his face suddenly white with rage. 'I told you – how many times? How many more times, huh?'

And, releasing her so sharply she almost fell over, he opened the door and left her gasping, still gazing at the photographs as if by so doing they might reveal the answer to the enigma that was Umberto Fabiani.

'What do you think of her?' Andrew asked Flora.

The object of his affection parked outside was a silver Wolseley Six Eighty which he had just driven from Edinburgh.

'Lovely,' said Flora. 'But I didn't know Sir James had ordered a new car.'

'He hasn't. I thought it was time I stopped relying on others. Hop in,' he said proudly, 'I'll take you for a spin.'

It was a perfect day, and as they climbed to the heights above Strathblair, Schiehallion glistened under its first frosting of snow. Spread out far below them, they gazed at range upon range of the Perthshire hills, dotted with castles and farms as minute as children's toys – a tapestry woven in a blaze of autumn colours, bordered by a silver ribbon with the River Tay twisting and winding its sparkling way to a far distant sea.

'Beautiful, isn't it?' said Flora. But winter could be cruel, relentless in its ferocity, while summer storms devastated harvests, springtime snow ruined farmers, destroying lambs, crops and fruit blossom. But this unreliable land was hers and she loved it with the passion and loyalty of an offspring for an adored, but capricious, parent. Her sister laughed at her alarming lack of sophistication. How could she resist Edinburgh? But after a few days there she wilted and longed for what she called fresh air and space. She had only been to England twice for family weddings and London was so alien she felt as if she should have a passport.

'I used to think of this view when I was in the desert. It kept me sane,' said Andrew, aware in that shared moment of the strength of the bond between them. They had both sprung from this land. He thought of the past generations of Clan Menzies who had lived and ruled these hills and valleys. It didn't matter that the laird and the Master of Strathblair no longer spoke Gaelic, nor even sounded Scots. Their Englishness was only a thin veneer and their blood had survived through history's blood-soaked centuries. Here men kept faith with their roots and proudly gave to the world a dazzling race of empire builders, explorers and scientists. On its better days, he had considered it a land well worth dying for.

Flora was silent for a moment. 'You've never told anybody else the full story – about Coriano Ridge, have you?' When he shook his head, she nodded. 'Then it'll be our secret.'

'And Alec Ritchie's,' said Andrew.

'And Alec Ritchie's,' Flora echoed.

He said thanks and moving closer, kissed her. She

responded with such eagerness and warmth, that releasing her he asked: 'How do you fancy a honeymoon in Italy?'

She blinked and then said with a smile: 'Oh, I've had a proposal of marriage, have I?'

'Certainly. Do you think you might consider it seriously?'

'Of course!' But she was teasing him. Their eyes had already signalled the love that grew steadily between them, where questions were silently asked and silently answered. As for Flora, even if she hadn't loved him, she would have agreed in order to belong to Strathblair for the rest of her life.

However, Andrew preferred to be cautious when he told Sir James who, in turn, retorted: 'I don't see why she has to think about it.'

'It's a big step for her, I suppose.'

'Nevertheless, whatever her feelings are for you now, are they liable to alter in the next day, week or however long it takes her to make up her mind?'

Andrew continued playing with Prince, the labrador. 'Perhaps she'd like to talk it over with her family. I suspect Janet will have something to say on the matter,' he added, knowing exactly how the elder sister whom he had loved and lost would advise the younger: have nothing to do with that family.

As if Sir James was thinking along the same lines, and conscious of his own part in the break-up of Andrew's first romance, he muttered: 'I dare say.'

Andrew stood up, calling Prince. As the dog bounded eagerly towards the door, Sir James said: 'The Fergusons are coming to dinner this evening, remember.'

'I'll ask Flora, shall I?'

'Please do. A good time to announce your engagement, if Flora could be persuaded to make up her mind by then.'

When Andrew suggested they make it official that evening, Flora kissed him and smiled. So, this was to be her début as the Master of Strathblair's bride, a prelude to the day when she would cross the threshold as the future Lady Menzies.

Lady Menzies. She liked the sound of it as she put on her prettiest dress and marcasite earrings. Letting down her hair, making up her face carefully, she looked in the mirror and was not disappointed at what she saw reflected there.

She decided she was very happy indeed, much happier than she had ever imagined possible after John's death. It was amazing how well time healed, cleanly putting the pieces together again. Once more she was to be a wife and all that entailed. The only difference was that this time she was going into it with her eyes wide open, experienced, with no virginal, first-night tremors.

Both she and Andrew had been starved of love for a long time and if his urgent embraces were anything to go by, she hadn't the least doubt about their perfect sexual harmony.

Gerald Ferguson worked for the Chamber of Commerce in Perth and he and Aline were old friends of Sir James's. As Strathblair's factor, Flora had met them on formal occasions and Andrew waited until dinner was over to make his announcement.

The Fergusons beamed on them both. They had known Andrew since he was a small boy and were delighted with the news.

'So you've made a match at last,' said Gerald.

Andrew took Flora's hand. 'Yes, she finally talked me into it,' he said lightly.

Shaking his head in mock severity Gerald said to Flora, 'About time someone made an honest man of him.'

'I'll second that, Gerald,' Sir James raised his glass.

'Have you set a date?' Aline asked Flora.

'It depends on Andrew really. His regiment and so on.'

'Of course,' murmured Aline sympathetically. 'This ghastly Korean business.'

'Well, let's hope it doesn't get in the way of a good thrash,' chortled Gerald. At his wife's shocked exclamation, he raised his glass to Andrew: 'Just joking, old fella.'

Flora awaited a signal from Sir James and then rose with Aline. In time-honoured fashion rigidly adhered to in Strathblair House, the ladies still retired to the drawing room after the cheese and biscuits were served, leaving the gentlemen to their port and cigars.

Flora, offering Aline a cigarette with her coffee, discovered she had left her evening bag on the table outside the dining room. Going back for it, she heard Gerald's voice through the open door: 'Andrew, you're a lucky man. She's an absolute charmer.'

Hearing Andrew's proud: 'I think so.' Flora, smiling, wanted to hear more, especially when Gerald said: 'You must be very proud too, James.'

Her future father-in-law had always seemed kindly disposed towards her and she was both curious and interested to know what his response would be.

'It's what I wanted,' he said.

She smiled. That was good.

'Flora's a good worker and has a sensible head on her shoulders. But more to the point, she's healthy and can still bear children.' Pausing, he added: 'And that is my principal concern —'

How dare he say such a thing? How dare he consider her as a breeding machine? Resisting with considerable difficulty the impulse to rush in and confront him, Flora returned angrily to the drawing room.

It was intolerable and she had no idea afterwards how she got through the next half-hour before the men rejoined them. Without hearing a word of Aline's conversation, she managed somehow to respond automatically, a polite smile rigidly fixed on her face.

She thought the couple would never leave, but at last waving them goodbye, Andrew put his arm around her.

'I'll see you home.' In the gardens, moonlight made a watery paleness among the shadows. A lover's night. 'Tired?' he said.

'Hardly. I'm strong and healthy.'

Andrew gave her a puzzled look. Why did she sound so bitter all of a sudden? 'Sorry, I'm not with you.'

'Never mind. Your father enjoyed himself.'

'We all did. Didn't you?'

'Oh yes, the meal was fine.'

She did sound odd. About to ask her what was wrong, she said: 'I'm sorry, Andrew, I'll speak to you in the morning.'

Before he could kiss her goodnight, she rushed away. And even as he said: 'Flora – wait,' the door was firmly closed against him.

· · · · **Thirty-six** · · · ·

Snow had fallen on the upper reaches of the hills and Alec viewed the scene which was as pretty as any Christmas card with considerable anxiety. If this signalled an early winter and possibly a long and severe one, then he must make sure that the sheep were safe and their shelters adequate. As soon as it was light, he set off with Fly to examine the fences and gates.

He left Jenny still in bed, glad of the luxury of an unexpected lie-in. She got up at eight, fed the hens and wondered why Puss's saucer of milk was still untouched. Calling her she felt slightly anxious at this non-appearance since the little wild cat came so promptly and regularly each morning.

She was working at what Alec called 'being sensible' about animals. After all he told her, they had survived pretty well up to now without wrist-watches or kitchen clocks to regulate their behaviour. Still, it wasn't easy.

As she opened the door to go to the barn and fetch an assortment of vegetables for some soup, a furry shape wrapped itself around her ankles with a frenzy of exaggerated miaows.

She picked her up. 'And where do you think you've been?'

she asked and was about to refill the saucer when she heard the insistent bleating of a sheep in distress. It came from the inby field and, looking over the fence, she saw a ewe lying on its back with all four feet in the air.

Oh, you silly beast, she thought. Without Alec to help her it was going to be quite difficult, but she knew that once sheep got on to their backs, gravity and four hopelessly inadequate legs make it impossible for them to roll over and get up again. She had to do something – and quickly.

She went up the field and far from realising that her arrival meant rescue, the sheep became more terrified than ever and struggled violently as she patted its head.

'Poor old girl,' said Jenny. 'I can't leave you here like this until Alec gets back, can I?'

Her attempts at soothing were in vain, so she knelt down considering how best to tackle the problem. There was a knack to it. She'd watched Alec and Macrae restore a fallen ewe back to its feet, using a flick of the wrist, just like tossing an oversized, grossly woolly pancake.

Well, here goes. Putting her hand under its back she realised that wasn't the way. The ewe refused to budge and was incredibly heavy. Moving her hands down, she closed her eyes and gave an almighty heave, which to her delight worked. The next moment the ewe struggled upright and was tearing away, bleating furiously as if the devil was in pursuit.

'Well, how's that for gratitude!' She set off back down the hill feeling inordinately pleased with her good deed for the day. Alec would be so proud of her great achievement. Smiling, she remembered her father's constant warning about lifting heavy objects. He was quite obsessive about it, and rushed forward if she picked up as much as a chair. It was ridiculous really. Obviously dear Daddy had no idea what was involved in being a farmer's wife, or that a woman had to be as strong as a horse, with an athlete's muscles.

She was pulling the gate back into place when it happened.

Her body was seized in a giant vice and steadily, relentlessly, crushed. The pain was so swift and unexpected that it took her breath away.

She clung to the gate for support. A moment later, as mysteriously and swiftly as it came, the pain was gone. She straightened up very carefully, very shaken. How extraordinary. Surely these couldn't be the baby's movements? After all, she was only four months pregnant. Up till now he had been singularly inactive and hadn't made his presence felt by as much as a solitary flutter.

Oh – no! Not again —

Doubled up, she took slow, deep breaths, sat down weakly once more and prayed for the onslaught to subside. Just when she thought she couldn't – couldn't bear it – it began to fade.

Dear God, what was it? She'd never experienced anything like this before. Stomach-ache was new to her, the worst she'd ever lived through were menstrual cramps, and they were nothing to compare with this.

Could there be some other reason? Food poisoning? As she staggered across the yard and into the house, she tried to remember exactly what she and Alec had eaten in the last twenty-four hours, hoping Alec wasn't suffering like this up on the hill away from everyone.

In the kitchen, miraculously free of pain for a couple of minutes, she began to consider more reasonable explanations. Perhaps the baby was just hungry. Getting up late she hadn't bothered to make herself any breakfast. Maybe he was just reminding her? She'd make some toast, sit down and have a cup of tea.

She was filling the kettle —

Ohh . . . God . . . Waves of pain surged over her body; she couldn't breathe, couldn't see. The kettle slipped out of her nerveless hands as she staggered to the door.

She must get help.

Help —

Leaning weakly against the doorpost, she saw the bicycle and thought that if she could cycle to Carnban, Pheemie would know what to do. Pheemie was sensible.

She made an unsteady progress down the sloping path and onto the road. Thank heaven the route to Carnban was mostly downhill for the first mile. She was feeling better now. That was fine.

Ohhh . . .

She fell off her bike and lay on the ground, her knees raised to her stomach, panting.

Again the pain receded, slowly. Suddenly she guessed what was happening. Her baby. He was in danger. That's what the pain is trying to tell me. In his little dark secret world, something has gone wrong . . .

If this was a preview of what labour and childbirth had in store, the textbooks had all lied and she was surprised there were not more only-children. She shuddered; if the pain of bringing her son into the world was to be worse than this, then she would never survive to hear him cry.

Oh please God, look after him – look after my baby. Please keep the pain away —

It seemed that her prayer had been answered and, in an oasis of calm, she took stock of her surroundings. She looked at the bicycle wondering if she still had strength enough to continue on her journey. Perhaps that wasn't such a good idea after all. Perhaps her cycling upset him. That was possible.

Alec had been right, of course, warning her against cycling during her pregnancy.

Staring over the fence she could see the outbuildings of Carnban about a quarter of a mile away. If she took the short cut through the potato field and hurried, she might get there before the next onslaught. Pheemie would know what to do.

She set off down the field. She was in sight of the farm, feeling confident again, believing that there must be some logical explanation for it all, when the vice closed in on her again, its jaws biting deep into her spine. As if felled by an invisible fist, she slipped to the ground and lay there, moaning, gasping for breath.

As she fell, she noticed there was a stone wall above her, and on the ground near by, two flat stones. They reminded her of tombstones, she thought dazedly. Was this where she was going to die? Out here on the hillside, all alone?

I'm being broken to pieces, no human body can endure this for long. And if I die, my baby, that I love so much already, he'll die, too. I'll never know what it would be like to hold him in my arms.

Oh God —

Another wave hit her so soon, she hardly had time to get her breath back. Her vision blurred with pain, she saw two figures in the yard. Pheemie and Umberto. With her last remaining strength she framed the word: 'Pheemie!'

The pain surged again, writhing, twisting like some unseen hand thrusting a spear into her. She could take no more and as the blessed blackness of oblivion surged over her, she felt the first warm trickle of life-blood oozing from her body.

When she opened her eyes she was in Pheemie's armchair. Bewildered, she looked around. What on earth was she doing here? Had she fainted or something? Then she remembered.

Figures were bending over her, Pheemie – Umberto hovering.

'The pain, such a pain,' she grasped Pheemie's hand.

'Get a towel, Umberto. And keep that fire going.'

'My baby, please look after him,' she whispered and closed her eyes. When she opened them again she was in Pheemie's bedroom, in a white nightgown that wasn't her own. A woman was hovering by the bedside. There was the sound of running water and over by the dressing table a man was putting instruments into a case.

'My baby,' she gasped.

The woman said: 'There, there. It's all over now, dear.'

Confused and only half-conscious, Jenny recognised Mrs Lovatt the midwife who always took such an interest in her when they met in the village. Now she realised what all those pains were about. She'd been in labour, had her son prematurely. She'd be all right now. But where was he? And shouldn't he be crying for her?

'My baby,' she said, looking round for the small white bundle she expected to be put in her arms. She hoped he was all right, that she hadn't hurt him.

'My fault,' she murmured. 'It was my fault. I did such silly things.'

'Come now, you mustn't blame yourself.' Mrs Lovatt moved aside to let the man approach the bed. It was Dr McGowan and as he took her pulse, she asked: 'Where is he? Where's my baby?'

The doctor shook his head sadly and she knew then that he was dead.

'I killed him. I killed my baby.'

'No, Mrs Ritchie. I assure you, you didn't. It probably aborted itself.'

But dazedly she repeated: 'I killed him.'

'Mrs Ritchie, it was a defective foetus. It would not have lived.'

Jenny stared at him. 'Don't lie to me, please.'

'I wouldn't do that, believe me. Now I want you to sleep. You must rest. Here, swallow this, it'll help you relax.'

She took the drink obediently and suddenly the room was empty. So empty, like her body. So empty that she wanted only to die.

Downstairs, three anxious faces awaited the doctor's reappearance, Pheemie, Umberto and Alec.

Alec, on his way down from the hill, had noticed an abandoned bicycle lying at the roadside. Curious, he'd gone to inspect it, only to discover it was Jenny's.

What the hell was she doing riding a bike against his express wishes when she was pregnant? What was she up to now? he thought, looking round angrily. No doubt she'd had a puncture, didn't know how to mend it and had had to walk. But when he examined the tyres they were all right. So why had she left the machine lying in the road where a car turning the corner could run into it?

Baffled, he looked over the fence, shouted: 'Jenny. Jenny.' But there was no answer.

If something had happened to Jenny, she would run to Pheemie for help. There might be some other explanation. First he must check. Seized by a sudden panic, he began to run across the fields to Corriebeg.

The back door was wide open, the kitchen empty.

'Jenny,' he called. She wasn't upstairs either.

'Jenny?' But he hardly expected an answer any more. Then he saw the kettle lying in a pool of water where she had dropped it. Sick with apprehension he rushed outside, remembered the bicycle – on the road to Carnban – and leaping onto the motorbike he hurtled down the road.

Umberto was in the yard. 'Jenny? Have you seen Jenny?'

In answer Umberto walked quickly into the house where Alec took one look at Pheemie's face and knew the news was bad.

'What is it? Where is she?' he demanded. The two of them exchanged glances. 'Will somebody tell me what's going on?'

'She's upstairs,' said Pheemie. 'It's the baby.'

As Alec made to rush past her, she grabbed his arm. 'Alec, wait. There have been complications. The doctor's with her now.' Gently she pushed him into a chair. 'We just have to wait. Maybe it'll be all right.'

Umberto thrust a glass into his hand. 'Here take this. A dram. Try to calm yourself.'

Alec downed the whisky. The passing minutes seemed like

hours and none of them had the heart for conversation or speculation.

'What's taking so long?'

At last a door closed above them and they heard footsteps on the stairs. Dr McGowan went straight over to Alec.

'I'm sorry, Mr Ritchie. She's lost the baby.'

Alec sank back into the chair. He could hardly believe it. She had been in such radiant good health and spirits. He remembered teasing her about all the nappies and Viyella nightgowns she was sewing. All for one baby? And, patting her stomach, he had asked: 'Do you think you have quads in there?'

And now it was over. The baby he had never quite believed in, would never be a reality.

Dr McGowan was talking to him. 'The foetus was abnormal, a spontaneous abortion. I'm sorry.' And, to Pheemie he added: 'Miss Robertson, I'd like her to stay here for a day or two. Let her rest properly.'

Suddenly Alec sat up and asked anxiously: 'Is she all right?'

'Yes. A warm drink would be a good idea though.' As Pheemie poured the tea he continued: 'Yes, of course you can see her, Mr Ritchie. But I should warn you, she's feeling guilty right now.'

'Guilty? What about?'

'Losing the baby. It's a perfectly normal reaction in the circumstances. But you must convince her of that.'

As Alec opened the bedroom door, Mrs Lovatt was adjusting Jenny's pillows and with a sympathetic smile left them together.

Alec sat down on the bed. 'Hello there, I brought you this.' Putting the tea on the bedside table, he took her in his arms. She began to cry: 'Our baby. Our baby, Alec.'

'I know, I know.' And he felt his eyes brimming with tears. He had no idea it would be like this. He'd never imagined Jenny might not carry a baby successfully. And now sharing the full measure of her agony, he too knew grief and disappointment, deprived of being a father, of proudly holding a baby, his son – or his daughter – in his arms.

'I'm sorry. I'm so sorry,' she sobbed.

'It's not your fault. It's not anybody's fault . . .' His voice broke and he wept, too. Regarding her through his tears, he whispered: 'We'll have another baby, you'll see. When you're well again. I promise, Jenny. I promise.'

· · · · *Thirty-seven* · · · ·

Janet Urquhart was surprised at this unexpected visit from her sister. Flora was meticulous about not 'dropping in' on people and she was fortunate to find Janet working at home, surrounded by a pile of first-year assessments from her students.

'It's the old man, I take it,' said Janet.

'Partly,' sighed Flora, putting down her case.

'Not good enough for his son. Like me, I suppose.' After she parted from Andrew, Janet had determined on an academic career. She'd prove to Sir James that not only was she good enough for his son, but a damn sight brighter intellectually. In that she had succeeded but Flora sometimes thought she detected a note of sadness about Janet's life. Although she presented her life as one hectic rush of exciting events, Flora suspected there were many sterile patches. Janet was attractive and had men friends, but there was no longer any hint of a serious suitor.

Waving aside her apologies for turning up on the doorstep and begging a bed, Janet poured out a couple of whiskies.

'Cheers! And don't be sorry. It's been months since the last time you were here. We don't see nearly enough of each other.'

'I thought you'd understand.' Flora paused awkwardly. 'Especially since you've been through it all yourself, as you might say.'

'That's all in the past as far as I'm concerned,' said Janet firmly. 'What was Daddy's ploy this time?'

'Only that I discovered he had suggested the marriage to Andrew. It was his idea!'

'Good Lord. Have we moved up the social scale then?'

'No. But apparently I'm intelligent. I can run the place and have children into the bargain,' she added bitterly.

'What about Andrew?'

'He says he loves me.'

But not enough to stand up to his father, thought Janet. How typical. He hasn't changed much with the years; all things considered, I had a lucky escape. Longing to tell Flora that she was far too good for him, she held her peace.

Janet's flat, a five-minute bus ride from the city centre, was small, compact and had been chosen for its magnificent view. From her window she could see the whole majestic skyline of Edinburgh complete with Castle, Arthur's Seat and Salisbury Crags.

A late diner, Janet had insisted they eat out at her favourite restaurant. The divan in the sitting room served as a comfortable spare bed, but that night sleep seemed impossible for Flora. She had just dozed off at last when the phone rang. Tempted to ignore it, she realised it would wake Janet.

'Flora?' She heard the relief in Andrew's voice as she spoke. 'Thank God you're there. I know it's late, but I had to call.'

'I need time. Time on my own,' she said desperately.

'Flora, you just can't do this – it isn't fair —'

'I'm sorry – I'm sorry —' She put down the phone.

So she really meant it. Andrew could hardly believe that she had walked out on him, without a word. After a frantic day trying to track her down, it suddenly occurred to him that she had most probably gone to Janet's. Fortunately he'd found the address in Flora's desk but the phone had rung unanswered.

Now at least he knew Flora was all right. Worried in case she had met with an accident, he didn't much care for the idea of her weeping on her sister's shoulder. He was uncomfortably aware that Janet would present her with a lot of home truths about himself from the past he would rather have forgotten.

With or without Flora, the business of factoring remained. The next morning, taking the car down to Strathblair for petrol, he met Todd cycling up with the mail. Always first with local news, the postman shook his head sadly.

'Ye'll no have heard, Major. Poor Mrs Ritchie, she's lost the bairn.'

Poor Jenny. But she was young. Years younger than Flora and there were still hazards in child-bearing. His father obviously hadn't taken into account that perhaps it was already too late for Flora to provide those sons and heirs. Not that he cared a damn personally, he just wanted Flora as his wife, his body yearning for her love. He was sick and tired of the subject that had caused so much trouble.

On his way back Andrew almost collided with Alec who was driving fast round the corner. He wound down the window.

'Alec, I've only just heard. I'm so dreadfully sorry.' Alec looked dazed, shocked. 'How's she taken it?'

'Badly.'

'Give her my best.'

'I will, sir. Thank you.' He paused. 'I don't mean to pry. But Mrs McInnes, is it true?'

God, thought Andrew, how quickly news travels here. The bush telegraph has nothing on us in Strathblair. 'I'm afraid so.'

Alec looked at him curiously. 'Does that mean the wedding —?'

Andrew nodded. 'For the time being, yes.'

'What will you do now?'

'God knows. If Flora doesn't come back, everything's going to be – well, I may just leave myself,' he added.

'Meaning what? The Army?'

Andrew shrugged. 'Meaning, if Flora wants me, I'll go with

her. Wherever she wants to settle.' And, letting in the clutch, he waved. 'Be seeing you, Alec.'

'Right, sir.'

In the factor's office, Andrew set to work sorting out the papers which Flora had left. When Sir James looked in, he was able to say: 'It appears that she's left everything in meticulous order. Just as well, since you'll need to be finding yourself a new factor,' he added grimly.

'You could do it.'

'I'm a serving officer in His Majesty's Armed Forces, or have you forgotten?'

'You can get compassionate leave.' Seeing Andrew's angry look, Sir James said smoothly: 'It'll only be for a short time, until Flora returns from Edinburgh.'

Andrew was having difficulty restraining his temper, especially when his father made it sound as if she had merely gone off on holiday instead of being driven away by his damned lack of tact.

'I doubt very much that she will return,' he said shortly.

'Where else will she get as good a job?' Sir James demanded. 'No one else will take on a woman factor.'

'Priorities in order, as usual, Father?' said Andrew, his voice heavy with sarcasm.

Sir James regarded him for a moment, then said slowly: 'You must go and see her, Andrew.'

Andrew sprang from the table and said: 'I'll go when I'm good and ready. And not under orders from you.' As he strode towards the door, Sir James uttered desperately: 'Does this place mean anything to you at all?'

Andrew looked round and shook his head. 'I'm really not sure, Father.'

'You'll be quite happy to see it fall apart? Because that's exactly what will happen if we're not very careful.' And conscious that his son's silence condemned him, he burst out: 'Oh for God's sake! How was I to know the woman would listen to my private conversations?'

'Hardly private, as I recall. There were others present. Besides – arranged marriages – in this day and age? You're behind the times, Father.'

And turning on his heel, Andrew left him. With a sigh, Sir James went round the desk and looking through Flora's address book, he wearily picked up the phone and dialled Janet's number. He had better apologise to Flora, get the silly girl to see reason.

The phone was answered immediately. 'Flora? Sir James here. I —'

But before he could murmur a word of apology or anything else, there was a click and the line went dead.

'Well, really,' he said huffily, 'no one could say I haven't tried to make amends.'

Preparing to leave for the university, Janet heard the phone ring and guessing it had been for Flora, she asked: 'Which one was that?'

'Sir James. I can't bring myself to speak to him. Oh Jan, tell me, am I being a fool?'

'I wouldn't think so. Women are entitled to a bit of dignity.'

Janet had been trying her best to convince Flora that she had done the right thing and that Andrew was weak and would never be able to stand on his own feet where his father was concerned. She knew what she was talking about. She was glad now she had got out while there was still time. And Flora should do the same. If she really wanted to get married again, there were plenty of other eligible men here in Edinburgh.

'Let's be practical. What's your financial situation?' When Flora said it wasn't bad, Janet asked: 'Can you keep yourself till you find another job?'

'Well, I've John's army pension and I've saved a bit. Depends how long I have to look really.' Then, with a despairing gesture, she said: 'But I liked it there.'

In the hall Janet pulled a newspaper out of the door, said firmly: 'Here's *The Scotsman*. Look up the job vacancies. Bye.'

'But I don't know what sort of job . . . Oh well.' And she turned to the vacancies section with very little hope and even less enthusiasm.

The local newspaper was of rather more absorbing interest to Robert Sinclair when his grandfather threw it down on the breakfast table.

'Todd's just brought it. Corriebeg – she's lost the baby.'

Robert felt sorry for Jenny. She'd take it badly.

'They're at Pheemie's,' said Macrae. 'I'll take a wander up to Corriebeg and check the stock.'

'Do you want a hand?'

'I'll manage fine. There's plenty to keep you busy here.'

But not for another ten minutes, Robert thought, watching him go. He always looked through the advertisements in the *Perthshire Advertiser* more out of curiosity than hope that there might be some irresistible high-salaried administrative job in the agricultural line, for which his meagre qualifications would be just right.

But there never was. Skimming idly through the pages, the name 'Macrae' caught his eye. 'In loving memory of Jeannie, died 13 October 1913, beloved wife of Alasdair and mother of Mary deceased. Always remembered.'

His grandmother. He put down the paper. Now he had the answer to the letter addressed to the newspaper he had posted for Macrae a week ago.

And 13 October was today. Robert did his own chores about the place and when his grandfather returned, he was already dressed in his best suit.

'Has something happened?' Macrae sounded anxious.

'No,' said Robert and added casually: 'I read the notice. I'd like to come to the cemetery with you.'

Macrae nodded. 'Then we'd better get going.' He went into the house and boiled a kettle of water. Half an hour later Balbuie came downstairs, much transformed. Not only was he sporting his best suit, but he was wearing an overcoat and a decent hat. The biggest surprise of all was that he had shaved and was rubbing his chin a little self-consciously.

'You're looking smart, Grandfather.'

Macrae regarded Robert's smile suspiciously. Then he noticed the bunch of flowers lying on the table, neatly wrapped.

'The last roses of summer,' said Robert, who had cut them from the bush outside the back door. They were the only flowers at Wester Balbuie.

As they walked out together, Macrae pushed back a tendril of the bush. 'She loved roses. Planted that when she was expecting your mother. It's the only damned thing I've ever got to grow here.'

Thrusting the flowers into Robert's hand, he said: 'Here, you put them on the grave, son.' And with the nearest he ever came to a tender smile, he explained: 'She'd like that.'

Together they walked down the hill without acrimony, in one mind, united by the ghost of a woman who'd been dead for nearly forty years.

The post that day also contained a letter to Flora in Edinburgh. Janet handed it to her.

'From Strathblair.' And, as Flora read it, she asked: 'Which one – man or boy?'

'Good Lord. An apology!'

'From Andrew? And about time!' Then, as Flora shook her head, she exclaimed: 'Not Sir James?'

Flora nodded. 'He says that he wanted the marriage but didn't influence Andrew. In fact Andrew resisted at first – huh! He understands Andrew has a very high regard for me and that was his only reason for proposing. But, best of all – listen to this – he regrets his own stupid, selfish remarks.'

Janet sighed. 'I believe him, thousands wouldn't.'

Flora threw the letter on to the table. She'd never imagined that Sir James was capable of saying he was sorry to anyone. 'Well —'

Janet looked at her, saw that the anger had vanished. Flora was smiling. 'He wants you back?'

And even though Flora gave a non-committal shrug, Janet guessed that she was happy again.

She loved Andrew and she loved Strathblair. All would be well.

· · · · *Thirty-eight* · · · ·

Jenny had been at Carnban for almost a week. Although Pheemie had taken good care of her she both longed and dreaded her return to Corriebeg. She had to face it sometime, put away the matinée jacket she had been knitting when it happened and sort out the drawer upstairs packed full of tiny garments and nappies.

Watching Pheemie ironing, she sighed. 'I almost don't want to go. You and Umberto have spoiled me.'

'You needed a bit of spoiling.'

They exchanged smiles as from outside the window Umberto's voice drifted up singing, in a rich tenor voice: '*La donna è mobile.*'

'I wonder why it wasn't normal. I mean we're both healthy,' said Jenny returning again, as she did so often these days, to the subject uppermost in her mind.

Pheemie went to get another hot iron from the stove. 'I doubt that counts much in these matters. Don't worry, next time it'll be all right. You'll see.'

'Perhaps.' Jenny frowned. 'But I feel so uncertain about things now.'

'Aye. I know how you feel,' said Pheemie sadly.

How could Pheemie know? Jenny looked at her sharply. She was standing very still, the iron poised in her hand, her face lost in sadness.

'I kept all its clothes,' she said softly.

'What?' And then realising what Pheemie was trying to tell her, Jenny whispered: 'When?'

Pheemie resumed her ironing. 'A long time ago.'

Jenny looked at her, trying to take in this new revelation. Had the baby been adopted? 'Where is it?'

'Dead,' Pheemie said bleakly.

'A miscarriage?' Of course, that was why she had understood so well —

Pheemie shook her head. 'No. It was born dead. That is – it lived a few minutes. My fault. I delivered it myself. I was working in the top field when I went into labour.'

'Couldn't you call somebody – surely . . .?'

'No.' Pheemie looked away.

'But —'

'I hadn't told anyone. You see, I wasn't married. My mother was dead, my father – oh, he was an elder in the Kirk. Very strict and narrow.'

'You had a brother.'

'Oh aye. I had a brother.' And Jenny heard the bitterness in her voice. Poor Pheemie. Two men, neither of whom would understand. It was terrible. But a brother —

'Surely he could have helped?'

'He was in Australia by then.' She paused. 'Nine months on.' And the harsh way she spoke as she looked at Jenny left her in no possible doubt of what she was implying.

Her own brother. Oh God, how terrible. 'What happened?'

'I wrapped it in a shawl, buried it out there by the wall, under the two white stones. It's out of the wind there and it catches the sun.'

'I saw those two stones. Oh Pheemie, I'm so sorry.' And stretching out her arms, Jenny held her friend close and they both wept for each other's grief. At last Pheemie said: 'It's me that should be apologising to you. I'd no right to bother you at such a time.'

'Oh, of course you had. Oh, Pheemie, what you must have been through. I'm glad you told me.'

'So am I.' She looked up and sighed. 'There's Alec for you now.' And drying her eyes, Jenny went upstairs for her coat.

Crossing the yard, Alec saw Umberto leaning against the wall. He held a bunch of flowers in his hand, but he was looking slightly dazed, lost in thought, as Alec walked towards him.

'Hello Umberto, how's things?'

Umberto came back with a start. 'Jenny. She's ready for you now.'

There was something strange in his manner, so Alec said anxiously: 'Everything OK, Umberto?'

Umberto's face was white, drawn. He looked sick, but he said: 'Yes, fine. Give her these, huh?'

And thrusting the chrysanthemums into Alec's hand he went up the steps to his bothy and closed the door as Jenny and Pheemie came out of the house.

The two girls hugged each other and Alec said: 'Thanks for having us, Pheemie. You've been great.'

As she got into the sidecar, Jenny looked around. 'Thank Umberto for me too, will you, Pheemie?'

It was strange to be home again, to be rapturously welcomed by Fly. She found herself looking round for the Jenny who had left it a week ago and would never return to that lost dream where babies are safely delivered, full term and healthy. Even her reflection in the mirror seemed different, sadder, older and she felt like a Mrs Rip Van Winkle who had been away for years and years.

Tactfully, Alec had put out of sight all traces of the baby, as if for him, too, it had never existed.

Putting Umberto's flowers into a vase, she went into the little garden she had made. Alec came out and found her staring at it, with Fly sitting at her side, both of them very still.

'I planted bulbs, for the spring,' she said.

They both looked down at the bare earth where deep in the soil the bulbs lay hidden. In the spring, the first green shoots

would appear followed by the golden glory of daffodils, crocuses and tulips.

'They'll look good,' said Alec encouragingly, not knowing
what else to say to comfort her.

'I just thought – flowers. For the baby.' Her voice broke and
then, as Alec put his arm around her, she looked up at him. 'We
will have another one?'

He smiled. 'I promised. Remember?'

They went inside and Jenny insisted on making tea. Pheemie
had given her some scones and oatcakes. But as he ate, Alec
kept remembering Umberto's odd behaviour – the way he had
dashed off without saying goodbye to them.

'Have Umberto and Pheemie been fighting again?'

Jenny stared at him. 'No. It's been all things bright and
beautiful, all the time I've been there. Why do you ask?'

'Oh, I just wondered. It's time those two got married.'

'I wish they would. Pheemie wants it so much but sometimes
I wonder about Umberto.'

After the Ritchies left, Umberto came down from his brothy,
gathered up a bag and a trowel and set off across the potato
field.

'Umberto!'

But he didn't hear Pheemie call him. He went to the wall
with its two white stones. There he dug some holes and taking
the bulbs from his bag, planted them carefully, patting the earth
gently back into place.

Pheemie was standing by the gate. As he straightened up,
regarding the tiny grave, he crossed himself and she realised
that someone else shared her secret. Umberto, working by the
open window must have overheard her talking to Jenny.

Now he came towards her and when he put his arm around
her, hugged her to his side, she saw tears in his eyes.

Silently they walked back together to the house.

November 1950

· · · · *Thirty-nine* · · · ·

As the ragged funereal shapes of rooks circling the stubble fields screeched a requiem for a dying year, the weather came out in sympathy with Jenny's dismal thoughts. The glory of autumn had vanished leaving Corriebeg a monotone of browns. Brown earth, brown fields, brown mud as the rain fell more persistently and lasted longer, finding a sad echo in the damp, drizzling November in Jenny's heart.

She regarded the coming months with apprehension. Working outside was much harder; she already had chilblains on her hands and feet. The onset of winter made its presence felt inside, too, making a warm bed on a dark morning particularly seductive – especially with nothing to look forward to but chopping up turnips for the winter feed. Gruelling monotonous work, which gave her plenty of time to go over endlessly the possible reasons why she and Alec, a healthy strong couple, could have produced an abnormal foetus.

On the hills the snowline crept steadily downwards, each day nearer Corriebeg. As a little girl she had loved and eagerly awaited the first snowfall, sitting in a warm room watching the huge flakes falling in the garden, longing to get her sledge out. Now she preferred to see it restricted to Christmas cards. For this snow wasn't gentle or romantic, it had joined forces with her enemy, the harsh bitter land that had robbed her of her baby. She knew this wasn't logical or true, but she needed something to blame for her cruel loss.

Seeing her so desolate tore at Alec's heart. Slicing turnips manually was a back-breaking task, but she never complained and in a way he would have been glad if she had turned upon him angrily, rebelliously. This mute acceptance was so out of character, the spark and fire that was his Jenny seemed to have been quenched for ever.

Often as he went out on the hill with Fly in the morning she was already at work, and when he returned, she was in exactly the same position as if she had turned into some kind of automaton, working the handle of the slicing knife, up and down, up and down. When he spoke to her, she looked up unsmiling, her gaze distant, as if her broken spirit had fled her weary body.

Once when he asked cheerfully: 'How are you getting on?' she replied: 'At this rate, I shall be slicing turnips for the rest of my life.' And when he suggested going to Carnban to see if there was an electric slicer they could borrow, she merely shrugged as if it would make little difference. She was beyond enthusiasm.

Pheemie couldn't help, her own machine was in constant use and she advised him to try the factor. As he expected, Mrs McInnes' office was closed.

While he was peering through the window, Andrew drove up. When Alec asked about hiring an electric turnip slicer, he said: 'Yes, of course. But I haven't the faintest idea where they'll be. That's really Flora's department, not mine.'

Alec looked at him curiously. 'Any word about Mrs McInnes?'

'No,' said Andrew quickly. With a rapid change of subject, he advised Alec to try the home farm.

'What's the hire charge?'

'I haven't the foggiest.' Walking in the direction of the house, he called out: 'Ask Pheemie Robertson.'

Alec stared after him. The major was remarkably uncommunicative today, no doubt he was worried that Flora had not returned.

Someone else, however, had returned to Strathblair House and Andrew was on his way to welcome his mother after an absence of many years.

'Indecent bitch,' was how Macrae described the re-appearance of the laird's ex-wife.

Her arrival off the Edinburgh train that morning with a load of expensive luggage had set a quiver of delighted anticipation through Strathblair.

Emerging from the Atholl Arms to be met by Sir James's car, she was obviously expected. They were intrigued. This was no repentant return of the prodigal wife. Considerable restraint was being exercised by shopkeepers and local residents. Those who remembered her tried not to come out and rudely gape. The Forbes had a ring-side seat, so to speak, as they stood at their shop door in the High Street talking to Macrae and Robert who had emerged from the bank.

Mrs Forbes looked at the elegant slim woman, with her high heels and silk stockings, and her expensive fur-trimmed coat.

'Just fancy, she must be past sixty. I wonder how she keeps so young looking. Especially after the kind of life she's led,' she added a little enviously, as if Lady Menzies' lapse from virtue should have left a permanent record on her face.

'Fancy the laird sending his car to pick her up.' When Macrae said she'd be after his money, Mrs Forbes, who had a keen ear for village gossip, said: 'No – no, her second husband left her well-off. He was some kind of a millionaire —'

'Then what does she want back here?' Macrae demanded.

'Maybe she's spent all her money. Why don't you lend her some of yours, Balbuie?' Forbes asked slyly and Macrae hastily pushed his wallet deeper into his pocket, as if it might be in some danger.

'Is she staying at Strathblair House?'

'Oh no, that wouldn't be proper,' said Mrs Forbes primly. 'She's booked in to the Atholl Arms.'

As their eyes followed the departing car, each one of the watchers would have given much to be a fly on the wall when Sir James met his estranged wife for the first time in over thirty years.

Their curiosity would have been richly rewarded.

Sir James watched her arrival from the sitting-room window.

At first glance the woman stepping out of the car was a stranger. She had changed, of course, and he was glad of that. There was little he could recognise of the Constance he had loved, or the self-portrait in Andrew's workroom.

He heard her voice in the hall greeting Mrs Mckenzie, recognised her familiar laugh. He braced himself for her entrance into his life again.

As she walked towards him, his first impression was of a still-lovely woman, but as she came closer he saw that what had once been natural was now reinforced by careful cosmetics. Eyes that had been tender were now narrowed and calculating; lips that had been dew-soft had thinned; the mouth tightened and finely lined. He realised he was looking at a brittle mask, a travesty of his Constance, who had died long ago.

She smiled as if sensing his discomfort. 'Shall we exchange platitudes, James?'

'How are you, Constance?' he said stiffly.

'Remarkably well. And you?'

'As well as can be expected.'

He had changed, too, she thought, time had blurred the fine features, his body had thickened with age but the clipped voice, so often raised in anger or frustration against her, was exactly as she remembered it. She was glad she had left him when she did. Had she sacrificed her new lover, Lt.-Col. Brad Hallenburg who had changed her feelings for James into indifference, had she stayed for their son's sake, she would have ended up hating him.

She had not been relishing this meeting and was pleased that James aroused even less emotion in her than she would have felt for an old acquaintance renewed at a cocktail party.

She smiled. 'Well, that's the easy part over. It was kind of you to send the car.'

'It was the least I could do,' he said, his voice cold, his manner correct. 'Are you comfortable at the hotel?'

'I expect I will be. It's amusing.' But she doubted whether

James would appreciate the joke. 'Mrs Hallenburg II' was how she signed the register, but to Strathblair who knew her when the Dowager Lady Menzies, James's mother, was still alive, she would always be 'Lady Constance'.

'You are welcome to stay here,' he said in the most unwelcoming voice she had ever heard.

She had been invited by his son for the wedding, the tradition which demanded both parents being present winning out over his own distaste, his most earnest wishes, that he never had to set eyes on her again.

'Would staying here be – appropriate?' she asked mockingly.

'I was suggesting that we sleep under the same roof, not the same ceiling,' he said coldly.

'That's a subtlety I fear might be lost on the locals. I imagine they already have their own views about the decadence of the upper classes,' she retorted.

'I doubt if they think about it very much. The society columns are not required reading in Strathblair.'

'But they did enjoy our scandal.'

Sir James's eyebrows shot up. 'That was all a long time ago. But the older ones remember your, er —'

'Transgression? Misconduct? Betrayal?' Constance was enjoying herself.

'Departure,' said Sir James acidly and rang for tea.

Pheemie heard it from Todd – first with the news as usual. A stern believer in passing on gossip while it was still fresh, she cycled up to Corriebeg.

'The major's mother?' said Jenny.

'The very same. She took up with this American officer during the First World War. I was only a wee lassie, but it was a fair scandal, so it was.'

'I can imagine,' said Jenny, handing her a mug of tea.

'Andrew was a wee lad at the time. The two of them were carrying on for months before Sir James found out.'

'Well, that was a long time ago.'

'Aye, but folk about here have long memories. I expect she's come for the wedding. If that's still going ahead.'

Jenny heard the sound of Alec's motorbike and, looking out of the window, she said: 'Oh, at last! He's got the electric slicer.'

'It'll make all the difference,' said Pheemie. 'I don't know how you've managed doing it by hand. Ah well, time I got on my way.'

'Write down that recipe for clootie dumpling, first, will you? I think I got it wrong somewhere.' Jenny's mind wasn't on food these days, or cooking either, when she came in dazed with tiredness.

Five minutes later waving Pheemie off, Jenny went over to Alec who was tinkering at the slicer with a screwdriver.

'How's it going?'

'The damn thing's bust,' was the furious reply. 'I think it's an electrical connection.'

'Can you fix it?'

'I'm trying my best.'

'Alec —' She put a hand on his shoulder. 'Alec, I'm sorry I've been such an old misery.'

'You haven't.'

'Yes, I have. And you've been very sweet about it. Tell you what. I'll take you to the pictures next week.'

'All right,' said Alec enthusiastically. It was great to see her smiling again. As they kissed he felt that maybe something of the old Jenny hadn't been lost for ever, after all.

Pheemie didn't go directly home after leaving Corriebeg. There were other neighbours who might not have heard the news.

As she passed Wester Balbuie, she saw Macrae making his way up the hill with his two dogs. Head down into the biting wind, he was moving slower than usual. She hailed him, but he didn't seem to hear her.

Och well, he probably knew already.

Having had a couple of good long gossips on the subject of Lady Constance, when she finally arrived home, she was met by a furious Umberto and found she had missed an unwelcome visitor.

He had been working in the yard when Sergeant Brodie wheeled his bicycle in and asked to see his work permit. When Umberto said he had been working at Carnban since 1943, Brodie had said grimly: 'So I'm told. Without a work permit. In contravention of the Aliens Order of 1920.' And letting that sink in, he added: 'And you haven't been registering at the police station.'

'Who told him, Pheemie?' Umberto demanded angrily. 'Who told on me? I would like to know.'

Trying to placate him, Pheemie said: 'Nobody around here would report you to the police.'

'Then how did he know?' Umberto persisted.

'Oh, he probably came across some old regulation and decided to be officious.' And she continued, explaining that Brodie was already getting a reputation for this kind of thing, for nit-picking and laying down the very letter of the law.

In his predecessor's time, life in Strathblair was rather more relaxed and the Atholl Arms took little heed of the licensing laws, closing when the customers finished drinking. These halcyon days were now replaced by the strict enforcement of 'Time, gentlemen, please' on the stroke of nine, when Sergeant Brodie was standing there ready to blow his whistle. Such behaviour was bitterly resented by the farmers and did nothing for the young policeman's popularity.

'Somebody told him about me,' said Umberto firmly.

'And I suppose you know who?'

'Could be lots of folk. They're jealous of me because I make money. That's why they want me deported.'

'Who are "they"? Come on, tell me.'

'Could be – could be Wallace. I always know how much to bid

at his auctions. Or it could be Forbes, because —'

'Because what —'

'Because he never liked me.'

'Och, away with ye. Next ye'll be saying it could be Alec Ritchie.'

'And so it could. We had that fight, remember? And all the others were on his side. Of course, in the pub in front of my face, they are all nice. But behind my back it's different.'

'Oh, don't be so daft, Umberto.'

'And what about the sheep stealing. Remember who was the first to be accused? Me!' He turned and started to stamp out.

'Where are you going now? Umberto!'

'I'm going to see if Alec has finished with the tractor.'

Pheemie sighed. There was no dealing with him in this kind of mood. However, if Sergeant Brodie was serious then she'd have to see what she could do.

She couldn't lose Umberto. It was unthinkable that he could be sent back to Italy. She'd do anything to stop that. Anything short of murder, she thought desperately.

Alec was still trying to fix the slicer when Umberto arrived. He wanted to keep the tractor until Monday, and once Umberto had agreed, he asked: 'Know anything about electric motors?'

'A little bit.' Umberto smiled modestly. He was a wizard with machines and hardly one existed in Strathblair that he couldn't mend, take to pieces and put together again. A quick worker, he had earned a reputation for producing first-class results for which busy farmers and tradesmen were willing to pay well.

Five minutes later the slicer was churning away happily.

Alec was lost in admiration. 'You've got the magic touch, Umberto. You're a handy man to have around.'

'I won't be around much longer. Someone told the policeman I hadn't a work permit.'

When Alec repeated the story of Umberto's dilemma to Jenny, she was horrified. 'He surely doesn't think it was you who reported him, does he?'

'Maybe he did at first. But not now. He's feeling pretty hurt though.' Fixing the plug into the kitchen socket, he switched on the slicer. 'Here goes.'

And it did – an almighty spark as the fuse blew!

'Damn.'

As he got to work repairing it once more, Jenny said: 'I wonder how Pheemie will take this, about Umberto, I mean. I can't see her letting him go without a struggle.'

At that moment, round one of Pheemie's struggle was taking place. She had decided to start at the top with the laird. Besides she wanted a valid excuse to visit Strathblair House, as she was determined to satisfy her curiosity with a glimpse of Lady Constance.

Sir James didn't keep her waiting. He saw her straight away in his sitting room and was very understanding about Umberto's problem. Although he told her it was outside his experience, he promised he'd do what he could.

As he showed her to the door, the hall was disappointingly empty. There was no sign of the prodigal wife, but as Pheemie cycled back up the road, she saw a car very like that of Mrs McInnes entering the estate road.

· · · · *Forty* · · · ·

Constance was sure of one wholehearted welcome in Strathblair: Andrew was delighted to see her.

As he kissed her fondly, Sir James, watching them cynically, saw that their son had inherited his mother's good looks. Unfortunately the genes hadn't included a stronger dash of her positive character.

'And where's the lovely Flora?' she asked.

'I'm sorry, Mother, it rather looks as if your journey was unnecessary.'

Andrew proceeded to relate the events that had led to Flora's abrupt departure while Sir James shuffled his feet uncomfortably.

'A complete misunderstanding, of course,' he said.

Constance looked hard at Sir James. 'Yes, I think I understand the situation. Your father has displayed his usual admirable tact,' she said sarcastically.

'I hardly think —' Sir James protested.

'I hardly think she would appreciate being thought of as a brood mare,' Constance interrupted sharply.

'I didn't realise she was listening —'

Turning her back on him, she said to Andrew: 'Why don't you just go through to Edinburgh and sweep the woman off her feet.'

'I've telephoned her several times.'

'Not quite the same thing, my dear.'

'No. Well, I have my pride, too.'

His mother sighed. 'And I seem to have crossed the Atlantic for nothing.'

'Oh come along, Constance, you've been making regular trips to London ever since the war ended,' Sir James put in irritably.

She smiled. 'You're well-informed.' But what he didn't know was that she and Andrew had met on quite a few occasions.

'I do take the daily papers,' said Sir James stiffly.

'So someone in Strathblair reads the gossip columns,' Constance beamed.

As Andrew prepared to drive her back to Strathblair, she said: 'If a stiff neck is all that you've inherited from your father, you're lucky.'

Andrew smiled. 'Oh – and a stiff upper lip, too.'

In answer Constance laid her fingertips against his mouth. 'Then let it relax a little. Don't tell Flora you're sorry. Show her.'

Still mulling over her advice, Andrew drove back to the factor's office. He'd better get down to work. There were still a lot of things to sort out, questions to which only Flora seemed to know the answers.

His heart leapt. Her car was outside.

She'd come back.

He opened the door and there she was, sitting at her desk looking through papers, just as if she had never been away. She hardly glanced up as he came in.

'You're back,' he said.

'Obviously.' She frowned, flicking through a file with an expression of annoyance.

'Father will be pleased,' he said.

She darted an angry look at him. 'And that's the main thing, isn't it?'

He realised too late that he had said the wrong thing and suddenly at a loss for words, he gestured towards the desk. 'I've, er, been doing what I can to keep things going.'

'So I see.' Her grim look indicated that he hadn't done that very well either.

Be casual, thought Andrew, and with a businesslike change of subject, he told her about Alec Ritchie's request for an electric turnip slicer and that he didn't know the hiring charge.

'I'll attend to it.'

'Right.' And, studying her unsmiling face, he asked: 'So, you're back for good, then?'

In answer she turned her back on him, pulled out another file from the cabinet. 'I suppose so.'

'I'm glad you changed your mind.'

She swung round to face him, flushed and angry. 'Your father did the changing, Andrew. In fact he was quite insistent about my duties and obligations. So – I'm back. As factor.' She paused to let the words sink in. 'Nothing more.'

Andrew looked at her helplessly. He loved her so much. 'Flora, I'm sorry.' The words sounded like a feeble bleat, totally inadequate to express all he felt at that moment.

'Don't say it, Andrew. Just don't say it.' Her voice broke, and for a second he thought she was going to cry.

'All right. I won't.' Seizing her roughly, he pulled her to him and kissed her. At first he thought she was going to resist, but then with a sigh and a moan, she relaxed and put her arms around his neck. After what seemed a long time, he released her.

'I know it was a deeply insensitive thing to say, but I didn't say it. My father did.'

She smiled at him. 'True.'

'And it's not my father you're marrying.'

'Also true. But I'm quite looking forward to meeting the woman who did,' she said.

'She doesn't eat lunch. Bad for her figure, she says. But she'll be with us for dinner. Now where were we?'

Flora smiled and with considerable zest and enthusiasm she started to kiss him again. This reconciliation seemed ripe for a lot more than mere kisses, but it was hardly opportune. There wasn't even a sofa in sight and delicacy forbade that he begin undressing her on her office floor. What if his father came in? Or one of the farmers? Such thoughts were enough to cool his ardour. But judging from Flora's response, neither of them would last out a long engagement.

What was lunch in Strathblair House was dinner for the laird's tenants and in Wester Balbuie, at two o'clock, Robert threw away the contents of the stew pan which had burnt to a cinder.

His grandfather was never late. He came in promptly at twelve-fifteen every day and gave Robert hell if his dinner wasn't all ready and waiting for him on the table.

Robert liked to eat and took a pride in cooking. He was becoming quite an expert and Macrae was glad to be relieved of this side of domesticity. He ate to live, he didn't live to eat, was his proud boast, allowing himself to be persuaded to second helpings.

At first angry as the meal had been ruined, by two-thirty Robert was becoming increasingly anxious about his grandfather's non-appearance. Going back and forth to the window, he saw that the drizzle which had threatened all morning had turned into a steady downpour. The tops of the hills with their snow coverings had disappeared in thick mist which was rapidly closing in.

An hour later, he put on his outdoor clothes and set off in search of Macrae. Halfway up the field he looked back. The farm, already shrouded in mist, was hardly visible. If there was some innocent reason that his grandfather had been delayed, such as a sheep in distress, and he came home hungry, to find no Robert and no food, there would be ructions.

As he began the ascent into the foothills, the rain had turned to sleet driving painfully into his face. Even at his fast pace, he felt half-frozen. As he climbed, the silence became all-embracing and terrible, as if the whole world had died out here on this shrouded hillside.

Soon there was nothing but desolation and a feeling of emptiness as if this land had never known the tread of a man's foot, nor the sound of a human voice.

All he could see through the mist from the high corries were steep slopes of slipping scree, gullies filled with water running deep and fast, and here and there a skein of rocky outcrop breaking loose from the hillside like bare bones.

Occasionally he stopped and shouted: 'Hello? Hello?' His call only seemed to arouse the bleating of a frightened ewe or the raucous cry of hoodie crow.

Higher and higher he climbed. What had happened to the old fool? Then he remembered that the old man hadn't been feeling very well lately, complaining about being out of breath. Sometimes when he came in, he looked exhausted, a bad colour. As Robert stopped to shout again, he wished he hadn't remembered that.

He began to panic. Something must have happened to him.

He listened. What was that?

A dog barking.

Tam perhaps? Heartened he began to run down the slope. There was a large boulder, with two dogs crouched next to it, whining. And behind the boulder, Robert would never have seen Macrae if it hadn't been for the dogs shivering beside his body.

He knelt down beside him. Ashen-faced, unmoving, his lips were blue. Convinced that he was dead, Robert cursed himself for arriving too late to save him. Then he detected the flutter of eyelids, signs of life, faint but unmistakable.

Guessing that he had suffered a heart attack, Robert looked round helplessly. He had no idea what to do but knew that somehow he must get his grandfather back to the farm. God knows what damage it would do, hoisting him on to his back, but that was the only quick way. He couldn't risk leaving him here getting steadily colder while he raised the alarm at neighbouring farms.

Robert was surprised to find that Macrae was lighter than he had imagined, with an old man's thin bones. He could carry him easily across his strong young shoulders; nevertheless he was thankful that it was downhill all the way.

At last he got him into the house and carried him upstairs to his bed. Phoning the surgery, the nurse told him to keep him warm until Dr McGowan arrived.

Removing his boots, Robert leant over him. He was still alive but only just.

He thought the doctor would never come as he sat by the bedside, blankets piled on the bed, a hot water-bottle at his grandfather's icy cold feet. He wished he knew how to pray, because chafing those gnarled old hands, he knew that he wanted his grandfather to live. He could hardly believe that all the hatred and anger of a few weeks ago had vanished. Lately he felt they had made their first faltering steps towards a deeper understanding, to healing the hurt that had warped Macrae's years with bitterness.

True, they would always spark at each other and have blazing rows, but in spite of these surface ripples, the bond of kinship was steadily growing. Robert no longer wished his grandfather would die so that he'd inherit Wester Balbuie. Some day he hoped it would be his, but not yet. He still had a lot to learn about farming and no one was a better teacher than Macrae.

At last the doctor arrived and Robert stood by as he carefully examined the old man.

'Well, it was a mild heart attack, but bad enough. I think he should go into hospital for a few days.'

Macrae, who had recovered consciousness during the doctor's examination, murmured: 'I'm going into no hospital.'

'Don't be daft, man. It's only for observation.'

'I'm going into no hospital.' And added in a voice growing steadily firmer and more obstinately like himself: 'I have a farm to run!'

'You won't be running it much longer if you get another of these attacks.'

'I can look after him,' Robert put in.

'He needs proper nursing.'

'He can look after me,' said Macrae with a look of near gratitude in his grandson's direction.

Dr McGowan sighed. 'Preserve me from thrawn old devils, like you, Balbuie. All right, you're to stay in bed for the next few days.' And turning to Robert, he scribbled out a prescription. 'You have this made up at the chemist's. And see that he takes it.'

After seeing the doctor out, Robert ran back upstairs and began tucking the clothes round his grandfather.

'Away with ye,' he grumbled. 'You're no going to take all that nonsense about nursing me seriously. Doctors aye talk a load of rubbish, try to frighten folk, just to make themselves important.'

That wasn't at all the impression Robert had been given by

McGowan. 'In that case, Grandfather, what will you be wanting for your supper?'

'Anything you can scratch together as usual. I suppose you ate all the stew yourself.'

Robert set his lips firmly together against the response that unworthy remark deserved. 'Aye, Grandfather, I fair enjoyed it trailing after you in the hills.'

Macrae grunted. 'A bit of bread and cheese will do me fine. I'm not all that hungry.'

When Robert came back upstairs later with another mug of tea, the tray was empty and his grandfather was sitting up in bed, the defiant look he gave Robert daring him to comment. It was effective; Robert knew any protest would be a mere waste of breath.

'Do you want anything else before I turn in?'

'Nothing. Oh, there's one thing. You can look out my good suit and a clean shirt. I'll need them for the morning.'

'And where do you think you're going?'

'The kirk, of course,' Macrae said sharply.

'The doctor said you were to stay in bed for a few days, remember —'

'I have never missed a Remembrance Day yet and I'm not missing tomorrow's.'

In answer Robert shook his head sadly. If his grandfather took a heart attack in church, then he refused to be held responsible. Anyway, come to think of it, the kirk was not a bad place for the thrawn old devil's last stand!

As he looked out one of the seldom-worn white shirts that smelt strongly of mothballs, Robert guessed that there'd be a lot of folk in the kirk that Sunday, not out of piety but out of curiosity. The whole village would be eager to see if Lady Constance would have the brass neck to sit beside her son and her ex-husband in the Menzies family pew, visible to the entire congregation below the pulpit and in direct line of fire for the minister's sermon.

Flora had just been introduced to her future mother-in-law, who wasted no time on preliminaries. Andrew listened anxiously. He didn't like the way Flora was being subjected to a barrage of rapid-fire questions, ranging from how old she was, who her parents were and where she went to school.

At one stage Sir James interrupted to remind Constance that Flora's father, Dr Urquhart, had brought Andrew into the world.

'Oh, him,' she said dismissively. 'Of course I remember.' She had been furious that she had had Andrew at home, instead of in the fashionable London clinic. However, her determination to go riding against Dr Urquhart's advice, had brought Andrew's birth forward by three weeks, much to her chagrin.

'He was a very good doctor, my dear,' said Sir James and with a smile at Flora. 'We all miss him.'

Andrew sighed. His father was on their side for once. Looking at Flora's rather stony expression, he had an uneasy suspicion that his mother's questions were not having quite the right effect. They indicated that the lady of the manor was interviewing a prospective servant, rather than chatting pleasantly to her future daughter-in-law.

'Where are you planning to get married?'

'Strathblair, of course,' said Flora.

'Oh yes, of course. Tradition. It would be expected, wouldn't it?'

'Actually, Mother, expected or not, that's how we want it,' said Andrew with a smile in Flora's direction.

'Did you discard tradition when you became an American citizen?' Sir James asked her.

'Heavens no. It's a great social cachet in the States. Nothing impresses them more than an English accent and some connection, however tenuous, with impoverished aristocracy.'

This remark revived unpleasant memories of Donald Telfer for Sir James. 'This chap Andrew's gone into business with. He's an American.' Obviously a text-book example, too, he thought.

'Try not to sound so disapproving, James. They are the same species, you know.'

'Indeed? He appears to think that Scotland is up for sale.'

'If anyone wants to buy it, take the money and run,' was her candid reply.

'That's a bit strong, Mother.'

Constance made an expansive gesture which took in all their surroundings, the antiques, the ancestral portraits. She gave them a scathing glance. 'It's finished, Andrew. Britain is finished. The glory days are over now. Your choice now lies between Moscow and Washington. And I don't think Washington will let you choose Moscow.'

'Perhaps we have a different perspective on this side of the Atlantic,' said Sir James.

'I doubt it. What are you trying to hold on to with this estate anyway?'

'I suppose you'd laugh if I said, "Tradition",' he replied.

Constance considered him. 'I think I'd feel a twinge of pity. By the end of this century, who do you think will be the laird of Strathblair?'

'One of Andrew's sons, I would hope.'

Andrew's helpless look in Flora's direction apologised, but her smile told him she didn't mind.

Constance shook her head. 'Or someone who can afford the indulgence of a Highland estate and a forelock-tugging peasantry.'

This was too much for Flora who had stayed out of the argument so far. 'The people in this district don't tug forelocks,' she reminded her.

'And it may surprise you to learn that I do not regard them as peasants,' said their laird.

'Oh, don't be so touchy, James. Peasants are simply people who work the land. How do they regard you?'

'With some respect, I should imagine.'

'As one of themselves?' she asked in a voice heavy with

sarcasm. 'Heaven preserve me from the scions of splendid old Highland families, educated at the best English public schools, members of the most exclusive London clubs.' Sir James winced as she added sweetly: 'James, you don't even sound like your – your —'

'Tenants,' Flora provided.

Constance turned and looked at her, severely and without affection. Flora met her gaze and for a moment the two women stared at each other, neither, it has to be said, with much enthusiasm.

The door opened and Mrs Mckenzie announced: 'Dinner is served.'

'Saved by the bell,' Andrew muttered taking Flora's arm.

As they shared a nightcap together later that evening, he said: 'You didn't exactly hit it off with her, did you? She was only trying to needle my father, you know.'

'It doesn't matter. It's not your mother I'm marrying either.' And she went into his arms happily, waiting to be kissed.

· · · · *Forty-one* · · · ·

Remembrance Sunday dawned with a pale sunshine filtering through menacing clouds, Wagnerian enough to remind mortals that the war-gods hadn't finished with them yet.

The church bells rang and Strathblair turned out wearing its poppies and medals to honour the dead of two world wars, but there were uneasy thoughts in the minds of those who had listened to the news on the wireless that their sons and husbands might soon be marching off to another conflagration not of Scotland's making.

Things were not going well in Korea, the 'insurrection' the generals had imagined could be speedily quelled using the strategy of two wars in Europe, had proved disastrous. Two weeks earlier the United Nations' troops had pushed through to the Chinese border and a nervous President Truman, threatened by the 'yellow peril', had reined in General MacArthur advising a more cautious policy where the might of China was involved.

And as conflicts bred yet more conflicts, King Farouk of Egypt had decided to assert himself and was demanding that the United Kingdom quit the Suez Canal.

Remembrance Day sermons throughout the land must have involved ministers in many busy searchings through the Scriptures for interesting and noteworthy parables and parallels.

A procession led by veterans and local dignitaries marched towards the church. Gathered to watch this impressive parade of war medals were the Ritchies, the Forbes and Macrae who had risen from his sick bed. He made light of it but agreed with Robert, for once, that he'd accept the lift Robert had arranged with Munro of Dalscriadan.

Pheemie arrived in her Sunday best, alone and looking flustered. Where was Umberto?

When Alec related the story of Sergeant Brodie's visit to Carnban, everyone was on Umberto's side with murmurs about that young Brodie getting too big for his boots.

'Aye,' said Macrae, 'put some folk in a uniform and they think they're Hitler.'

Pheemie was angry. Having expected Umberto to accompany her as usual to the Remembrance Day service, he appeared in his working clothes and announced that he wasn't going.

'Oh stop sulking, will you?'

'I'm not going, Pheemie,' he repeated firmly.

'You always go to the memorial.'

'This time I'm not going. If they don't want me, I don't want them.'

'Ah, you big bairn,' said Pheemie furiously. 'I told you that Sir James promised to do what he could.' She hesitated and then added casually: 'He happened to mention, just in passing, that you couldn't be sent back if —'

'If what?' Umberto interrupted eagerly, his face suddenly hopeful, ready to grasp at straws, however frail.

Pheemie shrugged. 'He said if you were married to a British citizen that could make a difference.'

Umberto gave her a bewildered look. 'But I'm not, Pheemie.'

'I ken that! But ye could be!'

He shook his head. 'I don't see how.'

That final insult was too much for Pheemie who thought she had delivered her little speech with great care and tact. She had expected – oh God, what had she expected? Certainly not this daft response.

'You big stirk!' she yelled at him. 'If you think I'm going to get down on one knee in the cow muck, you can think again!' And she stamped off down the road, unmoved by his astonished face at this strange outburst.

The church was more crowded than usual, not entirely from motives of piety, or patriotism, but rather from vulgar curiosity. All of Strathblair it seemed had turned out to see if the wicked Lady Constance would accompany her family that morning.

A great stir rippled through the congregation as she appeared in the doorway at Sir James's side and walked right down to the front pew running the gauntlet of curious eyes and whispered speculations.

The laird and his ex-wife were followed by Andrew and his fiancée, Flora McInnes. This was the first public appearance of the newly engaged couple, but all interest was focused on Lady Constance. Female heads were craned to see not only what she was wearing but, more importantly, how she had worn.

'It's a wonder the roof doesn't fall in,' muttered Macrae disgustedly.

A hymn, two minutes' silence, then an agreeably short and well-chosen sermon whose theme was love one another, which ended:

'. . . And so we are met here on this day which is set aside to the memory of the men and women of this parish who gave their lives in the two great conflicts that the generations present have endured. Already the guns are thundering in a land far distant from the peace and serenity of our Strathblair hills: again our young are being called upon to take up arms . . .'

The door opened and Umberto walked in, wearing his best suit and a battered Italian uniform forage cap. He crossed himself and took his place in a rear pew, behind Sergeant Brodie, in time for the last hymn, 'O God, our help in ages past' and the benediction.

Umberto last in was first out and defiantly donning his army cap again, he hurried through the kirkyard.

Alec followed him, seized his arm. 'Umberto – come on,' he said indicating a smiling group of folk Umberto knew, no longer his enemies but comrades who accepted him as a citizen of Strathblair. 'Come on.'

There was a moment's hesitation then he went back with Alec to where hands were eager to grasp his own. Macrae, Robert, Wallace, Munro . . . familiar faces, friendly, smiling faces.

Shaking hands with the minister, Sir James saw Sergeant Brodie grimly watching this little scene of camaraderie.

'If I could have a private word with you, Sergeant,' he said.

The film Jenny had promised Alec was *Passport to Pimlico*, a rollicking comedy. Alec was looking forward to it, especially as Jenny had really made an effort during the last few days. Occasionally catching a brief glimpse of the pretty happy young wife he had lost, he had hopes that someday she would be wholly restored to him as if these past weeks of suffering had never happened.

As they came out of the house together, Alec decided to check the turnip slicer. It had been behaving very well, so far. As he went over, Jenny shouted:

'Alec, you'll get your jacket all dirty. Come on, or we'll miss the start.'

Inside the village hall Jenny waved to the Forbes and to Andrew and Flora who were sitting behind them. Standing up she looked round the audience. As the lights dimmed, she whispered: 'Pheemie's not here. She said she was coming.'

'She's probably just late. Like we nearly were.'

The film started, so they sat back to enjoy what promised to be a rare treat with plenty of laughs. Any tears of mirth, however, were replaced by sombre faces as, the film over, fact took the place of fantasy – grim facts in the Pathe News with the latest newsreel from the Korean war front. Straight from the battlezone it showed the guns in action, bombs dropping, the devastation as stretcher bearers carried away the dead and wounded.

Flora felt Andrew move at her side and turning, saw him heading for the exit. She rushed out and found him leaning against the doorway. Her first thought was that he had been taken ill suddenly for he had been laughing with all the rest a few minutes earlier.

'Andrew. What's wrong?' She saw the cigarette trembling in his hand as he stared ahead.

'It's all going to happen again,' he said dully. 'I know it's all going to happen again.'

He walked swiftly to his parked car. Before he switched on the engine he handed her an envelope from the War Office. There was no doubt of what it contained.

'When?' she whispered.

'I report to Edinburgh on Monday. A couple of weeks to get into shape and then Korea.' Turning he gave her a searching look. 'So, what does that do to our future?'

'Oh God, Andrew —'

From inside the hall, she heard the sounds of the National Anthem. The show was over. When, she wondered, would she and Andrew ever enjoy a light-hearted film at the village hall again?

As Andrew reversed the car, Flora watched Alec and Jenny come out, arm in arm laughing. Envying their closeness, their happiness unthreatened, she was glad Alec was making such a success of Corriebeg. Since he was unlikely to be called up, their lives would not be devastated by Britain's eagerness to join the American warlords in yet another conflict. Thank goodness everything was going well for one young couple at least.

As they walked towards the motorbike, Alec said: 'We must do that more often.'

'Yes, we will,' Jenny frowned. 'I wonder what happened to Pheemie?'

'Maybe she got a better offer,' Alec grinned. 'She missed a good laugh. I really enjoyed that.'

'Me too. It's been a great night out.'

It was a night that Alec and Jenny would never forget. And it had only just begun.

What had happened at Carnban that night was a greater drama than the film Pheemie had missed. It had begun when she went up to the bothy to see if Umberto would accompany her.

'It'll cheer you up,' she said. He was obviously worried. Sergeant Brodie's threat still hung over him and up to now there had been no word from Sir James.

'I don't want to come.'

She didn't want to go on her own knowing she wouldn't enjoy the film as she would feel guilty about leaving him in such a miserable state.

'I'm not all that keen. I don't think I'll bother either. Especially if you have any of that Spaghetti Carbonara left,' she added with a grin.

At least the food was a success, which was more than could be said for her attempts to jolly Umberto along. At last, looking at his glum countenance, she said: 'Oh Umberto, for heaven's sake. Look, if the worst comes to the worst, at least you'll be seeing your family again.'

'No I won't.' Turning, he looked at her. 'They're dead. They're all dead, Pheemie,' he repeated.

'But your children?'

'All dead.' Umberto seemed to be having trouble breathing. 'Major Walter Reder, an Austrian. One day he came to the village, massacred more than a thousand people, mostly women and children, in retaliation for attacks on German soldiers by the resistance fighters. My brother was a partisan. The SS captured him. Under torture, he betrayed our family.'

Pheemie couldn't believe it, couldn't take it in. And yet it made sense of all the gaps she had tried to fill, the enigma of Umberto Fabiani. 'Why did you never tell me?'

Umberto's eyes were tear-filled. 'I never want to think about it. I just – pretend – that it had never happened.'

'These photographs are all I have left. So, you see, Pheemie, there is no one to go back to.'

He broke down, wept and taking him into her arms, Pheemie wept with him.

Hours later when she was deeply asleep, Umberto awakened her. Something about a fire. She thought it was part of a bad dream, but he was standing over her, shaking her.

'Pheemie! Corriebeg – it's on fire!'

· · · · *Forty-two* · · · ·

By the time Umberto and Pheemie reached Corriebeg, the fire which seemed to have started in the kitchen was well ablaze. Robert had been the first to see the glow in the sky from his grandfather's bedroom window. He had alerted neighbouring farmers and called the fire brigade from Perth.

As he dashed back and forth into the house dragging out whatever furniture and household effects were accessible, other neighbours formed a bucket chain in a futile attempt to douse the now-fierce flames.

Umberto seized Robert's arm as he rushed past. 'Alec? Jenny?'

'I don't know —' yelled Robert and with Pheemie screaming after them, Umberto and he dived into the inferno.

It seemed as if hours had passed, as timbers fell and the fire spread, before the two emerged blackened but unscathed.

'They're not there,' Robert shouted.

Suddenly Pheemie remembered what Umberto's revelations had put clean out of her mind. The Ritchies had gone to the pictures. She joined the bucket carriers. The fire brigade had just arrived when Alec's motorbike came hurtling into the yard.

Their faces distraught, he and Jenny rushed towards the house. Alec pushed past Umberto, who grabbed him, shouting: 'Don't. It's too late.'

'Get away!' He struggled free and Jenny made to follow him, but was held back by Robert.

'No. *No*, Alec!' she screamed. But he rushed into the house. Trying to reach the bedroom, he was too late. The stair had already collapsed. Looking round in despair, he knew there was nothing he could do, nothing more he could save. As he staggered out and Jenny ran sobbing into his arms, he heard the terrified hens and the cow.

'The barn. It's spread to the barn. Oh, Alec. Buttercup!'

Alec picked up the shotgun which Robert had saved, putting in a cartridge as he ran across the yard. But the mooing had stopped. All was silent but for the red hiss of flames. Buttercup was already dead. And the hens – all dead.

He thought he heard a dog barking. Fly. Where was Fly? But turning, he saw Jenny with Fly clasped in her arms.

They stayed until the end, helplessly watching their home reduced to a smouldering ruin and as the barn collapsed in a wall of flame, with it went the hay and all of Corriebeg. Still they remained unable to tear themselves away, staring unbelieving at all that remained of their dream, their hopes for a future, piled up in the few possessions Robert had salvaged.

'It isn't fair,' sobbed Jenny as Alec held her. 'Oh, Alec, it isn't fair.'

At last Pheemie and Umberto persuaded them to go back to Carnban. 'There's nothing more you can do here. Come back with us. There's a bed for you for as long as you like.'

There was a bed, but no comfort, or sleep for either of them as they whispered to each other about what lay ahead.

They went back to Corriebeg at daybreak. It was even worse than they had thought. As they walked through the charred ruins of what had been their kitchen, there were some survivors – ornaments on shelves, cups and saucers, blackened but whole. And most bizarre of all, there, on the middle of the floor, was a baby's knitted jacket.

It lay at Jenny's feet, with arms outstretched, delicate and helpless, in a feeble piteous cry for help. She picked it up, wondering had it fallen from the bedroom above when furniture was being carried out? Miraculously almost unmarked it had escaped the blaze.

She was still holding it tearfully against her cheek, that tiny symbol of joy for a life ended before it had begun when Flora's car drove up. Clearly Flora was shocked by the extent of the damage, the burnt-out steading, windows gaping and black with only part of the roof still intact.

'How bad is it?' she asked.

'You can see for yourself,' said Alec. 'There isn't much to be saved.'

'Where did it start?'

'In the house somewhere. The firemen thought it might have been a short-circuit. I had the turnip slicer plugged into a socket in the kitchen.'

Flora walked towards the barn with its charred, still-smouldering hay. She touched the blackened turnip slicer.

'Some sparks must have blown across to the barn,' said Alec. 'Once the hay caught, the fuel for the tractor would burn, too.'

'Quite an eventful night,' said Andrew who was waiting for

Flora in the factor's office. 'For everyone,' he whispered as he put his arm around her. She had been with him when he heard about the fire at Corriebeg.

As they returned from the pictures, Andrew had suggested she came in for a nightcap.

'If I come, I'll stay,' she had said and did. It had been a night of love, of fulfilment. They had crept upstairs to Andrew's bedroom at first overcome with giggles in case they met Sir James or the housekeeper.

With the door closed, Andrew had leant against it. 'That's the first hurdle over.' But even as he walked towards her she had already shed her coat, her blouse and was unfastening her skirt, discarding stockings.

Long afterwards Andrew was to remember that they had made love that night as if there was no tomorrow, with a fever induced not only by starvation but by imminent parting.

Flora lay awake in the darkness, pinned by Andrew's arm across her as he slept, his head on her breast. Sometimes she stroked his hair: fulfilment made her feel maternal. But it also brought darker shadows, as she realised that instead of comfort and consolation, bitter past memories had been unchained.

'You never did answer my question,' Andrew was saying. 'What happens to our future?'

Flora had known the answer to that for several hours now. She loved Andrew, loved him too much to lose him, to go through all the agonies and uncertainties of being a soldier's wife and then a widow.

'Andrew.' She didn't know quite where to begin. 'I have already seen one man I loved go down that road wearing a uniform, off to war.' Suddenly her eyes brimmed over. 'I don't think I can go through that again.'

Andrew looked at her. He knew only too well what she was talking about. How could he ask her to endure for a second time all the horrors and uncertainties of a wartime marriage?

He nodded. 'Well, I'll tell my parents that our wedding is – postponed?'

The phone rang on Flora's desk. 'Yes. The damage is pretty extensive. I imagine that you'll want to send someone along and if you could let me have a claim form. Thank you.'

When she turned, Andrew had gone. Five minutes later, she gathered up her papers and went across to the house where Sir James was waiting for her report. He listened carefully and when she told him Corriebeg was gutted, he shrugged. 'Then that's that.'

'Do you want me to get estimates on how much it will cost to rebuild?'

'Hardly worthwhile, is it? Balbuie ran the grazings well enough when it was empty. He can do that again.'

His reaction amazed Flora. Had he no feelings for the poor Ritchies, their livelihood gone, their home destroyed? How could he dismiss it just like that? 'So – that's the end of Corriebeg. Just another empty Highland steading. You do know Ritchie hired that machine from us?'

Sir James sat up. 'What?'

'Andrew gave him permission. The motor was defective.'

'He's not going to allege that we are responsible, I hope. You said yourself that the fire started in the house.'

'Who knows what happened? The cable was in the kitchen socket.' Flora paused. 'But I wasn't thinking about what Alec Ritchie might say.'

Sir James stared at her. 'The insurance company?'

'Exactly. They could contend that it was our responsibility to make sure the equipment was in a proper condition. It could affect our claim.'

Sir James tapped his fingers on his desk. 'Let me think about it, will you?' As she turned to leave, he said gently: 'Flora, Andrew told me about your decision.'

Flora summoned a smile. 'Our decision actually,' she corrected him.

'You won't reconsider.'

'No. We have both agreed it would be best to wait.'

Flora hoped to make her escape without an encounter with Andrew's mother, but at the door Mrs Mckenzie said: 'The major's mother is wanting a word with you, Mrs McInnes.'

Flora was amused by her tact and delicacy, at having got round the embarrassment of calling the laird's ex-wife 'Lady Menzies' or 'Mrs Hallenburg II'.

Mrs Mckenzie pointed across the hall. 'She's in the sitting room.'

It wasn't a conversation Flora was looking forward to and without even inviting her to sit down, Constance demanded: 'Is this true?'

Playing for time, Flora said: 'Is what true?'

Constance made an irritated gesture. 'That you've postponed the wedding.'

'Andrew —' Flora repeated: 'Andrew and I have decided it wouldn't be a good idea to get married until the war's over.'

'And Johnny comes marching home. If he comes marching home,' Constance added heavily.

'You seem pretty callous about the possibility of your son not returning.'

'Not callous, my dear.' Constance paused to look in the mirror and apply more lipstick. 'Realistic. Like you.'

There was nothing more to say. Feeling she had been dismissed like a rather unsatisfactory servant, Flora added pointedly 'If you'll excuse me, then. I have things to do.'

As she left she saw Sir James's car going down the drive.

After Flora left, he had suddenly decided to go to Carnban. He wanted a word with Pheemie Robertson about her orraman and it would be the decent thing to chat to the Ritchies whom he knew were staying with her.

Alec Ritchie had gone up the hill, he was told by Pheemie. But he'd find Mrs Ritchie at Corriebeg.

As the car drove into the yard, he saw her sorting through the pathetic few pieces that had been saved from the fire.

Opening the car door, he called to her. 'Hop in.'

She took a seat beside him and watched him frowning at the burnt-out timbers. 'Sorry we burnt it down,' she said.

'I will have to have it properly surveyed, of course. But I daresay it could be put back into commission.'

'Wouldn't that cost a lot of money?'

Ignoring the question, Sir James said: 'Your husband can resume the tenancy if he wants to, of course.'

Jenny paused to let the significance of this sink in. Then with a shake of her head, she said firmly: 'He doesn't.'

Sir James's smile was sympathetic, understanding. 'Tell him the offer is open. He might get a job at the sawmill, or we might be able to give him something else meantime, until we get things sorted out and the house ready for you. That shouldn't take too long.'

Alec had seen the car leaving and was coming down from the field with Fly when Jenny ran up to meet him.

'What did he want?'

They sat down together on the stone wall facing the house and holding Fly in her arms, Jenny told him: 'Don't you see by his offer Sir James shows how confident he is in your abilities. You've proved you could run Corriebeg successfully,' she added proudly.

Alec listened in silence. At the end he sighed. 'No. There's a time to cut your losses. And that's exactly what we're going to do now.'

Jenny smiled sadly. 'It'll be nice seeing the girls again. Mummy and Daddy too.' Mummy would be delighted to have her home again, whatever the circumstances. And there were plenty of farms in the surrounding area where Alec's experience might get him a job.

Hugging her to his side, he said: 'It's all been a bit of an adventure, hasn't it?'

'Yes. It has.'

Their decision made, there was no point in lingering. They had finished with Corriebeg; let Mrs McInnes sort it out. No doubt Balbuie would take on the sheep again as he had done before.

Alec had decided not to call in on his mother and sister. The catastrophe at Corriebeg would distress them too much. Instead he would write from Salisbury, softening the blow with some story of better prospects.

And so they began the rounds of goodbyes.

As Alec and Jenny for the last time visited the people who had first resented them as incomers, like Macrae, and were now their friends, there was another poignant leave-taking at Strathblair House.

Major Andrew Menzies was departing on the first step of his long journey to the battlezone in Korea.

Seeing him like this, vulnerable and sad, Flora said impulsively: 'Andrew, we still have time to marry with a special licence.'

He smiled ruefully. 'Now you tell me. No, Flora, we'll get married with all the bells and whistles when I get back.'

'When you get back,' she whispered with her heart in her eyes.

His parents emerged from the house. As father and son shook hands, Sir James wished him good luck and suggested they all accompany him to the railway station.

'No. I hate protracted farewells.' And, kissing Constance, who clung to him in that last moment, he said breezily: 'Cheerio, Mother.'

To Flora there still seemed so much to say, with no time left except to say goodbye. Andrew opened his mouth to speak and she put a finger over it, trying hard not to cry.

'Don't, please.' As he kissed her, she whispered, 'Take care, Andrew. For God's sake, take care.'

They watched the car drive off and looking at Flora's distraught face, Sir James said consolingly: 'He'll be all right,' and hoped it would be true.

Alec and Jenny had loaded the sidecar with their few surviving personal things. Pheemie was to store the rest until they had a place for them.

'Take care of yourself, lass,' said Pheemie. 'And stay in touch, will you?'

Jenny promised, thanking her and Umberto for everything.

'Och away. It was nothing. I'll miss you, Jenny.'

'And I you.'

'Well, we'd best be off,' said Alec, shaking hands with Umberto.

'*Arrivederci*. And good luck.'

'I hope your problems sort themselves out.'

'Och, dinnae worry.'

Alec hugged Pheemie and turned to Jenny who was cuddling a whimpering Fly who had watched every move they made. She seemed to sense that they were going away and not taking her with them. Her whines implored them.

'Oh, Fly.' Jenny kissed her. Parting with her dog was the hardest thing of all. But it was impossible to take her to Salisbury where a dog would hardly be welcomed into her parents' home. Pheemie would be good to her. But that was scant consolation.

Jenny hugged Umberto and got onto the pillion behind Alec.

'Goodbye – goodbye.'

They set off down the road and Jenny looked for the last time on all the places that had become so dear to her. Strathblair with its shops and houses, the main street and the green with its Celtic Cross. The smell of peat smoke would always awake nostalgic memories. Behind the stark outlines of winter trees, she studied the great undulating hills, the land she had thought of as her enemy, that she believed during the last few days of agony had taken her baby and her home.

But that land now felt like a friend with whom she was parting, a friend she loved and might never see again. No longer did she regard it as an enemy. She had been tested and proved herself worthy. Weaklings would have fallen by the wayside but she had been determined. And against all the odds she had won her long battle for Corriebeg. Only to lose it again, just when it was beginning to twine itself around her heart.

Dear hills, blue in winter sunshine, purple in summer heather. But she wouldn't be here for that annual awakening. She'd never see those bulbs she'd planted in their glory of spring flowering.

Goodbye, dear Corriebeg. I shall miss you.

At the crossroads she came to a sudden decision.

'Alec. Alec, stop a minute.'

Alec pulled over to the side of the road. 'What is it?'

'Will you take me home?'

'I am taking you home.'

She shook her head, smiled at him. 'No, Alec. I mean – home.'

He looked at her incredulously, knowing that it was what he wanted, too. Another chance, another battle to be won.

Pheemie and Umberto, feeling sad, were having a cup of tea in front of the fire. 'It'll no' be the same without her just up the road. There's no that many about here I can talk to. She was like the wee sister I never had.'

'Ah well, maybe she'll be happier back where she came from.'

Pheemie looked at him. 'Oh, by the way, the laird was here earlier. He's had a word with some folk and they say you'll likely no' be sent back to Italy. Och, you'll get a row and you'll have to sign some papers. But they'll not send you back.'

Seeing the beaming delight spread across his face, she said somewhat sourly: 'Looks like you won't have to marry me after all. Unless you want to, that is . . .'

She never got his answer for at that moment they heard Fly barking hysterically, followed by the sound of Alec's motorbike in the yard.

Together they rushed out. 'Did you forget something?'

'No, Pheemie. We just remembered something,' Alec called to her. 'Fly, here lass.'

And as Jenny bent over to gather a delirious Fly into her arms, she shouted: 'We've come home, Pheemie. Home to Corriebeg!'